THE ALPINE QUILT

THE
ALPINE
QUILT

A Novel

Mary Daheim

BALLANTINE BOOKS • NEW YORK

A Ballantine Book
Published by The Random House Publishing Group

Copyright © 2005 by Mary Daheim

All rights reserved under International and Pan-American Copyright Conventions. Published in the United States by Ballantine Books, an imprint of The Random House Publishing Group, a division of Random House, Inc., New York, and simultaneously in Canada by Random House of Canada Limited, Toronto.

www.ballantinebooks.com

Library of Congress Cataloging-in-Publication Data is available from the publisher upon request.

ISBN 0-345-47720-0

Text design by Susan Turner

Manufactured in the United States of America

First Edition: May 2005

1   3   5   7   9   8   6   4   2

With special thanks to Christine Thresh, whose quilt expertise kept me from making egregious errors while I pieced this story together.

ONE

IT WAS NEVER HARD TO INFURIATE *THE ALPINE ADVOCATE* readers. Even my mildest editorials could earn me such epithets as *pinko, nazi, or psycho slut.* But this time I'd gone too far. Without writing a single word, I'd managed to offend one of our business associates.

Buddy Bayard's photo studio had done our darkroom work for years. Unfortunately, technology had caught up with him. After Buddy cussed me out over the phone and damned progress as well, my ears were still ringing.

Sitting at my desk, I looked up at my reporter, Scott Chamoud. "I warned you," I said, "he'd be furious."

Scott's dark eyes—sable, I called them, the kind a woman could feel caressing her like the richest of furs—looked sad. "Maybe," he lamented, "I should never have suggested that we update our photography process. But Kip MacDuff thought it was a terrific idea, and said he could handle it. Kip's a real wizard when it comes to high-tech stuff, and you said there was enough in the budget . . ."

I waved a hand at him. "Stop fussing. It didn't make sense to keep farming the work out. It slowed us down. In the long run, we'll save money. And we can run more color. It isn't as if Buddy can't make a living without us."

"Ha!" The shout came from Vida Runkel, my House & Home editor, who had just tromped up beside Scott. "Buddy and Roseanna overcharge anyway. Do you have any idea what it cost for Roger to have his graduation picture taken there last month?"

If I'd been Buddy, I'd have paid Vida's grandson to go out of town for his photo session. Seattle, New York, London, Bombay—anywhere to put some serious distance between the obnoxious teenager and Alpine.

"Buddy will simmer down," I declared, though in recent years his once-amiable disposition had soured a bit. "Today's November first, All Saints' Day. I'm going to seven o'clock evening Mass. He and Roseanna may be there, too. I'll see if I can get Ben to soothe them."

"An able ally, your brother," Vida murmured. She flashed her toothy smile. "Really, Emma, I'm pleased that he's taking Father Kelly's place for six months. You're much more like your old self since Ben arrived in Alpine on the first of October."

My brother had finished his missionary assignment in Tuba City, Arizona. He hadn't quite reached burnout stage, but knew from his previous experience on the Mississippi Delta that he was due for a change. Still, his departure had been wrenching, not only for him, but for the entire community. He'd grown very close to his Navajo and Hopi parishioners. Indeed, Ben had confided that after over thirty years in the southern part of the United States, what he really yearned for was more temperate weather.

Temperate is a relative term, of course. Seattle is temperate. Alpine is more variable. At almost three thousand feet above sea level, the mountain town gets more rain, more wind, more snow. But November was starting off with mild temperatures and hints of sun. I needed only a light jacket when I left my little log house to head for St. Mildred's.

Father Dennis Kelly's last contribution before leaving on sabbatical was a paint job for the church's simple wooden exterior. The building had been white since it was built more than seventy years ago. Father Den had decided that the color wasn't practical, and after wrangling with the parish council, he had won the argument. Our church's exterior was now a deep navy with light blue and white trim. I liked it.

My brother was on the front porch, greeting members of his new congregation. Ben is two years older, seven inches taller, fifty pounds heavier, and a whole lot wiser than I am. I smiled as I watched him shake hands with Deputy Jack Mullins and his wife, Nina.

I waited for Clancy and Debra Barton to have a word with Ben before I approached him and Mary Jane Bourgette, who was scheduled to be the lector for the first two Scripture readings.

"Any sign of the Bayards yet?" I asked.

Ben made an adjustment to his white vestments. "They came to eight o'clock, you lazy twit."

"So the early twit gets to heaven?" I retorted. "You know damned well I had to be at the office by eight. Don't call me lazy."

Ben chuckled; so did Mary Jane. "Actually, Buddy and Roseanna had to leave for Seattle around noon to pick up his mother at the airport. She flew in from Spokane and wanted to spend a long weekend with them in the city. I guess she lived in Seattle for several years before she moved across the mountains."

Mary Jane's pretty, dark face wore a curious expression. "I didn't know Buddy had a mother. She must have lived here before Dick and I arrived."

The Bourgettes and some of their numerous progeny had

moved to Alpine several years ago. Dick owned a construction firm, and at least three of their children had made careers for themselves in town. Along with Mary Jane's involvement in church and civic activities, the family was a welcome addition to the local scene.

"I never met Mrs. Bayard," I remarked, nodding at pizzeria owner Pete Patricelli. "Or Mr. Bayard, either."

Mary Jane shrugged and patted Ben on the arm. "Short. Keep the homily short. I have to tape a TV program at eight for Dick. He's out of town on a job."

Seeing my former ad manager, Ed Bronsky, and his wife, Shirley, arriving in their Mercedes, I hustled inside. Years ago, Ed had inherited money. Last winter, he had toyed with the idea of running for mayor in the September off-year election against the longtime incumbent, Fuzzy Baugh. Along about June, Ed discovered he'd have to spend money and exert himself to woo voters. "Golly darn," he'd said to me, "I put in my time making nice with advertisers. I just can't see myself working hard to win an election."

Neither could I, especially the part about "working hard," a concept with which Ed was unfamiliar. He was currently slogging away on a sequel to his self-published life story, and had been nagging me to help with the manuscript. I'd been pestered to pieces by his requests on the first book, eventually feeling as if I'd rewritten the thing. At least I could spell and punctuate. But Ed then had to edit *my* work, resulting in a mishmash of turgid prose and about five hundred exclamation marks. This time around, I knew my Christian charity would flee at the sight of the word *preface*.

I sat down next to Jack and Nina Mullins.

Nina leaned across Jack. "Your brother is such a good-looking man. I was so afraid we'd get some crazy old coot to sub for Father Den. You know, with the priest shortage."

My response was cut short by Annie Jeanne Dupré's heavy-handed pounding on the organ. Annie Jeanne was a longtime fixture at St. Mildred's despite her lack of musical talent. She sounded as if she was playing with mittens. But she was a good soul, and had signed on as the parish house-keeper a few years back. The job had enabled her to move out of the old ramshackle family home, which had gotten too dif-ficult for her to maintain. Ben said she cooked better than she played.

However, I invited Ben to dinner whenever he was free, which wasn't often. Invitation or not, he knew he was always welcome, even if dropping in would get him a hot dog, potato chips, and some store-bought pickles.

Because of the holy day, the rest of Thursday night was open for my brother. By the time Ben came out of the rectory in his civvies, I was starved.

"You shouldn't have waited," Ben said in his crackling voice. "I'll drive my own car."

"That's a car?" I shot back, pointing to the beat-up Jeep Wrangler parked in the pastor's slot. "What did you do with that thing in Arizona? Play war games?"

Ben grinned. "You've seen the roads down there. What you haven't seen are the dirt tracks. See you." He got into the Jeep and zipped out of the parking lot before I could open the door to my Honda.

I took my time. My brother is not a good driver. He goes too fast and takes too many chances. Ironically, he didn't start out that way. Unlike many teenagers, Ben had been cau-tious and considerate. Of course, he'd also been in the semi-nary for part of his youth, but it was only after our parents were killed in an auto accident that Ben began to exhibit a more aggressive, reckless style behind the wheel. He'd just been ordained, and I wondered if his driving was an outlet for the suppressed anger he felt for Mom and Dad's untimely deaths. Sometimes I thought that he was subconsciously seeking revenge. In any event, he certainly hadn't improved with age. But I attributed some of that to the roads less traveled in Mississippi and Arizona. My brother simply wasn't used to driving in towns, let alone big cities.

As usual, Ben somehow managed to get to my house in one piece. I had visions of his guardian angel in the heavenly weight room, working out on a half-dozen apparatuses at once. That angel needed to keep in tip-top shape to keep up with Ben's driving.

"What's for dinner?" Ben called from the front porch as I came around from the carport.

"Shish kebabs," I replied, "with very good beef from the Grocery Basket. Jake and Betsy O'Toole don't skimp when they buy meat for their store."

"They were at eight o'clock Mass this morning," Ben noted as I unlocked the door. "One thing about Alpine, it doesn't take long to get acquainted with my flock."

"For better or for worse," I said, hanging my new red wool jacket in the front closet, "that's the way it is in a small town. It's different in the city. When I went to work for *The Oregonian* in Portland, I needed to recognize only the people I met on my city desk beat. But in the first week I was here, I had to memorize about a hundred names and faces—literally. A journalist has to know who's who in a little place like Alpine."

Helping himself to the cupboard where I kept my liquor, Ben nodded. "I did that in Tuba City. No easy task, since so many of my parishioners—and nonparishioners, for that matter—were spread out all over the place. Hence, my battered Jeep. You ever try to drive through what's left of a gully washer?"

Accepting a glass of Canadian whiskey and water from Ben, I shook my head. "Just blizzards, ice storms, and foot-deep puddles."

He held up his glass, which also contained Canadian whiskey but without the water. "To your recovery."

"Amen," I said, and clicked glasses.

"You are better, you know," Ben asserted, leaning against the kitchen counter while I put the prepared shish kebabs under the broiler. "Rome must have helped."

Ben referred to the trip we'd made the previous autumn. He'd felt it would elevate my emotional and spiritual state to visit the Vatican after my longtime lover and almost husband, Tom Cavanaugh, had been murdered before my very eyes.

"I think going to Rome was good for me," I said slowly. "It was hard at first. I saw Tom everywhere."

"You told me that," Ben replied. "Six, ten, twenty times." His smile was typically wry.

"Right." I shot him a rueful glance. "What I mean is, maybe that helped me get over my grief. Not that I'll ever stop grieving, really. But time—" The oven door slipped out of my grasp and slammed shut. "Damn! I've got to do something about that hinge."

"Sackcloth and ashes don't become you, Sluggly," he declared, using his childhood nickname for me. "You look good in red. I like your new coat."

"Benjamin Lord, the Common Sense Priest," I said with a touch of sarcasm. "Whither pity, compassion, mercy?"

"Up your oven," Ben retorted. "How long do you cook shish kebab? I didn't take a vow of starvation."

"As long as the rice that goes with it. Have another drink."

Ben shook his head. "Later, maybe. You know I'm a two-drink-limit kind of guy. I made up my mind before I got out of the seminary that I wasn't going to be one of those priests who fought off despair and loneliness by making Jim Beam my best friend."

"You're strong," I remarked, wrapping a buttered baguette in foil.

"Ornery," Ben put in.

"Darn." I'd turned on the oven light—which worked much better than the door—to observe the shish kebabs. "I know we're both hungry, but I've got a lot of food in here. I should've invited Vida to dinner. She's fond of you, you know."

Ben glanced at his watch. "It's almost eight-thirty. Being a staunch Presbyterian, she didn't have to go to church tonight. Vida probably ate a couple of hours ago."

"God only knows *what* she ate," I murmured. "She can't cook, despite all those recipes and culinary advice she hands out on her House and Home page. Of course, it's all filler she gets from the news services. She's doing the same thing on her weekly radio show, *Vida's Cupboard.*"

"I still haven't heard it," Ben said. "Too many damned meetings on Wednesdays."

The water for the rice had boiled. "You're right—Vida's probably eaten. But," I added, "I bought half of a coconut cake from the Upper Crust Bakery. I'll call her and see if she wants to come by for dessert."

"Vida's a real character," Ben noted, his eagle eye spotting the pink cake box on the counter. "I suppose every community has somebody like her. In Tuba City, there was Dolores Goodgrass. She knew everything about everybody, despite the fact that she lived way out past Moenkopi. Once a week, she'd come into the Tuba City trading post, and everybody would gather round to catch the gossip. On Sundays, she'd stand outside the church and grill all the parishioners, especially the kids. She's over seventy, but she has a way with young people. Dolores could get them to tell just about anything, including whose pa was stepping out on ma. Yet she was never malicious, just nosy. Dolo—as she's called—dished out advice, sympathy, and her own little sermons. I always felt she had more spiritual and moral influence than I did."

"I take it she wasn't as critical of others as Vida," I said.

"Only to their faces," Ben replied. "She never talked smack behind anyone's back."

"Unlike Vida," I remarked.

I poured rice into the kettle, put on a lid, and turned the burner down. Then I picked up the phone, which I'd left lying on the counter. Dialing Vida's number, I got her answering machine with its usual message urging any caller to leave as much information—translation: *gossip*—as possible. My own message was brief. "Thought you might like to have dessert with Ben and me, but I guess you're out for the evening. See you tomorrow."

I realized I'd been so hungry when I got home that I'd forgotten to check my calls. Sure enough, Vida had phoned shortly before seven. "I'm afraid I won't be in the office tomorrow, Emma. My daughter Beth is ill and has asked me to visit her in Tacoma. I'm leaving as soon as I can pack a few things. I'll try to be back to work Monday. But of course you never know with these things. That is, illness can be so unpredictable. Beth's husband, Randy, is so tied up with work, and their children are very busy with school and sports. Well— you understand, I'm sure. Good-bye for now."

It wasn't just the content of Vida's message that puzzled me, it was her tone. She sounded constrained and spoke slower than her usual staccato delivery. I was puzzled, and said so to Ben.

My brother shrugged. "She's probably worried about her daughter. Did Vida say what was wrong with Jo?"

"Beth," I corrected. "There is no Jo. Vida and Ernest had only three little women—Amy, Meg, and Beth." Amy, the unfortunate mother of Roger, was the only one of the trio who lived in Alpine.

Ben's keen brown eyes watched my every move, probably to make sure I didn't waste any time getting dinner on the table. "Vida's husband met a tragic end, right?"

"Totally tragic, but semicomic," I replied. "Ernest decided to go over Deception Falls in a barrel. Bad idea."

"People don't do that kind of thing much anymore," Ben remarked. "I guess it was a fad that lost its appeal. Especially when you don't make it to the bottom in one piece."

"That wasn't Ernest's problem," I explained, peeking at the rice. "The truck that had brought him to the falls ran over the barrel—with Ernest in it."

Ben winced. "That's a pretty ignoble way to go. Was Vida driving the truck?"

I couldn't help but laugh. "No. I don't think anybody was, or if Ernest had someone along, I never heard who it was. The brakes slipped. I don't believe Vida was even there."

"She's not the type to endorse daredevil activities," Ben declared. "Was Ernest always such a wild man?"

I shook my head. "I gather that Ernest was normally a most prosaic type. I suspect that this was his big chance to break out of his image—midlife crisis and all that. Unfortunately, it didn't turn out very well."

"Only in Alpine," Ben murmured.

"Risk-takers are everywhere and you know it," I said, sounding defensive. "But Ernest wasn't the first to try the barrel bit in Skykomish County. In the early years, several men had attempted the stunt, either at Deception or one of the other falls in the area. A couple of them also met a grim fate—though at least they got in the water."

Dinner was a success, judging by Ben's ability to eat not

only his share but whatever I might have had left over for Vida. While we talked of many things, including my son, Adam, who had followed in his uncle's footsteps and was now a priest in a remote part of Alaska, it was Vida who kept niggling at the back of my mind.

Finally, just as Ben was about to head back to the rectory at ten-thirty, I again expressed concern for my House & Home editor. "Vida never misses work," I asserted. "I can't imagine her not being on the job tomorrow and maybe not even Monday."

Ben, however, downplayed my anxiety. "Her daughter's sick," he reasoned. "If it were Adam, wouldn't you rush to his igloo?"

"You know it's not an igloo," I retorted. "And of course I would. What bothers me is that Vida sounded so . . . evasive."

Ben patted my head, another old habit. I'd hated it when we were younger because it was so patronizing: older, taller, smarter brother. He was still all those things, but the gesture no longer irritated me.

"From what you've told me," Ben began, "Vida is a very private person, at least when it comes to her personal life. If whatever is wrong with her daughter is serious, she may not want—or be able—to talk about it. Cut her some slack."

Ben was right. Vida would use every means short of torture to uncover other people's deepest, darkest secrets. But she guarded her own like the CIA. I told Ben I'd try to stop fussing about her.

I managed fairly well, in fact.

Later, I'd learn that I should have been worried to death.

TWO

THE OFFICE SEEMED EMPTY WITHOUT VIDA FRIDAY MORN-
ing. I wasn't concerned about having to do her work for
her. She had a backlog of at least two features, and she'd already written a wedding story along with a cutline for the
happy couple's photograph. If she didn't return until Tuesday,
Vida would have plenty of time to sort through her fillers and
to collect items for the front page's gossipy "Scene Around
Town" feature.

My ad manager, Leo Walsh, glanced over at Vida's empty
desk. "Where's the Duchess?" he inquired. "She's not on her
dais this morning."

No one, not even Vida, could make Leo stop calling her
Duchess. "She went to Tacoma to stay with her sick daughter," I replied.

Scott turned away from the coffeemaker. "You mean . . .
she won't be in today?"

Ginny Erlandson stopped just inside the newsroom door.
"I don't think Vida's missed a day since she went to Ore-
gon with you years ago," our office manager declared. "She
doesn't even take vacation unless it's family oriented."

I nodded. Vida's defection was tantamount to abdication by Queen Elizabeth II. "Well, this *is* family oriented. We'll have to struggle along without her."

"At least," Leo put in, lighting a cigarette, "I can smoke in peace."

Ginny, however, scotched that notion. "You really should quit, Leo. It's not good for you, and it smells bad."

"Half the people who come through this office smell bad," Leo shot back. "The cigarettes protect me. A smoke screen, you know." Happily, he puffed away.

"Ugh," said Ginny, with a shake of her stunning red hair.

So the day began, routine despite the void. By nine-thirty, the first person seeking Vida arrived. Ethel Pike, steel-gray hair, stout, and stern, stared at Vida's chair as if she could make our House & Home editor materialize like a genie.

"Out and about, I suppose?" I heard Ethel say to Leo.

"Ran off with the circus," Leo replied, grabbing his brief-case and standing up. "I'm going to join her. We've got a really amazing trapeze act."

Leo left Ethel still standing by Vida's desk. I realized that Scott had gone off on his regular city-county beat and that Ginny was at her usual post in the front office.

"Good morning, Ethel," I said pleasantly, emerging from my cubbyhole. "Vida's gone for the day. Can I help you?"

Ethel had no sense of humor. "Gone to the circus? I don't believe it."

I explained that Leo was joking. Ethel's round, rosy face didn't crack a smile. "Some joke. I'd like to see Vida in the circus. Especially on a trapeze." Judging from the grim expression, I guessed that Ethel was envisioning Vida working without a net.

"You can tell me what you have for the paper," I assured her.

Ethel delved into her big blue purse and pulled out a manila envelope. "I've got two stories." She opened the envelope and took out at least four or five sheets of handwritten ruled paper. "This first one is about me and Pike going to Orlando Tuesday. That's where our son, Terry, lives with his wife and our grandkiddies. We're taking the grandkiddies to Disney World, even though Terry's snippy wife, Dawn, says they've been there about a hundred times. Now to me and Pike, Disney World is a place where grandfolks take their grandkiddies. I don't care if they live within spitting distance, Terry and Dawn should have waited until we got down there. The kiddies are only six and eight. What's the rush?"

I was at a loss for words, maybe because Ethel had used up so many of them. "What's the other story?" I asked.

Ethel scowled at me. "Have you been to Disney World?"

I shook my head. "Only to Disneyland, years ago, when my son was about seven."

She waved the pages at me. "You see? You could wait. Did his grandfolks go with you?"

"My parents were dead," I replied.

"What about his daddy's?"

Having cut myself off from Tom Cavanaugh after he refused to leave his nutty wife, I had no idea where my son's paternal grandparents were at the time. They, too, could have been dead, or living blissfully in Seattle's Fremont district where Tom had grown up.

"I was a single mother," I finally said. "My brother—Father Lord—and I took Adam to Disneyland."

"Oh." Ethel may have looked slightly deflated, but with her stoic features, it was hard to tell. She handed me the first two pages. "Here's the story about our trip. I'll bring more after we get back." She held on to the other pages. "This is about the Burl Creek Thimble Club's big reunion party Sunday night."

"This Sunday?" I tried not to look miffed. "If you'd brought it in earlier in the week, we could have run the story in Wednesday's edition."

"We didn't know we were having it until today," Ethel asserted. "How could I tell you something I didn't know about?"

It was not an unreasonable argument. "Spur of the moment, huh?"

Ethel nodded emphatically. "None of us in the club knew Gen would be in town until yesterday."

"Gen?"

"Genevieve Bayard, Buddy's mama." Ethel regarded me as if I should be wearing a dunce cap.

"Oh, yes, I heard Buddy and Roseanna went into Seattle to meet her," I said in an effort to save face. "They're spending the weekend there, I understand."

"Hunh. I can't think why," Ethel grumbled. "All that traffic, all those people. I told Pike we should worry more about getting to the airport than having the plane crash. He don't like to fly, you know, which is why we haven't been to Orlando yet. I warned him if he went over thirty-five on that freeway, I'd divorce him."

I felt a pang for Pike, whose first name was Bickford. I also felt a pang for all the drivers who would be driven to despair—and possibly road rage—by the slow-moving Pike vehicle.

"As for Gen," Ethel went on, "why did she have to fly from Spokane? She could have driven here in the time it'd take to get through the airport with all that security they have nowadays. It isn't like there's snow to close the pass."

I didn't argue, nor did I point out that Genevieve Bayard apparently wanted to see something of Seattle since she'd once lived there.

"Anyways," Ethel continued, barely stopping for breath, "Gen used to be a member of the BCTC"—she pronounced

the initials as *Betsy*—"way back when. A fine quilter, that
was her specialty. She's getting to Alpine in the afternoon, so
we decided to have a party for her. We didn't want to wait
until she got settled, because I'm leaving Tuesday so it's kind
of a send-off party for me. Not to mention the BCTC is giving me a special going-away present for winning the blue ribbon in quilting at the Skykomish County Fair this fall."

Another action-packed article for the paper, I thought.
"There should be a follow-up on it," I pointed out, "since we
can make our deadline if we get the story by Tuesday afternoon."

Ethel shrugged. "Somebody else will have to do that.
Maybe Charlene Vickers. She has a way with words."

Charlene was married to Cal, owner of the Texaco gas
station. As a member of several clubs and organizations, she
was often tapped to write news releases. I nodded at Ethel.
"Charlene can handle it," I said, "but please remind her
about the Tuesday deadline."

Ethel frowned. "I'll try. I've got plenty on my mind as it
is, what with the party and getting ready to go out of town."

I was more than ready to have Ethel go out of the office,
which she did, just as Scott came in.

"Crime wave hits Alpine," he announced jauntily. "Lock
up your valuables. And your daughters, just in case."

"I have neither valuables nor daughters," I noted. "I'm
safe. What now?"

Scott handed me a copy of the police log. "A break-in last
night at Cliff and Nancy Stuart's house in The Pines," he said,
referring to the owner of Stuart's Stereo and his wife, who
happened to be Doc Dewey's sister. "Last weekend, the Vickerses got burglarized in Ptarmigan Tract, remember?"

"Sure," I replied, studying the log, which included a few
additions to the previous day's reports of Halloween vandal-

ism. "We ran the burglary article on the front page. Do you think I'm getting senile?"

Scott gave me his killer grin. "I was thinking that if we had one more before Tuesday's deadline, we wouldn't have to worry about a lead story."

"Ah." I smiled back at Scott. "Good thinking. Three break-ins this time of year would be real news."

"You mean as opposed to during the summer when the kids are out of school and at loose ends?"

"Exactly." I looked again at the log. "Whoever did this wasn't very bright. I see that a stereo system was taken along with some of Nancy's jewelry and the Dewey family's sterling tea set. If what they really wanted was the stereo, why not break into Cliff's store?"

"If it's the same guy—or guys," Scott said, dumping out his cold coffee and pouring himself a refill, "they took the Vickerses' stereo along with their brand-new flat-screen TV."

I sighed. "Money for drugs, I imagine. Does Milo Dodge have any leads?"

"The sheriff is baffled," Scott declared, sitting down at his desk.

"Another standing headline," I murmured, then felt a pang of guilt. "I shouldn't criticize Milo. He's really a fine lawman." The guilt wasn't only for my offhand remark. I always felt guilty about the sheriff for having dumped him years ago when he wanted to turn our affair into something more serious.

"You want me to write the story?" Scott inquired as I handed the log back to him.

I nodded. "We can play it up a few inches, given the previous burglary. I'm guessing there's a link, which is what Milo probably figures, too, even if he won't come out and say so."

"He allowed for the possibility," Scott said. "Both happened in the evening while the couples were out. Both break-ins were through a window on the first story near the porch. No prints, by the way."

I shrugged. "That doesn't mean it was a pro."

Ginny and Leo came into the newsroom together. Ginny had the mail; Leo had a sour expression on his face.

"I'm humiliated," he declared. "I missed a glitch in the Upper Crust's ad last week."

"Then I missed it, too," I said, though in fact, Leo made so few errors that I scarcely bothered to read his ad copy. "What was it?"

"Those new owners of the bakery changed their hours," Leo said, putting his briefcase down on the floor with more force than was necessary. "You wouldn't have caught the mistake. It was supposed to read, 'Open now on Sundays from noon to 5 P.M.' Instead, it read, '6 P.M.' Now they figure a bunch of pastry freaks will show up between five and six and get pissed off because the bakery's closed. Either that, or this Sunday they'll have to stay open late."

"You're right—I didn't know what the hours should have read," I responded. "The marvel is that they're open at all on Sundays. It's so un-Alpine."

"They're new," Leo said. "They're from Seattle. They figure they can make an extra buck, especially with the holiday season coming up. They admit they may change their minds come January."

I recalled the article on the new owners that Vida had written for her page. Vicki and Gordon Crowe had bought the Upper Crust in September from the longtime proprietors, who had decided to move back to their native California. So far, the Crowes' baked goods had proved not only equal, but better, especially when it came to cakes. The previous night I'd kidded Ben that the coconut slice he'd eaten was the size of Mount Baldy.

"If Vicki and Gordon are such go-getters," I pointed out, "they shouldn't mind putting in an extra hour on Sunday. Don't beat yourself up, Leo. Usually, you're infallible."

Leo merely grunted. I leafed through Ethel's articles before putting them in Vida's in-basket. Both stories were for the House & Home section. I could put my time to better use by going to the Upper Crust Bakery and making nice.

The Crowes had given the bakery a fresh paint job, both inside and out. They'd also hung a new purple, pink, and black awning over the storefront. I recalled from Vida's article that the couple had also installed a new oven and a state-of-the-art bread slicer. The sales section, however, remained much the same except for the pink walls with their purple trim. Best of all, they'd restored the old photographs that the Californians had removed and put into storage: a long-dead Petersen with a nineteen-pound steelhead; a young couple named Durning bicycling through a wide cut in a giant cedar stump; a half-dozen loggers standing next to a truckload of Douglas fir trees; the entire Alpine Lumber Company seated in the social hall for 1927's holiday dinner with the framed menu below it.

The aroma of fresh bread wafted my way as I went up to the counter. Vicki and Gordon both baked. They'd retained the counter help, which included Carrie Amundson, the teenage daughter of Wes, one of our park rangers. Carrie was a strawberry blonde with translucent braces on her teeth. She was waiting on Annie Jeanne Dupré when I arrived.

"Hi, Ms. Lord," Carrie said brightly. "I'll be just a minute."

Annie Jeanne turned around. "Emma!" she said in surprise. Annie Jeanne was always surprised, wearing a constant expression of amazement on her long, thin face with its wide-open chocolate-chip eyes. "What a coincidence! I'm here buying a coconut cake for your brother."

It was my turn to be goggle-eyed. "You mean he ate the chunk I sent home with him already?"

Annie Jeanne giggled, a shrill, girlish sound that didn't suit her advancing years. "For breakfast. Can you imagine?"

I grew stern. "You shouldn't let Ben—I mean, Father Ben—eat such an unwholesome diet. He'll get fat."

Carrie had tied up the pink cake box with purple string. She offered it, along with a pink paper bag, to Annie Jeanne. "Here you go, Ms. Dupré. That'll be twelve dollars and forty cents."

Annie Jeanne had taken a worn coin leather purse from her woven handbag. "I may have exact change," she said before turning back to me. "Oh, Emma, don't give Father Ben such a hard time. He's spent so many years in godforsaken places like Arizona and Mississippi."

"He grew very fond of the local cuisine in both places," I said. "Too fond. That's why he's working out at the high school gym."

"He is?" Annie Jeanne was surprised, as usual. "Oh, my! That's very energetic of him. Father Kelly used the college gym. Priests seem very different these days, don't they?"

"As opposed to Father Fitzgerald, who was about eighty-five when he left St. Mildred's?" Even as I spoke, I saw the hurt on Annie Jeanne's face. I patted her arm. "I'm not criticizing Father Fitz. It's just that when I knew him, he was elderly." And gaga.

Annie Jeanne seemed appeased. She finally counted out the money for Carrie, who was showing unusual patience for a teenager. "I don't remember any priest except Father Fitz," Annie Jeanne explained. "When I was a small child, we were a mission church out of Everett and had different priests you never really got to know. Then we got Father Fitz. I was nine, and starting piano lessons. We didn't have an organ in those days, just a piano, so when I got to be eighteen, he asked if I'd play it for the liturgies. Mrs. Barton—that'd be Clancy's grandmother—had developed very bad arthritis. Naturally, I said I'd play anytime he wanted me to. About five years later, we'd raised enough money to buy an organ. I was so thrilled when Father asked me to—'graduate,' as he put it—that I realized it was my vocation." Annie Jeanne smiled shyly. "And here I am, still playing after forty-odd years."

And very odd playing, I thought, but kept smiling. "And you're the housekeeper as well," I remarked, not wanting to have to lie like a rug if the organ topic was kept open. "I understand you're having a BCTC reunion party Sunday."

Annie Jeanne was wearing what looked like hand-knitted gloves, perhaps a product of her club membership. Maybe she did wear them while playing the organ. In any event, she put a hand to her face and giggled.

"My, yes!" Annie Jeanne explained. "For Genevieve Bayard! And after all these years! I can't wait. She was my best friend in high school." Suddenly, she looked at the clock on the far wall. The hour hand, which was a knife, was between nine and ten; the minute hand—a spoon—was on eight. "Oh! I must dash! I have to buy party favors for our fête." She nodded at me, thanked Carrie, and rushed out the door.

Carrie now became the resident giggler, though the sound suited her much better than it did Annie Jeanne. "Ms. Dupré's a funny old thing," Carrie said. "Every time she comes in, I have to try not to laugh."

"Actually," I said, "she's not all that old." Having reached the midcentury mark, I no longer considered anybody under eighty as old. "I figure Annie Jeanne is in her mid-sixties."

Carrie's expression indicated that she didn't understand my logic. But she merely smiled self-consciously. "What can I do for you today, Ms. Lord?"

"I'd like a loaf of your country white, sliced," I replied, "and, if I may, a word with either Vicki or Gordon."

"Oh. Sure," she responded, glancing at the open door that led into the bakery itself. "I'll get one of them before I take care of your bread."

Vicki Crowe was around forty, with shoulder-length curly black hair and a businesslike manner that didn't mesh with her pert good looks.

"Ms. Lord," she said with a smile as tight as her curls. "What can I do for you?"

"Accept my apologies for the mistake in this week's edition," I said. "Don't blame Leo. I'm the one who has the final look at the paper. And please call me Emma."

To my surprise, Vicki shrugged. "It's no big deal, Emma. We'll stay open until six on Sunday. We can use the time to get ready for Monday. But how about this?" She leaned toward me and lowered her voice as a young mother entered, pushing a sleeping infant in a stroller. "I talked it over with Gord after Leo left," Vicki went on. "We decided we could get some free promotional inches by asking you to run a brief item stating our Sunday hours and emphasizing that we'll probably change back to six days a week after New Year's. Frankly, I don't think we can keep up the pace in the long term. We didn't move to Alpine to kill ourselves."

The proposal sounded fair to me. "We'll place the story near your ad on the House and Home page," I agreed.

"Good." Vicki greeted the newcomer, but headed back into the bakery section.

Carrie had my bread ready. I paid for it and started on my way. I was almost to the door when I had an idea. The young mother was hemming and hawing over bear claws. She finally decided on the ones with apple filling. After she left, I informed Carrie that I wanted a dozen doughnuts, three each of cinnamon, frosted, plain, and glazed. The Crowes made doughnuts to die for.

The Upper Crust was right across the street from the sheriff's office. Alpine may not have bumper-to-bumper traffic on the main drag, but it's not wise—or legal—to jaywalk. I went to the corner and crossed at the new stoplight at Front and Third.

"Doughnut Lady," I announced, entering the reception area, where Milo stood behind the curving desk, jawing with deputies Jack Mullins and Dustin Fong. Toni Andreas was answering phones, but glanced up with an expression of expectancy.

"Gimme, gimme," Jack urged, his hands outstretched. "Nina says if I eat more than two a day, she's sending me to a fat farm."

Jack was, in fact, putting on some weight as he entered middle age. Milo, too, had added a few pounds in recent years, but on his six-foot-five-inch frame, it wasn't noticeable unless he took his clothes off. Not wanting to think about that, I opened the pink bakery bag and let the quartet dig in.

"So," I remarked, after everyone had a doughnut in hand, "tell me about the break-ins."

The sheriff had chosen a glazed doughnut. Toni was off the phone. Before answering my question, Milo asked her to get us all a cup of coffee.

"Fresh brew," he said.

Fresh or stale, it wouldn't matter. The sheriff's coffee was always awful—too weak or too strong, and sometimes tasting as if the inside of the coffeemaker had been scorched by a flash fire. "Break-ins?" I prompted.

"All two of them?" Milo retorted with an ironic expression on his long face. "What about them?"

I accepted a steaming mug from Toni. "Same MO in both incidents?" I asked.

"Right." Milo peered at me over the rim of a mug that had CRIMEBUSTER stamped on its side. "I told Scott as much."

"Yes," I agreed, and dared to take a sip of coffee. It tasted like asphalt. "Kids?" Trying not to grimace, I bit into a plain doughnut.

Milo shrugged. "Maybe."

"Come on, Milo," I said in an impatient tone, "don't be coy. You can tell a pro from an amateur."

"Yep." He sipped his coffee and bit off another chunk of doughnut.

Obviously, the sheriff wasn't going to cooperate, which made me all the more curious. But I knew from frustrating experience that the more I asked, the less he'd be inclined to answer.

"I'm taking my doughnuts and going home," I declared. Snatching the bag off the counter, I started for the door.

"Hey!" Jack cried. "Come back, sweet Emma! I didn't get a cinnamon!"

I relented. "Here," I said, but handed the bag to Dustin Fong, who was looking equally crestfallen. "I'm keeping one for myself," I added, removing a cinnamon doughnut for myself.

Dustin, Jack, and Toni all thanked me. Milo said, "You didn't finish your coffee."

With the acrid taste still on my tongue, I shot him a sharp look. "I *am* finished with your coffee."

I ATE MY CONFISCATED DOUGHNUT AS I WALKED THE TWO blocks to the *Advocate*. In the front office, Ginny looked up from her computer. "You have sugar on your face. Hank

Sails died this morning." She made both pronouncements in the same tone of voice. Despite the flaming red hair that often signaled a volatile temperament, Ginny usually kept herself on an even keel.

Brushing off the sugar, I stared at Ginny. Hank Sails's death wasn't really a shock. He was in his late eighties and had lived a long and satisfying life. The owner of six weekly newspapers until he'd sold out five years ago, Hank had been one of the people who'd advised me on buying the *Advocate*. He'd been a kind man, generous with his time and his knowledge. Hank had been a true independent, never following party lines or popular thinking. His peers as well as his readers regarded him as an icon in the newspaper business.

"When's the funeral?" I inquired.

Ginny shook her head. "I don't know. The story just came across the wire ten minutes ago. More to come, as they say."

The phone rang. Ginny answered, then called to me just as I started into the newsroom. "It's Vida," Ginny said. "Do you want to take it in your office?"

"Sure."

I hurried past Scott, who was listening to his tape recorder while typing on his computer keyboard.

"Vida," I said eagerly, "how are you? How's Beth?"

"About the same," Vida replied in a noncommittal tone. "I have a favor to ask. Would you please call Buck late this afternoon and remind him to take care of Cupcake? He sometimes can be absentminded."

I assumed she referred to Buck, not to Cupcake. Buck was Buck Bardeen, Vida's longtime companion; Cupcake was Vida's canary, who had been around longer than Buck. "Sure," I replied, jotting down a reminder note. "What's wrong with Beth?"

"Ooooh . . ." Vida paused, and I could picture her

familiar—and disturbing—habit of whipping off her glasses and rubbing her eyes so hard that I wondered how they stayed in their sockets. "You know these doctors nowadays. They hem and haw."

"It's nothing serious, I hope?"

Vida sighed. "We hope not."

Her reticence was driving me nuts. Vida might be close-mouthed when it came to intimate details of her private life, but it seemed to me that she was going too far this time. The least I expected was a string of complaints about the medical profession, the effort she was expending, and being forced to stay in a city the size of Tacoma.

"When do you think you'll come home?" I asked.

"I can't say just yet."

I realized I was grinding my teeth, so I surrendered. "Well, we certainly miss you. Do take care of yourself, as well as Beth. By the way, I put a couple of items in your in-basket. One's about a trip that the Pikes are taking to Orlando next week, and the other is about the Burl Creek Thimble Club's welcome-back party Sunday for Genevieve Bayard."

I thought I heard Vida's sudden intake of breath. But she didn't respond, and I wondered if we'd been disconnected. I was about to say something when she finally spoke in a husky, unfamiliar voice:

"Excuse me, I have to go at once."

Vida hung up.

THREE

M Y CURIOSITY GOT THE BETTER OF ME. I DECIDED TO call Amy Hibbert in The Pines. Maybe Vida's eldest daughter could explain her mother's behavior, or at least tell me what was wrong with Beth.

Before I could pick up the receiver, the phone rang.

"Where the hell were you this morning?" Ben demanded. "You lose your calendar along with your soul?"

"Oh, shoot!" It was November 2, All Souls' Day, and while not a holy day of obligation, I sometimes went to Mass to pray for the souls of our parents. "I blew it."

"Your penance is taking me to dinner at Le Gourmand out on the highway," Ben stated. "I hear they have food that's actually edible, not to mention more variety than the ski lodge's version of Scandinavian haute cuisine. I can only eat so much pickled herring at one sitting."

"The dining room at the lodge serves a lot more than herring," I asserted. "They have valet parking now. I'm sure they'd feel honored to drive your beat-up Jeep. Besides, I like pickled herring."

"Another black mark against you," Ben replied. "How about tomorrow night?"

I grimaced. "If I can snag a reservation," I said. "They get busy on weekends. Some people drive all the way from Seattle to eat there."

"Use your clout," Ben commanded. He hung up on me, too. I had no opportunity to tell him I had no clout.

Amy Hibbert answered on the second ring. It always amazed me that although Vida's daughters resembled her physically, none of them shared her personality traits. All three were somewhat timid and very careful not to offend. I assumed that while they might look like their mother, they had acquired Ernest Runkel's character. Given Vida's forceful qualities, they probably didn't have much choice. It had occurred to me that the only form of rebellion the daughters had ever shown was when Beth had settled in Tacoma and Meg moved to Bellingham. Though Vida never said as much, I was certain that their defection rankled.

I told Amy that I'd just finished speaking with her mother. "I'm worried, Amy," I admitted. "She doesn't sound like herself and she won't say what's wrong with your sister. I know I sound like a snoop, but I'm very concerned."

"Oh, dear," Amy said in a fretful voice, "I'm sorry you're upset. I spoke with Mother last night, and she told me Beth was doing fairly well. All things considered."

My shoulders slumped. Was I going to get the runaround from Beth, too? "Such as?"

"Such as what?"

"The things," I said. "All the things."

"Oh!" Amy uttered a lame little laugh. "I mean, recovering from surgery is never easy."

Dare I ask?

I dared. "What kind of surgery?"

"For hammertoes," Amy replied. "The doctors aren't

sure how soon Beth can walk. And when she does, she has to wear funny-looking shoes."

"Oh!" I said in relief. "I was afraid it was something serious."

"It *is* serious for Beth," Amy asserted. "She has kind of big feet—well, we all do—and she's very self-conscious about having to wear those ugly shoes that'll make her feet look even bigger."

The image brought Vida to mind as I envisioned her tromping through the newsroom in her splayfooted manner. "Yes, I can see how that would bother Beth," I remarked. "Excuse me, but I have a rather odd question for you, Amy. I wouldn't ask, but it may be affecting a couple of assignments I have for your mother. Is she feuding with Ethel Pike?"

"Ethel?" Amy evinced surprise. "Not that I know of. I haven't heard her mention Ethel lately, but when she has, it's just . . . the usual kind of comment."

In other words, Vida thought Ethel was a ninny. But Vida thought most people were ninnies. "Do you recall her ever mentioning Genevieve Bayard?"

"Genevieve Bayard?" Amy sounded stumped. "Goodness, I haven't heard that name in years. Isn't she Buddy's mother?"

"Yes," I replied. "She's coming to town for a visit."

"That's nice for Buddy," Amy said. "Usually, he and Roseanna have to visit her over in Spokane. That's quite a long, tiring drive. I mean," she added hastily, lest she offend the half of the state east of the Cascades, "it's pretty if you like all that farmland and rolling brown countryside."

"The two sides of Washington couldn't be much more different," I noted, distracted by what seemed to be Vida's overreaction to Beth's dilemma. "Forest on the west, prairie on the east."

"That's what I mean," Amy agreed. "Eastern Washington is like the Midwest in terms of weather."

The weather wasn't why I'd called. "Do you have any idea when your mother will be home? She was very vague with me."

"I suppose she'll come back when Beth can get around on her own," Amy said in an uncertain voice. "Really, I don't think it should be too long. You know how she hates to be away from Alpine."

I did know. That was the problem: For once, Vida didn't seem anxious to come home.

OVER THE WEEKEND, I TRIED TO PUT THE CONUNDRUM that was Vida out of my mind. Distractions, however, saved me from becoming obsessed with her behavior. Adam called from Alaska Saturday morning. As usual, the connection between Alpine and St. Mary's was transmitted via radio, which meant there was always a delay after each of us spoke.

"Guess what?" he said over a couple of crackles along the line. "I'll be home for Christmas!"

"Hooray!" I shouted. "This will be the first time in I don't know how many years! How did you manage it?"

Pause. "I got a sub," Adam finally replied. "The priest I replaced wants to visit his old flock. I'll get in at Sea-Tac around noon on the twenty-third. I have to be back here the twenty-ninth."

Airport holiday zoo. Curbside pickup, if there was room to park. Cars, cabs, limos, buses, shuttles clogging the lanes in front of the entrance. I didn't mind. I was too excited to see my son for the first time in almost two years.

"I'm so happy, I could cry," I said.

Pause. "You don't cry much. Don't do it on my account. You always end up with a really ugly sneezing and coughing fit. How's Uncle Ben There, Done That? If he e-mails me any more advice, I'm going to kill him."

"He's only trying to be helpful, and you know it," I responded. "He's fine. We're going to dinner tonight at Le Gourmand."

Pause. "Do they serve whale blubber? I can't remember what normal food tastes like."

"You're exaggerating. I sent you Omaha steaks last month."

Pause. "A walrus ate them. Then I ate the walrus. Got to go. I'll e-mail you the details, okay?"

It was more than okay, it was a minor miracle. I told him how excited I was and how much I loved him and to be careful, especially during the whiteouts where he literally couldn't see his hand in front of his face and had to follow a rope to move around outdoors. During one of those blinding snowstorms the previous winter, a local man had let go of the rope and disappeared. His frozen corpse was found in the spring, three miles from the tiny town.

Ben was also thrilled when I told him about Adam's plans. They would, my brother announced, concelebrate Midnight Mass and the Christmas Day liturgy. At that point, I almost did cry. I knew how proud Tom would have been to see his son on the altar.

The dinner at Le Gourmand was excellent as usual. We couldn't get a reservation until nine, but that was fine since Ben couldn't leave until after Saturday evening Mass. I drove. I didn't trust him on Highway 2 at night, especially since it had started raining.

When I got home from church Sunday I started planning for Thanksgiving and Christmas. I already had my Turkey Day guest list made out, including Ben, of course, along with Milo, Vida, and Buck. Amy and her husband were going to

Hawaii for the long weekend. I assumed—and prayed—that they'd take Roger with them. I tried to obliterate an unbidden image of Roger being roasted over a spit at a Thanksgiving luau.

Since I had the spare time, I started to reorganize Adam's old bedroom, which I'd used for storage since he'd moved away. It was a daunting task, and I ended up throwing out a bunch of junk I didn't know why I'd kept in the first place. My holiday decorations were in his closet, so I removed the Thanksgiving box and began putting the items around the living room. Figures of Pilgrims and Indians, various sizes of turkeys, a cornucopia, assorted pumpkins, squash, and corncobs made me feel downright festive.

That night I went to bed tired but feeling I'd accomplished something. I slept like a log.

Ben was already here. Adam was coming home. I had a family again.

B UT MY MOOD SOURED A BIT WHEN I LEARNED THAT VIDA would miss another day of work.

"She called early," Ginny reported. "In fact, I was just coming through the door when the phone rang. She said she wasn't able to leave Beth yet. What's wrong with her?"

I informed Ginny of the hammertoes surgery. She looked relieved but also puzzled. "Isn't that when your toes curl up?" she inquired.

"I guess so," I replied, trying not to sound unsympathetic. "I've never had that problem. I suppose it's something to look forward to."

"Oh," Ginny said, just before I went into the newsroom, "Hank Sails's funeral is Thursday. It's private, but that evening there's a memorial reception for him at the Columbia Tower in Seattle."

I smiled. Even beyond the grave, Hank seemed to be thinking of his fellow newspaper owners. After Wednesdays, which was usually publication day for most weeklies, Thursdays were always a little slow, a time to catch your breath.

"I think I'll go," I said. Vida, who wouldn't miss a grief-related occasion for the world, had known Hank and would want to come along—*if* she was back Thursday.

But of course she'd be in Alpine by then. I couldn't imagine her missing what would amount to an entire workweek.

Vida seemed to be on everybody's mind. I guess she always is. Charlene Vickers came by around eleven with the write-up of the party for Genevieve Bayard. I left my cubbyhole to greet her.

"Where's Vida?" Charlene asked.

I was getting tired of the question, but I answered patiently. One of the many groups Charlene belongs to is my bridge club. She's a nice woman, a little older than I am, and somewhat reserved. Being the wife of a service station owner is not easy in Alpine. Every time the price of gas goes up, the Vickers name is maligned by half of Skykomish County.

"How was the party last night?" I inquired, leaning my backside against Vida's desk.

"Lovely," Charlene replied. "Everyone was so glad to see Genevieve. Of course, some of us were quite young when she moved away after her ex-husband died. She's aged very well." Charlene grimaced, perhaps because since I'd known her, her hair had gone gray and her figure had expanded by several inches. "Anyway, Annie Jeanne was absolutely thrilled. She and Gen were very close friends since childhood. I've got pictures." She gestured at the envelope that she'd put on Vida's desk. "There's one of them hugging that's priceless. I hope Vida can use it."

"Yes." I picked up the envelope and removed its contents.

The story was two-and-a-half neatly typed pages, double-spaced. The photographs were all in color.

"Buddy stopped by to take some pictures," Charlene explained, "but I took these. I hope they're all right."

They looked usable, unlike in the past when everybody in town submitted badly posed Polaroids that not only didn't reproduce well, but couldn't be run in color because we didn't have the equipment.

I pointed to a group photo where a woman I didn't recognize sat in the middle. "That's Gen?"

Charlene nodded. "She's still a pretty woman, isn't she?"

The shape of her face and the fair hair—which I assumed was dyed—vaguely resembled Buddy. Charlene was right. Genevieve Bayard was attractive and didn't look more than late fifties.

"How old is she?" I inquired. "She hardly seems old enough to be Buddy's mother."

"I know." Charlene uttered a small laugh. "It's hard to believe that Gen and Annie Jeanne are the same age, but they're both in their mid-sixties. Gen married very young. I suppose it's not a surprise that it didn't last. Andre drank, I've heard."

"Andre," I repeated. I knew that was Buddy's real first name, but I hadn't known he'd been named for his father. "Andre died young?"

Charlene shook her head. "Not *really* young. Forties, I think. He may have died from drink—or a drunk-driving accident. I don't remember. They were divorced several years earlier but kept trying to reconcile. I suppose he promised to change but didn't. So sad. Gen never remarried because she's Catholic."

"She could have remarried as a widow," I pointed out to Charlene, who isn't Catholic but Methodist.

"I don't know," Charlene said. "Maybe Gen really loved him and never found anyone else."

"That happens," I said, trying to keep the bitterness out of my voice. I could never imagine marrying anyone but Tom.

"Here's a picture of Ethel with her prizewinning quilt," Charlene said, perhaps sensing what I was thinking and tactful enough to change the subject.

A grim-faced Ethel Pike was standing up, holding a large quilt in some kind of star pattern. The quilt was a lot better looking than Ethel.

"Oh!" Charlene exclaimed. "I forgot to add one thing. Gen brought homemade cookies for everyone. She baked them after she got to Alpine Sunday afternoon. She made a double batch for Ethel so she and Pike could eat them on the plane to Orlando. Nobody had the heart to tell Gen that Ethel has developed diabetes in the last few years."

"Gen sounds like a good person," I remarked. "I'd like to meet her. I'm sure Vida will want to interview her for a feature article."

Charlene hoped so, too. We parted with assurances of seeing each other at the next bridge club get-together.

Five minutes later, Milo Dodge loped into my office and put a big foot on the seat of one of my visitor's chairs. "Scott's still bugging me," he said in an irked tone. "Damn it, Emma, I get tired of you acting like I haven't told your reporter everything he needs to know. Or else you're asking about stuff that you think should be made public. As far as these break-ins go, I'm not holding back. If they keep up, I'm going to have to double the patrol cars in the evenings."

I couldn't resist. "And have *two* of them?"

Milo turned his head away from me. "Sheesh. You know our budget. What do you want, have me call in the frigging FBI?"

"A quote would work," I noted. "I need a minimum of two inches of copy. How about, 'Sheriff Dodge says he doesn't believe the break-ins are the work of a professional ring of thieves,' adding that if the burglaries continue, it will be easier to establish an MO and eventually capture the perps?"

Milo looked at me again, his hazel eyes serious. "That's not bad. Leave out *eventually*. It makes me sound slow."

No kidding, I thought. *Plodding* had been the word that came to my mind, though to be fair, it should have been *thorough*.

"Okay," I said, quickly writing down the quote I'd given him. "You're sure?"

"Sure of what?"

"That you want to say this in print."

He shrugged. "It can't do any harm, I suppose." Removing his foot from the chair, he stood up to his full height. With his Smokey Bear hat, Milo was close to six-nine. The top of the hat barely cleared my office's low ceiling. "Want to grab some lunch at the Venison Inn?" he asked.

It was only a little after eleven-thirty. "Now?" I said.

"Well . . ." Milo lifted his hat and scratched above his left ear. "Half an hour okay? That'll give me time to check on the weirdo at the Alpine Falls Motel."

I stared at Milo. "What weirdo?" I tried not to sound annoyed. Milo—along with most of Alpine—didn't recognize a potential news story unless it had HEADLINE stamped all over it.

"It's no big deal," Milo assured me. "Some guy checked in last night and won't come out of his room so it can be cleaned. He only paid for one night, and checkout was at eleven. We just heard about it. For all I know, he's gone by now."

I waved Milo off, thinking that maybe he was right. The guy was probably trying to sleep off a hard night at Mugs Ahoy. The motel had opened last May just off Highway 2 near the steel bridge over the Skykomish River. The two-story building looked like a cracker box, with cheap rates to compete with the two existing motels and the ski lodge. Scott had written a story in which he'd interviewed the manager who was running the place for a national chain of budget-rate hostelries. Leo couldn't stand the manager, whose name I didn't recall, and had had to practically hold the guy's head under water to get him to take out an ad for the grand opening. The motel hadn't advertised in the paper since.

Milo was waiting for me when I arrived at the Venison Inn a couple of minutes after noon. He already had his coffee, and was smoking a cigarette despite the ban on tobacco in the restaurant section.

"False alarm," he said. "The guy was gone. He took off about ten minutes before I got there."

"Did he leave any souvenirs?" I inquired, not needing to look at the menu.

Milo shook his head. "Not if you mean drugs, booze, or condoms. I guess he just likes to sleep late. It's not the souvenirs guests leave that bother Will Pace. He's the manager, and kind of a jackass. If anybody acts the least bit unusual, he's sure they're stealing the TV, the towels, and everything including the bathroom sink. That's why we get called in. Will's not exactly what I'd call a gracious host."

"Will Pace." I repeated the name. "I should try to remember that, even if Leo is trying to forget."

"How come?" the sheriff asked as Mandy, one of the inn's usual blond waitresses, brought Milo's standard order of a cheeseburger, fries, and a green salad.

I put in my own request before explaining to the sheriff

about the motel manager's reluctance to advertise in the paper. We moved on to other topics, including my excitement over Adam's Christmas visit.

Milo was happy for me. "By the way," he said, "I'm going to be a granddad. Or so Mulehide informs me."

Mulehide was Tricia, Milo's ex-wife, who had remarried and lived in Bellevue, east of Seattle. "Which kid is having the kid?" I asked.

"Tanya," Milo answered, looking bemused. "She and that sculptor she's been living with. Chipper, I call him. They figured if they had a baby, they might think about getting married. Jeez, what's with this younger generation?"

I had to laugh. "Don't ask me. I have a son and I've never been married."

Milo turned sheepish. "I didn't mean . . . That was different. Anyway, you were going to marry Tom. It just took you thirty years to get around to it."

Six months ago, I might have felt like bursting into tears. In fact, six months ago, Milo would never have said such a thing. On this rainy afternoon in November, I merely nodded. "When's the baby due?"

"In the spring," Milo replied after swallowing a big bite of cheeseburger. "Late May. How's Ben? I'd like to get together with him sometime. Does he still fish?"

"He used to," I said, recalling a long-ago outing with Milo that ended abruptly in a grisly discovery. "Ask him. He, too, can be cold, wet, and miserable while not catching any steelhead. Ben will consider it as penance."

"I'll give him a call," Milo responded.

I smiled. Milo and Ben had hit it off when they first met many years earlier. They'd be good for each other. They were both lonely men.

Shortly after I returned to the office, I received a call from Ethel Pike. "I wanted you to know that me and Pike are leaving this afternoon instead of Tuesday morning. We don't want to have to fight all that traffic and worry about getting to the plane on time, so we're going to stay at a motel by the airport. Just tell Vida to put that in her story. I wouldn't want her to make a mistake and say we left on Tuesday when we didn't. I remember the time she printed my rhubarb pie recipe and left out the salt for the crust. And didn't I hear about that! Everybody in town thought *I'd* made the mistake when it was Vida."

Apparently, that was before my time. Vida had worked for Marius Vandeventer almost twenty years before he sold the paper to me. Seeing my other line light up, I wished Ethel and her husband bon voyage.

The new call was from Ben. "Hey," he said, "I think I'll ask Adam to give the Christmas homily. He can soak the C&Eers for the home missions with a second collection. They'll all feel guilty anyway, so they might want to bribe their way to heaven."

C&Eers were Catholics who came to Mass only for Christmas and Easter, the two biggest feast days on the church calendar. "Good thinking," I replied. "How's everything at the rectory?"

"A-twitter," Ben said. "Annie Jeanne is scurrying around like a mouse in a cheese shop. She's invited Genevieve Bayard for dinner tonight so they can have a long one-on-one visit."

"That sounds sweet," I remarked. "Does that mean you won't get dinner?"

"I'm being treated this evening by Bernie and Patsy Shaw," Ben said. "They're taking me to the ski lodge. Bernie's probably going to try to sell me insurance."

"Do you have any?"

"No. Why should I?" Ben chuckled. "I'd end up leaving it to you or Adam, and neither of you needs it."

"Gee, thanks," I retorted. "Have you forgotten that if it

weren't for Don, my former fiancé, and his Boeing insurance policy, I wouldn't have been able to buy the *Advocate*?"

"That was a fluke," Ben scoffed. "The poor guy forgot to change the beneficiary when you dumped him."

"So? I wouldn't be here if he hadn't."

"I thought you didn't always like being here. In a small town, I mean."

I paused. "Well . . ." I paused again. "I definitely miss the city."

"Who doesn't?" Ben responded. "I haven't lived in a city for almost thirty years."

"I know." I looked up to see Leo standing in the doorway with an ad mock-up in his hand. "I have to get back to work, Big Bro. Say hi to the Shaws. And tell Annie Jeanne to enjoy her little dinner party with Gen."

"Oh, she will," Ben assured me.

Ben was wrong. His crystal ball was already clouded by a deadly shadow from the past.

FOUR

WHEN I GOT HOME THAT EVENING, VIDA HAD LEFT A message on my answering machine. "I'm staying with Beth another day. She isn't able to drive, so I have to pick up the children from school. I do hate to miss deadline tomorrow, but I'm afraid I must ask you—or Scott—to write up whatever has to go into this week's paper. Now if you'll look on my desk, you'll see that I've already done . . ."

It was a long message, instructing me about the holdover features, the recipe file, the gardening tips, the helpful hints, and all the other fillers that Vida used for her section. "As for 'Scene,' " she concluded, "I must apologize for not having any items myself. I'm sure that you and the rest of the staff can come up with enough to fill the column."

The call had come through at three-oh-nine. Vida had purposely phoned me at home when she knew I wouldn't be there. I considered calling her back, but since she had hung up on me during our last conversation, it appeared that she didn't want to talk to me. I grew more curious than ever.

Thus, I didn't dial Beth's number in Tacoma. Instead, I poured myself a bourbon and water, got out my laptop, and went to work. I could write Ethel Pike's story from memory, though I'd have to fill in her children's and grandchildren's names later. Vida could handle the follow-up article when the Pikes returned next week. On a big-city daily, only celebrities were given such coverage; in a small town, Ethel and Bickford Pike's itinerary made headlines.

I was also able to type up most of the article about Genevieve Bayard's welcome-home party. I should, however, set up an appointment with her for an interview sometime tomorrow.

Maybe she hadn't yet left for her dinner at the rectory. I dialed the Bayards' home number, and hoped I wouldn't get Buddy. I didn't want him hanging up on me again, either.

Luckily, Roseanna answered. She sounded pleasant enough, albeit a bit harried. Her mother-in-law was still there, changing her clothes for the dinner with Annie Jeanne Dupré. Roseanna summoned Gen to the phone, explaining first who I was and what I wanted.

"I'm flattered," Genevieve Bayard replied in a silky, if wary, voice. "After all, I've been away from Alpine for many years. Who cares about an old battle-axe like me?"

"I do," I replied. "I've heard you're not old, and no one has suggested you're a battle-axe. Returning Alpiners always make news, even if it's only for a visit. When can we get together tomorrow? Tuesday is our deadline for the Wednesday edition."

Gen hesitated. In the background, I heard Roseanna call to her. "Midafternoon would be best," Gen said into my ear. "My daughter-in-law just reminded me that we're going to visit some old friends in Index for lunch. The Briers, John and Jessica. Do you know them?"

The name rang a faint bell. Vida could tell me. *If* she was around. "I associate the name with logging," I said.

"Yes, John was in the logging business for many years,

as were his father and grandfather before him. But nowadays . . ." Gen's voice drifted away. There was no need to explain. The timber industry was in decline, and had been for an entire generation. Work in the woods was hard to find: The vocation was no longer handed down from generation to generation.

"Two o'clock would be fine," I put in. "Would you like to stop by the office?"

"Well—if you don't mind, could you come to Buddy and Roseanna's house?" Gen asked. "Actually, two-thirty would be better. We wouldn't want to rush our visit with John and Jessica. I'm sure you understand."

I did. The interview shouldn't take long, nor would it require more than fifteen minutes to write the story. I'd send Scott, who could also take a photo. But I didn't dare say so to Gen, lest Buddy get wind of it and pitch another five-star fit.

"Two-thirty is fine," I said. I didn't add that I wouldn't be there. My excuse would be the looming deadline, which wasn't a lie.

"I really must dash," Gen said. "Annie Jeanne's expecting me at six. She's always been so prompt. I'm sure dinner will be on the table the minute I arrive."

I wished Gen bon appétit, and rang off. Finishing my drink and a rough draft of the BCTC story shortly before six-thirty, I studied the contents of the fridge. Nothing inspired me. I took a can of oyster stew, a can of sliced peaches, and some soda crackers out of the cupboard. No frills for Emma. No ski lodge, no Annie Jeanne, certainly no Le Gourmand.

On the other hand, I love oysters in any form. I managed to slurp down my supper in less than ten minutes. I was closing the dishwasher a few minutes after seven when the phone rang. Vida? Not likely. Milo? Doubtful. Adam? Possibly. I picked up the receiver from the kitchen counter and said hello.

It was Ben. My immediate reaction was to wonder why he wasn't at the ski lodge with the Shaws. But it took only the tone of his voice to tell me that something was amiss.

"Emma?" he said, sounding shaken. "A terrible thing has happened."

I panicked. To Ben? To Adam? I thought I could hear a sharp wailing noise in the background. "What?" I asked, breathless.

"Genevieve Bayard just died. She collapsed at the dinner table." His voice was hushed, though it grew in strength as he spoke. "I anointed her, but she was already dead. Doc Dewey is on his way, as are the usual medical personnel. I've also called the sheriff."

"The sheriff?" I was stunned. "Why?"

Ben's voice dropped even lower. "I want to cover all the bases. A sudden death at the rectory could cause scandal. Got to run. Annie Jeanne is in a state of collapse."

For once, I hadn't changed clothes when I arrived home. Making sure that the stove was turned off, I grabbed my purse and my winter jacket before heading out to the carport. This was news, but that wasn't my first concern. This was Ben calling, and he needed me. I drove to St. Mildred's so fast that I forgot to turn on the windshield wipers. Fortunately, the rain wasn't heavy and traffic was light.

Approaching the church, I saw the flashing red lights of the emergency vehicles—one fire truck, one aid car. Pulling into the parking lot, I recognized Doc Dewey's black Volvo. I guessed that while Genevieve Bayard was beyond help, Annie Jeanne Dupré wasn't. Fortunately, the hospital was catty-corner from the church. There was no sign of Milo Dodge's Grand Cherokee.

The rectory door was wide open. So was the door to the parlor. I could hear moans and groans, apparently coming from Annie Jeanne. Ben, Doc Dewey, Del Amundson, and two firefighters blocked my view.

Not wanting to interfere, I kept my distance. The kitchen and the small dining room were down the hall, past Ben's study. I stepped back a few paces. Vic Thorstensen, another medic, was coming toward me from the rear of the rectory.

"You don't intend to take pictures, do you?" he asked without preamble.

"No," I replied, having forgotten—as usual—to bring a camera. "Why?"

Vic gestured over his shoulder toward the dining room. "It's kind of messy in there."

I assumed he meant that Gen had thrown up—or worse—before she died. "What was it?" I asked. "A heart attack?"

Vic shrugged. "That's what it looks like. Del and I tried to revive her, but she was too far gone. I'm wondering if we could've saved her if Annie Jeanne had called for help right away."

I was taken aback. "She didn't?"

Vic shook his head. "I get the impression she went to pieces and was running around like a chicken with her head cut off. Your brother didn't know anything had happened until he came out of his quarters to go someplace. Annie Jeanne was huddled in a corner, shaking and blubbering like a baby. Doc's sending her to the hospital. Frankly, I always thought she was kind of daffy."

I felt I should defend Annie Jeanne, even if it meant stretching the truth. "She's not daffy. She's merely excitable. It's because of her musical talent; it's artistic temperament." Vic was a Lutheran who wouldn't know the difference, probably never having had to endure Annie Jeanne's boxing-glove punishment of the organ. "Besides," I added, "her oldest and dearest friend died right before her eyes. That must have been horrible." I suppressed a shudder; I ought to know.

"Yeah," Vic responded, "I guess I should cut her some slack. Where are those two nuns?"

Sister Mary Joan and Sister Clare shared a small condo across the street. The convent had burned down years ago, and was never rebuilt because of the scarcity of vocations. "For all I know, they're at the movies," I said after filling him in on their place of residence.

Vic cocked an eyebrow. "The Whistling Marmot's showing *Texas Chainsaw Massacre*."

"So?"

"I didn't know nuns went to movies, let alone ones with violence and raw—" He stopped and looked beyond me. "Ah. Here comes the long arm of the law."

I turned to see Milo loping through the open door. He nodded abruptly at Vic and me before going into the parlor. My curiosity got the better of me, but first I dialed Scott's number. He'd recently moved in permanently with his fiancée, Tamara Rostova, who taught at the community college. Scott answered on the third ring. I asked him to grab his camera and come to St. Mildred's.

When I started to move into the parlor, I was forced to backtrack. Vic, Del, and Doc Dewey were putting a subdued Annie Jeanne on a gurney. After they tucked her in, Doc gave me one of his kindly smiles. Like his father before him, he was of the old school. He even made house calls. I gave them plenty of room as the medics wheeled Annie Jeanne away. Doc was right at her side, holding an IV bag aloft. The firefighters also trooped toward the exit.

"We'll be back in ten minutes," Del called over his shoulder to Ben, who had joined me in the hallway.

"No rush," Milo said from the parlor doorway. He was dressed in his civvies—blue jeans and a plaid flannel shirt.

"Okay," he said, after the others had left, "Gen Bayard's in the dining room?"

Ben nodded. "They'd just finished eating. Or at least that's what I got out of Annie Jeanne. She was pretty damned incoherent."

I lagged a bit behind my brother and the sheriff. I'd seen too many dead people in my time, but I hadn't yet grown the callous shell that protected other journalists.

A third firefighter was standing by, but he excused himself when he saw the sheriff. Milo bent down by the body, which was lying next to an overturned chair. I couldn't see Gen's face, only the tinted blond hair. She lay in an awkward position, as if she had died in agony. There was nothing gruesome about the sight, but the smell made me feel slightly nauseous—a combination of roasted meat, something very sweet, and sickness. Moving closer to Ben, I swallowed hard.

Milo stood up. "Her color's really bad. Doc thinks it was a heart attack?"

"That's his offhand guess," Ben replied. "He wants a good look before he signs off on the death certificate."

The sheriff got down on his knees, taking a close look at Gen's face. "Doc's cautious," Milo said slowly, "so he'll check with Buddy to see if his mother had a history of heart trouble."

Ben slapped at his forehead. "I haven't called them yet. I'll do that now." He left the dining room.

I wandered into the kitchen. Milo followed me.

"What're you looking for?" he asked, hands jammed into his pockets.

I hadn't realized I was looking for anything. "Who knows? I'm a professional snoop, remember?" I said with a shrug. "Maybe I just want to see if Annie Jeanne has been keeping my brother well nourished."

"He looks fine," Milo remarked. "It's good to see him. He's a solid guy for a priest."

I shot Milo a dirty look. "He'd be a solid guy if he were a sheriff. We come from solid stock." I waved a hand at the dirty pots and pans in the sink and on the counters. Bowls and measuring cups and spoons and spatulas littered the counters. Two soiled dinner plates were perched precariously on a butcher block in the middle of the room. "Annie Jeanne makes quite a mess when she cooks. I assume she keeps the rest of the place clean."

"Father Den never complained, did he?" Milo looked thoughtful. "Den's a good guy, too. I guess Alpine got lucky when it comes to priests."

I assumed the sheriff alluded to the sexual scandals that had been wracking the church. "Most priests are decent, holy men. How many nonpriests have you arrested over the years for misconduct?"

Milo chuckled. "At least four Boy Scout leaders, three camp counselors, and a couple of teachers. Not to mention the assorted nonprofessionals, who probably number a few dozen." He paused, gazing at a half-eaten cheesecake on the counter. "Mmm. Chocolate cheesecake. That's a great favorite of mine. It looks homemade."

"It is," I said dryly. "That's why it's still in the pan."

"Funny Emma." Milo, of course, wasn't laughing. "Roast chicken," he went on, pointing to a couple of small carcasses in the garbage can. "Kind of little, aren't they?"

"They're Cornish game hens," I said. "Haven't I taught you anything?"

The hazel eyes threw me a sharp look. "Yeah, in fact, you have. But it wasn't anything about chickens."

I ignored the remark. "What are we waiting for?"

Milo looked as if he was about to say something, but

changed his mind. "Just in case, Dwight's coming by to take some pictures."

"So's Scott," I replied, "but I'm not sure what of. I'm trying to think what we could run in the paper that wouldn't look morbid." I glanced toward the dining room. "Maybe after they remove Gen's body, Scott can shoot the dining room table. Gen's Last Supper. Or is that too ghoulish?"

"Not for me," Milo said, "but I'm not your average sensitive reader."

Looking grim and still holding his cell phone, Ben entered the kitchen. "I got hold of Buddy," he said. "He's pretty shaken up. I told him it'd be better if he and Roseanna waited until Gen was taken to Driggers Funeral Home."

The phone rang in Ben's hand. Milo and I kept quiet while Ben responded. "Yes. . . . You're certain of that. . . . It's up to you, of course. . . . No, they're not back yet. . . . Fine, I'll tell them." Ben clicked off. "That was Buddy. He doesn't want his mother sent directly to the mortuary. He says Gen has never had any heart problems and just had a complete physical a month ago over in Spokane. Buddy wants a full autopsy."

Milo was angry. "Goddamn it, why does Buddy want to make trouble? He knows we have to ship his old lady to Everett. Doc doesn't have the time or the equipment for a full autopsy."

Ben offered Milo a sympathetic look. "But you have to comply, don't you?"

"Hell, yes." Milo's voice was still raised along with his temper. "It's up to the immediate family," he continued, lowering the volume a bit. "That's the problem. At least twice a year a survivor wants an autopsy even if the deceased has a chronic history of high blood pressure, heart trouble, or has drunk enough booze to boil six livers. It costs the county money, and it's a pain in the ass. We're always at the bottom of the list when we have to ask Snohomish County for help."

"Gen wasn't that old," I pointed out. "I realize that you can get a clean bill of health one day and be dead the next, but I can't blame Buddy for wanting to know what happened."

Milo glared at me, and I think he said "candy ass" under his breath. Judging from my brother's slight smirk, I knew it was something derogatory.

Scott, Del, and Vic all arrived at the same time. For starters, I told my reporter-photographer to take a couple of outside shots first. It was dark, it was raining, but if he used color, the darkened church and the amber lights in the rectory might create a little visual drama.

I stood on the rectory steps while Scott worked, peering out from under the hood of his black peacoat. He was concentrating so hard that he didn't turn around when a beat-up SUV pulled into the parking lot. I recognized the vehicle as belonging to Dwight Gould. An ardent hunter and fisherman, the longtime deputy had a reputation for driving on any kind of surface short of straight up.

"Why me?" he called as he stepped down from the driver's seat. "Why do I have to leave my easy chair and a good Monday night football game to take a picture? You already got a photographer here."

"Ask Dodge," I called back. Dwight also had a reputation for griping.

Scott finished his exterior work. "Is this a story or just an obit?" he asked as we went inside.

"It's a front-page story," I replied. " 'Native Alpiner Comes Home to Die'—or something like that."

"Poor Buddy," Scott murmured as I beckoned him into the empty parlor. "This has been a bad week for him."

"I know," I agreed. "Now I feel guilty about taking our business away from him."

"You had to," Scott reasoned.

He looked around the room. Ben had added a couple of Hopi kachina dolls and a framed Navajo petroglyph from one of the canyons near Tuba City. Coupled with Dennis Kelly's Swahili masks and headdresses, the parlor was a far cry from Father Fitz's romanticized paintings of the Madonna and the saints. After seven years, Father Den had left his mark on Alpine in more ways than one. As the first African-American clergyman in town, he'd been every bit as much of a pioneer as the early miners, loggers, and railway workers. Over the next few months, I hoped Ben would put his own stamp on Alpine.

"Is this room worth shooting?" Scott asked.

"No," I replied, studying the petroglyph, which depicted two figures playing long, slim horns. "I just want us to keep out of the way until they remove Gen's body."

Ben poked his head into the parlor. "Where'd you go, Sluggly? Oh, hi, Scott." My brother grinned at the younger man. "I thought Emma was raiding the poor box."

Scott, who had met Ben only once before, didn't seem to know what to make of a priest who wasn't in a movie or on a TV show.

"Hi . . . Father," Scott said in a deferential tone. "I'm sorry for what happened here. It must be awful for you."

Ben shrugged. "It's life. Death, that is. I'm more concerned about Annie Jeanne Dupré. She was a real wreck when they hauled her out of here. I'm going to the hospital later to see her."

Rolling the gurney that carried Gen's covered body, Del and Vic went past the parlor door. I made the sign of the cross and said a short, silent prayer.

"See ya," Del called.

His jaunty farewell unsettled me. It seemed I ran into Del Amundson only at disaster scenes. He was a remarkably cheerful man, somehow wearing death and suffering as comfortably as his EMT uniform.

Milo and Dwight came along a few seconds later. The sheriff was still exasperated. "We're going to have to treat the dining room and kitchen like a crime scene until we get the autopsy report. That could take a couple of days." He grimaced at Ben. "Sorry. Maybe you can move in with Emma. Gotta run. I've got freaking paperwork to do tonight."

Ben rubbed at his forehead. "Damn."

"Hey, Stench," I said, calling Ben by my girlhood nickname for him, "it's no problem if you bunk with me. I've already started cleaning out Adam's room."

Scott looked aghast. *"Stench?"* he said under his breath.

I didn't enlighten my reporter. Maybe he'd think it was some kind of Catholic term, like *eminence.*

Ben grinned at me. "I'm not going to start a rumor that I'm sleeping with my sister. That's about all the church needs right now, a good case of incest. I'll eat with you, but dinner only. I'll go out for brunch. You know I always have a late breakfast after morning Mass."

"Deal," I said, grabbing Ben's hand.

Scott and I went out to the dining room so he could take some photos of the death site. "We'll do the kitchen next. We should hurry before Dwight comes back with the crime scene tape."

Scott eyed me with curiosity. "This really isn't a crime scene, is it?"

"It is until Milo says it isn't," I replied with a sigh. "You're right, though—the sheriff doesn't think Gen was murdered. This is all a formality to satisfy Buddy."

Scott looked relieved. "Got it." He started clicking off photos.

"Besides," I added, "if there was even the hint of foul play, Spencer Fleetwood would already have showed up with a remote setup so he could put the news on KSKY."

"Right." Scott kept moving, taking shots from every angle, including the overturned chair and the remnants of the meal. "Fleetwood never misses a beat."

"Don't use that word," I said drolly. "It equates with *scoop*."

Scott laughed. "It does, doesn't it?" He moved on to the kitchen.

I didn't want to follow him. The kitchen smelled bad. I went back down the hall to find Ben.

Dwight was coming into the rectory with his roll of black and yellow tape.

Spencer Fleetwood was right behind him.

FIVE

E MMA," SPENCE SAID IN HIS MOST UNCTUOUS VOICE. "I
see you're already on the scene. The brother connection,
right?"

I merely looked at him.

"So is this murder or what?" Spence asked, setting his
equipment case down in the hallway.

"It's 'or what,' " I said. "Buddy Bayard's got his bloomers
in a bunch because he thinks his mother was immortal.
Milo's ticked off. The autopsy's an exercise in futility."

Spence raised one eyebrow. "There *will* be an autopsy?"
He'd opened the case and taken out a tape recorder. "May I
quote you?"

"You may not. Quote Milo. Or grab Dwight when he
comes out."

"Okay," Spence said, dropping his radio personality fa-
cade. "What really happened?"

I shrugged. "Gen Bayard came to dine with her old buddy
Annie Jeanne Dupré. Gen keeled over right after dinner. Ben
made emergency calls. Buddy overreacted. End of story as far
I'm concerned."

Spence gazed down the hall with those keen brown eyes and the hawklike nose that always made him look like a bird of prey. "I've seen Annie Jeanne around town. She doesn't look much like Lucrezia Borgia to me."

"Exactly."

Spence and I both stepped aside for a grumpy-looking Dwight. "Just when I was planning to go home and catch the rest of the football game . . ." he muttered as he passed us.

"Now what?" I said aloud.

Spence chuckled. "Probably the break-in at the Shaws. I picked it up on the scanner. That's why I was late getting here."

I stared at Spence. "Another break-in? Weren't the Shaws at home?"

"A couple of alert joggers chased the burglar away." Spence regarded me with a patronizing expression. "The Shaws were supposed to be dining at the ski lodge with your brother. Apparently, he forgot to call the restaurant and tell them he couldn't make it. They got notified about the robbery attempt and came straight home."

One of Ben's faults is that he's sometimes absentminded, though I've never believed his tale that he once forgot his vestments and celebrated Mass in a T-shirt and boxer shorts. In this instance, however, he could be excused.

"Ben will feel terrible when I tell him," I said to Spence. "In fact, here he comes now."

After I'd relayed the message, Ben started directly for the phone. I cautioned him to wait; the Shaws probably still had deputies with them.

"Was anything stolen at the Shaws?" he asked after evincing dismay.

Spence shook his head. "Not that they know of. They were trying to break a window when the joggers spotted them and called us on their cell phone. The perps took off the back way."

Bernie and Patsy Shaw lived in a house on the east side of town, overlooking the river, and not far from Casa de Bronska, as I called the Italianate villa owned by Ed and Shirley. Maybe the next break-in would be at Ed's, and they'd steal his latest manuscript.

Spence got a quote from Ben, packed up his equipment, and left. But not before he needled me about how he'd gotten the stories of Gen's demise and the latest break-in before the *Advocate*'s pub date.

The next hour seemed anticlimactic. I waited for Ben to get hold of the Shaws around nine-thirty. They'd tried to call my brother from the ski lodge, but the line was busy. Bernie said he figured that some emergency must have come up at the rectory, but was shocked to hear of Gen's death, adding that he hadn't heard of her in years and had wondered if she'd already died.

"She wasn't insured with me," Bernie added, as if her life and death didn't matter unless he had to pay out on a policy.

"Go easy on him," Ben cautioned as we walked through the rain to the hospital. "Bernie's a good guy. He and Patsy are already upset, what with almost getting robbed."

"I'm in a grumpy mood," I admitted. "I hate having Spence gloat when he scoops me."

"There's nothing you can do about that," Ben said in consolation. "He always will. That's the trouble with owning a weekly as opposed to a radio station."

"I know." But it still grated.

Doc Dewey, looking tired, met us outside of the intensive care unit. "Just a precaution," he assured us. "Annie Jeanne's sleeping. I want to keep her under observation. She was quite ill when we brought her here."

"In what way?" I inquired.

Doc made a face. "Sick to her stomach, disoriented, complaining of a terrible headache, blood pressure dangerously low, and she'd started to turn blue."

Ben had brought his kit, which contained the oil for the Sacrament of the Sick. "Any way I can nip in and anoint her?"

Doc, who is an Episcopalian, considered briefly. "Why not?" He opened the ICU door for Ben.

"I don't get it," I said to Doc. "Are those symptoms of hysteria?"

"They can be," Doc said with a frown. "At least the headache, the stomach upset, and even the disorientation. But . . ." He stopped, glancing through the glass that separated the ICU from the corridor.

"But what?"

Doc hesitated again, before meeting my gaze. "I administered ipecac to cause emesis, and activated charcoal to prevent absorption, just in case."

I was puzzled. "Just in case . . . what?"

Doc looked distressed. "Just in case she'd ingested poison."

I didn't exactly reel, but I was certainly startled. "Accidentally, you mean?"

Doc, who was looking more and more like his revered father, nodded. "Of course." But he didn't meet my gaze.

On the way back from the hospital, I told Ben what Doc had said. My brother stopped short of scoffing.

"I suppose," he allowed, "that in her excitement and general ditzlike state, Annie Jeanne may have used the wrong kind of ingredient."

"That'd be terrible," I asserted. "It'd mean she poisoned her best friend. Assuming Annie Jeanne recovers, she'll never forgive herself."

Ben looked grim as we stopped by my Honda in the church

parking lot. "That's the trouble with the Sacrament of Penance. God can forgive people, but often they can't forgive themselves."

"At least the autopsy on Gen will show cause of death," I noted. "Maybe Milo shouldn't be so hard on Buddy after all."

Ben glanced through the rain toward the hospital. "Maybe if Buddy hadn't asked for an autopsy, Doc would have, based on Annie Jeanne's symptoms."

The rain was coming down harder and the wind had picked up. My brother and I were getting wet. But that wasn't the reason for the shiver I felt along my spine.

Homicide—accidental or otherwise—was nagging at the back of my mind.

PRECISELY AT TEN O'CLOCK, MY PHONE RANG. I FIGURED IT might be Ben, calling to see if I got home safely. Just as I left him, sharp gusts of wind had blown down from the mountains, snapping a few tree limbs along my route. Ben wasn't a worrywart, but he also wasn't used to the vagaries of weather in the Cascades.

The caller wasn't Ben. "Emma, I'm so happy to be home!" Vida exclaimed. "Tacoma! So big, so busy! How do people cope? And all those stoplights on the main streets! Really, I almost went mad!"

"I'm truly glad you're back," I declared. "How's Beth?"

"Limping, but able to get around," Vida replied. "Randy is taking tomorrow and Wednesday off since she can't drive yet. He has to prepare for a trial, so he can do that at home."

Beth's husband was a member of a law firm with offices in Tacoma and in Olympia, the state capital. His specialty was insurance fraud.

"I'm afraid I've got some bad news," I said to Vida. "Genevieve Bayard died this evening."

"No!" Vida sounded shocked. "What a shame! To think she'd just gotten here. Very sad for Buddy and Roseanna and the grandchildren. How's your dear brother, Ben?"

"Not as good as he could be, since Gen died at the rectory," I replied. "She was having dinner with Annie Jeanne Dupré."

"Really." Vida paused. "Quite upsetting for Annie Jeanne. I suppose she went to pieces. Such an emotional creature, I've always thought, and not really a very good musician."

Although Vida was a Presbyterian, she'd attended enough funerals at St. Mildred's—and every other church in Skykomish County—that she'd been subjected to Annie Jeanne's thumping.

"Annie Jeanne's in the hospital," I said, somehow put off by Vida's reaction to the latest grim news.

"Dear me," she remarked. "A nervous collapse, I suppose."

"Maybe." I hesitated before dropping my bombshell. "Doc Dewey thinks she may have been poisoned. I assume he's thinking that Gen was, too."

"Gracious!" Vida's cry almost ruptured my eardrum. "Poisoned! Isn't that far-fetched?"

"Please don't tell anyone until after the autopsy on Gen," I urged. "It wouldn't be fair to Gen—or to Annie Jeanne."

"Autopsy!" I could almost hear Vida smacking her lips. "Really, now!" She paused again. "If that's the case, it must have been an accident. My, my. I wonder if the funeral service will be held here?"

"I've no idea," I replied. "That's up to Buddy. I imagine most of Gen's current friends are in Spokane. Where's her husband buried?"

"Ex-husband, you mean," Vida huffed. "I have no idea."

"Did you know him?"

"Vaguely." Vida's voice had cooled. "I must go. I'll see you in the morning."

V IDA'S RETURN CAUSED A PREDICTABLE STIR. SHE PREENED a bit, obviously pleased by the reception. Leo even refrained from calling her Duchess, despite the red satin toque that lent her a regal aura.

But it was Scott who captured the limelight later that morning. He didn't get back from his usual beat until almost ten-thirty.

"Not one," he announced to Vida and me, "but two break-ins yesterday. The Shaws *and* the Pikes."

"The Pikes?" I said with a curious expression. "They're not home."

Scott nodded. "Right. Their neighbors, Roy and Bebe Everson, noticed a broken window by the Pikes' front door this morning when Roy left for work. Bebe called the sheriff, and Sam Heppner went out to take a look. Sure enough, the place had been ransacked."

I stared harder at Scott. "Ransacked? What do you mean?"

Scott hung his peacoat on the oak hat rack Ginny had recently purchased at a garage sale. "Just what I said, according to Sam. The place was really torn up. The funny thing was that nothing of value seemed to have been taken."

Vida was standing by her desk, tucking in the red-and-white-striped blouse that had inched its way out of her gray skirt. "I thought the Pikes weren't leaving until today."

I told her they'd changed their minds and had spent the night at the airport. Turning back to Scott, I asked if the Pikes had been informed.

"Dodge managed to have them paged at the airport," he replied. "They don't take off until around noon. Mrs. Pike said they wouldn't cancel the trip if nothing seemed to be missing. Roy Everson's going to fix the window for them and try to straighten things up before they get back."

Puzzled, I shook my head. "This doesn't sound like the usual MO."

Scott agreed. "The others have been quickies. The burglar gets inside, grabs whatever looks like it could be fenced, and takes off."

"I don't suppose," Vida put in, "that the Eversons saw anything. Roy may be the postal supervisor, but he lives in his own little world. And Bebe is even worse. I wonder sometimes if she doesn't have early Alzheimer's."

That seemed a trifle harsh. Bebe was the vivacious type with a short attention span.

"The fact is," Scott said, sitting down in his swivel chair, "Sam isn't sure when the break-in happened. Roy was at work all day, and Bebe went into Monroe for the afternoon. Neither of them got home until after six. It gets dark a lot earlier than that this time of year, especially when it's raining."

Vida also sat down. "Maud Dodd lives on the other side of the Pikes. She hardly ever comes out of the house anymore. Arthritis, you know. As for Ethel and Pike, I can't imagine what they'd have that was worth stealing. The last time I was in their house they still had a black-and-white TV."

"Then they still have it," Scott said, grinning.

Vida rested her chin on her hands and tapped her cheeks with her fingers. "Yes." She was looking thoughtful, even a bit worried.

Maybe she was thinking about Beth. Whatever the cause of her mood shift, I couldn't let it gnaw at me. This was Tuesday, and we had a paper to put out.

Scott went off to take pictures of both the Shaw and the

Pike houses. He'd already photographed the previous break-in sites. We could run the most recent shots on page two, with a jump from page one. For now, the burglaries were our lead story.

" 'Scene,' " Vida said, just as I was heading into my office after checking the wire service. "I have two items from Ginny and one from Leo. I need four more."

"How about you?" I asked.

"You mean my trip to Tacoma to take care of Beth?" Vida frowned. "Isn't that self-serving?"

"We ran an item about Leo a few years back when he slid downhill on the ice and sprained his ankle," I countered. "In September, you all but announced Scott and Tammy's engagement before they did."

"I merely hinted," Vida said with a sniff. "How did I put it? 'Which beautiful educator and which handsome journalist are hearing the tinkle of wedding bells in the distance?' Or something like that."

"I don't think you wrote *tinkle,*" I said dryly. "At least, I hope not."

"You're not helping me," Vida admonished.

I thought back over the weekend. I'd love to announce that my son was coming home, but that would definitely be self-serving, as if I had to see it in print to believe it. Anyway, it was a two-inch item for Vida's page when he got here. Or maybe twelve inches. Adam and his Alaskan adventures were worth a feature, publisher's son or not.

"We're in a bind," I admitted. "It'd be inappropriate to use the Pikes' early departure, because it'd sound as if they were to blame for the break-in. We should avoid the Burl Creek Thimble Party's event for Gen, since she died a day later. How about mentioning the old-time photos at the Upper Crust?"

"We did that in the story about the renovation," Vida reminded me.

"Oh. Right." I ruminated some more. "The wind blew down some branches on Third Street last night, and probably elsewhere in town."

"That's a brief story," Vida asserted. "You or Scott should check to see if there was any serious damage."

I made a face. "I already did. There wasn't any." My mind seemed to be turning to mush. I felt fragmented by the weekend's events, both happy and sad.

"You're a total loss," Vida chided. "Here's the sheriff. Perhaps he can help. Good morning, Milo. You've spilled something on your trousers. I can use that for 'Scene.' What is it?"

In surprise, Milo glanced at his pants legs. "Damn. Coffee, I expect."

If so, I thought, it was a wonder it hadn't eaten through the fabric. "What's up?" I inquired, after Vida told him not to curse. "Don't tell me you have news."

"Not yet," he replied, still studying the stain. "We sent Gen's body to Everett last night, but I don't expect to hear anything until late today."

"How late?"

Milo shrugged. "Five, six o'clock. Then again, maybe not until tomorrow."

"Milo," I said calmly and slowly, "we have a deadline today. Do you think it might be possible to see if you can goose the Everett MEs into hurrying just a little bit? After all, they owe you. Didn't you apprehend a bank robber for them last month?"

"Oh—right," Milo said, finally looking up. "The guy who ran off the road by Deception Falls. No big deal. He wasn't going anywhere. He had a broken pelvis."

"That's not the point. You caught him." I put on my most pitiful expression. "Please, Milo? Just for the sake of your hometown newspaper?"

"The SnoCo MEs don't care if I apprehended a perp," Milo noted. "But I'll see what I can do." He strolled over to the table that held the coffeemaker and what was left of the morning's pastries. "No doughnuts? No cinnamon rolls? What's this?" He picked up a knish.

I explained. "That one is filled with cheese. The Upper Crust is introducing a few ethnic pastries. We do, after all, have some diversity on the college campus."

Milo bit into the soft dough. "Not bad," he remarked, licking his lips.

"A 'Scene' item for certain," Vida murmured, scribbling on a piece of paper.

Milo poured himself half a mug of coffee. "By the way, this might be of interest to you, Vida. When Sam checked out the Pike house this morning, somebody had set a small fire in the backyard. The rain was down to a drizzle by then, so the fire didn't do much damage. It's kind of crazy, though. The parts that didn't get completely burned were some papers that looked like a kind of pattern. There was also a corner of an old quilt. What caught Sam's eye was that somebody had written on it. It was your mother's name, Muriel Blatt."

Vida turned white.

SIX

It's just the shock," Vida assured me after I'd quickly brought her a glass of water. "My mother. Her quilts. She was so clever with her fingers. Goodness." Vida dabbed at her eyes with a tissue. "Goodness," she repeated.

Milo was leaning over Vida's desk, his face filled with concern. "Would you like . . . what's left of the quilt?"

Vida vehemently shook her head and blew her nose at the same time. "No. No, not if it's half-burned."

"It's pretty much gone," Milo conceded. He stood up and framed a foot-wide triangle with his hands. "The only part is the border where her name is, and some red, white, and blue cloth."

Vida nodded and blew her nose again, sounding much like a herald using his trumpet to proclaim a big event. "Yes, Mother always signed her quilts. Most quilters do. Excuse me," she said, getting up from her chair. "I must go to the restroom."

"Poor Vida," I said when she'd disappeared. "She's had a rough few days."

"I guess," Milo allowed. "I've never seen her so upset."

"Did Mrs. Blatt date the quilt, as well?" I inquired, recalling some of my paternal grandmother's handsome quilts, three of which I still had at home.

Milo grimaced. "I almost told her what the whole signature deal said. I'm glad I didn't."

All at sea, I gazed up at Milo. "Why not?"

"Because," he said slowly, obviously trying to recall the inscription word for word, "it read 'Begun February 10, 1974, by Genevieve Bayard,' written in a different handwriting. Then it said, 'Completed October 21, 1978, by Muriel May Blatt.' I thought mentioning Gen's name so soon after she died might upset Vida. I suppose they were friends."

Milo and I didn't know it, but he couldn't have been more wrong.

INSTEAD OF THE INTERVIEW I'D SCHEDULED WITH GEN, I asked Vida if she would talk to Buddy and Roseanna about the dead woman's life.

Vida refused. She was polite but insisted she had too much catching up to do. In a way, that was true: Our House & Home editor collected potential news items via her vast network of friends and relations. Being out of the loop for the past four days was tantamount to having the Associated Press wire go down.

"Don't forget," she added, not quite looking me in the eye, "I have to prepare for my weekly radio show tomorrow night. I've already lined up Rosemary Bourgette to talk about her experiences as SkyCo's prosecuting attorney."

After eight months, Vida should know that I no longer harbored any resentment for what I'd initially termed her defection to the radio station. Last February she'd sprung *Vida's Cupboard* on me without warning. That wasn't fair, but after a few weeks, I got over it. She never used items that should have appeared in the paper first, and her sponsors divided their advertising budget between KSKY and the *Advocate.*

Scott, whose main flaw was not making deadlines, already had plenty on his plate. I called Roseanna and told her what I needed as background—if she and Buddy didn't mind.

Buddy had kept the studio open despite the tragedy, but Roseanna had taken the day off to cope with whatever arrangements might be necessary for Gen's funeral.

"Come over to the house at two-thirty when the original appointment was set with Gen," she said in a flat tone. "I'll make coffee. Or maybe something stronger. I could use a good jolt about now."

T HE RAIN HAD STARTED AGAIN WHEN I CLIMBED THE winding stone steps that led up to the Bayards' brick rambler on Pine Street near Icicle Creek. I felt as if I were going to interview a ghost: Same time, same place—but the subject was dead.

Roseanna met me at the door. Her usual high color was drained, her fair hair drooped, and the sparkle was gone from her blue eyes.

"Can you believe this?" she said in a tired voice. "The first time Gen comes to visit, she dies. Why do mothers-in-law have to be so contrary?"

It dawned on me that maybe I wasn't looking at grief in Roseanna's eyes, but frustration. I didn't know what to say. All I could come up with was, "It's sad for everyone."

Roseanna indicated I should sit on the big brown leather sofa, while she flopped into a matching armchair. "Gen wasn't your average mother or grandmother," she declared. "Oh, I shouldn't criticize, but in all the years our three kids were growing up, she never remembered a birthday. Christmas, yes, she could hardly miss that, but otherwise . . ." She waved a hand. "Our kids barely knew her. We hauled them over to Spokane when they were little, but after they got to be teenagers, we gave up coercing them into going with us. It's a damned shame, really."

I seemed to have sunk at least six inches into the soft leather. "Not the maternal type, I guess."

She shook her head. "No wonder Buddy is an only child. I honestly don't think she liked children. Of course, Gen was very young when she had him." Roseanna gave me a knowing look.

"Teenagers in love?" I remarked.

"You got it. Gen barely finished high school. Andy was two years older. They got married that June, and Buddy was born in October. You know how it was in those days—a backstreet abortion, a six-month stay at a home for wayward girls, or a shotgun wedding. One way or the other, unwed mothers didn't keep their babies." Roseanna's color suddenly rose. "Damn. I didn't mean . . ."

I waved away her apology. "I was 'wayward' several years later. Abortion was legal by then, but I wouldn't do it. Just think of me as a pioneer."

Roseanna smiled weakly. "The Poster Girl for Single Moms," she said. "Do you want something to drink? A gin and tonic sounds good to me."

"Go ahead," I responded. "I still have work to do this afternoon. I'll take a Pepsi or a Coke if you've got it—as long as it's not diet."

Roseanna went out into the kitchen. I hauled myself off the sofa and walked into the dining room, where one wall was covered with Buddy's photographs, most of which were of family and friends. I felt guilty as I studied his artistry.

Buddy was very good, although we rarely used his photos except in cases of Mother Nature gone wild. The most recent example was a July thunder and lightning storm where he'd captured some spectacular shots of the summer storm. Maybe I could appease him by buying more of his photographs for the paper. Financially, it wouldn't make up for the loss of the darkroom job, but he'd get more exposure, perhaps even have some of his work picked up by the wire services.

"The Rogues Gallery," Roseanna noted as she came out of the kitchen carrying two glasses and a can of Coke. "Did you ever see our wedding picture?" She nodded to her left. "Weren't we cute? It was our hippie phase."

Roseanna's fair hair hung down to her waist; Buddy's was almost as long, and his beard sprouted in every direction. Their clothes were conventional, however, though I peered closely at the bridal bouquet.

"It's an artichoke," Roseanna said. "We were into growing our own vegetables."

I laughed. "Not artichokes at this elevation, right?"

"Right. But I couldn't carry radishes or onions. Anyway, it was February. We convinced Father Fitz that the artichoke was an exotic tropical flower. I guess he'd never eaten one."

"I assume he enforced a dress code," I said as I accepted the glass of ice and the can of Coke from my hostess.

"You bet," Roseanna replied. "Of course, my parents were on his side."

"And Buddy's, too?"

"Gen and Andy had split up long before that," Roseanna said, no longer amused. "Andy didn't come to the wedding, just the reception, where he got so drunk he fell in the punch bowl. He died about four years after we were married. His truck went off the road somewhere south of Seattle and hit a tree. He probably passed out at the wheel. Andy had moved from Alpine just a couple of months before he died. Buddy refused to talk about him."

I nodded at the wall. "Are there any pictures of his parents here?"

"Just Gen," Roseanna replied. "One of the few along with our wedding photo that Buddy didn't take. Here." She pointed to what looked like an enlargement of a snapshot. Standing on a beach with the ocean or maybe the sound in the background, Genevieve Bayard was wearing shorts and a halter top. She looked as if she was in her mid-twenties, and pretty enough to be a pinup girl.

"She was a knockout," I said. "She certainly must have had her chances to remarry, especially after Andy died and she could have had a church wedding."

Roseanna was heading back into the living room. "She probably did. I know she had at least one guy she was living with for a long time, but they never made it official. When we'd visit her in Spokane, she was careful to make sure he wasn't around. But," she went on, sitting down again in the easy chair, "Buddy and I knew there was a man stashed somewhere. His belongings were evident around the house."

"But not in the spare bedrooms?"

"No. We figured they were sleeping together." Roseanna took a big drink from her G&T. "There were only two bedrooms. When the kids went with us, they had to bring sleeping bags and bed down in the living room. I really can't blame them for not going with us when they got older. It wasn't as if she made a fuss over them anyway. I'm sure they felt like excess baggage."

"That's sad," I remarked. Not that I'd ever know what it would be like to be a grandmother.

"Gen was an odd woman," Roseanna said with a wave of her hand. "What else do you want to know about her?"

Obviously, we couldn't run an obit with a headline that read ODD WOMAN DIES IN ALPINE. "Vida no doubt has the early background filed away in her amazing brain," I noted. "Why did Gen move away?"

Roseanna shrugged. "I think she got bored, not to mention sick and tired of getting drunken phone calls in the middle of the night from Andy telling her how much he still loved her. She left town about three years after we were married. She went to Seattle for a while, but didn't like it. Too big. Gen had friends in Spokane, though we never met them. She liked the sun, too, and of course they have more of that in eastern Washington than on this side of the mountains. I suppose Spokane was a natural choice—not really all that far, but smaller than Seattle."

"And more sun," I murmured. "More snow, too. Was this really the first time she visited here since she left?"

Roseanna nodded. "Yes. Gen always said she'd had enough of small towns. Her parents—they were the Ferrers, who died long before you came to Alpine—were her only other relatives here. The brother had been a commercial fisherman and drowned in Alaska years ago. Except for Buddy," Roseanna added on a bitter note, "there was no reason for her to visit. And apparently, he wasn't enough."

"She had friends," I pointed out, "like Annie Jeanne Dupré and the other women in the Burl Creek Thimble Club."

Roseanna gave me an ironic smile. "Gen and Annie Jeanne. The original odd couple. Yes, that's so, but she wasn't really close to the rest of them. Actually, I think she and Annie Jeanne wrote to each other quite often."

"Did Annie Jeanne ever go to visit Gen in Spokane?"

"Not that I ever heard of," Roseanna said. "You know Annie Jeanne; she's so timid. I'm not sure if she's ever been to Seattle."

If Annie Jeanne had ever visited the big city, I hadn't heard of it. That meant Vida hadn't, either: Vida would not only know, but put the item on her page or in "Scene." As for Gen, I knew more than I did when I arrived at the Bayards', but most of it wasn't fit to print.

"She was a quilter," I said after a long pause. "Gen must have been clever with her hands."

"Yes," Roseanna agreed. "She was good. When we visited, she always showed off the latest outfits she'd made for herself. She didn't just sew, she could do tailoring. Until a couple of years ago, Gen worked in alterations for women's stores in Spokane. But she never made anything for us, not even baby clothes when the kids were small."

"Ah." Finally we'd hit on something newsworthy. "Do you know what store she worked at?"

"Several," Roseanna replied, her hand swirling around what was left of her cocktail. "She never stayed long in one place, except for Frederick & Nelson before they closed. Gen always had complaints, especially with the owners of smaller stores. She was with Nordstrom when she retired. Do you need to know exactly?"

I shook my head. "That's good enough. I suppose she belonged to a parish in Spokane."

"Yes, the church on the Gonzaga University campus. She had a condo by the river."

It crossed my mind that the condo would be worth something. Maybe it had crossed Roseanna's mind, too. If so, she wasn't looking very happy about it.

"So," I said, "Buddy and your kids are the sole survivors?"

"Yes." She wore a dour expression.

Making notes, I nodded. "Full names in order of age are Kenneth, Anne, and Joseph, right?"

"Right." Roseanna finished her drink. "Kenny's waiting

at WSU to hear about the funeral. If it isn't held here, he might as well stay in Pullman since it's so close to Spokane."

"You don't know yet where the services will be held?"

"No. We haven't tracked down her lawyer yet—if she had a lawyer. For all we know," Roseanna went on in a grim voice, "she left instructions to be buried in Spokane. We're waiting for Doc or the ME or whoever to sign off on the death certificate. According to Al Driggers, she didn't have a plot in Alpine."

"Maybe," I said, putting my notepad in my purse, "we'll hear something later today."

Roseanna stood up. "I hope so. This is a real pain." She grimaced. "That sounds so callous. It isn't as if we'd been close to Gen. Buddy's never known what it's like to have a doting mother. Oh, she clothed and fed him when he was a kid, but she was never . . . *loving*. I guess that's the word. Gen was a very cold person, in my opinion."

I'd struggled out of the deep leather sofa and was moving toward the door. I smiled at Roseanna. "I can't put that in the paper, either."

"I know," she said with a heavy sigh.

"I can run a photo, though," I said. "Do you have one that's fairly recent?"

Roseanna snorted. "No. The only one we have is that cheesecake shot on the wall. Not appropriate, right?"

"Right. Didn't Buddy ever take pictures of her when you visited?"

"No," Roseanna said. "She didn't want him to. She was camera-shy, she told him."

I considered my options. "Charlene Vickers brought in some photos from the BCTC party," I said. "We can crop one of them and run a head shot."

"Fine." Roseanna sounded as if she didn't care if we ran a picture of Gen's rear end. "Oh—how's Annie Jeanne?" she asked suddenly. "I heard she made herself sick over Gen's death."

"I called the hospital this morning," I replied, my hand on the brass doorknob. "Doc Dewey was in surgery, and Dr. Sung was seeing patients at the clinic. The nurse told me that Annie Jeanne was stable but still very upset. Ben planned to see her this afternoon. I'm going to call again when I get back to the office."

"Poor lady," Roseanna said with a shake of her head. "Annie Jeanne's so high-strung. If she stays another day at the hospital, I'll go see her tomorrow."

"I should, too," I said. "In fact, I'll drop in after work."

"It's funny," Roseanna remarked as we stood on the porch, "I feel much sorrier for Annie Jeanne being sick than I do for Gen being dead. That's not right, is it?"

I couldn't answer that question. "It sounds as if Gen led a very private life," I said in a vague voice.

"Private?" Roseanna narrowed her eyes, though she didn't look at me but out into the rain that was falling on a slant. "More than private. It's almost as if she'd led a secret life. Maybe it's just as well that we don't know what she did all those years on the other side of the mountains. We might not like it if we knew the truth."

SEVEN

THE TRUTH. WHAT EVERY JOURNALIST WANTS TO KNOW. Roseanna had certainly piqued my interest in her mother-in-law's background, so much so that I'd forgotten to apologize for yanking our darkroom business away from Buddy.

The only problem was that if the Bayards didn't know what Gen had been up to for the last twenty-odd years, nobody else would either. Not even Vida. My House & Home editor's grapevine didn't grow as far as Spokane. I decided that I might as well let Gen rest in peace. *If* I could.

Instead of phoning the hospital when I returned to the office, I called Ben. I caught him just as he was about to meet with a parishioner whose troubles apparently came out of a bottle. I knew better than to ask who.

"Annie Jeanne's coming along okay," Ben informed me. "Doc's keeping her another day to make sure she doesn't go to pieces again."

"Thank goodness Alpine's hospital isn't like its big-city counterparts," I said. "Here they don't throw you out twenty-four hours after you've had brain surgery or broken every bone in your body."

"My, my," Ben said lightly, "do I hear you trumpeting the praises of small-town life?"

"There are *some* advantages," I said, sounding defensive. "Did Doc mention anything about . . . food poisoning?"

"If he did, it was said in confidence," Ben replied.

"He's not a parishioner," I pointed out. "You wouldn't break the seal of the confessional by telling *your very own sister.*"

"Hey, Sluggly, a confidence is a confidence. Ask Doc yourself. Gotta go, gotta tell a certain unidentified person that falling down drunk can make for a hard climb on the stairway to heaven. See you at dinner."

I took Ben's advice and called Doc at the clinic. He and his partner, Elvis Sung, were both seeing patients, according to the receptionist, Marje Blatt. The raw November weather was doing its dirty work, especially among the elderly. Bronchitis was rampant, along with colds that came attached with flulike symptoms.

Vida had just returned from making her rounds. The satin toque looked very wet and very wrinkled. She removed the hat and gave it a good shake. "Whatever was I thinking of this morning?" she muttered. "I should have worn my new sou'wester. I bought it at the Tacoma Mall. Such a busy place! You can hardly move without bumping into someone."

I was leaning in the doorway to my office. "You didn't happen to stop by the clinic today for a visit with your niece, Marje Blatt, did you?"

"What?" Vida set the battered toque on top of the radiator. "Well, as a matter of fact, I did. It would have been most thoughtless of me not to check in to see who'd been ill in my absence. I do send so many get-well cards, you know."

"And?" I coaxed.

"Marje was a clam," Vida declared with an expression of disapproval. "My niece knows better than to keep things from me. On the other hand," she added grudgingly, "Marje may not be aware of exactly what caused Annie Jeanne's severe reaction. Receptionists aren't always as well informed as nurses."

"It couldn't have been allergies," I pointed out. "Annie Jeanne did the cooking."

"True." Vida looked at the clock before sitting at her desk. "It's almost four. I assume you haven't had any word on the autopsy from Milo?"

Ginny had no messages for me from the sheriff. It was too soon to nag. There still was an hour to go before deadline.

"I'll call him before five," I said. But surely this time, Milo wouldn't forget our pub date. Or would he? "Are you certain you don't want to write the obituary part about Gen?" I asked Vida.

"Positive," she replied, peering at her own phone messages.

"Then I need your input on her early background," I said.

She looked at me. "Didn't you get that from Roseanna?"

"Roseanna wasn't born yet," I said dryly. "Furthermore, she wasn't at all close to Gen."

"I shouldn't think so," Vida said, and pursed her lips.

"Parents' names, schooling, marriage? Come on, Vida, help me out."

Vida whipped off her glasses and began pummeling her eyes. "Ooooh . . . very well." She sighed heavily, put her glasses back on, and stared into space. "Parents, Marie Curtis Ferrer and Paul Ferrer. He worked as a sawyer in the mills. I believe Paul was originally from Wisconsin, and Marie was born in Snohomish. Children, Peter and Genevieve. Peter, the elder of the two, died in his early twenties when his fishing boat capsized off of Ketchikan. Gen became pregnant when she was a senior in high school and married Andre—known as Andy—Bayard right after she graduated."

"I know that part," I put in.

Vida turned in my direction. "Then that's it. The rest is Buddy's birth, Andy's drunkenness, violent quarrels between husband and wife, and finally divorce. Andy died years ago in a tragic highway accident. He drank."

"Is he buried here?" I asked.

"What difference does it make?" Vida demanded. "You don't put that sort of thing in an obituary."

"I know," I agreed. "This is straight news, page one. But I was thinking about where Gen might be buried."

"In a ditch, for all I care," Vida said, picking up the telephone receiver, and with ruthless fingers, she punched in numbers.

I wrote the story, wondering if I still might have to insert a new lead. But when I called Milo at ten to five, he assured me he hadn't heard anything from Everett, and that he'd checked as recently as half an hour earlier.

"They knock off at five," he said, "or pretty close to it. I figure we'll get the results sometime before noon tomorrow."

"Okay," I said, disappointed. "But if you do hear anything in the next hour or so, call me at home or on my cell."

Milo promised that he would. As a precautionary measure, I told Kip to answer the phone if it rang. The sheriff might absentmindedly call the newspaper, forgetting that I wasn't still at work.

Ben wasn't due for dinner until after six. I'd planned on swinging by the Grocery Basket to pick up some lamb chops and fresh broccoli. I had everything else I needed at home.

But the hospital wasn't out of my way. I stopped there first and took the elevator to the second floor. The buxom, gray-haired nurse on duty was one of the Bergstroms. She informed me that Ms. Dupré couldn't receive visitors.

"Nerves, if you ask me," Olga Bergstrom huffed. "One of those excitable types. The kind of old maid who keeps medical coverage high. Every time they get a stomachache or a stuffy nose, it's off to see the doctor. I've no time for it."

I assumed a humble yet quizzical attitude. "You mean you don't think there was a medical cause for Annie Jeanne's collapse?"

"She ate something that didn't agree with her. Spoiled milk, I wouldn't wonder. You'd be surprised by how many people come into emergency, swearing they've been poisoned. Doctor—well, both doctors, really—humor them, especially if they're of a certain age. Mark my words, often as not, it's something they had in the refrigerator that they couldn't bear to throw out. Afraid to spend an extra dollar—they'd rather have their stomachs pumped."

"Goodness," I said in professed dismay, "perhaps I ought to run an article in the paper warning people to keep track of due dates on their perishable products."

"An excellent idea," Olga asserted with a sharp nod of her head. Unlike so many medical practitioners, she wore starched whites, white stockings, a cap with a double stripe, and a pin that indicated she'd trained at Deaconess Hospital in Spokane. Old Doc Dewey had insisted on proper attire, and his son carried on the tradition. I thought it wise. Call me fussy, but I prefer being able to tell the difference between a nurse and a barmaid at Mugs Ahoy.

"I can't discuss the case, of course," Olga continued, keeping one eye on the monitors at the nurses' station, "but a word to the wise is never wasted. Shelf dates, expiration dates, anything that a person has had on hand for over a year, particularly if it's been opened."

That qualified my food stores for condemnation by the health department. I should have felt doomed.

"We'll put that in the *Advocate*," I promised. It was a House & Home item, and actually not the worst idea I'd heard. Vida might even have a syndicated column on the subject in her files. "I understand Annie Jeanne is recovering, though."

"Certainly," Olga replied. "She should be up and doing by Thursday." The nurse's keen blue eyes scrutinized me. "That's right—she's the housekeeper at the Catholic church. Your brother is no doubt anxious for her to get back to work. I've heard that priests can be quite demanding."

"Ben's not used to having a housekeeper," I said. "I don't recall Father Kelly being a slave driver."

Olga's lips exhibited a faint twitch of amusement. "Strange you should say that, since he's black. But I'm talking in general, from what people say about priests. You might be surprised at the things I've heard, especially lately."

"No," I said, sounding weary, "I wouldn't. As a Catholic, I've heard it all."

Olga looked dubious, but was distracted by one of the monitors. "Ah. Elmer Kemp is having some respiratory problems. A smoker, you know. I must go. I'm all alone, it being the dinner hour."

Olga bustled away.

Fifteen minutes later, I was waiting in the express checkout line at the Grocery Basket when my cell phone rang. Despite a glare from the woman ahead of me, I answered the call. It might be Milo.

It was. "We got the autopsy report," he said in his typically unhurried manner. "It came in about ten minutes ago. Hang on." The phone crackled a couple of times as it sometimes does at Alpine's three-thousand-foot elevation. I tried to refrain from tapping my foot. "Sorry about that. Bill Blatt had a question for me about his overtime. Anyway, as I was saying, we got the ME's results back from Everett. According to them, Genevieve Bayard died from a—" The phone cut out again.

It was my turn with the checker, Ryan O'Toole, the teenage son of the store's owners. Ryan gazed at me with questioning hazel eyes after he rang up my seven items. The total was thirty-one dollars and forty-four cents. The express line was cash only. My wallet was short by four dollars. Preparing to beg and scrambling to find my credit card, I heard a mellow voice in the ear that wasn't glued to the phone.

"May I?" said Spencer Fleetwood, handing me a five-dollar bill.

"Jeez." I glanced at the half-dozen people behind Spence, gritted my teeth, and took the money. "Thanks," I murmured. "I owe you."

By the time I got my change and my bag of groceries, the cell had gone dead. I hurried out into the rain and dialed the sheriff's number.

"What happened?" Milo said. "I lost you."

I didn't take time to explain. He was the sheriff; he could figure it out. "How did Gen die?" I asked, as the rain poured down and I wondered if I could get electrocuted.

"What?" He sounded impatient. "Oh—you lost the connection. Gen was poisoned, an overdose of insulin. It was in the food she ate at the rectory. I'm afraid Annie Jeanne Dupré's in a bit of trouble."

My jaw dropped. "No! That's impossible! It had to be an accident!"

"We still have to investigate," Milo said reasonably. "I sent Dustin to the hospital to stand guard."

"You think Annie Jeanne's going to escape?" I asked in disbelief.

"No, of course not," he responded on a slightly sour note. "It's procedure. Besides, if Gen's death wasn't accidental, Annie Jeanne could be in danger. She was poisoned, too. And if it was an accident, she might be suicidal. I'll have Dwight Gould spell Dustin later on."

"Good grief," I murmured, realizing that I hadn't seen any sign of the law at the hospital. "When did Dustin go over there?"

"About fifteen minutes ago," Milo said. "Got to run. I'm on my way to Buddy and Roseanna's. Talk to you later." He clicked off.

As I opened the passenger door, Spence sauntered out of the store. "Emma!" he called.

I was putting the groceries on the floor of my Honda. Maybe I could pretend I didn't hear him. But his voice carried and he knew it; I swore he could broadcast without a transmitter.

"Just a minute!" I yelled. "Let me get out of the rain!" Rushing around to the driver's side, I frantically dialed the *Advocate*'s number. The phone rang four times, and I was afraid it would trunk over to the answering system before Kip could pick up.

He answered just as I was plunging into despair. "Hold everything!" I shouted—just as Spence slid into the passenger seat beside me.

"You owe me," he murmured, looking annoyingly amused.

"Ohhh . . ." But no matter how much I stalled, Spence would have the news before the paper was published. My shoulders slumped. I stopped shouting and briefly relayed the autopsy report to Kip.

"Are you coming to the office?" Kip asked.

"Of course, I'm on my way as soon as I call Ben to tell

him I'll be late getting home. We're going to need at least three inches, either on page one or in a jump to page two."

"Got it," Kip said. "See you."

I put the key in the ignition. Spence angled his long legs around the grocery bag and leaned back in the seat. "So Mrs. Bayard was poisoned." He glanced at his high-tech watch that seemed to tell him everything except the odds on the Super Bowl. "I just missed the six-o'clock hour turn. I'll have to break in with a bulletin."

"You can start by getting out of my car," I snapped. "I'm not a taxi."

"I've got my wheels here," he replied, reaching over to lift a strand of wet hair out of my right eye. "You need a haircut."

I was beyond annoyance, climbing fast to anger. Fury wasn't far behind. "Since when did I ask you to be my fashion consultant? Beat it, Fleetwood. I've got work to do."

With feigned sadness, Spence shook his head. "I thought we were media partners. I'm only trying to help your image."

I turned on the engine just as my cell phone rang again. I shot Spence a dark look as I fumbled around in my purse for the blasted phone.

"I know when I'm not wanted," he said with a self-pitying sigh. "Besides, I have breaking news to report. Ta-ta."

Spence got out of the car just as I found the phone and answered.

"Where the hell are you, Sluggly?" my brother asked. "I'm drowning on your front porch."

"Meet me at the paper," I said. "I'll explain then. I've got the lamb chops with me." I rang off, turned on the windshield wipers, and reversed out of the parking space. Someone honked behind me. I looked in the rearview mirror. It was Spence in his BMW. I felt like backing up and hitting him.

Instead, I drove a little too fast, but not fast enough to beat my brother, who had a straight shot down Fourth from my little log cabin to the newspaper office.

"What kept you?" he asked ingenuously as he stood by the entrance.

"You'll kill yourself someday," I muttered as I unlocked the door. "I'll gloat before I mourn."

"Hmm," he responded, "somebody's little sister is in a bad mood."

"Somebody's big brother is going to be in one when I tell you what's happened," I shot back.

"How's that?" Ben asked as I flipped on the lights in the reception area before heading into the back shop.

I was feeling perverse. "What do you think of having your housekeeper charged with murder?"

Ben looked at me as if I must be joking. But I kept walking until we were in the production area. Kip looked up from whatever he was doing with the optical character scanner.

"Hi, Emma, hi, Father." Kip stood up. "Are we talking poison as in murder?"

"We don't say 'murder' until Milo does," I replied. "Don't worry, I'm going to rewrite the story with great caution."

"What about *Annie Jeanne*?" Ben demanded, following me back into the newsroom and on into my cubbyhole.

"I'm sorry," I said, sitting down and turning on the computer. "I exaggerated. Let me do this first. Then I'll explain."

Ben glowered at me before turning around and going out into the newsroom.

It took me a couple of minutes to focus on the new lead. "Alpine native Genevieve Ferret Bayard died early Monday evening after ingesting what the Snohomish County medical examiners termed 'an overdose of insulin.' "

I stared at the sentence. It was as dead as Gen, and I'd

misspelled her maiden name. Changing *Ferret* to *Ferrer*, I deleted the rest of the lead. Then I deleted everything except Gen's name. Next, I called the sheriff's office.

"Milo's not there, right?" I said to Deputy Bill Blatt, who also happened to be Vida's nephew.

"He only left about ten minutes ago for the Bayards'," Bill said. "Can I help?"

Perhaps because of his kinship—not to mention constant reminders from Aunt Vida about deadlines—Bill was more aware than most about how we put out the paper. "Can you give me the exact wording of the ME's statement?"

"Want me to fax it to you?" Bill asked.

"Please. Thanks, Bill. I gather there isn't anything else that Milo didn't tell me?"

"Um . . ." Bill was as cautious as his boss. "I was standing right by him when he was talking to you. Until we start the investigation, I don't think there's anything else we can say yet."

That made sense. "Can I quote you as saying Gen's death qualifies as being caused by mysterious or suspicious circumstances?"

"Ouch." I could picture Bill flinching. "Gee, I wouldn't want to say that in the paper."

"I need a quote."

"Do you really?"

"Yes."

"Um . . . okay, how about this? I'll say, 'Mrs. Bayard's death will be under investigation.' "

It was feeble, but it'd have to do. At least it covered the backsides of the sheriff's office and the newspaper. "Thanks, Bill. Your aunt will thank you, too."

"I hope so," Bill said. "She's been out of sorts the last few days, even before she went to Tacoma. I guess she gave Buck Bardeen an earful because he hadn't put Cupcake to bed

Monday night. Luckily, she got home before it was really dark. Why do canaries have to have a blanket anyway? Other birds don't."

"Other birds don't live indoors," I said before ringing off.

Although the fax's official wording didn't add anything important, by the fourth try, I had a livelier, more up-to-date lead: "Skykomish County law officials are launching an investigation into the insulin poisoning death of Alpine native Genevieve Ferrer Bayard, who was stricken Monday evening while visiting here."

Explaining where Gen's death occurred was a delicate matter. Pending the outcome of the autopsy, I hadn't yet written that part. No blame must be attached in any way to St. Mildred's or to my brother. And, as far as I was concerned, to Annie Jeanne.

"Bayard died shortly after dinner with her longtime friend Annie Jeanne Dupré, who was hospitalized with similar symptoms of poisoning. Dupré is recovering at Alpine Memorial Hospital, but is expected to be released today."

So far, so tactful. But I hadn't finished the paragraph. Reminding myself of the five W's of journalism—who, what, when, where, and why—I took a deep breath and continued typing.

"The two women were dining at the rectory of St. Mildred's Catholic Church, where Dupré is employed as parish housekeeper."

I looked out into the newsroom. My brother was perusing a bound copy of past editions of the *Advocate*.

"Ben," I called, "I need a quote from you."

He slammed the volume shut and approached my office. "Why?"

"To save your ass and mine. Here," I said, quickly printing out the material I'd written, "what comes next is you exonerating the church, Annie Jeanne, and yourself while also expressing shock and sorrow."

Ben scanned the lines. "Shit." He bit his lower lip and scowled before signaling me to vacate my chair. "I do better if I write, not talk."

"Go ahead." I stood up and wandered around what little space there was in my cubbyhole. Ben typed in fits and starts. After five minutes, he shook his head and got to his feet. "See if this'll do."

I sat down again and read what my brother had written.

"Like the entire community of Alpine, I'm devastated by the untimely passing of Genevieve Bayard and by the suffering of Annie Jeanne Dupré. However, I have great confidence in Sheriff Milo Dodge, and I am certain that he'll be able to determine what might have caused such a horrendous accident. Personally, I blame the Baptists."

"That's not funny," I snarled, deleting the last sentence.

"Hey," Ben retorted, "don't lose your sense of humor. You're wound up like a Swiss watch."

He was right. I tried to relax. "It's going on seven. We're two hours behind already."

"No, you're not," Ben pointed out. "Kip hasn't been dozing in the back shop; he's been putting the rest of the paper together. Sure, you're worried about Annie Jeanne. So am I. But we know she wouldn't intentionally hurt a fly. So we'll have to see her through this."

I agreed. It wasn't hard to picture Annie Jeanne all aflutter, scurrying around the rectory kitchen and, in her excitement, using the wrong—and deadly—ingredient.

Just before I sent the complete story to Kip, I wondered if we should run a small head shot of Annie Jeanne on page two. There was one in our files, although it had been taken at least fifteen years earlier, before I bought the paper. But Annie

Jeanne was one of those people who never appeared to age; she seemed to have been born middle-aged.

I had seen the photo recently, just before Father Kelly left on his sabbatical. Annie Jeanne wasn't smiling, but looked uncharacteristically severe, with her high forehead and graying black hair pulled back into a tight knot: A cliché, really, of the repressed old maid who might slide off her rocker and do in her nearest and dearest. I decided not to run the photo. It was too easy for readers to imagine the cutline that wasn't there.

"Annie Jeanne Dupré: church organist, housekeeper—and ruthless poisoner."

EIGHT

I DIDN'T HAVE THE ENERGY TO CALL VIDA THAT NIGHT TO relay the latest news. She'd find out soon enough, if, in fact, she hadn't wormed the story out of Bill Blatt already.

Strangely enough, she hadn't. "You should have phoned me," she declared in a testy voice when I announced the autopsy findings to the staff shortly after eight o'clock Wednesday morning. "What got into you?"

I was standing in the middle of the newsroom. Vida was also on her feet, hanging up her mottled brown raincoat. Leo lounged at his desk, caressing his coffee mug as if it were a woman. Ginny was in the doorway to the outer office, and Scott was placing the Upper Crust's morning offering of elephant ears on our worn plastic tray. Kip, who worked late hours before pub day, was always allowed to come in when he felt like it.

"Why?" I replied in an indifferent voice. "You haven't had much input on Gen's Alpine visit, Vida. I didn't think you'd be that interested."

Vida stamped her foot. "Nonsense! Of course I'm interested when someone gets poisoned in my hometown!"

She made it sound as if anyone having the temerity to die of unnatural causes in Alpine was a personal affront. I shrugged. "Now you know."

Vida paced back and forth by her desk. She was wearing the sou'wester today and hadn't yet taken it off. I kept expecting her to announce she'd found a full lobster pot off the coast of Maine.

I decided to confront her. "Well? Does that mean you'll write Gen's official obit when we get the information?"

Vida stopped pacing, standing splayfooted by the hat rack. The sou'wester's brim had fallen over her eyes, and I could barely see them. "Well. I'll have to think about that."

"When you make up your mind, let me know," I said, and started back into my cubbyhole but stopped just short of the doorway and turned to Scott, who was sampling the baked goods. "Maybe I should take over this story," I told him.

He looked crestfallen. "I haven't gotten a really juicy assignment in a long time," Scott said quietly. "So far, this is just a dumb accident."

I made a face. "I know. But it involves my brother and my parish. Nobody knows him—or Annie Jeanne, for that matter—as well as I do. I feel a family obligation."

The gloom lifted from Scott's handsome face. "That's true." He gave me a sheepish smile. "I didn't think of it that way."

"I'll check the sheriff's log for you while I'm there," I said. And then, because I hate being at odds with Vida, I asked her to step into my office.

"I forgot to mention this earlier, but Hank Sails died. I'm going to a memorial reception for him in Seattle tomorrow evening at seven o'clock. Do you want to come with me?"

Vida evinced surprise and then sadness. "Hank," she murmured. "Such a fine, courageous man. Yes, I think I'd like to join you, though going to Seattle so soon after being in Tacoma is something of an ordeal."

But, I thought, not one she couldn't endure for the sake of sniffing some funereal atmosphere. To be fair, however, I was certain that Vida had genuinely liked and admired the longtime newspaperman. Most people in the profession did.

Fifteen minutes and one cinnamon twister later, I was walking through the rain to the sheriff's office, a block away on Front Street. Like many people who were born and raised in Seattle, I didn't own any bumbershoots, as my parents had called them. The rain in the city was seldom more than a drizzle, and the first stiff wind turned the umbrellas inside out. They were more trouble than they were worth. Despite the more severe weather in Alpine, I remained staunch—and often wet. No umbrella for Emma, but always a jacket with a hood.

"No," Milo said as soon as I came through the front door.

"No?" I flipped back the hood and went up to the curving reception counter. "You mean you have nothing new for me?"

"Yes."

Jack Mullins snickered and Toni Andreas smothered a giggle. Sucking up to the boss, I thought, at Emma's expense. "No break-ins?"

"No."

"No words of more than one syllable?"

Milo looked exasperated. "We're stalled until Doc Dewey releases Annie Jeanne from the hospital and lets us talk to her. Meanwhile, we've got Buddy on our necks. Not to mention half your damned parish has been calling us all morning. They heard it on the radio."

Milo made the last statement with a slight smirk. "Okay," I said, giving in, "let me see the log. I'm filling in for Scott this morning."

"What's wrong with Scott?" Toni asked, her brown eyes wide with concern.

"Nothing," I replied. "Forget it, Toni, he's taken."

She sighed. "I know. But still . . ." Her voice trailed off as she went back to making entries on the computer.

The log had only five entries: three speeders on Highway 2, none of them local; one DUI, a college student; and one shoplifting incident involving Myra Sundvold, our local kleptomaniac, whose husband, Dave, was a retired telephone company vice president and could afford to pay for the items his wife stole.

"Is Myra being charged?" I asked Milo, who was going over a schedule for target practice at the shooting range in Everett.

He shook his head but didn't look up. "Nope. She never is, but we still have to log it if the merchant calls in a complaint. This time it was a bottle of suntan oil from Parker's Pharmacy."

"Are the Sundvolds going on a trip?" I inquired.

Milo shook his head again before setting the schedule aside. "Not that I know of. Myra usually steals stuff she can't use, like paste-on tattoos and contraceptives and dog food."

"I take it they don't own a dog?"

"They don't." Milo looked bemused, then leaned one hand on the counter. "There was another complaint we didn't bother to put in the log. Will Pace from the Alpine Falls Motel called to say that the guy who didn't check out on time did steal something—a local phone book. That didn't seem worth our time."

Stealing an Alpine directory struck me as odd. "Where was the guy from?"

"California," Milo answered, as if that explained everything.

But his answer struck me as even more odd. "So this Californian comes to Alpine, stays one night, and steals a phone book? Isn't that a little weird?"

"I told you," Milo said doggedly, "he's from California, and those people can be really weird."

I pointed to the log. "Weirder than Myra Sundvold?"

The sheriff held up his hands to forestall an argument. "Okay, okay. So we have some oddballs here, too. I suppose the guy wanted to call somebody before he left town. Will charges three bucks for every call from the motel."

At that price, I didn't blame the guy for ripping off one of Will's phone books. "What was his name?"

"The guy?" Milo was looking annoyed again. "I don't know." He turned to Jack, who was pouring himself a mug of coffee. If that stuff hadn't poisoned anybody, I suspected that the sheriff's staff could withstand even an overdose of insulin. "Did Will give you the name of the motel guy?" Milo asked his deputy.

"Yeah," Jack replied, "I've got it somewhere. Hang on." He rummaged around on the top of his desk. "Here. It's Anthony Knuler of Sacramento, California."

I thought for a moment. "I don't know anybody by that name around here. I guess he wasn't visiting his relatives."

Milo shrugged. "Whatever."

I took the not-so-subtle hint and left. The rain had almost stopped. The gray clouds were lifting, swirling like phantoms across the base of the mountains. I could see Baldy, almost to the five-thousand-foot level. There was no new snow at that elevation yet, but the past few autumns had stayed warmer. Too warm, as far as the hydroelectric companies and the ski industry were concerned.

It was only a steep block up Third from the sheriff's head-quarters to the hospital. I decided to see how Annie Jeanne was doing. The old bank clock on the sidewalk down the street informed me it was just after nine. Annie Jeanne should have had her breakfast and be preparing to go home by eleven, the usual time for hospital releases.

Olga Bergstrom was on duty again, and so was Dwight Gould. Judging from the way they were glowering at each other, it looked as if they weren't getting along. As I approached the nurses' station, I noticed that Olga had her hands pressed over a copper-colored candy box.

"It doesn't matter to me if you're a law enforcement officer. You are *not* entitled to sample the staff's belongings," she declared with a harsh look for Dwight. "This was a Halloween present from Dr. Sung. And nobody sticks a thumb into the chocolates to see what flavor they are. That's absolutely taboo."

Dwight, who had put on weight in the past few years, glared right back, but noticed me and kept his mouth shut.

"How's Annie Jeanne?" I asked, directing my question to Nurse Bergstrom.

"Mopish," Olga replied. "I told you, one of those people who are all over the chart when it comes to moods. Really, I don't see why it's so difficult to maintain a happy medium."

Nurse Bergstrom might be medium, but she didn't seem very happy. "Is Annie Jeanne being released this morning?"

"Yes. Dr. Dewey has made rounds already," Olga replied, keeping her eye on Dwight, lest he attempt to vault the counter and snatch away the candy box. "I understand your brother is picking her up around eleven."

"May I see her for a moment?" I inquired in my most humble manner.

Peering at me as if I had HOSPITAL TERRORIST stamped on my forehead, Olga frowned. "To what purpose?"

"I'm a friend," I said, not quite so humble. "We belong to the same church, remember?"

Olga relented. "Very well." She shot a glance at Dwight, perhaps to make sure he'd watch my every move through the ICU window.

"Hell of a mess," Dwight muttered as I went past him. "You sure your brother's feeling okay?"

"As far as I know," I responded, none too amiably.

Annie Jeanne was still in bed, the single sheet rumpled and only half-covering her. She didn't look to see who had come through the door.

"Annie Jeanne," I said softly, "it's me, Emma."

"Oh." Her voice sounded faint, but she turned her head slightly.

"Are you feeling better?" I asked, standing close to the bed. There was no visitor's chair in the ICU. Even though Annie Jeanne had passed the crisis stage, Doc Dewey apparently had felt she'd be better off staying put. Or maybe that had been Milo's "procedural" decision.

"Oh, Emma!" Her voice was still weak, but it was charged with emotion. "How could I?"

I took her thin hand. Her color was still very bad, and she looked as if she'd lost ten pounds. The graying black hair was splayed all over the pillow, like small, dead twigs.

"Listen, Annie Jeanne, it wasn't your fault. How could it be? You'd never harm anyone. Please don't beat yourself up. Milo will get to the bottom of this, and Ben and I will help him."

"That's so sweet," Annie Jeanne said listlessly. "But it won't change things. I still killed my oldest friend."

"I find that hard to believe," I asserted, stroking the back of her hand. "What could you possibly have in the rectory kitchen that might be dangerous?"

The question only made Annie Jeanne look more dispir-
ited. "Deputy Gould says just about anything can kill someone if they take enough of it."

"But do you have insulin anywhere in the rectory?"

"Isn't that what they make bombs from?" Annie Jeanne
seemed bewildered. "No, of course not. I don't even keep rat
poison on hand. Or traps, for that matter. I haven't seen a rat
at St. Mildred's in years, and if I find a mouse, I use the
broom to shoo it outdoors."

Her skin was so dry. Annie Jeanne obviously was dehydrated. I offered her a drink from the plastic tumbler next to
the bed. While she took a couple of sips, I posed another
query.

"What did you and Gen have for dinner?"

Annie Jeanne flinched and set the tumbler down. "I can't
bear to remember it."

"But you have to," I said gently. "I'm sure it was all very
wholesome." Except for the poison, I thought to myself.

"Well . . ." Annie Jeanne's face displayed a lightning-
quick series of emotions—regret, sorrow, anxiety, fear, and
concentration. I imagined that her illness had been traumatic,
causing her brain as well as her memory to go off track. "You
must realize," she began slowly, "that Genevieve was always
very weight conscious. She used to tease me when we were
young about how I could stay so thin, while just looking at a
candy bar made her gain half a pound." The faintest of smiles
touched Annie Jeanne's mouth. "She always had a sweet
tooth, you see. But she was very disciplined. That's how she
kept her figure." Gazing down at her lean frame, Annie
Jeanne sighed. "I never actually had one."

"The majority of women in this country would envy you
for being so slim," I put in. "More than half of them are over-
weight these days."

"Oh?" Annie Jeanne didn't seem interested in fat females.

"Anyway, Gen told me at the BCTC party not to make a heavy dinner. And not to go to a lot of trouble, either. She was so thoughtful that way." Another slight smile. "So I kept it simple—roasted Cornish game hens with white and wild rice stuffing, fresh green beans, and—this is where I just had to splurge—chocolate cheesecake for dessert. I told Gen she was on vacation and should piggy up—as we used to call it when we were young—because nothing else in the meal was that rich. She couldn't resist. Gen had three slices to my one. I intended to send the rest home with—" Annie Jeanne stopped and began to cry.

I patted her arm and said soothing words. No wonder Annie Jeanne was dehydrated: Besides having her stomach emptied, she'd shed a couple of gallons of tears in the past twenty-four hours. I couldn't blame her; I tried to imagine how I'd feel if I'd accidentally poisoned Vida. Even when I was annoyed with her, the thought was unbearable.

By the time Annie Jeanne got herself under control, Ben was tapping on the glass. I motioned for him to come in. Apparently he'd passed muster with Nurse Olga.

"Hey, ladies," Ben said in his crackling voice, "it's checkout time. Let's blow this joint."

"Oh, Father Ben!" Annie Jeanne looked as if she was going to cry again.

"Hold it," Ben said with a smile. "We need to say our prayers. Come on, Emma, get down on your knees, you sinner you."

Ben wasn't one for long or even formal prayers. He kept it short, asking God to watch over Annie Jeanne, to give her courage, hope, peace of mind, and ". . . to keep her eye on the prize, which isn't of this world. Amen."

My brother and I both stood up. I noticed that neither of us did it as easily as when we were kids crawling around our backyard, trying to catch grasshoppers. But at least he hadn't kicked me in the rear end before I could get to my feet. Maybe we were growing up as well as growing old.

"We'll get out of here so the nurse can get you dressed," Ben said to Annie Jeanne. "I'll take the newspaper ghoul with me."

A second nurse had appeared on the scene, Constance Peterson, an LPN. Apparently she'd been summoned to guard the chocolates. After Ben and I came out of the ICU, Olga went in and immediately closed the shades.

I greeted Constance before I spoke to Dwight. "Are you coming along to stand guard at the rectory?" I asked him.

He shook his head. "Annie Jeanne hasn't been charged with anything. We're too short of manpower to put somebody at the rectory. It's up to you now," he added with a nod at Ben. "In fact, I might as well go. See you." With one last, longing glance at the copper-colored candy box, the deputy headed for the elevators.

I moved down the hall a few yards, hopefully out of Constance's hearing range. Ben followed me.

"How are you going to handle this?" I asked.

"I'm organized," Ben replied. "Betsy O'Toole is taking the eleven-to-four shift, then Mary Jane Bourgette's coming until nine. They both said they'd stay with Annie Jeanne through tomorrow at least."

"They're good people," I noted. "Hopefully, you won't have to bother them for too long."

"That's not my main worry," Ben said with a scowl. "That is, Annie Jeanne tops the list, of course, but I had a problem at Mass this morning."

I was taken aback. "What?"

"As you know," Ben explained, "we only get about twenty people—mostly old folks—at daily Mass. Today four of them refused to take communion from the cup. They were afraid of being poisoned."

"Oh, good lord!" I cried, loud enough that Constance Peterson looked up from the charts she was reading. "What are you going to do about that?" I asked, lowering my voice.

Ben's expression was wry. "They were all elderly ladies. It seems they thought the communion wafers were safe. Now I've got to convince them that the wine's just as untainted. I thought you might ask Vida to mention it on her radio show tonight. Everybody in town—especially the elderly—listens to *Vida's Cupboard*. She's not too Presbyterian to do us a favor, is she?"

"Of course not," I said. "Besides, it'll give her a chance to mention Gen's demise. Let's hope she does it without gloating."

Ben nodded once. "Has she ever told you why she's so pissed off at Gen?"

"No, and I won't pry. You know how closemouthed Vida can be when it comes to personal matters." A sudden thought popped into my mind. "The wine—it reminds me that I didn't find out from Annie Jeanne what she and Gen drank Monday night. They must have had some kind of beverage, even if it was only tea or coffee."

"The leftover food, most of the kitchen stores, and all the medicines were taken to a lab for testing yesterday," Ben said. "Did Milo tell you?"

"*No.*" I grimaced at Ben. "And neither did you."

"Sorry." He had the grace to look shamefaced. "I guess I had too many other things on my mind."

I sighed and patted his shoulder. "I shouldn't snap at you. But I'd like to kick Milo's butt halfway to Gold Bar."

"He may want to keep the tests under wraps for legal reasons," Ben said as Olga emerged from the ICU.

"Maybe," I allowed, but I was still mad at the sheriff. "I'm going to yank Milo's chain. Unless," I added, "you want me to go to the rectory with you and Annie Jeanne."

"You're a working girl," Ben said. "Besides, Betsy O'Toole is waiting for us."

I practically ran down the hill to Front Street and the sheriff's office. My mind was a muddle: I should have known that the sheriff would have the dinner remnants tested; but it hadn't occurred to me that he'd make a clean sweep of the rectory. The idea terrified me. What if Ben—not Genevieve or Annie Jeanne—had been the intended victim? Priests, like judges and lawyers and doctors, were often a target, even if their only offense was being an authority figure.

In my agitated state, I slipped on the wet pavement at the corner and had to steady myself on—ironically—an empty *Advocate* newspaper box. It was going on eleven; Kip's delivery crew should start putting out this week's edition any minute.

Toni was the only employee in the sheriff's front office. She was talking to Charlene Vickers.

"Oh, Emma," Charlene said when she saw me, "isn't it awful about Gen Bayard! To think we were all having such a good time at Nell Blatt's house Sunday night!"

Nell was one of Vida's sisters-in-law, the wife of Osbert, one of Vida's two brothers. Vida had never gotten along with any of the in-laws in her own generation, including Ernest's family. She was on much friendlier terms with her many nieces and nephews.

"Just be glad," I said to Charlene, "that you were all together and happy with Gen for one last time. Had you kept up with her over the years?"

"Somewhat," Charlene replied, looking guilty. "Christmas and birthday cards. An occasional note. I blame myself. I've always been so busy raising the children and keeping the books and handling the money matters for Cal and the service station."

I nodded. "You also belong to several organizations, like our bridge club and the thimble club."

"I know." Charlene sighed. "There's never enough time to do everything."

In my opinion, there was too much time in small towns, which was why residents joined so many clubs and organizations. It was also why there were so many feuds and backstabbing. Too much propinquity. And yet there was a genuine sense of community, of belonging. Maybe living in Alpine wasn't the worst thing that could happen, even to a transplant like me.

"Everyone must have been thrilled to see Gen after all these years," I remarked as Toni handed a sheet of paper to Charlene.

"My, yes," Charlene replied, "they were agog." She turned to Toni. "Thanks so much. I assume Harvey's or someone else in town carries these alarms?"

"If you're going with Brink's, you'll have to call the 1-800 number listed under their name," Toni advised. "Unfortunately, we can't recommend any particular alarm service company."

"I understand," Charlene said. She folded the list and slipped it into her canvas shopping bag. "Honestly, Emma, with all these break-ins, you have to take extra precautions. We don't want it to happen again at our house, even though the stereo was old and our insurance will cover the new TV. I feel so sorry for Ethel Pike having to come home to a big mess. The thieves didn't do much damage at our place. I wonder if some of us Betsys should try to clean up the Pikes' house before they get back from Florida."

"That'd be a nice gesture," I said, edging away from Charlene to reach the half door in the reception counter. "That is, as long as it's still not a crime scene."

"Oh, dear." Charlene looked chagrined. "I hadn't thought of that." She turned back to Toni while I made my escape through the counter's opening.

Assuming the sheriff was in, I had the courtesy to knock. From the other side of the door, I heard Milo's gruff response. "What now?"

"I'm the one who should ask that question," I snapped as I entered his office and slammed the door behind me. "Why didn't you tell me about the leftovers going to the lab?"

Milo shrugged. "Because it was in-house. Do you want it to get out that your church's kitchen is stocked with poison?"

I grimaced, recalling the women who had refused to take communion from the cup. "Okay, I'll try not to kill you this time. Have you got the results yet?"

"Just in," the sheriff replied complacently. "We may not be able to do a full autopsy in SkyCo, but we *do* have enough equipment to detect poison, in case you've forgotten."

I had. It'd been some time since anyone—that we knew of—had been poisoned in Skykomish County. Clumsily, I sat down across the desk from Milo. "Well?"

He seemed determined to be aggravating. For at least thirty seconds, he shuffled papers around on his desk, then stubbed out his cigarette in a clamshell ashtray. "I don't want this broadcast all over town," he said with a warning look.

I was surprised. "Do you mean you're not telling Fleetwood yet?"

"That's right." His hazel eyes were steady as he stared at me. "You got it? Not even Vida should hear this, especially since tonight she has her radio show. I'm doing this as a favor to your brother. You can pass it on to him, but that's it."

"Okay." I remained surprised. Maybe Milo and Ben had a fishing date coming up. Fishing partners tend to trust each other.

The sheriff cleared his throat. "I won't read the scientific gobbledygook. What it comes down to is that the insulin was in the cheesecake dessert, probably the chocolate crust."

"Good lord!" I cried.

"Seems that way," Milo said in his laconic manner. "But there it is. The stuff is called glipizide, and comes in white tablets. They were crushed into a fine powder. Gen must have eaten more of the cheesecake than Annie Jeanne did."

"That's true," I said, remembering what Annie Jeanne had said about Gen eating three times the quantity as her hostess. " 'Piggy up,' " I murmured.

"Huh?"

I shook my head. "Nothing. But Gen ate three slices. I assume they were fairly large. I vaguely recall seeing the leftover cheesecake on the counter. It was more than half-gone."

"Does Annie Jeanne have diabetes?" Milo inquired.

"No, I'm sure she doesn't." In truth, I wasn't sure, though Annie Jeanne wasn't one to keep a secret.

"Ben?"

"No." Nor, thankfully, was there any history of the disease in our family tree. "And certainly not Dennis Kelly," I added. "On his busiest days, he survived on Twix bars."

We were both silent for a few moments.

"All those women in the Burl Creek Thimble Club were friends of Annie Jeanne's and Gen's, weren't they?" Milo noted as he lighted another cigarette. "How many of them belong to your church?"

I thought back to the article we'd done and the photo we'd run. "Only one," I finally said. "Debra Barton." Debra was married to Clancy, who owned Barton's Bootery, and despite being fellow parishioners, I'd never gotten to know her very well.

"Hunh." Milo again became silent, fading slightly behind a cloud of gray smoke. "Who else was at the party for Gen?"

I reached for a tablet and a pen from the desk. "Let

me think—Annie Jeanne, Gen, Debra, Ethel, Mary Lou Hinshaw Blatt, Charlene Vickers, Darlene Adcock, Edith Bartleby, Nell Blatt, Grace Grundle, Darla Puckett, Ella Hinshaw . . . oh, and Jean Campbell. Ethel was given a special award named after her for winning the blue ribbon at the county fair. It's called the Sweet Betsy from Pike."

Milo looked as if he wanted to gag. "Women do weird things," he said. "It's like they're still little girls."

"Men don't do weird things, too? What about Jack Mullins giving Ed Bronsky an atomic wedgie after Mass three weeks ago?"

Milo guffawed. "Jack did that? Damn, why didn't you put it in 'Scene'?"

"Because it was dumb," I replied. "Although not too dumb, considering the victim was Ed."

Sharing my opinion of Ed Bronsky, Milo snorted. "That's the truth."

"What was the crust made of?" I asked.

The sheriff consulted the lab report. "Crushed cookies, butter, powdered sugar, and salt. Not to mention glipizide."

"Ah." The powdered sugar would camouflage the white tablets. The extreme sweetness of the cheesecake would mask any bitterness from the insulin. A picture of Annie Jeanne loomed in my mind's eye: bustling around the kitchen, stuffing game hens, tip-and-tailing green beans, adding lemon juice to creamed cheese, crushing cookies into tiny bits, sprinkling glipizide into the mixture . . .

What was wrong with that picture?

Everything. But how could I prove it?

NINE

"ANNIE JEANNE IS *NOT* A POISONER," I DECLARED, LOOKING Milo straight in the eye, "and it couldn't have been an accident. That scenario doesn't play for me. Someone had to introduce glipizide into that kitchen."

"I'll admit," Milo conceded, "it seems weird. But you know how these old spinsters get sometimes. Gaga."

I gave the sheriff my most pugnacious stare. "*I'm* a spinster. Am I gaga, too?"

Milo was irked. "You know what I mean. You've had a kid, you're not as old as Annie Jeanne, you've been—" He stopped, apparently embarrassed.

"Around the block?"

"I didn't mean that."

"Yes, you did. You're talking about sexual repression. You're saying that women who don't have sex get goofy. I'm saying that some people are . . . well, asexual. They either have no sex drive or it's barely perceptible. In Annie Jeanne's case, she's an old-fashioned Catholic girl born and raised in a small town. She was a dutiful daughter; she's always been a loyal friend. When she wasn't taking care of her invalid parents before they died, she put all her energy into the parish, starting with playing the organ."

"From what I've heard you say, Annie Jeanne should have practiced using a different kind of organ," Milo said dryly. "If you get what I mean."

I had to laugh at Milo's uncharacteristic use of a double entendre. "Yes, I'm not completely dense. But music—even god-awful music—is an outlet for many people. Really, Milo, do you honestly believe Annie Jeanne murdered Genevieve Bayard?"

"I can believe almost anything after all these years in law enforcement." The sheriff paused, staring at my chest. "This sex talk is making me horny. Where'd you get that red sweater?"

"On sale, at Francine's Fine Apparel," I retorted. I closed my jacket and stood up. "Good-bye, Milo."

"Is your brother coming to your place for dinner tonight?" he asked as I headed toward the door.

"Yes." I stopped with my hand on the knob. "No. He'll probably stay with Annie Jeanne." Milo was the sheriff; he could probably figure that out for himself. I turned around. I couldn't stand it when Milo looked dejected and defeated. "I've got two rib eyes in the freezer. I was saving them for Ben, but I can buy some more."

His long face brightened. "Yeah? Okay, I'll be there."

"Fine. We can listen to Vida's program together."

"What about making love *during* Vida's program? Wouldn't that be kind of—" He winced. "Maybe not."

"I'll see you around six," I said, and left.

Back at the office, I called Ben to tell him I'd bring lunch to the rectory. He said not to bother; Betsy O'Toole had brought a bunch of deli items from the Grocery Basket. Would I like to join them?

It was going on twelve. I said I would, and drove off to St. Mildred's twenty minutes later.

Betsy had settled Annie Jeanne onto the sofa in the parlor.

"Lying in bed won't help her get better mentally," Betsy confided as soon as I entered the rectory. "Your brother can use the office for meeting with people. He's in there now, trying to catch up on his workload. Father Ben and Bernie Shaw are going over the books. The Sunday collections are down since Father Den went away."

We were almost to the parlor. "That's natural, I suppose. The parishioners have to make sure they can trust a new priest and that he won't make off with the Sunday envelopes." Or worse.

Annie Jeanne was gazing into space when we walked into the room. She gave a start when I said hello.

"Emma! You shouldn't take time away from work to tend to me!" she exclaimed. But before I could say that I was on my lunch hour, she tugged at the bright green, yellow, lavender, and orange quilt that covered her slight body. "Look! Gen made this for me years ago, before she moved. I've been using it ever since. Isn't it lovely? She designed it herself."

It was certainly colorful. The pattern was either suns or stars or maybe both, which, I guess, made sense, since the sun is a star. "Very nice," I said, pulling a side chair up close to the sofa. "How are you feeling now?"

"Oh . . ." Annie Jeanne sighed. "Better, physically, I guess. Otherwise . . ." She lifted her hands in a helpless gesture.

"Give yourself some time," Betsy said in her practical if unimaginative manner. "Once your body's recovered, your mind will get better, too. You shouldn't feel guilty about something you didn't do."

"But I made the dinner," Annie Jeanne protested, her voice rising.

Betsy put a firm, freckled hand on the other woman's shoulder. "Stop that. You weren't the one who added the poison."

I realized that Betsy and Annie Jeanne didn't know about the lab results. Milo had ordered me to tell no one but Ben.

"That's the problem," Annie Jeanne asserted, though her voice was calmer. "Who would have put insulin—or whatever that poison is called—into the ingredients? No one was here that afternoon, at least not in the kitchen."

"You were here the whole time?" I asked.

"Yes." Annie Jeanne nodded vigorously, then put a hand to her mouth. "Well, no, not the entire afternoon. I had to run to the store to get vanilla. I wanted the white kind, not the dark. But I wasn't gone more than twenty minutes. Father Ben was here while I was out."

But not in the kitchen, I thought. Father Fitz had always kept the church unlocked. He'd felt that anyone at anytime should have access to the Blessed Sacrament. As times changed, Father Den had locked the church as well as the rectory at night. Ben followed his lead, but had decided to lock the rectory during the day when neither he nor Annie Jeanne was on hand. To gain access, church volunteers had to wait until one of them was around. Otherwise, the door was open. Consequently, if Ben was in his office and Annie Jeanne stepped out, a mischief maker could come right through the front door.

"You see?" Betsy said to Annie Jeanne. "The poisoner could have nipped in while you were gone. Father Ben would never know."

"That still makes it my fault!" Annie Jeanne insisted. "I should have locked the door!"

"But you don't do that," Betsy argued. "Why would you change the routine in broad daylight as long as the rectory was occupied?" She didn't wait for an answer. "I've got to serve lunch. Jake and I have donated staples and some extras to replenish the kitchen."

"You're so generous!" Annie Jeanne called after Betsy before turning to me. "Aren't the O'Tooles wonderful?"

"They're good people," I said, and meant it. It was easy to overlook their habit of feuding in public. To Betsy and Jake, it wasn't a quarrel, it was foreplay.

Wheedling answers out of Annie Jeanne was tricky, not only because by nature she had a difficult time keeping focused, but because I couldn't reveal the glipizide's source on the dinner menu.

"I don't think you ever mentioned what you ladies had to drink," I said as casually as possible. "You never know these days what gets put into products before they ever get off the shelf."

The thought seemed to buoy Annie Jeanne. "Oh, isn't that the truth? Those aspirin tamperings a few years back were so dreadful! Innocent people dying!" She paused, apparently ruminating about past poisonings. "Drink," she finally said. "We had sherry before dinner. It wasn't a new bottle; I use it mostly for cooking. I made coffee to go with dessert, decaf from a canister I've been using for the past few days. Gen took hers black. I used sugar and cream. Well, not real cream—milk. That was all."

Bernie Shaw was saying good-bye to Ben in the hallway. Both men peeked into the parlor.

"How're you doing, Annie Jeanne?" Bernie inquired in his hearty style. "You'd better get well quick. You don't want to leave Father Ben here in the lurch." He winked, as was his habit.

"Oh, no, of course I don't!" Annie Jeanne looked as if she'd never considered her parish responsibilities until now. "You're right, I must regain my strength."

"You will," Bernie said cheerfully. "You have a good

heart and a good constitution. Be well. I'll see you later."
Bernie and Ben proceeded to the front door.

It had occurred to me that if I threw out a couple of hints
to Annie Jeanne, she might be able to figure out for herself
which part of the dinner had been poisoned.

"Do you know what glipizide tablets look like? That's the
name of the insulin form that was used," I added for clarifi-
cation.

Annie Jeanne frowned, then wagged a finger. "I do know.
Ethel Pike takes glipizide. I was with her once when she had
to take her medicine. She wasn't happy about me seeing her
do it, though. Ethel hates to admit she's diabetic. I can't think
why; there are worse things than diabetes."

"What did her tablets look like?" I asked.

"Um . . . they were white, like aspirin, but a different
shape. Squarish or triangular. I forget."

I waited for Annie Jeanne to put two and two together.
But she merely sighed and shook her head.

"You could disguise the pills somehow," I mused.

"I suppose." Annie Jeanne didn't seem interested. Instead,
she was fingering the various fabrics that made up the quilt
Gen had given her. I was getting impatient. She didn't seem to
understand that her situation was awkward, if not downright
precarious. But I suspected that this had always been Annie
Jeanne's way of dealing—or not dealing—with life.

Betsy entered the room, pushing an old-fashioned tea cart
laden with sandwiches, chips, raw vegetables, and potato
chips. "Luncheon is served," she announced, and bobbed a
curtsey. "I made you some of our soup from the deli, Annie
Jeanne. It's turkey noodle. I've got crackers here, too. I'll
bring tea and coffee later, unless you'd like juice or milk."

"Tea's fine," Annie Jeanne said meekly.

My pastrami and Swiss cheese on light rye was delicious.

Maybe I should make the effort to pick up more lunch items from the deli at the Grocery Basket. Ben and Betsy both had roast beef on whole wheat. Annie Jeanne toyed with her soupspoon.

"I'm sorry," she finally said in a lackluster voice, "I simply have no appetite."

"And I simply have no time for excuses," Betsy snapped. "You eat that soup or Jake and I won't donate any more food to the parish, not even the food bank. I mean it. You won't get well if you don't eat."

Startled, Annie Jeanne tasted the soup.

My brother looked amused. "You can't work if you don't recover," he said lightly. "Then I'd have to fire you."

"Oh, Father Ben . . ." Annie Jeanne slurped some soup.

After we'd eaten, I asked Ben if I could speak to him in his office. He led the way. Dennis Kelly had been well organized. My brother wasn't. In fact, when it came to tidiness, his work ethic resembled mine. Maybe that was because our parents had been very neat people and we had rebelled.

Once the door was closed, I gave him the results of the lab tests. As I knew he would, Ben said he'd keep his mouth shut.

"The cheesecake, huh?" he said in a thoughtful tone. "Do you remember if Father Fitz had diabetes?"

My mind went back to my early years in Alpine. It seemed so long ago, much longer than it felt. Maybe that's because I measured time by deadlines, not months and seasons. Had I really spent almost fourteen years in this semi-isolated town deep in the forest and perched on a mountainside?

Ben must have sensed my ruminations. "Only yesterday," he murmured. "Except that it wasn't."

I smiled at my brother. "How true. Did I really expect to stay here so long?"

Ben shook his head. "You expected Tom Cavanaugh to carry you off on his milk-white charger."

"No!" I wasn't smiling anymore. "When I moved here, I hadn't spoken to Tom in almost twenty years!"

Ben said nothing; he merely tipped his head to one side.

I shifted in my chair and put my brain back on track. "I don't remember if Father Fitz had diabetes. He might have, since he was elderly and the problem often develops in old age. Were you thinking he might have had insulin tablets stored away in the rectory?"

"It's possible," Ben said, "but unlikely. Fitz went to a retirement home for priests, right? He'd take his medications with him. And the tidy and orderly Dennis Kelly—no doubt because his father was a career army officer who inspected his room every morning—would have thrown out anything that was no longer useful."

"Except in the kitchen," I pointed out. "Sometimes people keep their medicine there because they take it with food or before eating. But the kitchen's always been the housekeeper's domain. Unfortunately, none of the previous housekeepers who served before Annie Jeanne are still with us. I doubt that Annie Jeanne ever throws anything out."

"Milo took all that stuff," Ben said.

"He wouldn't have it if it was used up."

"That's true." Ben clasped his hands and frowned. "That's odd."

"What?"

Ben moved in his swivel chair and accidentally knocked over a pile of pamphlets from the Knights of Columbus. He didn't bother to pick them up off the floor. "Something Annie Jeanne said that day . . . damn, what was it?" He grimaced and stared at the hand-carved statue of Saint Joseph in a niche above his desk. "It was about the crust," he finally recalled. "Annie Jeanne told me that Ethel Pike had given her some chocolate cookies at the party for Gen Sunday night. That gave her the idea to make a cheesecake for her old pal because she could use the cookies for the crust."

I was startled. "That's strange. Charlene Vickers mentioned something about cookies at Gen's party." I stopped, trying to resurrect the conversation. "Where's your copy of today's *Advocate*?"

Ben looked around his cluttered desk, the serviceable carpet, on top of the filing cabinets, the bookcases, and the homely pine table that had once been used as an altar by Father Fitz but was now a catchall.

"Maybe," Ben said sheepishly, "it's still in the box outside."

"Never mind." I knew he had had other things to do than retrieve our weekly edition. "I wrote the party story. I should remember it." I paused again, trying to visualize what I'd typed. "Ah. Gen brought homemade cookies for all of the guests. Some of them were served, but not the ones she made for Ethel Pike. Ethel has diabetes, and gave her cookies to Annie Jeanne. Of course, I didn't include most of that in the article because Ethel doesn't want people to know she's diabetic. Unless there really was insulin squirreled away somewhere in the rectory, we've come full circle back to Gen."

Ben leaned back in his chair. "You're kidding."

"I wish I were," I said grimly. "The worst of it is, I can't make any sense out of it."

Ben gazed indifferently at the hole in the sleeve of his blue cardigan sweater. "The problem is when the insulin was added to the cookies, right?"

"Yes, and who did it."

"Were all the cookies Gen brought the same kind?"

"I don't know. I could ask Charlene, or someone else who

was at the party. In fact," I went on, realizing I'd been remiss in making plans for a follow-through of the investigation, "I should ask someone else. Several of them, in fact."

Ben twirled in his swivel chair. It was a novelty for him. When I'd visited my brother in Tuba City a few years back, he'd had a very uncomfortable-looking straight-backed chair with a wicker seat. "Will Vida help?" he asked. "She must know the members even better than you do."

"That's the problem." I gave my brother a vexed look. "Three are related to her—Mary Lou Hinshaw Blatt and Nell Blatt, who Vida usually doesn't speak to, and Ella Hinshaw, who's kind of gaga. Frankly, Vida doesn't seem too interested in Gen's death. It's not like her to be so lacking in curiosity. I'm pretty sure that Vida and Gen had a falling-out a long time ago."

"Vida can hold a grudge," Ben remarked. "That's too bad."

"I know," I agreed. "Don't you remember when I told you a few months ago about Thyra Rasmussen and how Vida loathed her because she'd once stepped on Mrs. Blatt's prizewinning gourds?"

"Which happened fifty years ago at least?" Ben's expression was wry. "Yes, I remember. I suppose this rift with Gen was over some trifling thing, too. It's a shame, but it happens."

"Yes, it does," I said. "But in fact, Mrs. Rasmussen was just plain mean. I knew her, too. She was a magnet for hostility."

"Hostility needn't always be hatred," Ben pointed out.

"True." I knew what my brother was thinking. *Hate the sin, love the sinner.* That was easier said than done with someone like Thyra.

But Genevieve Bayard didn't strike me as being cut from

the same cloth as Thyra Rasmussen. On the other hand, I didn't know her. I'd only spoken to her once on the phone.

Maybe, judging from Vida's attitude toward Gen, once was enough.

NOR HAD VIDA'S ATTITUDE CHANGED. "OF COURSE ANNIE Jeanne didn't poison Genevieve," she asserted when I asked her to come into my office after lunch. "But I can't say I'm grieving. I've no time for that Bayard woman, dead or alive."

I'd closed the door behind Vida to give us privacy. "Why not?" I asked in what I hoped was a casual tone.

Vida looked away, gazing at the calendar from Harvey's Hardware with its full-color picture of Tonga Ridge. The photo, like all those that had graced Harvey Adcock's calendars over the years, had been taken by Buddy Bayard.

"I'd rather not discuss it," she finally said, looking back at me. "It was a long time ago, but there are some things that are just too despicable to talk about."

That didn't sound like Vida. "Gosh," I said innocently, "Gen must have made a lot of enemies in the old days. How did she manage to keep her buddies in the BCTC?"

"I have no idea." Vida was looking very prim.

"Were you ever a member?" I asked, still hoping to sound casual but not succeeding very well.

Vida took umbrage. "Are you interrogating me?"

"Of course not." My expression was ironic. "I'm doing what I always do when there's a local homicide. I'm trying to figure out whodunit. In the past, you've always helped me— tremendously. I'm just curious why you don't seem interested this time around."

"Genevieve hadn't lived here for years," Vida replied.

"Nor do I think she was purposely poisoned. And, no, I never belonged to the Burl Creek Thimble Club. My mother did, but she was clever at crafts. I wasn't." Vida looked down at her big hands with their stubby fingers, as if to blame them for her lack of talent.

"Let me fill you in," I said. "Then maybe you'll be more interested."

"I doubt it."

Nevertheless, I told her everything, even breaking my promise to Milo not to reveal the part about the cheesecake crust containing the glipizide. I hated doing it, but I was that desperate to engage Vida in the crime.

"My, my," Vida said after I'd finished, "that *is* rather intriguing."

"Then you'll work on the story with me?"

Vida blinked twice behind her big glasses. "I didn't say that."

"Why not? You said the case was intriguing."

"I wasn't referring to the case," Vida responded. "I meant the homemade cookies. I don't think Genevieve ever baked so much as a cupcake as long I knew her."

My shoulders sagged. "That's hardly the point. She was in Spokane for over twenty years. She could've been baking marzipan and Russian rye and marble cake for all you know."

"That's highly unlikely."

"Okay, so maybe Roseanna baked the cookies for her," I allowed, and sent my mind off on a different, frightening tangent. I pushed the thought aside. "Maybe she bought them at the Upper Crust, or even at the airport. There wasn't much time in between her arrival in Alpine and the party that night."

"That sounds more like Genevieve," Vida conceded. "You should ask Roseanna. Of course, Milo will do that as well. I assume he'll have to search the Bayard kitchen, if, in fact, the cookies were made there."

Did I sense that the fish was cautiously circling the bait? "I'd think," I said slowly, "that if you and Gen didn't get along, there'd be others who didn't, either. Like your mother, for instance."

"I told you," Vida said adamantly, "I don't wish to discuss it. Please, Emma, let's stop talking about Genevieve Bayard. I don't even like to mention her name."

The fierceness in Vida's gray eyes told me that she wasn't going to nibble after all. I couldn't believe it. But I had to let it go.

"Fine, I'll shut up." I rose from my chair. "I'm going to see Buddy and Roseanna now."

Vida also stood up. "I have several stories for next week. The Skylstads are going to Boise to spend Thanksgiving with their daughter, who owns a pet-sitting service. Edna Mae Dalrymple just returned from a library conference in Yakima. There are two weddings over the weekend. My page will be full, I assure you."

I didn't doubt it. But I was still irked.

B UDDY AND ROSEANNA WERE BOTH AT WORK. SHE WAS behind the front desk; Buddy was in the studio, photographing a newcomer to Alpine High School who hadn't yet had his senior picture taken.

"It's Jason Crowe," Roseanna explained, "the son of the Upper Crust owners. It's hard for kids to change schools in their senior year."

"That's true," I said. "By chance, I bought the paper right after Adam graduated in Portland. How are you and Buddy doing?"

"Ohhh . . ." Roseanna ran a hand through her blond

curls. "It's rough. We've finally tracked down somebody in Spokane who knew Gen's attorney. We're waiting to hear back from him. Then maybe we can find out if she had special wishes about her burial. Meanwhile, we're still going nuts trying to understand what happened. Our sheriff isn't very forthcoming."

I gathered that the Bayards didn't know exactly how Gen was poisoned. "It's a mess," I allowed. "It's a hard story to cover, but at least we have several days before the next edition. You're on a tighter schedule, I'm afraid."

Roseanna grimaced. "Gen's not going anywhere. As Janet Driggers told me, Al doesn't hand out weekend passes at the mortuary."

That sounded like Janet. She was a rambunctious woman with a runaway tongue, and I couldn't help but like her for it. "Gen must have had some fine qualities," I said. "Obviously the women from BCTC liked her."

"I guess so," Roseanna said without enthusiasm. "Maybe it was my fault that I never warmed to her. Who knows?"

"Gen certainly went out of her way to bake all those cookies for the club members," I remarked. "She must have had to hustle."

Roseanna grinned, the first smile I'd seen since before the tragedy. "Bake? Gen? We stopped at the Upper Crust after we got back from Seattle. She practically cleaned the place out. It's a good thing we called ahead. Ah." She turned around as a medium-size adolescent with straight black hair and rimless glasses emerged from the studio. He was already undoing the tie that he wore with a white shirt and navy slacks.

"All finished, Jason?" Roseanna inquired. "We were just talking about your parents' bakery. Have you met Emma Lord, the newspaper owner?"

He looked at me as if I were cat dirt, but put out a hand. "Hi."

"Jason works at the bakery, too," Roseanna said, poking keys on the computer that sat just below the reception counter. "How's that going?" she asked the youth as his invoice was printed out.

Jason shrugged. "Okay."

I kept my distance as Roseanna explained the billing procedure to Jason and told him how soon he'd see the contact prints. After the transaction was complete, Jason Crowe slouched out the door.

"Typical for his age," Roseanna murmured. "What else can I do for you?"

I'd hoped Buddy would come into the reception area, but he didn't. "I wanted to make amends with you two for pulling the darkroom business," I said. "I know it won't be the same in terms of immediate cash, but I'd like to ask Buddy to take some color photos for the paper. Stock shots, that we could use anytime. That'd give him exposure—excuse the expression—to wider markets so that he'd eventually make more money."

Roseanna looked thoughtful. "That's considerate of you, Emma. Are you talking about the kind of scenic stuff he does for Harvey Adcock's calendar?"

"That, plus more arty-type pictures," I replied. "He could show off his creativity."

Buddy emerged from behind the velvet curtains that led into the studio. "Is this appeasement?"

I should have guessed he'd been eavesdropping. "Call it what you like," I said, trying not to be annoyed. "Let's face it, Buddy—you've pretty well cornered the market in Alpine. Losing our darkroom business won't put you and Roseanna and the kids out on the streets. I just don't want any hard feelings."

Buddy came over to where I was standing by the reception desk. "Oh—hell, Emma, I don't want to end up in a feud, either." He offered his hand, which I took. "It was just bad timing. And now, with Ma's death . . ." He released his grip on me and threw both his hands into the air. "Heck, life's too short. I think you've got a good idea. I'd like to try some different kinds of photography. I get into a rut, especially after taking almost a hundred high school senior pictures. I feel stale."

"I understand," I said. It was true: I could do only so many county commissioner reports, weather stories, and local features before I felt like a robot. One of the things that kept me going was that it could be worse: I might be rewriting Ed Bronsky's autobiography.

"How's Annie Jeanne?" Buddy inquired. His voice was noncommittal, as if he wasn't sure whether she'd purposely killed his mother or not.

"She's back at the rectory, but still very distraught," I replied. "I'm sure she's completely innocent, though that doesn't make her feel any better. She seems so genuinely fond of your mother. I don't suppose you'd know of anybody around here who wasn't?" Except Vida, I thought to myself.

Neither of the Bayards could name anyone who hadn't been on good terms with Gen. Vida wasn't mentioned, which I found curious. She certainly made no secret of her dislike.

"Ma had been gone from Alpine long enough," Buddy added, "that she never got involved in some of the local feuds. As for Spokane, I wouldn't know. She was such a private person."

Roseanna was leaning on the counter. "I don't ever recall Gen mentioning anyone she'd quarreled with except for disagreements at work. But they weren't serious. On the other hand, I don't remember her talking about friends, either."

"What about the man she had living with her?" I asked. "Do you think he's still around?"

Roseanna shook her head. "The last few times we visited, there was no sign of him. I guess they broke up. For all I know, he could be dead."

"Surely the attorney must know who he is—or was," I pointed out.

Buddy and Roseanna exchanged glances. "We didn't ask," Roseanna said. "I mean, Gen didn't want us to know about him when she was alive, so what's the point of finding out who he was now?"

"She could have left her money to him," I said.

"No," Buddy responded. "About two years ago, she made a simple will and left it all to me. Not that it's any fortune. Ma liked nice things, especially clothes. That's why she always worked for apparel stores; she could get discounts. And she wasn't an investor, except for some Nordstrom stock. I suppose in the end we'll get around ninety thousand dollars, including the condo sale, the stock, and her savings."

That sounded like a substantial sum to me. Roseanna, however, spoke bitterly. "It'll help pay for the kids' college tuition when they get beyond Skykomish Community College. It's only fair, since Gen didn't do diddly-squat for them when she was alive."

Buddy frowned at his wife. "Don't harp on that. Let's forget all the negative stuff. Ma's gone, it's over."

But it wasn't over. There was a killer in Alpine, and it wouldn't be over until he or she was found. What really bothered me was that Buddy and Roseanna didn't seem to care.

I wondered why.

TEN

Bayard's Picture Perfect Photography Studio was located next to the state liquor store. I decided to replenish my bourbon and Canadian whiskey supply, which had been depleted by the arrival of Ben. I was also low on Scotch, the sheriff's drink of choice. As soon as I walked in the door, I saw Darlene Adcock, Harvey's wife, mulling over wine selections.

"For company," she said after we'd exchanged greetings. I assumed she felt an explanation was needed lest I think that Darlene and Harvey spent their evenings getting blotto and rolling around on their Turkish carpet. "The Campbells are coming."

I tried not to smile, since the phrase reminded me of an old Scottish song. "That's nice," I remarked. "I suppose you and Jean will speculate on what happened to Gen."

Darlene, who is petite and very slender, grimaced. "There's a rumor going around town that she was poisoned on purpose by Annie Jeanne. Is that possible?"

"No," I asserted. "Do you honestly think Annie Jeanne is

capable of such a thing, especially since Gen was a dear friend?"

Darlene wore a bewildered expression. "I can't imagine. . . . Certainly Annie Jeanne was thrilled to get together with Gen. You're right. It's impossible. But you know how people talk."

I did indeed. "I suppose Annie Jeanne's considered something of a character with Alpiners who don't belong to St. Mildred's." And with some who did, I thought unhappily. "She's been a pillar of the parish for years."

"Well . . . yes, I'm sure she is," Darlene agreed. "We're Methodists, so we don't hear much about what goes on at St. Mildred's. Your Debra Barton's the quiet type. Edith, of course, keeps us up-to-date on the Episcopalians."

I'd almost forgotten about Edith. Edith Bartleby was the wife of Trinity Episcopal's pastor. Her refinement was such that I couldn't possibly imagine Edith being involved in anything as sordid as murder.

"I assume Edith doesn't carry gossip in her sewing bag?"

"Oh, heavens no!" Darlene giggled. "Edith is the soul of discretion. Of course, she didn't know Genevieve. The Bartlebys have only been here sixteen years."

Relative newcomers, I thought. "But the rest of the club did?"

"Yes, I think so." Darlene was mulling again. "I've having a lamb roast. What do you think? A rosé?"

"Try a pinot gris," I advised, though I hadn't the faintest idea what it was, but the name sounded good.

"Oh." Darlene appeared to be checking prices. "Here's a pretty label. It's on special. I'll get two. Not that Jean and Lloyd are big drinkers, but Harvey and I hate to look cheap."

"Had Jean been close to Gen in years past?" I inquired.

Darlene put the bottles into her cart. "Not particularly. Gen's best friend in the group was Annie Jeanne, of course. She also was friendly with Nell Blatt and Grace Grundle and Ethel Pike. Although . . ." Her voice trailed off as we pushed our carts out of the wine section.

"Although what?" I asked, steering in the direction of whiskeys.

"Well . . . I seem to recall a spat—nothing serious—years ago between Ethel and Gen. But they must have made up. Gen brought a double batch of cookies for Ethel so she and Pike could eat them on the plane and have some left over for the grandchildren in Orlando. Of course, nobody had the heart to tell Gen that Ethel had developed diabetes in the past few years, but the gesture shows that they must have made up any differences."

Or not, I thought.

Eleanor Blatt—or Nell as she was more familiarly known—was now on my list of contacts. So was Grace Grundle, though I dreaded paying her a call. Grace had such a large feline menagerie that she could give my neighbor Edith Holmgren a run for the crown as Cat Queen of Alpine.

First, I had to check back at the office. As I walked in the front door, Ginny handed me a half-dozen messages and, with an apologetic look, told me that Ed Bronsky was waiting in my cubbyhole.

Not, pray God, with his manuscript, I thought as I trudged through the empty newsroom.

But there was no sign of a book-in-the-making. Ed turned in my visitor's chair, making the wood creak and groan. "Hey, hey, hey," he greeted me, "I was about to give up. Long publisher's lunch, huh?"

I shook my head as I squeezed past Ed to get behind my

desk. "I had some stops along the way. What can I do for you, Ed?"

He wagged a finger at me. "Ask not what you can do for Ed, but what Ed can do for Alpine."

My face froze in what I hoped was a pleasant expression. "Oh? And what's that?"

"First off," Ed began, suddenly very earnest, "I'm putting the sequel on hold for a while. It's not writer's block, but yesterday I was working on chapter twenty-six and I had a brainstorm. What does this town really need?"

Not a brainstorm from Ed. "What?"

He leaned back in the chair, which made more agonized noises. "A museum!"

"We have one," I pointed out. "The logging museum at Old Mill Park."

Ed waved a pudgy hand in dismissal. "That thing's about the size of our living room and not half as interesting. Old donkey engines, saws, miniature trucks, a bunch of photos—I'm talking state-of-the-art, animation, interactive—the whole bit."

My expression grew curious. "My goodness—what will it feature?"

Ed cocked his head to one side and looked exceedingly pleased with himself. "Me. What else?"

On purpose, I knocked a pen off my desk. I had to duck my head to keep Ed from seeing the dismay on my face. When I regained control, I bobbed up again and, for a change, decided to show enthusiasm. It might be fun to egg Ed on. It certainly wasn't fun just to listen to him being a blowhard.

"What will be in the museum?" I finally managed to ask.

Ed waved his hands in the air. "That's the beauty of it. All of a sudden, these ideas flew out of my head. It'll be family oriented, because that's what *Mr. Ed Gets Wed* is all about. Oh, sure, there'll be the usual memorabilia. Childhood stuff, like my teething ring, my favorite blankie, my booties. Then we'll move up to grade school and high school and the year I spent at Everett JC. That'll all be in side rooms. The centerpiece will be a replica of our dining room at Casa de Bronska. We'll have wax dummies to represent Shirley and me and the kids."

Why not use the real dummies? I thought.

"You've been to Disneyland, right?" he inquired.

"What?" My head was spinning with ideas of my own. "Oh, yes, years ago with Adam."

"You know how they have that animated life-size replica of Abraham Lincoln that recites the Gettysburg Address? Well, we'll have one of me, greeting visitors and reciting some of my favorite sayings."

Like pass the pork chops?

"Then we'll have some tab blows," Ed continued. "I haven't—"

"Some what?" I interrupted.

"Tab blows," Ed repeated, emphasizing the space between the two words. "Like the dining room scene, only taking up less space."

"Oh." There was no point in correcting Ed. After he called a tableau a tab blow, I was waiting for him to refer to a diorama as an Armani Aroma. "This all sounds very intriguing," I lied. "Are you asking me to put it in the paper?"

"Not yet, not yet," Ed responded quickly. "This is background. What I'm thinking about now is going to the county commissioners or the mayor and suggesting a bond issue to raise funds. It's just too darned bad I didn't come up with this sooner; it could've been on the ballot for the September off-year election. Now we'll have to wait for March or even the primary next September."

Whew.

Ed, at his most earnest, leaned forward. The chair made

more ominous noises. "The thing is," he said, lowering his voice, "I want this to be a community project. Oh, I could put up some of the money, of course. But the Mr. Pig Museum will bring in big tourist bucks and help the economy. Everyone will benefit."

Especially Mr. Pig. "You're going to call it after the animated Japanese cartoon based on your book?"

Ed looked surprised. "Of course." He frowned. "You think I should call it after the book, *Mr. Ed*?"

"It was just a passing idea," I said, assuming a thoughtful expression. "What about rides? One of those things with little cars that sail around? You could call it When Pigs Fly. A merry-go-round with pigs instead of horses. Cutouts of pigs that visitors can put their heads through and have their picture taken with the Bronsky family. A tunnel of love—call it Pig of My Heart—with cars that look like small pigsties. A chorus line of dancing pigs. Name the restaurant the Trough. Feature little pig sausages, pigs in a blanket, pork sandwiches, pork chops, pork roast, pork rinds, bacon burgers, ham on rye; the possibilities are endless. Let kids root through mud for prizes—"

"Wow." Ed looked awestruck. "You're really getting into this, aren't you, Emma?"

I nodded vigorously "You bet. Pig races. Piggyback races. Hog-calling contests. Stuffed pig toys. Piggy banks. The Oink Meter."

"The what?"

"You know, like those things where you hit a bell—only this one oinks, and see who can make the loudest squeal." I was beginning to run out of steam.

"I should be taking notes," Ed declared. "Could you write all this down and e-mail it to me?"

"Sure." I started to regret my feigned enthusiasm. "It might take me a day or two. That is, I may get some more ideas."

To my relief, Ed was unwedging himself from the chair. "It's all worth considering. I'm sure glad to have you on my side."

Side of pork, side of bacon, side of . . . I had to stop.

SIFTING THROUGH THE PHONE CALLS I'D RECEIVED, I began returning them in order of priority: Rita Patricelli at the Chamber of Commerce; Shawna Beresford-Hall, the new dean of students at the college; Bunky Smythe, forest ranger; and three complaining readers who thought I was an idiot. I was dealing with the last crank when Ginny came into my office.

I finished with the crank and gazed at Ginny. "What's up?"

Ginny was looking even more serious than usual. "Some man has called you twice—once while you were out and again while you were on the phone. He wouldn't leave his name or a number, but he said he'd try you at home. I didn't recognize his voice, although he sounded fairly young, like maybe twenties or early thirties."

I shrugged. "It may have something to do with the memorial for Hank Sails tomorrow night. You know—we should all come up with our favorite memory or something like that. By the way, Vida and I will be leaving early, probably around four."

"Oh." Ginny brightened a bit. "Okay, you could be right. He sounded anxious to talk to you, so maybe he had a deadline of his own."

I dithered briefly over whether I should pay a call on Nell Blatt or Grace Grundle. I couldn't face Grace and those cats, so around three-thirty, I phoned Nell and asked if I could stop by.

"Sorry," she replied in her brisk voice. "I'm washing the

living room and the dining room. The holidays are just around the corner, you know. What about the day after tomorrow?"

"Well . . ." I hesitated. The longer the wait, the shorter her memory. "Could I ask you a couple of questions now?"

"Make them short," Nell retorted.

I could see why Vida and Nell didn't get along. The sisters-in-law were both imperious, and no doubt had always rubbed each other the wrong way.

"I'll try," I promised, and decided to be blunt. "Who do you know who'd want to poison Gen?"

The question didn't seem to faze Nell. "Nobody, offhand. Except Vida, of course."

I was shocked. "Are you serious?"

"Of course. The two of them were archenemies after . . . Well, let's say for a couple of years before Gen left town."

"What was the problem?"

There was a pause at the other end of the line. "You don't know, do you?" Nell finally said.

"No," I admitted. "Although I'm aware that Vida didn't like Gen."

"If you don't know—if Vida's never told you—then I certainly won't. We may not be real close, but we *are* kin," Nell declared. "We keep ourselves to ourselves. If you want to know, ask Vida. I've got walls to wash." Nell hung up.

A SKING VIDA WOULDN'T DO ME ANY GOOD. IF SHE HADN'T told me by now, she wouldn't. My only hope was to spike her drink at Hank Sails's memorial and make her spill the beans.

What bothered me most was that in a town the size of Alpine tales of a feud between Vida and Gen would be fodder for gossip. Yet no one—except Nell and Vida herself—had suggested a problem between the two women. Such quarrels have long lives in Alpine. Was it possible that whatever had happened was really a family secret? Would any of Vida's daughters know? And if so, would they betray a confidence? The answer was a resounding *No*. I didn't think a call to Amy or Beth or Meg would do any good unless I could figure a way to wheedle the story out of them.

So I turned my thoughts to next Wednesday's editorial. Ben compared my weekly task to his weekly sermons: mull, discard, mull, revise, mull some more, and finally write the damned thing. He had the Sunday readings to rely on; I had the town. We were both expected to be fresh and inspiring.

My mind was a blank.

All I could think of was Ed's proposed museum. Images of pigs—standing pigs, sitting pigs, talking pigs, singing pigs—clumped across my mind's eye. I gave up, and concentrated on possible feature stories instead.

As soon as I got home, I removed the rib eye steaks from the freezer and defrosted them in the microwave. Then I checked my messages. There was only one, and it had come in just five minutes before I got home. But when I keyed in the actual call, it was a hang-up. I looked at my caller ID: it read PAY PHONE and registered the number, which was local. Could it be the man who had tried to reach me at the office? If so, he'd probably call again.

I went into the bedroom to change clothes. No seductive costume was necessary, so I put on a pair of jeans and a UW sweatshirt. Milo and I were way past the Language of Love. Indeed, I wasn't sure we'd ever learned it. Looking at myself in the bedroom mirror, I wondered if that hadn't always been a big part of the problem between us. It wasn't just that our backgrounds were different or that we didn't share many interests. We'd reached a stage in our relationship that was one step above using our bodies as convenience stores. Sometimes I felt like a charity, providing comfort for lonely sheriffs.

The mirror showed me smiling ironically. Maybe I should do something different. Not exotic, not erotic—but funny. The puckish mood that had beset me during Ed's visit hadn't yet evaporated.

I had some balloons in my kitchen junk drawer. They were left over from a baby and his mother who'd temporarily lived with me several years ago. I also had a couple of squeaky toys that had belonged to the little tot. One was—appropriately enough—a pink pig. The other was a mangy-looking orange cat.

Fortunately, the sweatshirt was baggy, a necessity in Alpine winters when I put a sweater under it in order to keep warm. I blew up the balloons and laid them over my bra. I looked a little weird, but not outrageous. Using a strip of Velcro, I attached the squeaky pig to my waist and the cat to my backside. I thought it was a funny idea; Milo might not agree. I'd have to wait and see.

The sheriff arrived five minutes early. He gave me a perfunctory kiss on the cheek before heading into the kitchen. Apparently, he didn't notice my expanded bust.

"Don't ask me anything until I get a drink," he said, taking an almost-empty bottle of Scotch out of the cupboard. "You got any more of this stuff?"

"It's right next to that bottle," I said, amazed anew at men's inability to see what's practically bumping their eyeballs.

"Oh. Good." He took down the new bottle. "You got yours yet?"

I pointed to a full glass on the counter about two inches from where he was standing. "I just made it. Are you going to get a glass or just drink it straight out of the jug?"

The sheriff looked as if he was considering the idea, but

finally got a glass, added ice, a stiff shot of Scotch, and a dash of water. "I'm having a job crisis," he announced.

I stared at Milo to make sure he was serious. Judging from his doleful expression, he was. "Why?"

"Over this poisoning deal," he replied, leaning against the fridge. "I'll have to question Annie Jeanne tomorrow. I know damned well she'll deny anything to do with the insulin in the cheesecake, but she's the only person who's a real suspect."

Cocktail glass in hand, I looked Milo straight in the eye. "Not so."

Milo stared back, but at my face, not my bosom. "How do you mean?"

"Let's sit down," I said. "I don't need to put the steaks on yet."

"I like mine pretty well done," the sheriff reminded me as we went into the living room.

"I know, I know, bootlike."

"Your steaks look like you could put a tourniquet on them and they'd go out to pasture," he said as we assumed our accustomed places—he in the easy chair, me on the sofa. He still didn't seem to notice anything unusual about my person. "What do you know that I don't?" he asked, taking a pack of Marlboro Lights out of his pocket. "About the poison, I mean."

I got out the ashtray and handed it to Milo, who promptly lit up, but not before offering me a cigarette, too. With a show of reluctance, I accepted. Why not? I was in for an evening of semidebauchery, even if smoking was a much graver social sin these days than sex outside of wedlock. "The cookies that made up the crust weren't homemade. Gen bought them at the bakery and gave them to Ethel Pike, who couldn't eat them because of her diabetes and handed them over to Annie Jeanne."

"Hold it." Milo was obviously trying to follow the cookie trail. "So the Crowes made the cookies?"

I nodded. "I doubt that they put insulin in them, however." I winced. That seemed to bring us back to Annie Jeanne. You can't make a crust without breaking the cookies.

The same thought struck Milo. "So Annie Jeanne was the only one who could have put the insulin in the crust," he mused.

"Well—no. Annie Jeanne left the rectory for what she called just a few minutes to go to the store. Knowing Annie Jeanne," I continued, "she may have been gone for an hour. She tends to dither."

"The rectory wasn't locked?"

"No." I hesitated. "Ben was there."

To my relief, Milo laughed. "I don't consider your brother a suspect."

"I'm so relieved," I said, only half joking. "Say, do you remember if Father Fitz had diabetes?"

Milo frowned. "How would I know? I was never a member of his flock."

"You'd remember if the EMTs had ever been called to the rectory because he'd gone into a diabetic coma," I said.

"Well . . . I might at that," Milo admitted. "But his tour of duty at St. Mildred's goes back to before I was on the force. Hell, when did he come here? It must have been back in the fifties, when I was still a kid."

"That sounds about right," I agreed.

We were both silent for a few minutes, sipping and smoking. It was moments like these when I could almost imagine myself saying, "What time are the kids coming home tonight?"

But there were no kids; nobody was coming home. I offered Milo a refill. He accepted. I went into the kitchen, put his steak on to cook, and returned with a full glass for him and a few more sprinkles of bourbon for me.

As I handed him his drink, he stared up at me. "You look different. Putting on some weight?"

"I don't think so," I replied, hastening to sit down on the sofa. "I stay around a hundred and twenty, a hundred and twenty-five. Frankly, I hardly ever weigh myself."

"Hunh." Milo was looking puzzled. "It must have been the way you were standing. I'm used to looking down at you."

I'd draped my arms across my chest. "I suppose."

"Hunh," Milo repeated.

During dinner, we spoke of topics unrelated to poisoning or my shape. The main subject was the string of break-ins. It was Wednesday; there had been no further reports since the Pikes' burglary Monday. Milo, however, wasn't sanguine about the thief—or thieves—giving up the crime spree.

"Too many houses in this town that can't be easily seen, what with all the trees and bushes," he said, making good headway on his dinner. "Not enough streetlights, either."

The sheriff was right. Despite numerous editorials on my part, Alpine had adequate lighting only in the commercial district. As for sidewalks—for which I'd also beaten the *Advocate*'s drums—they didn't exist south of Tyee Street or north of the river. My own front lawn dwindled into a strip of gravel between my property and the pavement. According to Vida, my street hadn't been paved until the mid-eighties.

"You must have some suspects," I pointed out. "There's always a few bad boys with nothing better to do than break into houses. Not to mention the druggies who are trying to support their habit."

"It used to be easy," Milo said with a sigh. "We knew who all the bad kids were—they'd usually grown up in Alpine. But now, with the college, we've got ten times as many outsiders. Plus, they come and go."

I glanced at the clock. It was ten to seven, almost time for *Vida's Cupboard*.

I started clearing away the dirty plates and putting them in the dishwasher. Milo had wandered out into the living room, where he turned the radio on. Spencer Fleetwood didn't usually work the weeknight shifts, leaving the DJ responsibilities to Tim Rafferty or some of the college students with an interest in broadcasting. But he was deferential to Vida, and always gave her a live introduction. The hour turn had just concluded as I joined the sheriff, who was now sitting on the sofa. *Milo's version of foreplay,* I thought, flopping down next to him. He threw a long arm around my shoulders. I moved a couple of inches closer.

"We're back with you on KSKY-AM, the voice of Skykomish County," Spence announced in his best radio voice. "This is Wednesday, a special night for our listeners. Without further ado, let me introduce the voice of the people, Vida Runkel, as she opens *Vida's Cupboard.*"

A creaking sound that symbolized the cupboard's opening was followed by Vida's unmistakable slightly nasal tones. "Good evening, dear listeners. This has been such a busy week for me, and not entirely pleasant." Pause. Was she going to mention Gen's demise? "I was forced to leave town for a few days to help take care of my daughter Beth, who had foot surgery. I left early Friday morning, and was— thankfully—back in Alpine late Monday night. I'm not only delighted to be home, but also happy to tell you that Beth is recovering nicely. While I was staying with her in Tacoma, I had the opportunity to spend time with my grandchildren, which is always such a joy. . . ."

Vida continued for at least three minutes discussing the charms and talents of Beth's offspring. Milo and I exchanged puzzled looks just before his hand began exploring my balloons. His expression became downright mystified.

"You haven't . . . gotten one of those boob jobs, have you?" he asked.

"Of course not," I replied, sounding indignant.

"You feel . . . different."

"Not to overlook my grandson right here in Alpine," Vida went on. "Roger Hibbert is attending Skykomish Community College and hopes to become an actor. He's taking English 101, drama, and music in his first quarter on campus."

"He also took remedial math in summer school," I said to Milo out of the corner of my mouth.

He put his hand under the sweatshirt. "Jesus!" he exclaimed. "What the hell?"

The left balloon popped. We both jumped.

"My God!" Milo cried, and tugged at the sweatshirt.

"Roger," Vida said in a proud voice, "is writing a paper for his English class. The students were asked to research an important historical figure. Roger chose Billy the Kid, which I think is very original of him."

Milo saw the other balloon. "Emma!" He poked it, and it, too, blew up. The sheriff started to laugh.

"Speaking of studies and books, in this coming edition of the *Advocate*," Vida resumed, giving the paper its usual plug, "I'll be telling you about Edna Mae Dalrymple's adventures at the library conference in Yakima. The article will focus on the conference itself, but I won't have room to include Edna Mae's adventure at a service station in Yakima. She stopped on her way into town to fill up the tank and was amazed when . . ."

Milo and I were both laughing so hard we barely heard Vida. The gist of the anecdote was that Edna Mae had encountered one of the many Hispanics in Yakima and couldn't understand a word he said. She thought he asked her if the car took soup or realtor, and if she needed hair or fodder. Vida continued in this vein until the commercial break for the Grocery Basket.

"This doesn't sound at all like her usual show," I said,

controlling my mirth. "Vida hasn't announced a guest, though I thought she told me she'd invited Doc Dewey to urge people to get flu shots."

"Maybe Doc had an emergency," Milo suggested, now caressing my real breast and pulling me closer. The pig went off.

Milo pulled away. "Is that your stomach growling?"

I was laughing so hard I couldn't answer. The sheriff yanked my sweatshirt up to my armpits. "It's a pig!" he cried, and gave me a swat on the bottom.

The cat meowed.

"Oh, Jesus," Milo groaned, falling back on the sofa. "You're really booby-trapped!" He started to guffaw again, holding his sides.

I'd never seen him laugh so hard, which practically sent me into hysterics. I was afraid I'd wet my pants, though that wouldn't be a bad encore, all things considered. Instead, I rolled off the sofa onto the floor.

Vida was on the air again. "I've been talking to some of our friends and neighbors about their Thanksgiving plans. Clancy and Debra Barton have already ordered a twenty-two-pound free-range turkey from Jake and Betsy O'Toole's Grocery Basket. Dot and Durwood Parker plan to have three kinds of stuffing—traditional, mushroom with oysters, and fresh fruit. Molly and Karl Freeman are traveling to a turkey farm near Centralia to pick out their bird. The Freemans have gotten their turkey from the same farm for the past three years. They tell me it's actually a very difficult task. Some of the turkeys look grumpy, which they think indicates that the meat won't be tender. Then there are the ones who look friendly and have such a cheerful gobble-gobble-gobble. You can imagine how Molly and Karl want them spared. Last year they chose what they considered the perfect bird: It looked bored, and the Freemans decided it didn't have much to live for anyway."

By this time, Milo had laughed so hard that he'd rolled off the sofa, too, but his lanky frame knocked over the coffee table, and the ashtray fell on my head. Milo took one look at me and laughed some more as I picked dead butts out of my hair and brushed off ashes.

But Vida wasn't done. "I'll be running some of Alpiners' treasured family recipes—and some new ones, too—in upcoming issues of the *Advocate*. I already have six cranberry ideas, including a . . ."

The Thanksgiving theme lasted until the end of the show. Milo and I finally regained our control and sat on the floor staring at each other.

"What's going on?" I said, finally getting up and turning off the radio just as Vida's cupboard creaked shut. "That wasn't anything like her usual program. She always manages to elaborate on the big news stories around town. But she never so much as alluded to Gen's death, the break-ins or mentioned that St. Mildred's parishioners shouldn't be afraid of drinking communion wine."

"Say," Milo said in a wondering voice, "now that I think about it, how come Vida hasn't been badgering Bill Blatt about Gen's poisoning?"

"Good question." I turned to face Milo, who was now standing up. "She claims she's not interested. Apparently, she and Gen had a big falling-out years ago. Do you know anything about that?"

"Nope. I sort of remember when Gen moved away, but that's it."

I took some deep breaths. I was weak from laughing. To my surprise, Milo wasn't making any moves.

"Are you okay?" I asked.

"Well . . ." He put a hand to his back. "I think I pulled something when I fell off the couch."

"Oh—I'm sorry. Does it feel serious?"

The sheriff shrugged as he looked at me with a wry expression. "No," he replied as the phone rang.

I waved at the receiver on the end table. "They'll call back," I said. "Are you sure you're okay?"

"I'll be fine." The wry expression remained. "But somehow I don't think I'm in a bedroom kind of mood anymore. I should probably head home and go over my tackle box. I may go steelheading Saturday."

Fishing. Sometimes better than sex. I understood.

Awkwardly, Milo patted my shoulder. "Great dinner. Thanks."

He put on his jacket, kissed the top of my head, and opened the door. I went out on the porch to see him off.

"Hey," I called when he was halfway to his car, "was it as good for you as it was for me?"

He stopped and turned to look over his shoulder. "Yeah, I think it was. But can you make balloon animals?"

A N HOUR LATER, I REMEMBERED THE UNANSWERED PHONE call. Suddenly I was anxious to check the message. It could have been Adam or Ben. It might even have been Vida.

The caller was none of the above. It was another hang-up. The caller ID informed me that the number had been dialed from a pay phone.

It wasn't quite nine o'clock, over two hours away from my bedtime. I phoned Ben to see how he and Annie Jeanne were doing.

Fine, he said. Doc Dewey had provided Annie Jeanne with some sleeping pills. "She went to her room about twenty minutes ago, and I haven't heard a peep out of her. I imagine she'll sleep like a rock. This has been pretty exhausting as well as traumatic for her."

"It hasn't been easy on you, either," I said.

"Hell, this is nothing," he replied. "Except for all the damned phone calls, including the cranks."

"The usual anti-Catholic witchcraft and idolatry stuff?"

"That, and a couple of cradle Catholics who left the church and wanted to tell me how justified they feel about it," Ben said dryly. "I tell them that's fine, they'll be back for their funerals."

I smiled into the receiver. "I like your style, Stench. By the way, I had Milo over to dinner."

"Does that mean you'll be coming to confession Saturday?"

"As a matter of fact, no," I said. "I'm going now. Good night."

The phone rang as soon as I put the receiver down on the end table. Thinking it was Ben delivering another smart crack, I answered with a breezy "Yeah?"

It wasn't Ben.

"Is this Emma Lord?" the hushed male voice inquired.

"Yes, it is," I said, regaining formality. "Who is this?"

"My name's Tony Knuler. I have to meet with you right away. It's urgent. How do I get to your house?"

I didn't know anyone named Tony Knuler, and I certainly wasn't letting a stranger come to my house at ten o'clock at night. On the other hand, it wasn't the first time that a stranger had contacted me with a news tip.

"I'm sorry," I said, "it's late. Why do you need to see me so soon?"

There was a long pause. "You own the newspaper, right?"

"Yes."

"I really need to talk to you now."

"Then talk."

The next pause was so lengthy that I wondered if he'd hung up. While I waited impatiently, I turned his name over in my brain. *Tony Knuler.* I'd heard it somewhere, and recently, too. But I couldn't place it. I hear so many names every day. Most of them are familiar, but some are not. They're contacts with state and government agencies, college students, tourists, out-of-town journalists checking background.

"How early can I meet you tomorrow?" the mystery man finally asked, his voice still hushed.

"I'm usually in the office around eight," I replied.

"I don't want to come to the office."

I was getting exasperated. "Can you tell me what this is about?"

"No, not over the phone." Tony Knuler was beginning to sound panicky. "Can I come to your house before you go to work? Say, around seven?"

"No, you can't."

Another long, long pause. "What about breakfast at a restaurant?" he finally asked.

Now it was my turn to hesitate. "Okay," I said. "The Venison Inn, seven-thirty." I wasn't going to get up early to meet this bozo. At least I wouldn't have to make breakfast at home.

"That's right near the newspaper office, isn't it?"

"Yes, just a block away."

"What about that diner near the bridge into town?"

The Bourgette boys' fifties-style diner just off Alpine Way served breakfast. "Fine," I said. "How will I recognize you?"

"I'll bring a copy of the *Advocate*," Tony Knuler said.

"So will I," I responded, "so that you know me."

"Don't bother," he replied. "I already know you."

He hung up.

ELEVEN

Sleep eluded me that night. Trying to remember where I'd heard Tony Knuler's name was driving me nuts. By midnight, I turned on the bedside lamp, picked up a book on the Plantagenets, and attempted to read myself to sleep.

It wasn't working. The Plantagenets, especially Henry II and his consort, Eleanor of Acquitaine, were fascinating. I thought about the movie *The Lion in Winter*, with Peter O'Toole and Katharine Hepburn as the royal couple. In a very small role, Anthony Hopkins had played the king's quavering son and heir.

Anthony Hopkins. Anthony Knuler. Tony Knuler. He was the guy who'd stolen the phone book from the Alpine Falls Motel. What the heck did he want with me?

I was too tired to figure it out. At last, I went to sleep, and dreamed not of strangers, but of Vida, wearing a cloche hat pulled down over her eyes and receding into a misty November morning.

There was fog when I woke up at seven. Dawn had barely broken with a murky gray light in the east. The dampness seeped through the evergreens in my backyard and settled just above the ground. I plugged in the coffeemaker, got dressed, and put on my makeup. Staring into space until I got my first jolt of caffeine, I sat down at the kitchen table and drank my coffee. Five minutes later, I was backing out of the driveway, with headlights on. The short trip to the diner took longer than usual, due to slow-moving traffic on fogbound Alpine Way.

The diner was busy. Many of the customers were workmen, though few these days were loggers. Blue jeans and plaid flannel were the costume du jour, accessorized with heavy shoes and tool belts. Terri Bourgette, one of Mary Jane and Dick's daughters, greeted me at the front desk.

"I'm meeting someone I don't know," I told her. "Has a man carrying a copy of the *Advocate* come in?"

"Not yet," Terri replied, flashing me her big, friendly smile. "Do you want to wait here or be seated?"

"I need coffee," I said. "I'll sit. Send him my way when he gets here."

Terri led me to a booth that was festooned with stills from *I Love Lucy* TV shows and glossy photos of Tony Curtis and Janet Leigh. At home, I skimp on breakfast, usually having toast and coffee with maybe a rasher of bacon or a scrambled egg. But the odors coming from the kitchen—as well as the stack of pancakes being served to an elderly couple across the aisle—accelerated my appetite. As soon as the waitress had finished, I waved at her. Suddenly, I was starving.

After ordering the pancakes with ham, an egg over easy, and coffee, I looked at my watch: It was seven thirty-five. Tony Knuler was late. He might know me, but he might not know exactly how to find the diner. I thanked the waitress as she filled my coffee mug and kept my eye on the restaurant's front.

A young man I didn't recognize came in alone a couple of

minutes later. But he didn't have a copy of the *Advocate* as far as I could tell, and judging from his suit and tie, I figured him for a salesman. Terri seated the new arrival at the chrome counter.

By seven forty-five, I was squirming a bit on the bright red plastic seat cover. A minute later, my order arrived—but still no Tony Knuler.

His tardiness didn't spoil my appetite. I ate as if I were related to the Bronsky family, but still watched the diner's front. It wasn't quite eight o'clock when I finished my meal. Sated, but becoming annoyed, I decided to give the Mystery Man another five minutes.

He never showed.

"Did you get stood up?" Terri asked as I paid my bill.

"I guess so," I replied, adding a tip and signing the receipt for my Visa card. "I'm not heartbroken. I have no idea who this guy is."

Terri's pretty face showed interest. "Really? Should I keep an eye out for him in case he comes in?"

I nodded. "Tell him to call me at the office. Thanks."

"He's got your number?" Terri inquired as I started to turn away.

I looked back over my shoulder. "Oh, yes. He's got my number."

Maybe, I wondered, in more ways than one.

JUST TO MAKE SURE, I LINGERED FOR A FEW MINUTES IN THE parking lot, watching for a man with a copy of the *Advocate*. There were new arrivals, but I recognized all of them: Skunk and Trout Nordby from the GM dealership, Shawna Beresford-Hall and Clea Bhuj of the college faculty, and County Commissioner Leonard Hollenberg with his wife, Violet. I gave up and drove away.

By the time I arrived at the office, the staff was in place, and most of the Upper Crust's coffee cake was gone. I didn't care; I was full of pancakes.

There was, however, a frosty air in the newsroom. Vida and Leo were obviously annoyed with each other. My ad manager was purposely blowing smoke in my House & Home editor's direction, while she was speaking much louder than usual on the telephone and rattling papers at the same time. Scott sat low in his chair, hiding behind his computer.

"Good morning," I said to all. "Sorry I'm late. I had a breakfast meeting."

Vida was all but shouting into the phone. "Now, now, Darla, you know perfectly well that I've never seen your underwear."

Leo looked at me and shook his head. "Rough start," he murmured.

Vida hooted with laughter. "Really, Darla, if it's genuine Belgian lace, I wouldn't sell it at any price, especially not on eBay."

I signaled for Leo to step into my office, but didn't ask him to close the door. We couldn't possibly be overheard with Vida's trumpetlike conversation.

"What's up?" I inquired.

"The Duchess's dander," Leo replied with a droll expression. "I dared to criticize her program last night. Did you hear it?"

"Oh, yes. I'm afraid so."

"What's with her lately?" Leo asked. "She's been acting strange for the last week or so."

I admitted I didn't know. "I wonder if I should ask her daughter Amy or Buck Bardeen. Frankly, it's getting to the point where she's disruptive in terms of the paper."

"Spence isn't happy with her, either," Leo confided in a low tone. "He called you first thing this morning, and when he found out you weren't here, he had Ginny transfer him to my line. Naturally, I couldn't say much—don't know much, for that matter—with Vida sitting ten feet away."

"What did Spence tell you?"

Leo stubbed out his cigarette in the ashtray I kept on the desk for him, for Milo, and for a few other local puffers. "The station got a bunch of calls right after the program went off the air. Two of the complaints were from Hispanics at the college who resented the Edna Mae service station bit, one was from another librarian who thought the item made her co-workers sound bad, and the rest wanted to know why Vida didn't talk about the local news—like Gen croaking at the rectory." He gestured in the direction of the newsroom. "She's been on the phone ever since she and I got into it. I think Vida's avoiding incoming calls. Ginny's already handed her about a half-dozen messages."

I had no solution to the problem. As long as Vida wouldn't confide in me, I was at a loss.

She was out most of the day, returning just after three o'clock. I had spent the morning on the phone talking to state and federal agencies about a proposal to create a new wilderness area just north of Highway 2 between Sultan and Alpine. The legislation, which covered 106,000 acres of forest and mountains, was called the Wild Sky Wilderness bill and was being studied by Congress. Because a wilderness area is the most stringent of all designations, Alpiners were divided between the environmentalists and those who had commercial interests. So far, I'd been siding with the former. Civilization was creeping ever farther along the Highway 2 corridor. I didn't like that.

Milo had no new developments regarding our local crimes. I told him about Tony Knuler, but he merely chuckled. "Publicity shy, huh? I'll bet he's some kind of promoter who came to town with big ideas. It happens."

That was true. Alpine had had its share of new arrivals who thought they'd found a place to make a buck. Some had succeeded; others had barely gotten a foot in the door. And in one case, a California developer had ended up dead.

Ben informed me that Annie Jeanne thought she might get out of bed by the afternoon. He was still getting the occasional crank call, but, as I'd expected, seemed unruffled.

When Vida finally showed up that afternoon, she dismissed the messages that Ginny had piled up for her. "I'll tend to them tomorrow. We really should be leaving soon if we want to avoid that dreadful rush-hour traffic into Seattle."

"I thought we'd head out around a quarter after four," I said, checking my watch, which informed me it was ten after three. "It shouldn't take more than two hours to get from here to downtown."

"Ha!" Vida exclaimed. "You obviously haven't been to the city lately! I can tell you what it's like in Tacoma, and Seattle is much larger."

We compromised, setting our departure time at four o'clock. I hated to admit it, but I was buying time to see if Tony Knuler would try to contact me and apologize.

He didn't. I had to wonder if, since he'd left the Alpine Falls Motel, he might have checked in somewhere else in town. Just before it was time to go, I reluctantly dialed Will Pace's number and asked what he knew about his recent guest.

"That creep?" Will wasn't exactly a gracious host. "He steals my property and you want to know about him? Well, I'm telling you—he's scum."

As far as I was concerned, Will might as well put up a sign on his reader board saying, WELCOME, SCUM. Between his attitude and the motel's no-frills policy, that was the type of guest he might expect.

To cut to the chase, candor might be my best ally. "I'm asking because he was supposed to meet me for breakfast this morning. He didn't show. Have you any idea where I could find him?"

"Hell, no." Will paused, and when he spoke again, his gravelly voice was suspicious. "What do you mean? Why did he want to have breakfast with you?"

"I don't know," I admitted. "I was hoping you might enlighten me. Did you speak to him much when he stayed at the motel?"

"I don't get chummy with the clientele," Will retorted. "If you do, the next thing they're asking for is special treatment."

Like heat and electricity. "I understand he was from California," I said.

"Yeah. So what?" Will shot back. "I'm from Riverside."

"Look," I responded, growing short on patience as well as time, "just tell me what you know about him. I'm sure you're busy and I am, too."

"Yeah, well, it is about time for guests to start arriving," Will mumbled. "I repeat, I didn't talk to him, even though he asked a bunch of questions."

"Like what?"

"Hell, I don't remember. Just about Alpine and stuff like that. Hey, a car's pulling up, gotta go."

"What kind of car did Knuler drive?"

"Huh? Oh, a beat-up Jap car. A Nissan, I think." Will hung up.

The car's make and year and license plate should be in the guest registry. So should Tony Knuler's home address. My natural curiosity was getting the better of me.

But I could do nothing more about my Mystery Man that afternoon. It was almost time to leave for Seattle. At four o'clock sharp, Vida appeared in my doorway, wearing a sealskin derby and her black swing coat over a black dress, which featured sprays of bright orange poppies.

For the first twenty minutes of the drive, Vida chattered away, mostly about her three daughters and their families. Beth's feet were healing; Amy worried too much, especially about Roger; Meg was auditing a history course at Western Washington University in Bellingham.

We were passing by Sultan's old cemetery next to the river when she finally stopped for breath.

I couldn't stand it another minute. "Vida," I said firmly, "what happened between you and Genevieve Bayard? I've never known you to be so callous or disinterested about what appears to be a murder."

Vida stiffened in the passenger seat. "Really!" She sniffed a couple of times. "I certainly didn't mourn Thyra Rasmussen's passing."

"Thyra wasn't murdered," I pointed out. "There was no mystery to her death. We were present when she died. She was just days short of being a hundred." I didn't add that a horrendous quarrel between Vida and Thyra might have precipitated the old girl's passing.

For a few moments, as we passed quiet farm country outside of Sultan, Vida remained silent. We were on the outskirts of Monroe when she spoke again.

"I don't like to speak of my relationship with Genevieve," she finally said in a flat voice. "It was most unpleasant."

"It was also twenty years ago," I noted. "More than that, wasn't it? It couldn't have been too awful. In fact, I've never heard one person in Alpine refer to it."

"Perhaps not," Vida murmured. "It wasn't something you'd broadcast."

I tried another angle. "Did it affect your daughters?"

Vida seemed to be withdrawing emotionally and physically, pulling farther away from me in her seat. "They never knew."

Something very personal, I conjectured, something that would not get talked about, that no one else would ever know—except Vida and Gen. Yet there had been a time when the Runkels—or at least the Blatts—had been close to Genevieve. Otherwise, Vida's mother would never have made Gen a quilt. Somehow, Gen must have betrayed the bond of friendship.

We were on the interstate that passed through the Eastside suburbs—Redmond, Kirkland, Bellevue. I planned to take the I-90 floating bridge, which would lead me into downtown, close to the Columbia Tower or the Bank of America Building or whatever the locals called the skyscraper these days. Not having lived in the city for so long, I couldn't keep up with all the takeovers and real estate deals that had transpired in my absence.

Neither Vida nor I had spoken for several minutes. We were getting into heavy traffic as we approached the bridge. The digital clock on the dashboard informed me it was five o'clock, the middle of rush hour. We were moving at a crawl by the time we took the Seattle exit from I-405.

"We have plenty of time, even in this mess," I said, breaking our long silence. "Do you want to get something to eat before we go to the memorial?"

"There will be food at the reception, I assume," Vida replied. "Eating in Seattle restaurants is very pricey."

"We're going to have over an hour to kill," I pointed out. "If you don't want to eat, we can shop a bit after we park."

"*Shop?*" Vida sounded horrified. "Have you any idea what things cost in the city? Why, last month Beth went to the Nordstrom's at the Tacoma Mall and saw a red wool coat that was priced at eleven hundred dollars!"

"I wasn't suggesting that you buy anything, Vida," I said,

inching toward the floating bridge. "We can merely look around."

Vida was fanning herself. "Oh, my. You realize that it's raining."

A torrential downpour wouldn't stop Vida in Alpine. The rain that was spattering the windshield was a typical Seattle drizzle. "You decide," I said in an impatient voice. "As I recall, there aren't a lot of shops at the lower end of town where the Columbia Tower is located. We'd have to take a bus up to the main stores, but it's a free zone."

"Free?" Vida turned to gaze at me. "I suppose we could go to that sports store. I could look for a Christmas present for Roger."

I assumed she meant Niketown. "We could."

But I'd been optimistic about our arrival time. No sooner had we gotten across Mercer Island and onto the bridge than westbound traffic stopped. I turned on the radio to find out what had happened. Not that it mattered—there was nothing to do but wait.

A cheerful young woman informed us that there was a stalled vehicle at midspan. The good news was there were no injuries; the bad news was that the car would have to be towed out of the way. That took over twenty minutes. Vida griped and groaned the entire time.

At last, we crept across the bridge. The lights of the city glistened through the rain. To me, it was a beautiful sight. To Vida, it was anathema. She likened our drive through the tunnel at the bridge's end to entering Dante's Inferno.

We reached the parking entrance to the Columbia Tower a little after six. That didn't give us enough time to take the bus uptown and do any shopping.

"I'm stiff," Vida announced after we got out of the car. "Let's walk a bit."

We went downhill, toward the waterfront. There were

shops along Western Avenue, including home design stores. Vida spotted a red leather sofa in one of the windows.

"Wouldn't that be perfect for Amy and Ted?" she enthused. "They're still open. Let's go inside."

The display floor was filled with rich woods, fine fabrics, and a sense of prosperity. The very air reeked of affluence. Or maybe it was all that leather.

A chic young woman of Asian descent approached us discreetly. "Isn't it handsome?" she murmured in a seductive voice. "Feel the leather. It's soft as a baby's skin."

"How much?" Vida asked without preamble.

"Ten-five," she murmured, as if the price were a secret. "It's on sale."

Vida goggled. "Ten-five *what*?"

"Ten thousand five hundred dollars." The saleswoman sounded embarrassed by her own admission. Clearly, she was conveying incredulity at such a bargain. "It's from Italy, all hand-tooled."

Vida cleared her throat and regained her composure. "That's a bit high," she said. "Does that include the pillows?" Apparently Vida wasn't going to lose face.

The saleswoman waved a hand at the three black satin pillows with their gold braided tassels. "They're sold separately. A well-known local designer made them."

"Perhaps something a bit less expensive," Vida said. "By the way, I'm Vida Runkel. What is your name?" The personal touch on Vida's part, perhaps an attempt to dispel the faceless factor of the big city.

"Michele." The saleswoman put out her hand.

"I'm Emma," I said, feeling as if I should add "the small and meek."

We all shook hands before Michele began retreating toward the rear of the display floor. "Back here," she murmured. "We have a red velveteen-covered sofa that's quite nice."

Apparently, Michele had calculated the net worth of Vida's pocketbook. "This is only two thousand dollars, but it's very comfortable."

Vida was looking not at the sofa but at the red, white, and blue quilt that was slung across its back. She froze in place before slowly lifting her hand to point at the quilt. "Where did you get that?"

The saleswoman looked puzzled. "The sofa? Or the quilt?"

Vida's expression was grim. "The quilt."

"It also was made by a local person, all hand-stitched, no machine work as some quilters use," Michele replied, keeping her aplomb. "This one's a steal at eight thousand dollars," she added in a confidential tone. "The price is about to go up because the artisan died recently. You see, it's an original Bayard design."

My jaw dropped, though I said nothing. Vida, however, squared her broad shoulders and stared down at Michele. "No, it's not. That quilt pattern was created by my mother."

TWELVE

I BEG YOUR PARDON?" MICHELE SAID, HER COMPLACENT FA-
cade finally cracking.

Vida had assumed a bulldog expression, though I thought
I caught the glimmer of tears in her eyes. "You heard me.
That quilt pattern was originally designed by my mother thirty
years ago. She won first prize for it at the Skykomish County
Fair. I have the same one at home in my bedroom, but in dif-
ferent colors."

"I don't understand," Michele replied, turning slightly as
a well-dressed young couple entered the store.

"There's nothing to understand," Vida snapped. "My
mother was a quilter, just as Genevieve Bayard was. Genevieve obviously used my mother's pattern and took credit for
it. I can bring my quilt down from Alpine to show you." Vida
winced slightly, no doubt at the thought of returning to
the city. "Or I could take a photograph."

A suave, dark-skinned young man had glided onto the
floor to assist the newcomers. They, too, were admiring the
red leather sofa.

"I'll have to talk to the manager," Michele said, focusing completely on Vida. "He's gone home for the day."

"Do you have any other so-called Bayard originals?" Vida asked archly.

"Ah . . . yes, we do. They're quite popular. Clients tend to like the homespun accessories these days." Michele led us to a green leather armchair. "Here's one," she said, indicating a green, brown, and white quilt resting on the chair's back. "And there's another, over on that fireplace settle. I believe that's all we have in stock now. Each quilt took almost a year to make. I doubt that we'll get any more since Ms. Bayard has passed away."

I thought I heard Vida snort. But when she spoke, her tone was thoughtful. "The other two quilts look familiar, but I don't believe my mother designed the patterns. Templates, I believe, is the proper term. How long have you been carrying the—the Bayard items?"

"Ever since I started working here three years ago," Michele replied warily. I imagined she was thinking about lawsuits. "Mr. Dreizle—that's the manager—would know."

"Do you have his card?" Vida inquired.

"I can give you mine," Michele said. "I'll put his name on it. Can you tell me yours again?"

We had gone over to an oak desk by the back wall. Vida and Michele exchanged information. With a curt nod, Vida tromped out of the store. I trailed along like the stooge I was, realizing that I hadn't uttered a word—other than to identify myself—since we'd entered.

"So," I said as we started back up the hill, "that's why you can't stand Gen? She was a pattern thief?"

"She was," Vida retorted. "I understand some quilters have their designs copyrighted. My mother never bothered. That's not the point. Genevieve was a fraud, a cheat, a completely phony person."

"But you must have known that for years," I said. "Is that why you despised Gen?"

Vida, who I swore could climb Mount Baldy without taking a deep breath, was a few steps ahead of me on the steep incline. "Certainly," she answered.

I couldn't see her face. I wished that I could. For once, I believed that Vida was lying.

Or at least not telling the whole truth.

WE ARRIVED IN THE TOWER'S EXCLUSIVE TOP-FLOOR club a few minutes after seven. More than thirty attendees were already on hand, including Hank's widow, Henrietta—or Hank-Too, as she was known. Vida immediately embraced her.

"Such an outstanding man!" Vida cried. "One of the finest journalists I've ever met! He taught me everything I know!"

That wasn't quite true, either, although I did recall that Marius Vandeventer had sent Vida to a newspaper seminar conducted by Hank when she first came to work for the *Advocate*.

I'd met Hank-Too only once, at a Washington State Newspaper Association conference at Lake Chelan. Tom had also attended the gathering. It was where we'd made love for the first time in almost twenty years. I hardly remembered Hank-Too, or much of the conference, for that matter.

But I paid my respects, which Hank's widow graciously accepted.

Vida seemed to know half of the mourners, although I couldn't figure out how. I let her prowl the room while I secured a bourbon and water from the bar and stuffed my face with crackers covered in crab and avocado dip.

"I knew you'd come," a low masculine voice said from behind me. "You want me, don't you?"

Even before turning around, I recognized the Associated Press's Rolf Fisher from our telephone conversations. He'd provided some important background on a murder case the previous winter. We'd exchanged business calls a couple of times since, though they were always peppered with Rolf's lascivious remarks and boasts of his successful womanizing. I didn't believe a word he said. I pictured the wretched lecher as about five foot two, shaped like a barrel, and with a bad comb-over.

He was none of those things. When I swiveled on my heel, I had to look up: If this was Rolf, I must be dreaming. He was six foot three, lean, sinewy, and wore a well-tailored black pinstripe suit. There was gray in his short dark beard and full head of wavy hair. He had chiseled features and black, black eyes. His expression was amused. I got the feeling he knew exactly what I was thinking. It was probably easy to discern: I'd just spilled dip on my black cashmere sweater.

"You certainly have trouble with hors d'oeuvres," Rolf remarked, gesturing at my bosom. "The first time we met, you dropped your earring in the crab dip. Now you're wearing it. How do you decorate your house, with mayonnaise and some garlic cloves?"

Luckily, I had a napkin in hand. "Drat," I muttered, trying to clean myself and ignore his remarks at the same time. *Did I have food stuck between my teeth? Was my lipstick smeared? Could I have gotten crab dip in my hair?* I hadn't been so self-conscious since I met Tom Cavanaugh.

"You don't remember, do you?" Rolf said, still amused.

I didn't. At least, I didn't remember him from our earlier meeting. Those were the days when I had eyes only for Tom. Sean Connery could have made a pass at me and I wouldn't have noticed.

But that was then and this was now.

"You're blushing," he said. "You blushed that other time, too. It's cute."

I was still wiping away at the crab dip. "I never blush," I declared. "It must be the lighting. Besides," I babbled, "we got stuck on the floating bridge."

" 'We'?" Rolf frowned. "I thought you were single."

"I am." I gestured at Vida with my elbow. "See the tall woman in the sealskin hat?"

Rolf gazed across the room where Vida was talking to an older man I didn't recognize. "You brought your duenna?"

I laughed. Actually, I giggled. God, I was making a fool of myself. "Yes. He's my Souse & Some editor. I mean *she's*—"

Maybe I could just jump out the window. The building was over seventy stories high. It would be better than dying of embarrassment.

Rolf was gazing at Vida. "I know who she is. Everybody knows Vida Runkel. She's quite a character, isn't she?"

Trying to be discreet, I took a backward step so I could dispose of my hors d'oeuvre remnants in an empty glass someone had left on a tray. I missed, and knocked the glass over, spilling the dregs, which included a lime slice.

"Oops." I righted the glass. "Goodness, I seem to be—" I didn't finish the sentence. *A mess* was what had popped into my mind.

"Let's see," Rolf said in a musing tone. "You're either overcome with emotion at Hank Sails's passing, or you're the clumsiest woman I've ever met. If it's the former, I don't blame you. If it's the latter, it's *really* cute."

"I don't get out much," I murmured.

"Vida is derelict in her duty," Rolf said. "She shouldn't let you out of her sight. On the other hand . . ." He shrugged.

"I'm allowed some time on my own," I responded.

"Good." Rolf's gaze shifted from Vida to a barrel-chested older man who was coming through the door with a willowy blonde on each arm. "Excuse me, there's Nick Anaconda. You know, the Snake. I worked for him on one of his small dailies thirty years ago in eastern Washington."

I knew the Snake only by reputation, so I stayed put. I certainly wasn't going to trot after Rolf Fisher like a bitch in heat. The shreds of dignity I still possessed must be guarded like gold.

I observed him from afar. He and the Snake exchanged hearty handshakes. He and the blondes hugged and kissed. Maybe everything Rolf had ever told me was true. Maybe he was a womanizer. His wife had died of cancer a few years ago. He had a right to pursue the ladies. Assuming he hadn't remarried. Anyway, who was I to judge?

I finally ambled over to a couple of publishers I actually knew. For the next hour I engaged myself in chitchat flavored with a bit of gossip. It was not uninteresting, since I had something in common with virtually everybody in the room. Vida continued to roam among the crowd, now grown to perhaps two hundred people who had known, admired, and respected Hank Sails.

I was considering a third drink when Nick Anaconda called for our attention. What followed was a half-dozen tributes to Hank, all true, mostly moving, and mercifully brief. Hank never did like overwriting.

It was just after nine, and time to hit the road. I didn't really need another drink. I spotted Vida on the far side of the room regaling a clutch of older women—no doubt former society editors themselves.

Edging my way through the throng, I was halfway to Vida when I felt a hand on my shoulder.

"Have you seen the view?" Rolf Fisher asked.

"It's hard to get near the windows in this crowd," I replied.

"I don't mean from here. The view's spectacular, but you

can't really see it unless you look out of the full-length windows in the restrooms."

I was trying to figure out if he was teasing. But for once, he looked serious.

"Come on," he said, the hand still on my arm. "Go take a look. I'll wait outside." He paused a beat. "Of course."

"Okay." I needed to use the restroom before we left town anyway.

Rolf escorted me out through the foyer, then pointed to the door marked by the woman symbol. "Only members and invited guests can use these restrooms. Take your time."

I had to admit, the view was everything that Rolf had promised. The tall floor-to-ceiling windows presented an unblemished panorama that I'd seen only from an airplane. I was looking east, far beyond the downtown area, practically into the foothills of the Cascade Mountains. The rain had stopped. I could almost believe we were above the clouds; on a foggy day, we would be. Maybe my head was already in the clouds. I certainly felt like a giddy teenager.

Rolf was waiting outside, standing by a table that held a huge arrangement of stargazer lilies, irises, freesias, asters, and alstroemerias. "What do you think?" he asked.

"Amazing," I declared. "Thanks for the suggestion."

He took a couple of steps toward me, lowering his voice as a couple of mourners headed for the elevator. "How often do you get to Seattle?"

"Not very often," I said. "Being my own boss means I don't get much time off."

Rolf cocked his head to one side. "Okay. I'm not my own boss. What are you doing weekend after next? Doing in Alpine, that is?"

"Are you serious?"

He looked it. "Sure. Why wouldn't I be?"

"But . . . All those women . . . The blondes . . ."

Rolf looked affronted. "Hey, I've got time for everybody. Those blondes are yesterday's news. You know—birdcage liners."

I didn't know what to think. Rolf was definitely attractive, but the last thing I needed in my life was to be part of a rake's progress. "I'm pretty tied up these days. We've got a big story—"

He pressed a finger to my lips. "I'm irresistible. I'll call you over the weekend." He dropped his hand. "Gotta run now. It's redhead night for old Rolf. See you in Alpine." He strode off toward the elevator.

Flummoxed, I returned to the herd, now increasingly noisy and more than adequately celebrating Hank Sails's life. After I managed to pry Vida away from a growing coterie, we said our farewells and departed.

"Honestly," Vida said as we took the smooth ride down to the lobby, "I didn't realize I knew so many people! Why, I met . . ."

She continued in that vein until we were passing through Monroe. I, however, barely heard her. All I could think of was the brazen Rolf Fisher. Or was he enigmatic? I couldn't tell. But he wasn't the least like Milo.

Or was he?

I DIDN'T THINK VIDA HAD NOTICED MY BRIEF ENCOUNTER with Rolf Fisher, but I was wrong. Shortly before we made the turn off Highway 2 for Alpine, she inquired about "the handsome man with the beard." Keeping my tone neutral, I'd reminded her of how Rolf had helped us discover some highly pertinent information concerning the murder of a local college professor. She made only one comment.

"I don't know him. Should I?"

I merely shrugged.

■   ■   ■

THE NEXT MORNING, I NOTICED THAT VIDA WAS BEING very selective about returning the phone messages in her in-basket. She made two stacks, which stood about even. Then she tossed one pile into the wastebasket before starting to answer the calls in the other. I assumed she didn't like critics, especially of her radio program.

Meanwhile, I made a call of my own, to Roseanna Bayard. I asked if she knew that her mother-in-law sold quilts commercially.

"She could have," Roseanna allowed. "I keep telling you, we weren't close. For all I know, she could have been in the black-market baby business."

"Did she ever make a quilt for you and Buddy?"

"Actually, she did," Roseanna replied. "It was our wedding present. We got it just before our second anniversary. Hang on, Emma, I've got another high school senior, and she's violating the dress code six different ways."

I could catch a few words of the conversation, which grew fairly heated when Roseanna informed "Stacie" that she couldn't wear her newsboy's cap, the plunging neckline was out, as was the belly button—even though it wouldn't appear in the photo—and the bare arms were verboten.

"But I have to show off my tattoo," Stacie wailed. "I got it just for my senior picture. See—it's a picture of my boyfriend, Dex, and it says, 'Forever Together.' "

"If you wanted to show it off, you should have had it put on your face," Roseanna snapped. "Go home, change clothes, and get back here in fifteen minutes so I don't have to charge you a cancellation fee."

I couldn't catch Stacie's dwindling protests, but she was obviously giving in.

"Sorry about that, Emma," Roseanna apologized. "God,

these kids. The girls come in here half-naked, and the boys look like they got their clothes at a rummage sale."

"That's okay," I said. "But you ought to know that Gen still has quilts out there that aren't sold. The attorney should know, too. The profits are part of the estate."

After giving Roseanna the name and number of the Seattle store's manager, I decided to call Edmund J. Dreizle myself.

Mr. Dreizle sounded as self-satisfied as his employees. "Ah. The Bayard works. You say you knew Genevieve?" He pronounced her name the French way, Jahn-vee-ev.

I told him I knew her family quite well.

"We had an exclusive contract with Genevieve," Dreizle said, a note of regret in his voice. "Alas, I'm very saddened by her passing. Such nimble fingers. It required months for her to make a quilt—terribly painstaking work—but they fetched a marvelous price."

"Who told you she died?" I asked.

There was a pause. "Let me think—I believe it was her son."

"Buddy?" I said in an incredulous voice.

"Buddy?" He made the name sound distasteful. No doubt he was used to clients who were known as Travis or Stanford or something that ended with III.

"Yes, he's the only Bayard son I know."

"No, not anyone called *Buddy*." I could hear Dreizle sigh. "I don't recall the name, to be honest. I was so shocked when he told me that Genevieve was gone. And not that old, either. Her heart, wasn't it?"

I ignored the question. "Did Gen sell them on consignment?"

"No, no, no," Dreizle responded. "We bought them directly from her. We've carried her items for almost ten years."

"I liked that green and brown and white one," I fibbed. "How much is it?"

"I'm afraid we marked it up a bit this morning," Dreizle hedged. "With her demise—you understand, of course. The well has gone dry, so to speak. But since you were in the store yesterday, I could let you have it for the original price. Fifteen hundred dollars. Believe me, that's quite a bargain."

Not for Emma. I wondered what Dreizle and Company had paid Gen. Four, maybe five hundred. I knew better than to ask. Either he wouldn't tell me or he'd lie.

It was my turn to hedge. "You say it's an original pattern?"

"Yes. All of Genevieve's quilts were original. She was not only a marvelous craftswoman, but a creative genius."

Don't say that to Vida, I thought. "I don't suppose you have pictures. That is, of her earlier work. I'm sure the needlework group she belonged to in Alpine would love to see what those quilts looked like."

"Why . . . certainly. We take photos of all our inventory, for insurance purposes," Dreizle explained. "I don't know that I'd have all the quilts, though. Once they're sold, we tend to dispose of the pictures after a while. Would you like me to send you some? Perhaps you could run them in your newspaper."

"That would be very nice," I said. Naturally, Dreizle would expect a free plug for the store, though I doubted that many Alpiners would race into Seattle to buy his pricey homewares.

"It may take a few days," Dreizle cautioned. "Our records aren't organized as efficiently as they might be. Michele says we should put everything on a computer, but that seems so . . . *cold,* doesn't it?"

"I'm not clever with computers myself," I confessed, before giving Edmund J. Dreizle the *Advocate*'s address. I thanked him and hung up.

My next call was to Ben. I got his voice messaging, so I asked if he wanted me to pick up lunch for him and Annie Jeanne. I felt as if I'd been neglecting my brother.

But I couldn't wait for him to return my call. I had an appointment to interview the new college president, May Hashimoto. She'd barely been in place when fall quarter had started, and couldn't take time out for the *Advocate*. I'd considered assigning the story to Scott, but since May and I hadn't yet met, I deemed it a courtesy to do the interview myself.

My route took me onto Burl Creek Road. I was halfway to the college when I saw two women hailing me some fifty yards ahead. Charlene Vickers and Darlene Adcock were standing by the new Jeep Liberty that Cal had bought for his wife.

"Emma," Charlene said, as I pulled onto the dirt verge, "have a look at what Dar and I've done. You can put it in Vida's 'Scene' column."

I suppressed a smile. Both women were self-effacing—except when it came to promoting the family businesses. Harvey's Hardware and Cal's Texaco would benefit from a front-page mention.

"What have you been doing?" I asked, gazing out the window at the modest frame house set back from the road. Neither Char nor Dar, as they were known to intimates, lived there.

"It's Pikes' place," Darlene said, and giggled. "At least that's what we call it. We've just finished cleaning up after the break-in."

"I thought you did that earlier in the week," I said.

"We did," Charlene chimed in. "That is, we got rid of most of the mess and clutter, but the Pikes aren't the greatest when it comes to housekeeping or gardening. He has a triple hernia, you know, and Ethel isn't in good health, either."

"The diabetes," I murmured.

Charlene put a finger to her lips. "Ssshhh. You know Ethel doesn't like people to know that."

I hesitated, not knowing how much information Milo had leaked about the poisoned cookies. Or maybe I should say the poisoned crust. We'd phrased it in the paper so that it was a simple poisoning. If there was such a thing.

"Come look at the yard," Darlene urged. "We cut back a lot of the berry vines and holly and forsythia. The place was really junglelike."

I checked my watch. It was a quarter of eleven. I'd allowed myself plenty of time to get to the college and had fifteen minutes to drive not quite a mile.

"Okay." They were nice women, and their husbands were faithful advertisers. I turned off the engine and got out. For the first time, I noticed a half-dozen large refuse bags on the edge of the weed-choked lawn. "Did you do all this today?" I asked.

Both women nodded. "We've been at it since eight o'clock," Darlene said. "Come look out back. We've got bags we haven't brought up to the road."

I complied. The Pikes' backyard wasn't as big as the front, but just as neglected. However, I could tell that it had been much worse before Char and Dar arrived on the scene. There were yellow patches of grass around the edges where shrubbery had taken over, and by the side of the house I could see the scorched area where the quilts and templates had been set afire.

"I don't know if the Pikes pick the berries on those vines we cut back," Charlene remarked. "There are several kinds— blackberries, thimbleberries, salmonberries, maybe even some boysenberries. It's a jelly and jam maker's paradise."

Darlene was pointing to a gnarled old apple tree. "They should cut that down. We raked up all the leaves and the rot-ting apples. Most of the apples were deformed and wormy. The tree's way past its prime."

"Caterpillars," Charlene said. "If they'd get rid of the caterpillars, the tree might do well." She fished into the pocket of her windbreaker. "I found this under one of the apples. It's some kind of religious medal."

I peered into Charlene's open hand. She held a Miraculous Medal that was etched with the image of the Blessed Virgin. "There's an inscription on the back, but it can't belong to the Pikes," Charlene went on, turning the medal over. "They aren't Catholic."

I picked up the medal to examine the inscription more closely. It read, "To MAR—First Communion, May 14, 1978."

"Last name beginning with *R*," I murmured. "The only parishioners I can think of are the Raffertys and the new couple—he works for the highway department—Romanelli, that's the name. Of course, it could belong to a woman whose maiden name started with an *R*. Do you mind if I take it to St. Mildred's and see if anyone claims it?"

Char and Dar shook their heads in unison. "Go ahead," said Darlene. "I suppose there'd be some sentimental value?"

"Probably." I slipped the medal into my handbag. "I'd better get going. I'm due at the college in five minutes."

Navigating the curves on Burl Creek Road, I thought about the Miraculous Medal. Charlene and Darlene had more in common than their rhyming names. They were both good-natured, kindhearted—and somewhat naive. To them, the discovery of the medal was simply somebody's bad luck or carelessness.

To me, it sent a different message: Had the Pikes' burglar dropped it when he ransacked the house?

It might take a miracle to find out.

THIRTEEN

MAY HASHIMOTO WAS A BRISK MIDDLE-AGED WOMAN whose mother had served in the army during the occupation of Japan. Dorothy Brooks had fallen in love with a Japanese translator and married him. Turning the tables on the norm of postwar unions, May's mother had brought a Japanese peace-groom home to San Jose.

The interview lasted almost half an hour. May had another appointment at eleven-thirty. She outlined her background, her philosophy of education, and her reasons for accepting the post at Skykomish Community College instead of remaining as chancellor of a small private four-year school in Colorado.

"I grew up near the ocean. I felt landlocked," May asserted. "I may not be able to watch the waves, but there's a river within walking distance of the campus, and lakes and streams all over the place. Furthermore, I believe in public education. I got tired of sucking up to alums for donations and endowments."

Those were valid reasons from my point of view. Besides, I liked the white streak of hair that ran from her forehead to the back of her neck. May told me her colleagues in Colorado nicknamed her "Skunk." I assured her that wouldn't happen in Alpine. We already had Skunk Nordby, and one Skunk was enough.

I CALLED BEN FROM MY CELL PHONE BEFORE I STARTED THE car in the college parking lot. He answered, but informed me that Mary Jane Bourgette was still on duty.

"She's a saint," he declared.

"It's hard to believe that her mother was Thyra Rasmussen," I replied. "Can I bring dessert?"

"Sure," Ben said. "Bring lots of it."

At the Upper Crust Bakery, Vicki Crowe waited on me. She didn't seem to be in a very good mood. Maybe it was because she was waiting on the Dithers sisters when I showed up. They were buying apple strudel—more apple strudel than two people could possibly eat before it went stale. I suspected that it wasn't for them, but for their horses.

"What's with those two?" Vicki demanded after the Dithers sisters left. "They hardly ever talk. They just point and sort of grunt."

"Did they whinny?" I inquired. "They own horses, you know."

Vicki looked flabbergasted. "Do you mean they're going to feed those apple strudels that I baked at three o'clock this morning to a bunch of dumb animals?"

"Consider some of your other customers," I said. "You know, the kind who stand on only two legs."

"Hunh," Vicki snorted. "There's some truth in that." Then, even though there were no other customers in the store, she lowered her voice. "Speaking of nitwits, Gordon and I are damned upset. There seems to be a rumor going around town that we bake poisoned goods."

I was startled, even though I knew what Vicki was talking

about. "You mean, the poison that killed Genevieve Bayard? What have you heard?"

"That Gen bought some cookies here—which she did— and was poisoned by them," Vicki whispered. "That's a rotten thing for anybody to say, especially when we're just starting out in this town."

I wondered how the rumor had started, but I didn't dare reveal too much. "It doesn't make sense," I finally said. "If the cookies were poisoned here, why didn't somebody else die or at least get sick?"

"Good point," Vicki responded. "Lord knows, Mrs. Bayard bought a bunch of them, and different kinds, too. Oatmeal, sugar, snickerdoodles, gingerbread, peanut butter, chocolate, and chocolate chip. Nine, ten dozen. We almost ran out. Of course," she added after a pause, "that Dupré woman did get sick. Gen must have taken some of the leftover cookies to her the next day."

I didn't enlighten Vicki. I couldn't in any event, because Edith Bartleby was coming into the store.

The Episcopal vicar's wife was a tall, rangy woman with gray hair that was always a bit untidy. It was the kind of hair that I associated with affluence, not unkempt, but more "I don't care, I don't have to." I knew that Edith had come from a wealthy family, though she was no lavish spender. She couldn't be, in her role as vicar's wife. Like Calpurnia, she had to be above reproach.

"Emma," she said in her pleasant manner, "how nice to see you. How is your brother? He and Regis are having dinner this weekend. Or did you know?"

I didn't. But that wasn't surprising. I couldn't keep up with Ben's hectic schedule.

"Tell me," Edith said in a confidential tone, "when is Genevieve's funeral going to be held? Even though I scarcely knew her, Regis and I would like to attend."

I didn't know that, either. "I think they're waiting to find out if she left instructions concerning her burial," I said.

"Really." Edith was too well bred to let her disapproval show. "You would have thought . . . But of course Genevieve appeared to be in excellent health."

"And good spirits, I understand. I mean," I added, "at the party in her honor Sunday night."

"Very much so," Edith agreed with a faint smile. "And so delighted to see her old friends, especially Annie Jeanne Dupré. They giggled like schoolgirls. Mary Lou Blatt told them she was going to have to get out her ruler to calm them down. Mary Lou taught grade school for years, you know." Edith paused, again quite serious. "It's comforting to think that Genevieve enjoyed her last hours in this world."

A young couple I didn't know entered the store. Vicki Crowe was drumming her nails on the counter.

"Excuse me," I said to Edith, "I think we're holding up progress."

I turned to Vicki and asked for half of a devil's food cake. I paid for my purchase and continued on my way to St. Mildred's. Annie Jeanne was sitting up in the parlor, visiting with Mary Jane Bourgette. Apparently Ben was tucked away in his study.

"Oh, Emma, how nice of you to come!" Annie Jeanne gushed. "I haven't seen very many friendly faces lately."

"Now, Annie Jeanne," Mary Jane admonished, "don't be so hard on people—or on yourself. You haven't been well enough to have visitors until now."

Annie Jeanne sighed heavily. "That's so. I must admit, I still feel a bit weak."

"That's natural," Mary Jane said before excusing herself to bring lunch from the kitchen.

I perched on the sofa's arm. "Annie Jeanne, may I pester you with a couple of questions?"

Annie Jeanne's eyes widened with alarm. "What kind of questions?"

I shrugged. "Mainly some details about the thimble club's party. Were there many cookies left over? Besides the ones Ethel Pike gave you, I mean."

She looked relieved. "Oh, yes. Everyone ate quite a few. Except Ethel, of course. I believe she ate an oatmeal cookie, probably to be polite. I suppose that might not bother her too much."

"What did Ethel do after Gen gave her the cookies to take on the trip?"

Annie Jeanne looked puzzled. "Do?"

"Where did Ethel put them?"

"Oh." Annie Jeanne stopped to think. "She took them into the hall closet and put them with the coats and things. Then, as we were leaving, Ethel gave me the bag on the sly. Not to hurt Gen's feelings, you see. Ethel seems brusque, but she's very good-hearted."

Thus, the cookies had been left unattended, but surely they wouldn't have been poisoned during the party. The insulin had to be put into the crust, which could have occurred only at the rectory. There was opportunity, with Annie Jeanne going to the store and Ben at work in his study.

"Had you started making the crust before you went to the Grocery Basket?" I inquired.

"It was Safeway, actually. Yes. That's when I realized I was out of white vanilla. Not for the crust, of course, but for the cheesecake itself." Annie Jeanne bit her lower lip. "Imagine! But I haven't done much baking recently. Father Kelly was always watching his weight."

I tried another route. "Did you know Gen was selling her quilts to a store in Seattle?"

"No!" Annie Jeanne smiled sadly. "How clever of her. I often wondered how she filled up her time after she retired when she had no family nearby. She didn't join clubs, either, not even a quilt or a needlework group. Yet she never complained of being bored. Or lonely." The sadness had overcome her thin face. I felt it was not so much for Gen, but for Annie Jeanne herself.

Ben entered the parlor, looking unusually tense. "Hello, ladies. How's everybody?"

"Better, I think," Annie Jeanne replied. "Thank you for asking, Father. You're so kind."

"No, he's not," I put in. "He's really a pill. Hi, Ben." I got up from the sofa's arm and went over to kiss his cheek.

"How was the big city?" my brother inquired. "Did you get chased by white slavers?"

"It was . . . nice," I said. "Naturally, Vida couldn't wait to get back."

"Naturally." He looked amused, but I still sensed that something was wrong.

Mary Jane arrived with our food—tuna sandwiches, potato chips, and a fruit salad. She'd taken the cake with her when she'd returned to the kitchen. The next half hour was devoted mainly to my experiences in Seattle. Or most of them. I mentioned Rolf Fisher only in passing, and avoided my brother's gaze during the brief account.

But Ben was very shrewd. As he saw me out, he asked what I should have guessed was the inevitable question.

"So you met a guy you like. Is he eligible or are you still in your Impossible Man phase?"

"He's a widower," I snapped. "And I hardly know him. It's just that he's not at all what I thought he was from talking to him on the phone."

"Were you hoping he'd look like a toad?"

"I wasn't hoping anything," I said. "I hadn't given it a thought. Come on, Ben, I had no idea he'd be at the memorial. I'll probably never see him again. Why should I? He's a big talker, which means he's not a big doer. You know—a guy with some snappy patter. He's probably been doing that for years."

"Go on."

I realized that I was overreacting. "Damn."

Ben shrugged. "Hey, it'd be great if he really was someone you could see occasionally. I sense that you're getting bored with Milo, or is it just because there's no baseball this time of year and the two of you have nothing to talk about?"

"You can talk baseball any time of year," I asserted. "The Hot Stove League, for instance."

"It sounds like you're more interested in the Hot Rolf League," Ben said dryly.

"You're being mean." Before he could respond, I poked a finger in his chest. "What about you? Something's up, I can tell."

Ben grunted. "Just part of the pastoral perils, Sluggly."

I surveyed him closely. "In other words, you can't talk about it."

My brother inclined his head. "Go back to work. Your readers need you."

"Wait." I took the Miraculous Medal out of my purse. "This was found outside of the Pikes' house this morning. Someone may be looking for it."

Ben took the medal and read the inscription. "MAR? Do those initials mean anything to you?"

I shook my head. "The date is 1978. The recipient might have been someone who lived here and then moved away shortly before I arrived."

"It's too late to get it in this week's bulletin," Ben said, "as you well know, since you print it. But I'll make an announcement from the altar Saturday and Sunday."

I hesitated. "I wonder."

"What?"

I grimaced. "Maybe I'm jumping to conclusions, but maybe the medal was dropped by the person who broke into the Pikes' house. It was found not far from where the bonfire was set off."

Looking thoughtful, Ben fingered the tarnished gold. "Unlike a lot of other religious items, this one comes with a perpetual enrollment in the Association of the Miraculous Medal. If you really think this is some sort of clue to the break-ins, you might be able to contact the association and see if someone with these initials was enrolled in seventy-eight."

"Good thinking," I murmured, realizing that if I gave the medal to Milo, a tiresome explanation would be required. Or maybe the sheriff would simply look at me with a blank—possibly even skeptical—stare. For now, I decided, I'd hold on to the medal. Ben could advertise its discovery from the pulpit. If some innocent soul claimed it, no harm would be done.

Half an hour after I returned to the office, I received a phone call from Terri Bourgette.

"Emma," she said in a frazzled voice, "I have to apologize for being such a dimwit yesterday morning. We had a tour group coming in from Wenatchee for brunch, and my head was full of all the details I still had to work out. Then, on top of the lunch regulars, it was a zoo around here. I didn't remember to call you until now." Terri stopped for breath; I waited. "Anyway," she went on, "I realized after you left that a man I didn't recognize got here around seven-fifteen. He sat in a booth near the front, had coffee, and took off just before you arrived." She laughed weakly. "He wasn't carrying a copy of the *Advocate* when he came in. In fact, he asked Erin, one of our waitresses, if she could get him a paper. I guess the box was all out."

"Did Erin find one for him?" I asked.

"Yes, we had this week's edition in the office," Terri replied. "He certainly didn't take time to read much of it, though. He must have left five minutes later."

I was silent for a moment. By Thursday morning, most of the newspaper boxes were empty. I didn't believe in overruns, and held back just enough copies each week for subscribers who wanted to mail articles outside of the area and for our archives. "What did this guy look like?" I finally asked.

Terri sighed. "Ohhh . . . ordinary. That is, average height, light brown hair, no beard or anything like that. Thirty, thirty-five, I'd guess. The only unusual thing for Alpine was that he was wearing a black leather jacket."

"Like a biker?"

"No. It was more of a coat. But not real long." Terri paused. "He had on a baseball cap when he first came in."

"You mean the kind with a team logo?"

"A logo?" Terri still sounded tired. "Like for the Mariners?"

"Like that," I said.

"It *could* have been," she allowed. "I'm not a big sports fan except for tennis. The cap was green with an *A* on it, sort of in script."

Oakland green, *A* for Athletics. "If you think of anything else," I said, "call me. I assume he paid cash."

"Yes. He never ordered breakfast, although he'd asked for a menu when he first sat down." Her tone turned apologetic again. "I feel so stupid for not thinking about him being here, but I was all wrapped up in that tour group."

"Don't worry about it," I said. "We all get sidetracked now and then." I thanked Terri and hung up.

Two minutes later, I realized I'd gotten sidetracked, too. I hadn't thought to ask her what the tour group was doing in Alpine besides having brunch. Whatever and whoever they were, it was news. Like Terri, my head was also too full.

I TURNED THE WENATCHEE BIT OVER TO VIDA. SHE SEEMED to be in a good mood, despite her complaints about Gen Bayard passing off the quilts as her own designs.

"I could sue, I suppose," Vida mused. "But what good would it do? Gen's dead, and it would only offend Buddy and Roseanna, since any monies would come out of the estate."

I shrugged. "That's true. And you'd have to have proof. Do you have your mother's quilt patterns stashed away somewhere?"

"No," Vida admitted with a rueful expression. "I gave them away after she passed on. Those templates were made of cardboard from cereal and gift boxes. Very bulky, and I'd never use them. Honestly, I don't recall who I gave them to. I was quite upset after my mother died. But I certainly didn't give them to Gen. Indeed, I believe she'd moved away by then." Vida frowned in concentration. "I might have donated them to the Burl Creek Thimble Club itself."

Bravely, I posed a question: "Could you ask Mary Lou Hinshaw Blatt?"

"Mary Lou?" Vida grimaced. "I wouldn't ask my sister-in-law for the time of day. In any event, she's a pill."

I had been leaning against Vida's desk. Scott was busy at his computer and Leo was on the phone. I moved closer to Vida and lowered my voice. "Would you be mad if I talked to Mary Lou?"

Vida bristled. "Why would you want to do that? I told you, she's a pill. Haven't I always said she was difficult? She hasn't changed."

"I'm trying to sort out this whole poison thing," I replied quietly. "For Annie Jeanne's sake. For Ben's."

"For Ben?" Clearly, Vida was dismissing Annie Jeanne as another ninny. But she liked my brother, even if he was a

Catholic priest. She'd once said that he wasn't as "Romish" as most. "Well . . ." Vida frowned. "I appreciate your concern. Gen did die at the rectory and people do talk. If you feel you must, go ahead and speak to Mary Lou. But I warn you, she won't be any help. She's a—"

"Witness," I finished for Vida. But I smiled and thanked her for giving permission.

Mary Lou Blatt was home, having just come inside from raking leaves. She sounded suspicious when I asked if I could stop by her house in the Icicle Creek development. But after I finished flattering her upside and downside, she agreed to let me call on her.

"I'm at the end of the cul-de-sac by the golf course," she informed me. "It's a blue house, with a cottonwood tree."

I knew the place. Mary Lou lived only a few doors down from Milo. The Blatt residence looked much like many other homes at Icicle Creek—a compact rambler built in the sixties with a big picture window and just enough yard to satisfy an occasional gardener.

"Come in, come in," Mary Lou urged in her slightly gruff voice. Like her sister-in-law, she was a big woman, but she lacked Vida's commanding presence. "If that windbag of a Vida sent you here to snoop around," Mary Lou said as she led me into the overdecorated living room, "you're wasting your time."

"Vida doesn't send me anywhere," I declared. "I'm the boss at the *Advocate*."

"Hunh." Mary Lou didn't comment, but motioned to a floral-covered loveseat. "Tea? Coffee? Juice?"

I shook my head. "I don't want to impose. You look as if you've been busy."

Mary Lou, who was wearing wool slacks and a sweatshirt that displayed the American flag, glanced down at her rubber boots. "I have. I'm sick of raking leaves. I still burn them like a lot of folks do around here instead of fussing with all that recycling. Since my husband died, I keep up this place by myself. It's not big, but there's plenty of work to be done. Luckily, I can fix the plumbing and the electricity. Ennis taught me. He thought women should know how to do things. Just in case," she added with a grim expression.

"You taught school, I understand," I said.

Mary Lou nodded. "Off and on for forty years. Third and fourth grade, mostly. I'm glad I retired when I did. Pupils these days are spoiled brats. No discipline, no sense of responsibility. What are their parents thinking? If they think at all. Most of them are as bad as the children. It must be even worse in the city."

I could easily imagine Mary Lou wielding the ruler with which she had—teasingly, I assumed—threatened Annie Jeanne and Genevieve. "You've racked up a lot of accomplishments. Are you a quilter, too?"

"No," Mary Lou replied, looking slightly defensive. "I crochet." She pointed to several antimacassars and table covers that were scattered around the room. "Not many of us Betsys quilt anymore, except Ethel Pike and sometimes Darlene Adcock. But there's no quilting group in Alpine. No knitting club, either, so we all do what we like to do best and enjoy each other's company."

"It sounds like a congenial bunch," I remarked as a large white Persian cat strolled into the living room.

"As a rule."

The cat had sidled over to my feet. It looked up at me with probing green eyes, as if wondering about my worthiness to occupy space on the loveseat. "Did you know that Gen sold her quilts to a store in Seattle?"

Mary Lou raised her sparse gray eyebrows. "No! That's interesting."

The cat jumped up and landed beside me. "In what way?" I asked.

Mary Lou shrugged. "That she made money off of them, I guess. Clever of her."

I was steering the conversation down a tricky road. The cat seemed to be growling at me, so softly that I assumed Mary Lou couldn't hear her pet's displeasure. "Gen must have been very creative. I heard the quilts were all designed by her."

Mary Lou frowned. "I'm surprised. Gen hadn't much imagination. I remember once years ago that she and Ethel Pike got into a row because Ethel thought Gen was copying her patterns. Gen finally had to start over. Ethel didn't like being copied."

"But they remained friends?"

"Oh, yes, they both got over it. Ethel can be sort of grumpy sometimes, but she doesn't hold a grudge."

"I hate to bring this up," I went on as the cat moved so close that I could feel its breathing, "but Vida believes that Gen actually stole some of her mother's designs and passed them off as her own."

Mary Lou hooted with laughter. "That sounds like Vida! What does she know about quilting or any other kind of handicraft? I always figured poor Ernest had to sew on his own buttons. Vida's all thumbs—and mouth."

"Vida says she has a quilt her mother made that's the exact same pattern as the one of Gen's we saw in the Seattle store," I said.

Mary Lou grew serious again. "Vida does? Well, either she does or she doesn't." There was a pause. "I have to admit, Gen wasn't the kind to dream up her own designs. I suppose it *is* possible. On the other hand, Vida and Gen didn't get along."

The cat was encroaching on my lap. I assumed I was sitting on its turf. "Ever? Or did they have a quarrel?"

"You know Vida." Mary Lou shot me a knowing glance. "She's so danged critical. And she *does* hold a grudge. Still . . ." My hostess suddenly clamped her lips together. "But all that's in the past. Gen's gone. I don't speak ill of the dead. Vida does, of course."

I noticed that Mary Lou had assumed a self-righteous air. I didn't know whether I should pretend to know what she was talking about or just be forthright. Since the damned cat was starting to knead its paws on my jacket, I opted for the direct route.

"Did Gen hurt Vida's feelings, or was it the other way around?"

Mary Lou studied me closely. "You don't know?"

I shook my head. "I never heard Vida mention Gen's name until she—Gen—came to town."

"I see." Mary Lou stared at her hands, which were roughened by hard work. "The truth is, I'm not sure what really happened. I won't go telling tales, either. But mark my words, there was trouble between them. I think that's why Gen moved away from Alpine. Just up and left. Didn't even finish the quilt she was working on. I think Vida's mother took it over not long before she died."

That must have been the quilt that had been burned at the Pikes' house, but there was no point in mentioning it. "What kind of trouble did Vida and Gen have?" I inquired, inching toward the end of the loveseat and away from the cat.

Mary Lou pursed her lips. "I was never sure, but I could guess." She grimaced. "The usual, I suspect. Ennis thought so, too."

"The usual?" *Not more gourds,* I thought. With Vida it could be almost anything that besmirched her name or dishonored her family.

"Yes." Mary Lou nodded three times, very slowly. "You know."

I didn't, but I kept quiet. And then, as Mary Lou continued to stare at me with an expectant expression, I made a wild guess. *"Ernest?"*

Mary Lou nodded once more.

FOURTEEN

I COULD HARDLY BELIEVE MY EARS. "ARE YOU SUGGESTING that Ernest and Genevieve had an affair?"

Mary Lou regarded me as if I were the class dunce. "Well, people do, you know."

But Ernest? That model of rectitude? He'd been an elder in the Presbyterian church, involved in Future Farmers of America, a member of the Rotary and Kiwanis clubs, president of the Chamber of Commerce, and a volunteer firefighter. I'd never known Vida's husband, but he sounded like an unlikely candidate for adultery.

Yet as I gathered my wits, I realized I could have misjudged his character. I had only Vida's word for his goodness. Ernest may have been ripe for an affair. His married life might not have been easy. Vida was critical, domineering, opinionated, and she couldn't cook. She was a doting mother and grandmother, but had she been a devoted wife? Of course, she always spoke of Ernest in the most glowing terms. Vida made him sound like a man without a flaw. But that was only in retrospect, after he was dead.

I shook my head. "It just . . . jars me. I'd never considered such a thing. And Vida never ever hinted at it." I looked Mary Lou in the eye. "Are you sure?"

"Of course not," Mary Lou replied frankly. "You can't ever be sure of such a thing unless you catch the couple in the act. But where there's smoke, there's fire."

The cat was still kneading my jacket, growling disdainfully, almost covering my lap, and shedding long white fur on my black slacks. "What was the smoke?"

"Attitude. Mannerisms. What do they call it nowadays? Body language." Mary Lou displayed some of her own as she folded her arms across her big bust to indicate disapproval. But there was also a touch of satisfaction in her expression. No doubt anything that might upset Vida would please her sister-in-law. "Not to mention that my late sister, Marguerite, saw them drive away from a motel in Monroe."

Hearsay, I thought. "But the . . . gossip was never confirmed?"

Mary Lou didn't answer directly. "The motel sighting happened around Thanksgiving. It was my turn to have the family dinner. Vida and Ernest always dropped by before we served. They had their own dinner on the Runkel side. But that year Vida called and told me they weren't coming. Ernest had a cold, and couldn't make both events. I happened to run into Ernest the next day at the Sears catalog pickup. He certainly didn't act like he had a cold. Furthermore, he wasn't anything like himself. He practically tried to hide from me. I figured he knew that I knew. I didn't see him and Vida again until Christmas. They weren't very friendly, not just with me, but with each other. It wasn't long after New Year's that Gen moved away. Add it up. You'll get the correct sum. Gen was quite a looker in those days, I might add."

"And Ernest? Was he attractive?"

"You've seen pictures?"

I nodded. "Vida has one of him in the living room, but it

must have been taken when Ernest was very young, even before they were married. He was what I'd describe as nice-
looking. The rest were snapshots, and not close-up. I mean,
was he attractive in middle age?"

"I suppose," Mary Lou responded. "A big man. Still had
his hair. A pleasant smile. Yes, I imagine some women would
consider Ernest easy on the eyes."

I stifled a sigh. If the story was true, Vida had my sympathy. Despite her faults, I could imagine how difficult it would
have been for her to discover that her husband had been unfaithful. The fact that no one seemed to know for certain that
the affair had occurred indicated that the Runkels had managed to weather the storm. The worst thing for Vida would
have been being the subject of tawdry, demeaning gossip. Her
pride must have been wounded deeply. If Ernest had really
strayed, she had kept the fact to herself all these years and put
on a brave front.

"I suppose," I mused, "that even a mild flirtation would
have caused a serious rift between Vida and Gen."

"Hunh." Mary Lou gave me a baleful look. "What do
you think, knowing Vida?"

"Yes." I managed—with effort—to move the cat off my
lap and stand up. "Thanks for your time, Mary Lou. Of
course, I won't breathe a word of what you've just told me."

"Good." Mary Lou was also on her feet. "As I said, I
don't like to tell tales. Especially since Ernest got himself
killed in that foolish waterfall stunt not long after."

"Oh?" The damned cat was following me to the door. I
felt as if I were under surveillance. "That's sad. I hope that if
the story's true, Vida and Ernest had mended things by then."

Mary Lou shrugged. "I wouldn't know."

The cat sat down in the doorway, blocking my path.
"Pretty animal," I remarked. "What's its name?"

Mary Lou smiled in a spiteful kind of way. "That cat is

proud, ornery, self-centered, and more curious than most of her species. What do you think I call her? Vida, of course."

I WOULD KEEP MY WORD TO MARY LOU AND NEVER MENTION what she'd told me about the rumors of a romance between Ernest Runkel and Genevieve Bayard. People talked, especially in small towns. The tale might not be true.

But I could see how it could be. Gen a lonely widow, Ernest a badgered husband, two aging babes in the woods. Until now, my sympathy had rested only on Vida. But compassion rose in my breast for Ernest, whose life had ended so tragically in that crazy barrel at Deception Falls. Certainly that stunt was an indication of midlife crisis.

Vida was out when I returned to the office just before three-thirty. Scott was in the back shop with Kip, working on a layout of autumn color photos. Leo was at his desk, looking smug.

"The Thanksgiving issue is shaping up," he announced. "That is, the ads are."

"Oh!" I slapped myself on the head. The holiday was always awkward, with merchants wanting their wares in the paper a full week ahead, while editorial content and Happy Thanksgiving ads ran on the Wednesday before the big event. "I'm not keeping up. Turkey Day is early this year, right?"

Leo nodded. "I'm talking about next Wednesday, the fourteenth. This week we've got a bunch of tie-in ads for Veterans Day." He gave me a scrutinizing look. "Are you okay? You seem kind of frazzled."

"Murder has that effect on me," I replied. "Especially when it happens right under my brother's nose."

Leo's well-worn face broke into a grin. "Dodge hasn't collared Ben yet?"

"Frankly," I said, trying not to steal the cigarette that my ad manager was lighting, "it's a wonder that some of the more prejudiced locals haven't demanded Ben's head. For the anti-Catholics, he's a perfect suspect—not to mention that he's a newcomer."

"Even the goofballs recognize that he didn't know Gen Bayard from a kumquat," Leo noted.

"That's true," I agreed, "but people aren't always reasonable. Some of Ben's parishioners have acted kind of weird."

"That's what happens when you go to church all the time," Leo declared. "That's why I only go a couple of times a year. I don't want to be weird."

I stared at Leo in exasperation. "You don't go to church because you're lazy."

"Me? Lazy?" Leo assumed an offended manner. "After Ed Bronsky, you're calling *me* lazy?"

I smiled. "It's different. Ed goes to church, but he'd go anywhere if he could sit down and nod off."

Ginny poked her head into the newsroom. "There's a call for you on line one."

"Who is it?" I asked.

Ginny looked apologetic. "He won't say."

"I'll take it." Wondering if Tony Knuler was trying to get in touch with me again, I rushed into my cubbyhole.

But it wasn't my Mystery Man—even though he said he was.

"This is your Mystery Man, Brenda Starr," Rolf Fisher said. "What's the hottest spot in Alpine on a Saturday night?"

Somehow, I was both disappointed and elated at the same time. "I didn't think you'd call."

"I never disappoint a lady," he replied. "You didn't answer my question."

"Ah . . ." I'd forgotten the question. "Oh! Well, there isn't a hot spot in Alpine on any night. Unless you consider the big stone fireplace at the ski lodge."

"Do they serve viands and potables?"

"Yes."

"I'll pick you up at five," Rolf said. "I have your address, but you better give me directions."

I was so flabbergasted that I got my lefts and rights mixed up, and had to go over the relatively simple route twice.

"See you tomorrow. Wear something irresistible. If we never leave your house, just perfume will do." Rolf rang off.

I felt giddy. I was going to have an *actual date*. And with an *eligible man*. Not only eligible, but *attractive*. I could hardly believe it.

"Now what?" Leo inquired, leaning against the door frame. "You look like you won the lottery."

I forced myself to appear normal. "Do you know Rolf Fisher from the AP?"

Leo shook his head. "I only know dreary advertising types, like me."

I didn't explain my reason for asking, and Leo didn't probe. Vida returned a few minutes later, holding her head.

"So sad," she said, flopping into her chair. "So confusing. So few veterans left. At least, from World War Two. Do you realize there are only seven here in Alpine, and of those, only three of them make sense?"

"What about the county commissioner troika?" Leo inquired. "They're old enough to have served."

Vida waved a hand in dismissal. "Did they *ever* make sense? Besides, only Alfred Cobb was in the military—intelligence, of all things. I can't believe we won with someone like him serving in such a capacity. It's a good thing we had the Korean and Vietnam wars. Otherwise, I couldn't write a readable feature for Armistice Day."

"That certainly justifies all those deaths in Korea and 'Nam," Leo remarked. "And by the way, they've been calling it Veterans Day for the last forty, fifty years."

Vida glared at Leo. "You know what I mean. We need to honor our veterans, to let them tell us what war was really like. Then maybe we wouldn't have countries at each other's throats."

" 'What if they had a war and nobody came?' " Leo murmured, paraphrasing an old protest slogan.

"Ernest enlisted in the navy when he was sixteen," Vida declared. "He lied about his age. He was sent to the Pacific, but the war ended before he saw any real action. I've always blamed Mr. Truman for that, though I suppose that rogue of a Roosevelt would have done the same thing and dropped the horrid bomb."

Vida was a staunch Republican. Indeed, she would probably have made a wonderful Whig. She gave me her gimlet eye. "Why are you looking at me like that, Emma? You know my feelings about the Democrats."

"Hey—I'm an independent," I replied. "It's my duty as a publisher to be unbiased." But of course, I wasn't staring at Vida because of her politics. I was thinking of Ernest and Genevieve.

I FELT GUILTY. IT WAS STUPID OF ME, BUT I COULDN'T MAKE the feeling go away. I was still arguing with myself when I left work ten minutes early and walked down Front Street to the sheriff's office.

"It's Friday," I said upon entering Milo's inner sanctum. "Let me treat you to a drink. Can you leave right now?"

The sheriff was doing paperwork. "I could if I didn't have to fill out all these damned forms. Right now I'd rather go out and bust somebody's chops."

"How come?" I asked, perching on the desk's one clear space.

Milo shrugged. "It's the homicide. I'm nowhere. And

we're not doing any better with the break-ins. We haven't had one in days. Were the crooks out-of-towners who've moved on? Or did they get scared?"

It wasn't like the sheriff to volunteer his frustration. I suffered even more guilt. Especially after his next remark. "I need a woman."

"Oh, Milo!" I gave him a compassionate look. "You know that if . . . I mean, when you want or need . . . I don't have any more balloons!"

Milo made a face. "I'm not talking about sex, for God's sake. I mean in the office. Toni can't handle all this crap. Face it, she's kind of slow. What I want is a female officer, someone who can deal with battered women, wives whose husbands are doing time, even hookers. But we don't have the funds. It's a damned shame."

"Oh." I think I blushed. Rolf Fisher would have accused me of blushing, though I rarely did. "Sorry. I felt bad about the other night."

Milo shrugged. "Hey—it was a good laugh. That does me good, too. I'm not laughing much on the job these days. Maybe I'm getting stale." He scooped up the paperwork and shoved the pile in a drawer. "Let's hit the bars. I can do this over the weekend. Or Monday. It's an official holiday, since Veterans Day falls on Sunday. Maybe the local perps will take it off, too."

"We're doing our homage to the vets a bit late this year," I said as Milo took his regulation jacket off of a peg by the door. "Too many holidays all bunched together. We decided our advertisers needed a break after Columbus Day and Halloween. The problem is, Thanksgiving comes early . . ."

Milo put a big hand on my shoulder. "Hey—how come you're so wound up?"

I sighed before turning to look him in the eye. "I've got a date."

"Good for you." If Milo was wounded, it didn't show. "Who's the guy?"

"Rolf Fisher, from the AP in Seattle." As we progressed through the outer office, I reminded Milo how Rolf had helped us with background information in a homicide case the previous winter.

"I thought you told me he was a creep," Milo said as we walked against the wind toward the Venison Inn.

"He may be," I responded, "but I'm willing to give him the benefit of the doubt. At least he's not as hideous as I thought he'd be." *That* was an understatement, but the sheriff didn't need to know.

"Hell, Emma, you don't have to apologize for going out with some guy," Milo assured me. "I've seen other women over the years."

Entering the restaurant, I gazed up at him. "How about now?"

Milo shook his head after removing his Smokey Bear regulation hat. "Maybe it's like you. I'd have to leave town to find somebody."

"It's a small pond," I commented, leading the way into the bar.

"And chances of getting skunked are pretty damned good," Milo said, commandeering a table away from most of the other after-work drinkers.

The sheriff ought to know. He'd picked some real local lemons. "Maybe we're getting too old to fish for love," I noted as Milo signaled to the bartender, Oren Rhodes, to bring our usual cocktails.

"Maybe," Milo agreed.

I scowled at him. "No, we're not. I don't know why I said that. I don't feel old. I don't feel much different than I did thirty years ago."

"I do," Milo asserted. "I'm not as quick. My reflexes

aren't what they used to be, and my joints feel stiff sometimes. Not good for a lawman. In a face-off, I'd get gunned
down in the middle of Front Street before I could get my
weapon out of the holster."

"You still look fine," I declared. "Solid, strong." Those
guilt pangs still nagged at me, but the words were true. The
sheriff had put on some weight over the years, there was gray
in his sandy hair, and the lines in his long face were deeper. Indeed, he was aging slowly and aging well. If I kept telling myself these things, I'd end up canceling on Rolf Fisher and
never budge from Alpine again.

Oren brought my bourbon and Milo's Scotch-rocks.
"Doubles," the bartender said. "House special to honor veterans. You were in 'Nam, right, Sheriff?"

"So I was," Milo replied, cradling the glass. "Wish I'd
had more of this stuff there."

Oren nodded at me. "You're a veteran of the newspaper
wars. Don't let the bastards get you down, Emma." He
flipped the bar towel that had been slung over his shoulder
and trudged back to his post.

"I suppose you've been sleuthing," Milo said after taking
a deep drink and lighting a cigarette. "Any luck?"

It wasn't like him to ask me about an ongoing investigation. Either he believed I might have some insights because
the death had occurred under my brother's nose, or the sheriff was more frustrated than I thought.

"Not much," I answered slowly, still not wanting to
bother Milo with the lost Miraculous Medal. "Mostly talking
to people who knew Gen, especially the women at the party.
She seemed well liked. Except by Vida."

Milo gave a brief nod. "They had some kind of falling-
out years ago. I heard about it later. I was either in college or
'Nam at the time."

I assumed an innocent expression. "Do you know what the row was about?"

Milo frowned and puffed out his cheeks. At least a minute passed before he responded. "It had something to do with Ernest. I think Vida thought Gen was making a play for him. Probably a lot of bullshit, but you know Vida. Once she gets something in that head of hers, it doesn't come out."

"You never thought it was true?"

Milo started to answer, but apparently changed his mind. "Well . . . no. I was young, mid-twenties or so, and Ernest seemed like an old man to me. I suppose he wasn't more than late forties, younger than I am now. As for Gen, she was good-looking, but everybody knew she had an eye for the men. Ernest wouldn't have been the first guy she'd come on to."

"Are you saying Gen was promiscuous?"

"No." Milo gazed at me as if I could have qualified for the Salem witch hunt. "She was just lonely. Her husband—what was his name?"

"Andy. Andre."

"Right. He was a drunk, and probably abused Gen. People didn't talk about battering those days like they do now. I remember seeing Gen once on a dark winter day wearing sunglasses. I was still a naive teenager, and all I thought was that she looked like a movie star. In reality, she'd probably gotten a shiner from Andy."

"Has Buddy ever talked to you about his dad?" I asked before giving in to my weakness and slipping one of Milo's cigarettes out of the pack he'd put on the table.

"Not really." The sheriff offered me a light. "In fact, Buddy hardly ever mentions him. He didn't talk much about his mother, either. I'm guessing Buddy wasn't raised in a happy family."

"And Dad left when Buddy was still young," I murmured. "Do you remember Andy Bayard at all?"

"Oh, sure, I'd see him around town. He was kind of a snappy dresser, at least for a town like—" The sheriff's cell phone went off. "Damn. I'd better take that," he said, reaching into his jacket, which was resting on the back of his chair.

I watched and listened. Milo's face registered surprise, then puzzlement. "Have you talked to Buddy?" he asked into the phone. "Sorry," the sheriff said after a pause, "I can't do much about it. It sounds like a couple of lawyers are going to make a few bucks off of this one." Another pause. "Keep me posted. Talk to you later."

"Well?" I said as Milo put the cell back in his jacket. "What's up?"

Milo gestured at Oren to bring us another round. "That was Al Driggers. You knew he's got Gen's body at the mortuary. Well, some dude who claims he's Gen's *other* son phoned Al and asked to claim the remains and have Gen buried in Citrus Heights, California. Al was suspicious and Buddy went ballistic. He insists he was his mother's only child."

"Is the alleged offspring also named Bayard?"

Milo shook his head. "No. He gave his name as Anthony Knuler."

FIFTEEN

I CHOKED ON MY DRINK. "ARE Y-Y-YOU K-K-KIDDING?" I sputtered.

Of course Milo wasn't. "Have you heard of this Knuler guy? The name sounds kind of familiar."

I wiped my mouth with a cocktail napkin and then began to explain Anthony Knuler's role as the Mystery Man.

"So this guy from the motel may still be in Alpine," Milo remarked after I'd finished telling him everything I knew. "You say Terri Bourgette saw somebody who might have been Knuler at the diner yesterday morning?"

"He must have given Al a phone number," I said. "Will should have an address in California."

"Al told me it was a don't-call-me-I'll-call-you situation. He wondered if this Knuler was using a pay phone. There was a lot of noise in the background, like cars and trucks going by."

"A rest stop, maybe," I pondered aloud. "Tony Knuler may be heading south. But if so, why didn't he request Gen's body while he was in town?"

Oren whisked away Milo's empty glass and delivered the

second round. Since the drinks were doubles, I was taking my time.

"How old did Terri say this guy was?" Milo asked.

"Thirties," I replied. "Younger than Buddy by at least ten years."

Milo lit another cigarette. "Bastard? Adopted? A husband Gen never told Buddy and Roseanna about? A divorce not long after the marriage but a baby as a souvenir?"

"Roseanna did mention that she thought her mother-in-law had a live-in boyfriend for a while," I recalled. "But she and Buddy never saw him, and Gen never spoke of him. Then, a few years ago—if I'm remembering this right—it looked as if the guy had moved out."

"Or died," Milo noted. "I'll have to talk to the Bayards about this deal." Milo sighed as he checked his watch. "It's not quite five-thirty. Maybe I can catch them at the studio. Damn. I thought I was done for the day."

I finished my first drink. "May I tag along?"

Milo frowned at me. "The visit's official, not social."

"You're right."

The sheriff was suspicious of my docile manner. "You'll show up anyway."

"Finish your drink," I said. "I'm paying for it, remember?"

Milo sipped in silence. I guessed that he was mulling over this latest, surprising development. Halfway through his second Scotch, he reached again for his cell phone.

"Dwight? Hey, do me a favor. Look up Anthony Knuler in the database. I'm guessing at the spelling. Check with Will Pace at the Alpine Falls Motel. The guy stayed there the other night."

"Has Knuler become Suspect Number One?" I asked after Milo clicked off. "Or merely a Person of Interest?"

"What do *you* think?" Milo's flowing bowl wasn't giving him much cheer. "He's either a swindler or the X factor."

"Or a killer," I put in.

Milo said nothing.

W̲E̲ PARTED COMPANY AT A QUARTER TO SIX. MILO, PRE-
sumably, was still going to see if the Bayards were at
the studio. I decided to wait until they went home. After two
doubles, I didn't want to drive in what was turning into a
wind and rain storm.

The office was empty, locked up for the weekend. I
wasn't inclined to give my employees three-day weekends. Instead, I paid them double for working holidays. We needed
both Monday and Tuesday to make our deadline.

I considered phoning the Bayards before Milo could
reach them, but he was probably already there, having
walked the three blocks from the Venison Inn to the studio.
Besides, it would be impolitic to usurp the sheriff's official du-
ties.

I'd never heard of Citrus Heights, California. Turning on
my computer, I entered the town's name. Sure enough, it
came up, appearing on the site map as being very close to
Sacramento, which was what Tony Knuler had listed as his
hometown at the motel.

Next, I dialed the number of the Alpine Falls Motel. A
harried-sounding Will Pace answered on the fourth ring.

"A quick question," I said.

"It better be," Will snapped. "I'm busy. A bunch of people are checking in because they don't want to go over the
pass in this crappy weather."

"How many nights did Tony Knuler stay at your motel?"

"Hell! Why do you care?"

I didn't respond. I wasn't the one pressed for time.

"Just one," Will said after my silence. "Tuesday, the
sixth." He hung up.

Gen had been poisoned on Monday, the fifth. Had Tony Knuler arrived in Alpine before the murder? If so, where had he been? And who on earth was he?

At precisely six o'clock, I punched in the Bayards' business number. Roseanna answered, sounding only slightly less harassed than Will Pace. I asked her if the sheriff was there.

"How did you know?" she demanded, lowering her voice. "And how the hell did you get involved with this Knuler creep?"

"I didn't," I replied. "If Milo hasn't explained that part, I will when I see you. Should I wait until you get home?"

"Not tonight," Roseanna retorted. "This is going to take some sorting out. I'll call you tomorrow." She, too, hung up on me.

I considered driving to the studio while the sheriff and the Bayards were still there. But I'd already offended Buddy and Roseanna by pulling our darkroom work. Maybe I should do as she wished.

It wasn't easy. I fidgeted at my desk for a few minutes before calling Dwight Gould. Hopefully, Milo's deputy wouldn't provide me with a hat-trick hang-up.

"We didn't find Knuler in the database," Dwight said in answer to my question. "Fact is, we didn't find him or any other Knulers anywhere. Maybe we're not spelling it right."

"Maybe Will Pace didn't spell it right," I suggested.

"No, he gave it to us right," Dwight said in his cheerless manner. "I was the one who stopped by the motel after Will made the complaint. I saw the registration that Knuler had filled out. Guests have to print their names and write their signatures."

"Yes, that's so," I agreed. "Have you got a Sacramento address for Knuler?"

"Sort of. It was hard to read." He paused, perhaps looking up the address. "It was something like 1112 H Street, or maybe A Street. Or the ones could've been sevens. It was really hard to tell. Dodge won't be happy about that."

I wasn't, either. Tony Knuler either had poor penmanship or was deliberately trying to obscure his place of residence.

At loose ends, I called Ben. Betsy O'Toole answered.

"Your brother just left for an ecumenical dinner with Regis Bartleby," Betsy said. "Is there a message?"

"No, not really. I forgot he was dining with the vicar this weekend." The truth was, Edith Bartleby hadn't mentioned which night the two pastors were getting together. "How's Annie Jeanne?"

"Fine," Betsy said tersely. "As far as I'm concerned, Doc Dewey should give her a dose of gumption."

"Are you saying she's malingering?"

"I won't say that," Betsy replied, "but I don't think the woman's ever put in a hard day's work in her life. Believe me, Jake and I know what work is. The Grocery Basket wouldn't have survived if we didn't. But Annie Jeanne's been what you might call a dilettante most of her life. She's been a clerk in some of the stores off and on, but she's been able to get by on next to nothing. Being the housekeeper here at the rectory doesn't require much more than a swipe of the broom and a flip of the duster. Any real labor is done by parish volunteers. Oh, she cooks, but she'd have to do that anyway unless she intended to starve."

"Her parents left her some money," I recalled. "She was an only child, and probably pampered. They could afford music lessons, for one thing." *Better they should have bought her a chemistry set,* I thought to myself.

"She says she isn't well enough to play the organ for five o'clock Mass tomorrow or Sunday, for that matter," Betsy complained. "Not that that's any great loss," she went on, reading my mind, "but what she suffered from was just a big stomachache."

"And shock," I pointed out. "The emotional toll on her has been far greater than any physical damage."

"Tell me about it," Betsy said in a grim voice. "And if I hear one more word about the 'dear Betsys' and how much they love each other, I'm going to legally change my name to Buttsy."

"Do you want me to relieve you? I'm not doing anything tonight." Ah, but tomorrow was a different matter. . . .

"Oh—Jake's working at the store until seven, seven-thirty." Betsy sighed. "Father Ben said he'd be home around eight. I've fed Annie Jeanne—though she eats like a damned bird. I suppose I could go home and get a start on our dinner. Do you mind?"

"Not at all," I replied. "I'll be there in five minutes."

And I was, despite the pelting rain and hard-driving wind.

"I'll finish that," I said to Betsy, who was cleaning up the kitchen. "I see Ben left the rectory door unlocked. Maybe that's a tradition he should change."

"Dubious," Betsy replied. "Your brother's dead set against making any kind of changes, lest the parishioners rise up and take arms. He doesn't want to look like he's sabotaging Father Den."

I uttered an ironic laugh. "I remember when Dennis Kelly came here, and most of the parish was shocked to see that he was black. Father Den's overcome some big hurdles in Alpine."

Betsy wiped her hands on a dishtowel. "I'll be honest," she said with a wry expression. "Jake and I were put off by him at first. Back then, before the college was open, we'd never had an African-American living here, let alone being an authority figure." She made a face. "It's funny, isn't it? Once you get to know someone, you stop thinking about the color of their skin."

Betsy's tardy insight might be forgiven. Alpine had been all-white for decades, with a traditional Scandinavian majority.

"Where's Annie Jeanne?" I inquired as Betsy put on her hooded coat.

"In her room. She's spending more time in there the last day or so." Betsy paused to rummage for her car keys in her leather purse. "I don't know if that's good or bad. But we haven't had many visitors, so there's not much point in her staying in the parlor and holding court."

"What about the thimble club members?" I asked, walking Betsy to the door.

"Char and Dar stopped by once—Wednesday, I think. Edith Bartleby phoned; so did Jean Campbell. Oh, Debra Barton brought a hot dish for last night."

"That's it?"

"There've been cards," Betsy said, inching through the door. "Grace Grundle and Ella Hinshaw don't drive much anymore. I don't think Ella ever did. And of course Ethel Pike is out of town."

"Yes. Not to mention that the ones who aren't old as dirt keep busy." I shut up at that point, sensing that Betsy O'Toole was anxious to be off.

But after she left I locked the rectory door.

So kind," Annie Jeanne declared from the rocking chair in her room on the second floor. "Betsy O'Toole, Mary Jane Bourgette—oh, and Debra Barton. Such a lovely casserole! Crab and shrimp and mushrooms!" She burst into tears. "Emma, Emma," she groaned through the thin hands that covered her face. "Am I going to prison?"

I hadn't yet sat down. "Of course not," I assured Annie Jeanne, putting an arm around her quivering shoulders. "Why would you? You haven't done anything."

"But I did! I made the cheesecake!" She sniffed a couple of times, pulled a crumpled handkerchief out of her housecoat pocket, and wiped her eyes. "I was the one who killed Genevieve," Annie Jeanne went on, her voice dropping. "If nothing else, I should have locked the door behind me when I went to the store. I just keep waiting for Sheriff Dodge to arrest me."

"I don't think he's even considered such a thing," I said, stepping away and sitting down on the single bed. It was covered with a well-worn quilt. I guessed aloud that Gen had made it.

"Yes, yes." Annie Jeanne attempted a smile. "Years ago, before she moved. It's still lovely, isn't it?"

I supposed that it was, but the pieces in the wedding ring design had faded and the edges were frayed. "Did Gen work in Alpine after she and her husband divorced?"

"She did," Annie Jeanne replied after blowing her nose. "At the dress shop. It wasn't Francine's then—before her time. It was Helen Jane's. Bernie Shaw's mother owned it, and sold out to Francine Wells. Gen worked in a yarn shop for a short time, too, but it went out of business."

"Gen must have been lonely after she and Andy broke up," I said in a thoughtful tone. "Raising a son on your own is hard to do. I know, because I've done it. And from my own experience, it's difficult to meet eligible men in Alpine when you're older."

"I suppose," Annie Jeanne agreed in a disinterested manner.

It was hard to picture Annie Jeanne stalking bachelors at

any age. "Gen was very good-looking," I went on in the same thoughtful voice. "She must have had an occasional suitor."

"If you could call them that," Annie Jeanne said scornfully.

"What would *you* call them?" I inquired in a mild tone.

Annie Jeanne frowned. "Lechers, perhaps. Skirt-chasers. Stepping out on their wives."

Her words seemed to crawl up from out of the past. "Surely Gen wouldn't fall for men like that."

"Oh, she made short shrift of them, all right," Anne Jeanne asserted. "But that doesn't mean they didn't try. Sometimes they were hard to discourage."

Or did it take a while before Gen tired of them? I tried to keep such evil thoughts at bay. "I would think," I said, watching Annie Jeanne carefully, "that somewhere along the way, Gen would have found a man she could love."

Annie Jeanne lowered her eyes. "That wasn't easy."

"But did she?"

The black eyes still didn't meet my gaze. "I really couldn't say."

Couldn't or wouldn't? I forced a laugh. "Oh, come on, Annie Jeanne, I'll bet you and Gen stayed up late at night, drinking cocoa and sharing confidences. You were such good friends. If anyone knows, it's you." I managed another chuckle.

Her skin darkened slightly, and she cast a swift glance in my direction. "That doesn't mean I can talk about it, not even after she's gone. You mentioned 'confidences'; that's what they were. I won't betray them."

I suppressed a sigh. "Of course. I understand." An uneasy silence settled over the room. It wasn't a large space, but Annie Jeanne had filled it with furniture, knickknacks, and other décor that presumably had come out of the family home. Two baby dolls on the end of the bed looked as if they were from the pre–World War II era. The outfits they wore were pristine, as if they had been much admired, but seldom engaged in play. There was no television set, only a small radio on the bedside table.

"You're not a TV fan," I remarked, for lack of anything more cogent to say.

Annie Jeanne shook her head. "Television is the source of moral depravity in this country. If there's something I want to see on the news, I go to the parlor. Father Dennis had a set installed there for people who had to wait to see him. He paid for the satellite dish out of his own pocket. I understand that reception in Alpine is poor because of the mountains. Frankly, I think those dish things are very ugly."

"They are," I agreed, as always trying to ignore the fact that one stood in my own backyard. "How do you spend your spare time, Annie Jeanne?"

"I knit. I listen to the radio. I read. The time passes."

I glanced at a bookshelf across the room. The dozen or more books that sat between praying pixie angels were mostly paperbacks. "What do you read?"

Annie Jeanne flushed again. "Love stories, mostly. Some biographies."

Even from twenty feet away, I could see the paperbacks' spines: romances all, of the sweet rather than steamy variety, except for the photos of Marilyn Monroe and Elizabeth Taylor on the two biographies.

"You're feeling much better, I hear." It was an exaggeration, of course.

The response was an uncertain nod. "Yes," Annie Jeanne said, "every day, I seem to get a bit stronger."

I stood up. "Good for you. Betsy O'Toole told me you wouldn't be able to play the organ for the weekend Masses. You have to be ready for next week. We all miss you so much." That wasn't an exaggeration; it was close to an outright lie.

"We'll see," Annie Jeanne replied in a pessimistic tone.

"You can do it," I declared with a pat on the shoulder for Annie Jeanne. "Try to eat more. You need to build yourself up."

She didn't reply except for a noise that was half sniff, half grunt. I returned to the kitchen. Talking about food had made me realize how hungry I was, and no wonder—it was almost seven-thirty. I opened cupboard doors and the fridge. It looked as if most of the items that the sheriff had confiscated for testing had been returned: There were partially used spices, bags of flour and sugar, and jars of various condiments. All were presumably innocent, poison-free. It also appeared that the O'Tooles had generously donated some staples.

I decided against raiding the rectory. Ben wouldn't return for probably half an hour. There was no point in waiting, especially since I was starving. I locked the door behind me and left my brother a note under a rock I placed on the mat: "Use your key, unless you forgot it. If so, use a window. Love, Sluggly."

VIDA CALLED SHORTLY AFTER I GOT HOME. "I HEAR VIA the grapevine that you actually did see Mary Lou this afternoon. Whatever could that idiot have had to tell you that might be of interest?"

"Not much," I hedged. "I wasn't keeping it a secret. You weren't around when I got back, and then you seemed to be on the phone until I left a few minutes early."

"I don't see why it was necessary to talk to her in the first place," Vida huffed.

"I'm trying to contact all of the club members," I replied. "If you'd help me out, I wouldn't have to do this."

There was a pause. "Very well. Who's left?"

I ticked the names off, including yet another shirttail relation of Vida's, Nell Blatt.

"Oh, dear," Vida sighed. "Nell is somewhat gaga. I really
think you should talk to Debra Barton. She belongs to your
church, after all. I'll do Grace Grundle over the phone. I simply can't stand to step foot in that cat menagerie of hers. I'm
told she had nine of the little beasts at last count. Besides,
Grace is addled—as is Darla Puckett, so I might as well handle them both, since I'm better at translating their nonsense
than you are. Who else? Oh, Jean Campbell. She and Lloyd
are leaving for a week in Hawaii. Imagine, sitting around in
all that awful sunshine this time of year! How can you possibly get into the holiday spirit in weather like that?"

"It sounds like they'll be back before Thanksgiving," I
noted dryly. "Surely then they'll have enough rain and maybe
even snow to set them straight."

"Don't be smart," Vida admonished. "You hate hot
weather as much as I do. It's unnatural. Why do you suppose
they describe hell as hot?"

"I think it's supposed to be more than ninety degrees
there."

Vida ignored my latest comment. "Is that everybody?
What about Edith Bartleby? Butter wouldn't melt in her
mouth, of course."

I related my brief encounter with Edith at the bakery. "In-
cidentally," I added, "Ben was having dinner with Regis
Bartleby this evening."

"He won't know anything," Vida asserted.

"Ben isn't sleuthing," I pointed out. "This is a pastoral
get-together."

"Your brother should be sleuthing," Vida insisted. "He
has to clear the parish's good name. Does Father Kelly know
what's happened?"

"I'm sure Ben e-mailed him," I said. "Frankly, I didn't ask. Ben and I haven't had much time together lately. We've both been busy."

"Yes. Yes, of course." Vida suddenly sounded vague. "Just what did that idiot of a Mary Lou have to tell you?"

"I talked to her mainly about the party for Gen," I replied.

"That's it? We already knew that, didn't we? I mean," Vida went on, "how everyone was so lovey-dovey."

"Pretty much," I allowed.

"Hunh." She paused. "Was that all?"

"She traced the route of the cookies," I said.

"We knew that, too," Vida said in a disdainful voice. "Nothing more?"

"Nothing important," I fibbed.

There was another pause. I heard the wind whistling down the chimney and the rain pelting the windows—but nothing from Vida for so long that I thought we'd been disconnected.

When she did speak again, it wasn't about Mary Lou or the mysterious death of Gen Bayard. "I hear you're going out with that Rolf Fisher."

"Yes, he actually called."

"So Leo told me. I hope you know what you're doing."

"I'm going to dinner, that's what I'm doing."

"You know what I mean. I met him at the memorial for Hank Sails. Rolf Fisher is definitely not to be trusted. He's far too smooth, not at all like Tommy or Milo."

It had always irked me that Vida referred to Tom as "Tommy." She'd done it to his face, and although he seemed amused, I never was. "Tom was fairly smooth," I asserted.

"He was poised, not smooth," Vida countered. "There's a difference."

A vision of Rolf Fisher looking like an oil slick came to my mind's eye. "Rolf simply has a line. I'd like to see if there's something more to him. He may not be as slick as you think."

"We'll see."

I T TOOK ALL MY SELF-DISCIPLINE NOT TO CALL BUDDY AND Roseanna Bayard that night. But I respected their wishes to wait until morning. I called Milo instead. It was well after nine, and he'd just gotten home.

"The Bayards never heard of a half brother or anybody named Knuler," Milo said, his voice weary. "We ran the name through the computer again, not just the perp database, but every other site we could think of. No Knulers anywhere, at least not in this country or Canada."

"That doesn't mean there aren't any," I pointed out.

"He sounds like a guy who doesn't want to be found," Milo said glumly.

"He'll have to reveal himself if this ploy of his is all about inheritance."

"Ploy? What the hell do you mean by that?" Milo demanded.

"I'm not sure," I admitted. "Look—the guy comes to town, checks into a motel, spends one night, steals a phone book, makes a date with me, then takes off after he's looked at a copy of the *Advocate*. Did he come to Alpine to meet his alleged mother? Did he come to kill her? Did he arrive before or after she was poisoned? Did he know she was dead when he got here?"

"Slow down," Milo cautioned. "You're going too fast. And you're speculating."

"Well?" My tone was impatient. "Can't you track Knuler from his California plate and driver's license?"

"We could if they were real," Milo retorted. "The address

is illegible, the driver's license hasn't checked through yet, and we got word from Sacramento just before I left the office that the plate number belongs to somebody who drives a Bentley in L.A. Knuler probably reversed the numbers or letters, and that dim bulb of a Will Pace never checked it out. It'll take time to run through different plate combos— and even then, a letter or a number might be omitted or changed."

"So his name may not be Knuler," I murmured. "He definitely sounds wrong. Say, I looked at a map. Citrus Heights is right by Sacramento—a suburb, from the looks of it. Don't you have somebody in the state capital who could find out if Knuler was a troublemaker? Assuming he really lives in Citrus Heights, of course."

"I might be able to give someone a shove," Milo said in a reflective voice. "I looked at a map, too. You know what else is close by?"

"Not offhand," I admitted.

"Folsom Prison," Milo said.

SIXTEEN

MILO WASN'T IN THE MOOD TO CONTINUE OUR CONVERsation. He said he'd let me know when they heard anything more from Sacramento—or Citrus Heights. Knowing how much he hated guesswork, I had to smile at his own speculation that Anthony Knuler might be an ex-con. It was possible. Down Highway 2, the Monroe Correctional Complex sat cheek by jowl with the town itself. Many wives and girlfriends moved into the area while their loved ones were serving time. When prisoners were released, they often moved into established residences. The same might be true for Folsom's ex-inmates.

The possibility—not to mention Knuler's own activities over the past few days—kept me awake until almost two A.M. I sensed that some missing piece of the puzzle was right before my eyes. But I'd be darned if I could figure out what it was.

Saturday brought less wind but harder rain. There was a small rock slide on Highway 187, above the old mine shafts. I called Scott to ask him to take some photos of the slide and the work crew that was going to clear it.

After breakfast, I went through my wardrobe, seeking an appropriate outfit to wear to dinner with Rolf Fisher at the ski lodge. Not a dress—though I had but two of those. Not a pantsuit—too formal, and the only good one I owned required a trip to the dry cleaner. Besides, I'd worn it to Hank Sails's memorial. The sweater I'd worn with it also needed to be cleaned. Slacks and a sweater—but nice slacks, pretty sweater. None of my slacks were nice, and none of my clean sweaters were pretty. My clothes were definitely suited to my working lifestyle.

I recalled that Leo had shown me the mock-up of a Francine's Fine Apparel ad that would appear in the next edition. Francine Wells was having a Thanksgiving sale. Maybe she could come to my rescue if my credit card would bear it.

I arrived at the shop just after Francine opened the doors at ten o'clock. Three other women were also eager beavers: May Hashimoto from the college; Sherry Medved, the local veterinarian's wife; and Marisa Foxx, an attorney and a fellow parishioner. We all went straight to the sale rack. Apparently, word of the upcoming sale had leaked out. But the sight of the trio brought back memories of a Saks Fifth Avenue sale I'd gone to in Beverly Hills when Ben and I took Adam to Disneyland. It was a war zone. Women exchanged blows over blouses, shoves over shoes, and punches over purses. I hadn't seen anything like it up close since the protest rallies of the seventies. Customers had to share dressing rooms, and a saleswoman shrewdly paired me with another intimidated tourist. Alpine was another world, at the opposite end of the frenzy scale.

But Francine managed to stay in business. She never tried to deceive her customers. If she had, she wouldn't have lasted long in this up-front town. "I haven't marked anything down yet, but I'll give you the discount anyway if you don't tell anybody." She winked. "All the sale items are from the first fall shipments. Times are tough, and I overbought on the Anne Kleins and Ellen Tracys. Those two Tahari suits are knockouts, by the way."

They were, but not intended for a five-foot-four woman with no waist and too much bust. Along with Marisa Foxx, I browsed through the Ellen Tracys.

"Who around here is a size four, Francine?" Marisa demanded.

"I am," piped up the petite May Hashimoto. "Where did you find a four?"

"I'm a six," Sherry Medved, former Washington State University cheerleader, declared in her perky voice. "Usually," she added, not quite so perkily.

Separates, I thought, trying to focus. Separates were so versatile.

"Your poor brother," Marisa murmured as we both searched the size tens. "I understand that some of the parishioners are afraid to attend Mass this weekend."

"That's ridiculous," I declared, keeping my voice down.

But Francine, also a parish member, had overheard us. "Stupid rumors," she said, not bothering to be discreet. "Does anyone really believe that Father Ben or Annie Jeanne, for that matter, would go off on a poisoning spree?"

"It's mostly the elderly," I said. "Fuddled, maybe."

"That's no excuse," Marisa snapped in her best courtroom manner. "Have you had much negative feedback at the paper?"

"The usual cranks," I said. "I'm used to them. Ben—or Den—is the Antichrist, and I'm Satan's handmaiden. Blahblah, misspell, wrong punctuation, incorrect word usage, et cetera."

"You should run them," Francine asserted, "to show your readers what you have to put up with and how stupid they are."

I shook my head. "I only run letters if I can verify the signature. The real cranks are either anonymous or use a pseudonym. But I still know who most of them are." And the irony was that when I met them on the street or in the store, they smiled and greeted me as if I were their best buddy. Maybe, in a pathetic way, I was.

But suddenly, I was distracted, as if a powerful spell had been cast over me. The three pieces were hung together, but sold separately: a long brown cashmere cardigan, a long-sleeved taupe cashmere pullover with a halter neckline, and taupe wool cuffed slacks.

Francine was quick to note a customer's rapture. "There's a belt that goes with it on the accessory sale table. Brown calfskin, with a gold medallion."

"I don't wear belts," I reminded Francine.

"This is a hip belt," she responded. "Come, take a look. You have slim hips. You could wear it with real flair."

"Yikes!" I'd looked at the price tags. "Out of my league."

"Oh." Francine was unfazed. She brushed at her carefully coiffed blond hair before taking all three garments off the rack. "Just try them. Obviously, I haven't marked everything down yet. I was going to do that tomorrow when we're closed, since the ad won't run until Wednesday. You're getting the preview."

I was dubious, but like a sacrificial lamb, I allowed Francine to lead me into a dressing room. I was putting the cardigan on over the rest of the ensemble when she appeared with the hip belt.

"It's meant to cover the sweater hem," she informed me, putting what I considered the useless accessory around me. "There! Now have a look."

It was certainly a different me, if not a radical renovation. Ignoring the wash-and-wear hair and the lack of makeup, I looked taller and even younger. The brown and taupe tones complemented my brunette coloring. I was still in love, even with the low-slung belt.

"How much?" I squeaked.

"Let me see." Francine checked out all four price tags. "I won't kid you, this stuff's expensive, even on sale. But damn, Emma, it's worth it. When did you last spoil yourself? Before the turn of the century?"

That was true. I hadn't bought anything really nice since Tom died. "How much?" I repeated.

Francine slipped a calculator out of the pocket of her wine-colored wool jersey dress. "Just a sec . . . a little over nine hundred. But think of how you could play off of this outfit. I've got a beige blouse that would look wonderful with it, and a brown sweater with a funnel neck that—"

"Stop." I'd turned solemn. "I can't. For one thing, the slacks need to be taken up. I wanted something I could wear tonight."

"Tonight?" Like a sleek cat, Francine's ears seem to lie back. "Is he worth nine hundred dollars?"

"I don't know yet."

"You won't find out unless you look good," Francine declared. "Let me get the blouse and the sweater. I'll give Marcella Patricelli a call to see if she could alter the slacks today."

My protests were feeble. The two additional pieces worked beautifully with the slacks. I was surrendering like an unarmed soldier in the face of an enemy battalion. Besides, Francine was right. A little pampering was in order. I'd look very chic in debtors' prison.

Twenty minutes later, and almost thirteen hundred dollars poorer, I walked happily, yet dazedly out of the shop and headed for Paul and Marcella Patricelli's home in Ptarmigan Tract. Marcella had married into the large Patricelli clan shortly after I arrived in Alpine. Unlike his brother, Pete, who owned a pizza parlor, Paul didn't believe in hard work. He took the occasional odd job, and let Marcella support him and their four kids with her sewing.

"How come," I asked as she measured the slacks, "you've never joined the Burl Creek Thimble Club?"

"I sew for money, not gossip," Marcella replied, after taking pins out of her mouth. "I have to be professional. That means concentrating without a bunch of old bags talking my ear off."

She stood up, ordering me to run around in front of the full-length mirror. "Besides," she added, "I'd rather not get poisoned."

"Genevieve wasn't poisoned during the club's party," I pointed out.

Marcella, who was short and stocky with beautiful curly black hair, shot me a dark look. "It's a wonder. I did go to a meeting once, years ago. It soured me on joining. They talked about other women in town in the most awful way. Criticize this one, rake over that one, make mean remarks about another—including one of the members who hadn't been able to come. I sure didn't want to join a group like that. They should call it the Cat Club."

"They were that vicious?"

Marcella motioned for me to turn around slowly. "That's good. These slacks are really beautifully made. I'll have them done by four." She picked up some fallen pins while I stepped out of the slacks. "Yes," she continued, "they were. I hadn't gone there to hear how so-and-so drank on the sly, or such-and-such was having an affair. I don't know how they ever accomplished anything. Of course, most of them don't."

"Ethel Pike did," I said. "She won a blue ribbon at the county fair."

"Ethel must have done some of her work at home," Marcella stated. "She had one of the sharpest tongues. A bitter woman, I'd say."

"How long ago was this?" I asked, putting on my worn black slacks.

"Oh—seven, eight years ago. It was while I was expecting Paul Jr. He was eight in August."

"I don't suppose they talked about Gen that night," I remarked.

Marcella frowned. "I honestly don't remember who all they shredded. Except your Vida Runkel. Her sister-in-law, Mary Lou Blatt, was especially nasty."

"In what way?" I inquired, hoping to sound casual.

"In every way," Marcella replied, hanging my new two-hundred-and-fifty-dollar slacks from a hanger. "I don't remember specifics, I just recall that she raked Vida up and down from every angle—as a wife, a mother, a grandmother, a journalist, you name it."

"Did anyone defend Vida?"

Marcella shrugged. "I don't really recall that, either. It's been a while. Maybe Nell Blatt made some feeble protest. She seemed to be the nicest of the bunch, though a bit vague."

"Certainly Edith Bartleby wasn't cruel," I said.

"Edith? Oh, the vicar's wife." Marcella was leading the way to the door. "Edith wasn't there. They made cracks about her being standoffish and a snob, not to mention holier-than-thou."

Maybe when Edith was present, cutting remarks about others weren't acceptable. It was possible that Marcella had been there on one of those rare nights when the Betsys had let loose.

My next stop was the Bayards. On Saturdays, Buddy and Roseanna worked until noon. Then Roseanna took the paperwork home while Buddy spent the rest of the day in the darkroom. I arrived at the studio fifteen minutes before their early closing time.

"Buddy's taking pictures of the Erlandsons for their Christmas card," Roseanna informed me. She looked tired and unkempt.

"Bad night?" I said.

"Terrible." She ran a hand through her red-gold curls. "I don't think either of us slept for more than a couple of hours. What next? Another supposed sibling for Buddy? This is all just crazy."

"What about birth records?" I asked. "Surely they can be checked out."

"Not over a weekend," Roseanna replied in disgust. "And how do we search? Dodge already told us that they can't find any Knulers anywhere. Checking out Bayards is useless; all our kids had to do that in sixth grade when they put together a family tree. We saved the projects, and I checked them over last night. No Anthony. I'll admit, only Annie went beyond using the Internet. She contacted the Mormons in Salt Lake City."

Ginny, Rick, and their two young children exited from the rear. They all looked harried, if festive, in their red and green elf costumes.

"Hi, Emma," Ginny greeted me. "Are you having a portrait done?"

"I'm on the job," I said. "Your editor and publisher never sleeps."

Ginny smiled. Rick grabbed their youngest, Brett, who apparently had decided he wanted some retakes and was running back into the studio's inner sanctum.

"I'm lucky I work only five days a week." Ginny glanced at Roseanna. "Did you and Buddy get our sympathy card?"

Roseanna said they did indeed, and offered appreciation. Rick and Ginny, each with a boy firmly in tow, completed the process at the front desk. After they'd left, I asked Roseanna if they'd heard from Gen's attorney in Spokane.

"Yes, finally," she replied with a grimace. "Gen left no in-

structions about her burial or any services. Bogus claim or
not on the part of this Knuler jerk, we're going to have a funeral Mass at St. Mildred's and bury Gen here. I'm calling Al
Driggers and Father Ben this afternoon to make the arrangements."

"How about Tuesday?"

Roseanna shot me a knowing look. "So you can have it
in the paper Wednesday?" She shrugged. "Why not? The
sooner the better."

Assuming my most confidential manner, I leaned against
the tall desk. "Can you recall even a *hint* that Gen might have
had another child or remarried?"

Roseanna shook her head. "She had a guy—maybe guys,
over time—living with her. I told you that. But Gen never
mentioned a male friend. He was like a phantom."

"The lawyer didn't know anything, I suppose?"

"No. He—his name is George Vaughn—only saw Gen a
couple of times," Roseanna said as Buddy came into the reception area. "When she made her will, and when she needed
a copyright for her quilts."

Buddy was scowling, not at me, but at the world in general. "I stopped by the diner this morning," he said. "Terri
Bourgette figured this Knuler character for mid-thirties at
most. That'd mean that my mother would have had him—
not that I think she did—when she was in her forties, after
she moved to Seattle." He scowled, apparently considering
the possibility. "But I saw her a couple of times when I was in
the city. I think I'd have noticed it if Mom had been pregnant."

Maybe, maybe not, depending on how far along Genevieve had been. "Did Roseanna go with you on those trips?"

Glancing at his wife, Buddy shook his head. "They were
for photography classes. I was about to go off on my own.
Flash Avery was on his last legs. He had the photography

business in Alpine for years. He sold it to me six weeks before he died."

I'd heard Flash's name over the years. His real name was Edgar, but he'd gotten his nickname from his flashbulbs that Vida swore threw sparks when they went off. He was a drunk, she'd informed me, and insisted that all her own wedding pictures were out of focus and made her look enormous. At one time, Flash had worked for the *Advocate*. Marius Vandeventer had had to fire him, according to Vida, because some of the sparks from his flashbulb had set fire to a Bergstrom bride's veil. The newlyweds had threatened a lawsuit, but abandoned it six months later when the marriage collapsed. Vida had blamed Flash for getting the couple off to a bad start.

Roseanna looked grim. "Early forties," she murmured. "Childbearing still possible—and nowadays, even popular, especially in big cities like Seattle. I don't get it. I'm glad I had our kids while I was still young."

"Did you ever visit your mother's place in Seattle?" I asked Buddy.

Buddy scowled some more. "No. We always met at a restaurant." He turned a little bleak. "I never thought about it at the time. She told me her place was a mess. I figured she had her quilt frame up in the middle of the living room or something like that. Mom was actually a good housekeeper."

"I'll give her that," Roseanna muttered.

"What about the will?" I queried.

"It's a simple will," Buddy said. "No names, just 'my rightful heirs' or something like that."

Which meant Anthony Knuler could share in the inheritance if he could prove Gen was his mother. "You're certain," I said slowly to Buddy, "that no one you don't know has ever contacted you claiming to be a relative? I'm talking about in the last twenty-odd years."

"Never." Buddy was emphatic. "It's not the kind of thing I'd forget."

I believed him, but it didn't help solve the puzzle. Maybe that was up to a computer in Sacramento.

V IDA WHISPERED INTO THE PHONE. "PLEASE PUT THE TEA-kettle on. I'll be at your house in five minutes."

She hung up, leaving me puzzled, though hardly surprised. Vida enjoyed a little subterfuge. Sure enough, she pulled up in her almost-new green Buick Regal just after I'd finished putting away my new treasure trove of clothing.

"Well!" Vida stamped her galoshes-clad feet on the door-mat. "I was right. As usual."

"About what?" I asked, closing the door behind her.

"My mother's quilts." She paused as the teakettle sang. "Wait until we sit down."

While Vida was removing her coat, galoshes, gloves, and water-repellent derby, I made tea.

"Such a cheerful sound, the teakettle," she remarked, entering the kitchen. "Especially on a dark day like this. Poor Cupcake is getting confused about his bedtime."

I poured tea into our mugs. Vida always used English bone china, but I didn't have anything so elegant. Instead, I thought with a wince, I owned thirteen hundred bucks' worth of new clothes. I was growing increasingly guilty.

"Well?" I ventured. "Did you confirm that Gen stole your mother's patterns?"

Vida nodded vigorously. "Certainly. I rose early and phoned Jean Campbell before she and Lloyd left for the air-port. The Betsys—such a gagging name—usually meet at Jean's because the Campbells have the biggest house—imagine the markup on Lloyd's appliances!—and they have room in their basement for all the supplies. The party for Gen

wasn't supposed to involve sewing, merely eating and fawn-
ing over that awful woman. That's why Mary Lou Blatt was
the hostess instead of Jean." Vida paused for breath and took
a sip of tea. "I asked Jean what happened to my mother's
quilt templates. In retrospect, I'm sure I gave at least some of
them to the club. Jean told me she didn't have any, but she recalled the one I was talking about that we saw in the Seattle
store. It was very unusual, she said, but of course the colors
Gen used were different. It seems that Mother had made the
quilt to honor Carl Clemans, the town founder. She used his
initials in a double-C design, back-to-back. I don't think I ever
knew that." Briefly, Vida looked embarrassed and a little sad.

"Yes," I put in. "I remember the design in Gen's quilt. But
I thought it was parts of a circle."

Vida added more sugar to her already sweetened tea. "I
took my quilt to Nell Blatt's to show it to her. It's still in the
car. I covered it in plastic, but I'd rather not bring it out again.
The rain is coming down in buckets."

So it was, coursing like tiny creeks down the kitchen window. "So," Vida continued, "I must admit, Nell is addled as
an egg, but like so many older people, she remembers forty
years ago much better than yesterday."

I had gotten up to pour more tea. "She married your
brother Osbert, right?"

Vida nodded. "Osbert and Ennis were several years older
than I was. Mother wanted a girl so desperately—and finally,
I came along."

I paused while Vida reflected on her birthright. "Nell
mentioned that Mother didn't bother to copyright her quilts,"
she continued. "Apparently, that's what serious quilt-makers
do, particularly the ones who enter competitions or have ex-
hibits. I gather it's like writers or musicians or other creative
persons. It's a shame Mother didn't bother to copyright hers,
but the part she loved best was the sheer joy of making them.

As Nell put it, no one could ever imagine any club member stealing another's designs. It was unthinkable. Then she backed up my recollection that I'd given some of Mother's sewing materials—cardboard templates included—to the club. Ethel Pike, who was the only serious quilter after Gen left, took them. But according to Nell, Ethel never stole any of Mother's ideas. She simply used the materials and pieced them into her own quilts. Nell swore that Ethel had one quilt that was full of my old frocks from high school days."

Another pause. We seemed to be going down memory lane. Indeed, I could imagine Vida's bittersweet reaction.

The lights flickered, as they often do at the three-thousand-foot level. Neither of us made a comment. We were used to it; we were also used to having the lights on at midday in November.

"That's interesting history," I remarked, "but it doesn't throw much light on why Gen was poisoned."

Vida shook her head, making her fat gray curls bounce. "I still believe it was an accident. Annie Jeanne's scatter-brained. You told me how excited she was at having her—ugh—friend to dinner. Can't you see her sailing around the kitchen, doing heaven-knows-what while she cooked?"

I admitted that was true. "But she surely couldn't have mistaken diabetes pills for chocolate squares."

"Yes, she could."

It was useless to argue the point with Vida. She was convinced she was right, and in fact, I hoped she was. "Why," I said, "would anyone break in to Ethel Pike's house and destroy her materials, as well as your mother's quilt? Ethel must have had those things for twenty-odd years."

"That *is* curious," Vida responded. "What time of day was it?"

"Nobody knows for sure. The Pikes had already left for the airport."

Vida made a face. "All these people flying here and there. Hawaii, Florida—what next, Albania? Why can't they be satisfied to stay home in Alpine?" She set her mug down on the table and went over to the phone, which I'd left on the counter. "I'm calling the Eversons. And Maud Dodd, if I have to."

I was momentarily puzzled. Then I remembered that the Eversons and Maud were the Pikes' neighbors. I sipped tea and listened to Vida talk on the phone.

"Bebe? It's Vida here. I have a question for you about that break-in at Ethel and Pike's house. Are you sure you didn't see or hear anything unusual?" Scowling, Vida paced the floor. "Yes, of course. I knew you'd gone into Monroe for the day and that Roy would be at the post office. Thank you so much. Bye-bye now." She clicked off. "Idiot."

"Nothing?"

Vida was already dialing Maud Dodd's number. "Bebe wasn't home all day, didn't hear or see a thing after she returned around six. I swear she wouldn't remember if she did. Early Alzheimer's, that's what— Maud? It's Vida here. I have a . . ." She repeated the spiel she'd given to Bebe Everson. "Oh, I'm so sorry to hear it. Arthritis is so painful. . . . Yes, the damp this time of year. . . . Dr. Sung suggested what? . . . I'm certain he has all the latest treatments. . . . I know he isn't Doc Dewey, but still . . ." Vida looked at me with an impatient expression. "Melons? Everyone needs fresh fruit, Maud. . . . Then have the courtesy clerks fill the bags more lightly." She whipped off her glasses. I wondered how she could grind away at her eyes with one hand holding the phone. "But to get back to the break-in. It was at the Pikes', remember?" Vida held her head with her free hand and paced faster. "I understand you don't like going outside, but . . . You did? When was that?" She gave me a wave, apparently indicating that progress was finally being made.

"You're sure it was early in the afternoon? Around two? Yes, Marlow Whipp likes to keep to a schedule on his route."

Vida looked at me and put her hand over the receiver. "Marlow is a very erratic postal carrier," she whispered before speaking back into the phone. "Could you tell where the smoke was coming from . . . ? Drifting, you say. But from which direction . . . ? Like a fog. I see. . . . Yes, thank you, Maud, that's very helpful."

Vida rang off, replaced her glasses, and uttered a deep groan. "Maud's in a fog! But if she can be believed, she went out to the mailbox around two and smelled smoke. She figured someone was burning leaves, which makes sense this time of year. But she couldn't pinpoint where the smoke was coming from. Still, it's a peculiar time to have a break-in."

"It doesn't follow the pattern of the other break-ins," I noted. "They were all at night."

Vida remained silent for a few moments. At last she sat back down at the table. "I must admit, I'm more interested in finding out who burned Ethel's templates along with my mother's quilt than learning who poisoned Gen Bayard."

"Maybe," I said quietly, "the culprit is one and the same."

SEVENTEEN

B Y FIVE O'CLOCK, I WAS A NERVOUS WRECK. I'D WAITED ALL afternoon for the phone to ring. And I wouldn't have blamed Rolf Fisher if he'd canceled. It was almost pitch-black outside and the rain continued to pour down. Highway 2 could be tricky, with its narrow lanes and sudden curves.

But after I returned from picking up my altered slacks, I'd checked for messages. There were none. Apparently, Rolf wasn't intimidated by bad weather. I began to prepare myself for the evening.

First off, I lost control of my eyeliner and made a diagonal streak across my eyelid. Remove, retrace, react with annoyance. Then I spilled my liquid foundation all over the bathroom sink counter. Last but not least, my grasp on the lipstick went awry, leaving me with what looked like a two-inch gash on my right cheek. I scrubbed it off and started over, careful not to mar my eye makeup. It took me fifteen minutes instead of the usual five.

The phone did ring just as I was stepping into my new slacks.

It was Rolf.

"You chickened out," I declared, feeling my spirits sink.

"I did not," he replied, taking umbrage. "I'm at something called Cal's Texaco. I drove the last two miles with a flat tire. Nothing can puncture our romance. Fortunately, Cal stays open until six."

"Did you damage your rims?" I asked as relief swept over me. Rolf was actually in Alpine, less than five minutes away. I couldn't believe it.

"Don't get personal," he responded, but quickly went on. "No, but it's going to take him a while to find another tire. He's busy with customers gassing up for the weekend. Haven't you people ever heard of 'Open All Hours'?"

"We haven't, as a matter of fact," I admitted. "Alpine is not a hotbed of ambition."

"A pity," Rolf said. "Would you mind picking me up? Cal—a most accommodating man—says that since I have an extra key, I can collect the car after . . . whatever we end up doing."

I told Rolf I'd be there in ten minutes. I actually made it in eight, since all I had to do was put on my two sweaters and throw a raincoat over my ensemble. The coat spoiled the effect, but it was better than ruining the outfit.

I spotted my date standing inside the service station. In his beige raincoat and black hat, he looked as if he'd stepped straight out of a movie role as foreign correspondent. I should have laughed with derision. Instead, I smiled with pleasure.

"Sorry," I said after I'd honked and he came out to the car. "I forgot to tell you what I was driving."

"I know a chariot when I see one," Rolf said, settling into the passenger seat. "I heard you drove a Lexus."

I turned back onto Alpine Way. "I did," I said tersely. "I sold it."

"Ah."

I glanced at Rolf. He looked satisfied with my answer. Maybe the newspaper grapevine was as efficient as Alpine's.

I took Tonga Road to the ski lodge. "Have you ever been to Alpine?" I asked.

"Never," Rolf replied. "In my skiing days, before I tore up a knee, I skied at the summit, but we always went past the town. You must like it here."

I shrugged. "I'm trapped. Having bought the paper, I don't have much choice, at least until I retire—*if* I retire. After the first few years, I guess I've found a certain comfort level in Alpine."

Rolf was gazing at my new togs, displayed by the open raincoat. "Something tells me you're a city girl at heart. You don't dress like Smalltown USA."

"I do, though. Usually." I winced. Damn. I was admitting that I'd gone upscale for Rolf's benefit.

Again, he made no comment. I'd reached the narrow winding road that led to the ski lodge. I had to focus on my driving, so I couldn't look at Rolf. Was he laughing at me for being a silly nincompoop? Was he feeling smug? Was he lurking like a lion whose prey was in sight?

"Tell me about the timber history," he said. "I'm doing some research on alternatives to clear-cutting."

"I'll tell you what I know," I replied. "Are you planning a series of articles?"

"No. A book."

"A book?" We'd arrived in the parking area. I darted a glance at my companion. He looked serious.

"I've already published one book," he said wryly. "I guess you haven't read it. That was four years ago. I wrote about the history of the timber giants. It was fair, factual, and judicious. Or so one critic called it. I didn't get rich, but libraries and business schools bought enough copies to send it into a second printing."

"The local library should have it," I said, pulling into the valet parking lane. I wasn't going to further expose my new clothes to the rain. Besides, there was no charge, though a tip was expected.

"Don't knock yourself out," Rolf remarked as he got out of the Honda. "You might find the writing tedious."

I accepted a receipt from the young valet, who might have been a college student. "I'd expect a livelier style from you," I said as we entered the ski lodge. "You have a way with words," I added in an ironic tone.

"You'll have to see for yourself," Rolf said as I led the way into the Nordic-themed dining room.

Heather Bardeen Bavich couldn't quite hide her surprise at seeing me with a strange man. But she made no comment as she led us to the quiet corner table I'd reserved on Friday. The restaurant was beginning to fill. I watched as Rolf cast appreciative eyes on the waterfall by the bar, the etched glass with its depiction of Nordic myths, and the woodcarvings of various Norse gods and goddesses.

"I'd expected something more rustic," he confessed. "Hewn timbers. Crossed axes. Paul Bunyan."

"The ski lodge is a monument to survival," I explained. "Back in the late twenties, Carl Clemans, who founded the town, had finished logging off Tonga Ridge and Mount Baldy. There was no reason for Alpine to go on. There wasn't even a road into the town from Highway 2. The plan was to move everyone out and burn the buildings so they wouldn't attract hoboes who came through on the train. But Rufus Runkel and a guy called Olaf the Obese decided to borrow some money and build a ski lodge. That's when the road and the bridge were put in."

"Hmm." Rolf smiled at me. "Maybe my next book should be about the smaller mills and logging businesses."

"Maybe. There's considerable human interest in those stories."

Heather returned to take our drink orders. I inquired how married life was treating her. Before she could answer, I noticed she was pregnant. The long black jacket she was wearing had hidden her condition. Indeed, I suddenly re-called that Vida had told me that Heather and Trevor Bavich were expecting in February. The item had also appeared in Vida's "Scene Around Town" column. Heather was the daughter of Henry, the ski lodge manager, and the niece of Buck Bardeen. My brain seemed muddled, either by Rolf Fisher or my extravagant expenditure.

"I'm taking maternity leave right after New Year's," Heather confided. "The commute from Monroe is just too hard in the winter."

"So," Rolf remarked after Heather had departed, "this is where Alpine's elite meet."

"Not entirely," I replied. "You passed a very fine French restaurant just before turning off the highway."

"I didn't notice. I must have been too busy driving on a flat tire." He gave me an insinuating look. "We'll go French next time."

Our drinks arrived, courtesy of the latest blond waitress, Becky Erdahl. I'd ordered my usual bourbon and water; Rolf had requested a vodka martini. He ate the olive first.

I asked him if he'd been born in Seattle. He had, although he'd moved several times in his job with AP. "Six years ago," he said in a subdued voice, "when my wife got cancer, I asked for a transfer back to Seattle. She was from there, too, and wanted to be with her family. We were in St. Louis at the time."

"Children?" I asked.

"A son, Melchior."

I know I looked as if I thought he was kidding.

"No, really. We named him Melchior after Miriam's grandfather. We call him Mel, of course."

"It's unusual. If you'd had two more, I'd have figured you'd call them Caspar and Balthazar."

"Not suitable for Jewish boys," Rolf said.

He's Jewish. Not an insurmountable problem. Obviously, I was getting ahead of myself. "Where is Mel?"

"At Stanford," Rolf replied. "He's going to be a doctor. He was always leaning that way, but when Miriam got sick . . ." Rolf raised both hands. "That made up his mind. Mel wants to become involved in cancer research."

"That's a wonderful ambition," I said. "But it must cost the world to send him to Stanford."

"It does. That's why you're paying for dinner."

This time, I thought he was serious. But he laughed and held up a hand. "No, Emma, this is my treat. How's your son? The last I heard, he was freezing his digits off in Alaska."

"How did you know that?" I asked, taken aback.

"I work for AP, remember? Word gets through, even from remote outposts, like Alpine and Alaska."

I supposed that it did. I—or Scott—talked to other people at the Associated Press upon occasion.

"I also heard you made a pilgrimage to Rome," Rolf said. "How was that?"

"It was lovely," I said. "I went with my brother, Ben."

"The priest?"

"I only have one sibling. In fact, he's here right now, filling in for our pastor who's on sabbatical."

"So Rome was lovely." His tone was wry.

I tried not to grimace. Rolf seemed to have a knack for reading my mind. "Yes—but at first it was . . . hard."

"Because of Tom Cavanaugh?"

Damn, the man seemed to know all about me. I should be flattered. I was. "Yes." I looked him straight in the eye.

"I knew Tom," Rolf said quietly. "I worked with him at the *Seattle Times* for about a year before I joined AP. He was a great guy."

"Yes."

"I can't tell you how sorry I was when he was killed," Rolf went on in that same quiet voice. "I was sorry for you, too. I understand you two were getting married. How are you doing?"

"I'm recovering," I said, trying to sound casual.

Rolf signaled for another round. "Then we'll order, if you like."

We didn't speak for a few moments. It was an awkward silence, at least for me. I was feeling foolish, even shallow. I'd blown thirteen hundred dollars on new clothes to impress a man I scarcely knew. I hadn't expected the conversation to touch on Tom. Somehow, it took the sheen off my ensemble and the glow from my vision. I couldn't help making comparisons.

"I was with my wife when she died," Rolf said, breaking the silence. "I wonder what's worse—watching someone you love go through so much suffering in a futile attempt to stay alive, or dying swiftly and unexpectedly. Personally, I'd much prefer the latter."

I'd grown tense. "Do we have to talk about it?"

"Yes." His dark eyes held mine in an unblinking gaze. "We have to because if I intend to keep driving eighty-five miles to Alpine in rotten weather, I want to make sure there's a reason for it. I don't want our ghosts kept in the closet."

I lowered my eyes. Our drinks arrived, giving me time to

think. Would Tom have been this forthright? No. I had to be honest. In the early stages of our illicit romance, Tom equivocated. He'd leave Sandra and marry me. He couldn't leave Sandra, because she needed his emotional support. After I got pregnant, he promised he'd get a divorce or an annulment. A week later, he learned that Sandra was pregnant, too. He couldn't possibly leave her. And on and on, for thirty years. Comparisons weren't all in Tom's favor.

"Maybe you're right," I finally said. "I've only talked about Tom's death with my brother and my son." For once, Vida had respected my privacy. She'd still been a comfort because she, too, had been fond of "Tommy." I avoided the subject with Milo, who had an irrational sense of failure for not being able to protect a private citizen on a public street.

"Then we've gotten past one big obstacle." Rolf raised his glass. "To Miriam. To Tom."

I lifted my glass, too. "Amen," I said.

"Now that we've opened the door to our ghosts, we can talk about other things," Rolf declared. "Name your ten favorite movies."

"What is this?" I asked. "The Rolf Fisher version of speed dating?"

"You bet. Let's hear your list."

And so the time passed, through the salad course, the trout and salmon entrees, the after-dinner drinks. Movies, books, and a short course in sports. Rolf liked only baseball, which was fine with me. There was the backgrounding, too. He was another UW graduate, receiving his degree just before I entered the journalism program. He'd managed to miss being drafted during the Vietnam conflict, and still harbored guilt about it, even though he hadn't approved of the war. He considered himself a political liberal and a fiscal conservative. He loved apple pie, kosher dill pickles, and old-fashioned pot roast. His favorite color was green, any green. His most admired historical figure was Abraham Lincoln.

"We have some common ground," he said, summing up our likes and dislikes. "I trust we'll have things to discuss."

Smiling, I shook my head. "Do you always approach a woman this way?"

Setting down his brandy snifter, he grew serious. "You're the first woman I've asked out since my wife died."

Believe? Or not? I tried to find the answer in his eyes. But they revealed nothing. "You've certainly got the verbal foreplay down pat," I said in a reproachful voice.

"I've always done that," he said, still solemn. "It's gotten me into trouble a couple of times. Once, I was sued for sexual harassment."

"Who won the case?"

"It got thrown out of court," Rolf replied with the hint of a smile. "The poor lady was one of the homeliest women I ever met. I thought my remarks would make her feel good. Instead, she got mad. But the judge took one look at her and knew I couldn't be serious."

"You're making this up."

Rolf didn't respond directly. "I'd seen you. I knew you weren't homely. I also knew you had a sense of humor. You had to, because Cavanaugh wouldn't have still been nuts about you if you'd been another grim female like his poor wife. I once heard that Sandra Cavanaugh hadn't laughed in twelve years before she died. And I assumed she didn't laugh then."

Tom had never mentioned such a thing. But this time, I could believe Rolf. Sandra's mental problems were no laughing matter to any of the Cavanaughs, including their two children.

I rested my cheek on my hand. "Why me, O Lord?"

"I've already told you." Amusement gleamed in Rolf's dark eyes. "I think you're cute."

"I hoped I was beyond cute," I said.

Rolf shook his head. "Thirty years from now you'll be one of those little old ladies who rams her grocery cart into the backside of the person in front of her and then smiles and bats her eyes and everyone says 'What a cute old lady. She can't mean any harm.' "

"Thirty years from now we won't have grocery carts," I said.

"Probably not." He grew silent before signaling for our bill.

The truly awkward moment had arrived. "It's going on nine o'clock," I noted, sounding a bit strained. "Shall I drop you off at Cal's?"

He laughed. His laughter was sharp-edged, but not jarring. "Isn't this where you should ask me back to your place for a cup of coffee so that I become sober and thus a safe driver?"

I considered. "Okay, I'll take you to Cal's, you can pick up your car, and follow me back home. For coffee." I kept telling myself I wasn't a complete fool. Knowing that Rolf's favorite movie was *Citizen Kane* and that he thought Abe Lincoln had a higher IQ than Thomas Jefferson didn't yet qualify him as a full-fledged lover. I wasn't a trusting person, a virtue—or lack thereof—that stood me well in my profession. Maybe, I thought briefly, it hadn't always been a plus in my personal life.

A different valet—also young and probably a college student—brought my Honda to the entrance. In the last few minutes before we left the ski lodge, Rolf had been rather quiet. Maybe he was disappointed in my reaction. Maybe he'd lost interest. Maybe he was a big phony.

"Do you smoke?" Rolf asked after we pulled out of the parking lot.

"No," I replied. "At least not anymore. Except . . ." I'd

braked for the arterial at the end of the ski lodge road. "Why do you ask? Do you?"

"A cigar once in a while. I thought I smelled cigarette smoke when we got in the car just now. I didn't notice it on the way here, though." He grinned at me. "I was probably too excited."

I sniffed at the air. There was a faint aroma of tobacco smoke. "The valets," I said. "I'll bet the kids sneak a cigarette in the cars sometimes. They probably aren't allowed to smoke while on duty. Check the ashtray."

"It's empty," Rolf said after taking a look. "How hard does your fair town come down on smokers?"

"Not too hard, since the sheriff frequently lights up in a nonsmoking area. You have to remember," I continued, "that many of the politically correct issues of the day aren't as popular in a place like Alpine. They like their guns not only because they hunt, but because wild animals who consider humans a tasty treat come to visit. For decades they voted a straight Democratic ticket because the party supported the worker. Then the environmentalists were mainly liberals. Now the natives feel deserted, and tend to be much more conservative."

Rolf sighed. "It'd take some getting used to. Not to mention suffering fools gladly."

"I find the fools represent all parts of the political spectrum," I replied. "The other thing to keep in mind is that small towns are always ten or more years behind the rest of the country. I still haven't figured out if that's good or bad."

"Wholesome. Family values. I noticed several American flags on the way up here."

"That's part of it," I agreed, turning onto Alpine Way. "They're proud of their country, though historically the flip side has been that they don't like newcomers."

"The college must have made a difference," Rolf remarked as I pulled into Cal's Texaco.

"It has, thank goodness. When I first came here, there were no people of color. Now we have a growing racial mix. Is that your car parked by the water hose?"

"Yes, that's my Bug buggy," Rolf replied. "You should see it in daylight. It's very lime."

"I'll wait until you get it started," I said as he edged out of the Honda. "I shouldn't lose you, but if I do, take a left on Fir Street. I'm on the right, three blocks down. It's a log house, set back in the trees."

"Cozy," Rolf said as he went out into the rain. "See you shortly."

With little traffic, it took only three minutes to get to my place. I pulled into the carport; Rolf pulled the VW up behind me.

"*Very* cozy," he emphasized. "All that's missing is a light in the window."

I frowned as I opened the kitchen door. "I could have sworn I left at least the kitchen light on. Maybe it burned out."

But even as I stepped across the threshold, I sensed that something was different. For one thing, the log house didn't feel cozy. It felt cold and smelled odd. The light went on in the kitchen, however, but I wasn't reassured.

Rolf looked at me in a curious manner. "Are you okay? Is something wrong?"

"It feels wrong," I said. "Let's go into the living room."

I turned on the lights in the dining alcove. The first thing I noticed was that the front door was wide open. Then I saw that my TV, my CD player, and the laptop I kept on a side table were gone. The cupboard where I stored tapes, CDs, and some classic vinyl records was empty.

"Good God!" I said, low and angry. "I've been robbed!"

EIGHTEEN

DON'T MOVE," ROLF URGED, PUTTING BOTH HANDS ON my shoulders. "They might still be here."

"No. The door's open. There wasn't anybody parked outside. And it's very cold, which means they must have been gone awhile." I slammed my purse down on the sofa. "Damn!" I was rattled. What was there to steal in my bedroom?

I started into the small hallway that led to the two bedrooms and the bath. Rolf stopped me. "Take a deep breath. Sit down." He all but pushed me onto the sofa next to my purse. "Collect yourself. Relax." He grinned at me, which seemed highly inappropriate. "I knew it would work. I attempt to seduce you while my accomplices steal your most priceless items."

"Not funny," I muttered.

"Semifunny," Rolf retorted. "If you can't laugh, you won't survive."

I knew he was right, but it didn't cheer me. He spotted the phone on the end table. At least the thieves hadn't stolen that. Dazedly, I watched Rolf pick it up.

"What are you doing?" I asked in a voice that had become shaky.

Rolf gave me an encouraging look. "What we do in the big city. I'm calling the cops."

While we waited for whoever had drawn Saturday night duty, Rolf and I went through the rest of the house. Adam's old skis were gone, so were the tapes and CDs he'd left behind, and the digital camera I'd never figured out how to use. Lastly, I checked in the bottom of the closet for my father's handgun. It was still there, in a Nordstrom shoebox.

"So you've had a series of break-ins around town," Rolf noted as we returned to the living room. "Does your sheriff have some usual suspects?"

"As a rule," I replied, continuing on into the kitchen. "But apparently he doesn't have any evidence. Only the dimmest of thieves would try to sell their ill-gotten gains in Skykomish County. In the past, whenever stolen items were recovered, they showed up in Monroe, Everett, or Seattle and its suburbs." I saw that my coffeemaker was still there. At twenty bucks, it wasn't worth stealing. "I'll make coffee now."

"You'd better put some whiskey in yours," Rolf said. "You're white as a sheet, to coin a phrase."

"Maybe I'll drink the whiskey separately," I responded, plugging in the coffeemaker, which I'd readied for morning. "How about you? I've got vodka."

"No. Really, I shouldn't," Rolf replied. "I make it a rule never to drink past ten."

I poured myself a short shot of bourbon over ice. To hell with the mixer. Just as I was about to suggest we wait in the living room, there was a knock at the kitchen door. I looked outside and saw Milo's tall figure looming under the carport light.

"Emma," he said in disgust, "you got hit?"

"Yes, damn it," I answered angrily, "I did."

The sheriff, who was wearing civvies, loped into the kitchen. He took one look at Rolf and stopped. "Are you the date?" Milo asked, sounding more like my father than the local lawman.

Rolf, who was some two inches shorter and twenty pounds lighter, put out a hand. "Rolf Fisher, middle-aged journalist. I'm keeping Emma in protective custody."

Milo's returning handshake was brief. "Yeah. Emma told me about you." He scrutinized Rolf as if he were a suspect in a long line of serial killings. "Okay, tell me what happened here."

"Are you on duty?" I asked in formal tones.

Milo gave me a dirty look. "Just answer the question."

I'd taken a big gulp of bourbon. "Can we sit down in the living room? I'm making coffee."

"Fine." Milo led the way out of the kitchen.

It didn't take long to relate what had happened, at least from my point of view. When I mentioned the theft of the TV set, his eyes went straight to the vacant spot across the room. I wondered if he was thinking of all the times we'd watched sports together, sometimes as a prelude to sex. For one fleeting moment, I wished Rolf Fisher were as ugly as sin.

I'd just finished when Jack Mullins arrived, complete with evidence kit. "Sorry," he apologized after I'd made the introductions, "we had a medical emergency. Man bites wife, wife stabs man, dog hides under bed."

"Anybody I know?" I inquired.

"Check the log Monday," Jack retorted. "Cooper's the name. They live way out past the fish hatchery in a double-wide."

No bells rang. My brain was still addled. "I don't get it," I said to Milo while Jack began to collect possible fingerprints and anything else that might be evidence. "Except for the value of the recordings, which I can't estimate, the only brand-new item I had was that blasted digital camera."

"Did you ever use it?" Milo asked.

"No." I didn't look at him. "I was going to have Scott show me how to install it or whatever you have to do. Or Adam, when he comes for Christmas. But it cost over two hundred dollars."

"So," the sheriff said in a reflective voice, "you were having dinner at the ski lodge."

It sounded like an indictment. I merely nodded.

"Did you park your own car?" Milo asked.

"No. It was raining too hard." I glanced down at my high-priced outfit. What I was wearing probably cost as much as the thieves—or thief—had stolen. Suddenly it dawned on me what Milo was getting at. "You think there's a connection between the valet guys and the thefts?"

Milo shrugged. "Just about everybody except the Pikes and maybe one other break-in took place while the victims were at the lodge. You like to sleuth. Work it out."

"Someone," Rolf said, speaking for the first time in ten minutes, "had been smoking in Emma's car."

Milo inclined his head.

Another knock sounded. Another deputy? The thieves returning my belongings because they wouldn't fetch a good price?

The sheriff beat me to the door. Ben came rushing into the room.

"Emma!" he cried, enfolding me in a bear hug. "Are you all right?"

"Yes, yes," I said in a muffled voice against his chest. "I'm mad, that's all."

Ben sensed my emotional temperature and let go of me. Milo had wandered off to the kitchen. Rolf regarded my brother with curiosity. Ben was dressed in blue jeans and a brown pullover. I realized that my date had no idea that the newcomer was my brother.

I introduced them. Milo returned with a shot of Scotch on ice. *Some first date in eons for Emma.* Any chance of romance was seeping away with the sheriff making himself at home and my brother the cleric on hand. If the thieves were ever caught, I'd reconsider my anti-death-penalty stand.

"Good idea," Ben remarked, seeing Milo's drink. "You must not be on duty."

"Right." He looked straight at Ben. "I picked up the call on my scanner at home. I figured I could get here faster than Jack since he was working a domestic violence incident."

Jack poked his head out into the living room. "Hey, Father, if you want to spend the night with your sister, I'll send Nina to stay with Annie Jeanne. I'm working until seven A.M. Not," he added with an impish expression, "that it matters. Our bedroom's the coldest place in Alpine."

Jack's barbs at his wife's expense always annoyed me. Nina Mullins seemed like a warm, loving woman. But to listen to her husband, she was the Ice Queen of Skykomish County.

"I'll let Emma decide," Ben said, then turned a dubious look in my direction. "Do you want company?"

"No. I hardly expect them to come back. What I want to know is how they got in."

"Bathroom window," Jack said. "Did you leave it open a crack?"

I'd only given a cursory glance at the bathroom. I had none of the drugs that would entice a thief. "Yes. I usually do. I grew up in a family with gas."

Milo smirked; Rolf looked away; Jack burst out laughing.

"My sister," Ben said in his most formal manner as he glanced at Rolf, "means that we had a gas furnace and gas appliances. She was always certain that we'd die of carbon monoxide poisoning unless there was fresh air coming into the house someplace."

"Sensible," Rolf commented. But he didn't look at any of us.

Ben also strolled off to the kitchen, apparently following Milo's example. It looked to me as if nobody was going anywhere.

Except Rolf Fisher. He'd shed his raincoat, which was slung over the back of the chair where the sheriff had parked himself. "I should head on out," Rolf said, giving the raincoat a tug that made Milo jump. "Sorry, Sheriff. Are you sitting on my hat?"

"Your hat?" Milo twisted around. "I don't think so."

"That's right—I put it on the mantel." Rolf retrieved the hat.

I joined him at the door, opening it for him. Despite the rain, which was blowing in onto the covered porch, I went outside and left the door slightly ajar.

"I feel terrible about all this," I confessed. "Really, it's not always like tonight."

"Oh." Rolf looked bemused. "How many chaperones do you need?"

The anger I'd felt toward the thieves now boiled over onto Rolf. "Are you trying to make me feel worse? Were you really expecting me to start pawing your body as soon as we got inside my house?"

"I could but hope."

Again, I couldn't tell if he was serious or not. But he certainly was aggravating. I always believed Tom. Even when he made promises he couldn't possibly keep.

I waved an arm. "Okay, okay, run off to the big city. It's not as if you don't have plenty of crime there."

"Then be prepared when you come to see me," he said,

and before I could step aside, he took me in his arms and kissed me, a long, hard, soul-wrenching kiss. When he finally pulled back, his eyes studied my face. "I'm not going away completely empty. And damn, but it felt good."

Rolf let go of me, turned on his heel, doffed his hat, and headed for his car. I stayed on the porch, despite the fact that the rain was probably ruining my new clothes. I already smelled like a sheep.

Or a lamb, being led to the slaughter.

J ACK WAS THE FIRST TO LEAVE. BEN AND MILO REMAINED, sipping their drinks and talking about fishing. I wanted to kill them both.

"Don't you two have something better to do?" I demanded.

Ben wore an innocent expression. Milo frowned, as if he'd missed some important event on his social calendar.

"No," the sheriff finally replied. "Can't think of a thing. I'm going steelheading at first light tomorrow. I'm trying to talk your brother into joining me for a couple of hours before he does his church thing."

"Martin Creek," Ben said. "I've never fished it. How long is the drive?"

Disgusted, I went into the kitchen. The coffee hadn't been touched. I could warm it up in the morning. Briefly, I considered a second drink. But like a moronic adolescent, I didn't want to wipe away Rolf's kiss.

Instead, I began straightening up the house. The thieves— or thief, I kept reminding myself—hadn't done much damage. They—or he—knew what was desirable and what wasn't. When I reappeared in the living room shortly before eleven, I was wearing my ratty old blue bathrobe. My guests had ob-

viously raided my liquor cabinet again and were growing
rather merry.

"Are you enjoying yourselves?" I asked in voice coated
with sarcasm.

"We're fine," Ben replied airily.

Milo ignored the question. "See," he was saying, "a
priest and a rabbi and a minister go into a bar. They see a
woman sitting next to a goat. A real goat. The rabbi looks at
the goat and . . ."

I went out into the kitchen again.

MILO WENT HOME HALF AN HOUR LATER. BEN INSISTED I
shouldn't stay alone, but I was firm. After all, I still had
our father's gun. My brother gave me a disparaging look, but
finally left.

I admitted to myself that I didn't like being alone that
night. The house still felt cold and strange. My cozy sanctu-
ary didn't exude its usual comfort. Houses were curious
things, I thought as I lay wide-eyed in bed. They provided so-
lace while you lived in them. But the home in which I'd
grown up in Seattle had ceased to be of any interest the moment my parents died in a car accident. The Portland bunga-
low that I'd bought for Adam and me became merely
eighteen hundred square feet of real estate property as soon
as I decided to move to Alpine. In both cases, strangers would
climb the steps and walk the floors as soon as I was gone.
And now, strangers had entered my little log house and
turned it into a stranger. It wasn't right; they'd taken only
things. And *things* could be replaced. But it still felt as if
they'd stolen part of *me*.

B EN HADN'T GONE FISHING. I DIDN'T SEE HIM BEFORE
Mass started, though our eyes met as soon as he finished
processing and turned on the altar to face the congregation.
Annie Jeanne, looking frail and timid, sat on the aisle in the
second row, next to the O'Tooles. No one played the organ.

After Mass, I started to approach Ben but saw Bernard
and Patsy Shaw, who had been sitting in the back. I decided
to inform Bernie about my loss so he could start the insurance
ball rolling.

"Not you, too, Emma!" Patsy cried. "Are they picking on
us Catholics?"

"We're not the only ones who've been hit," I replied. "It
seems to be a random thing."

"I'd like to know," Bernie said, looking vexed, "what
Dodge is up to. He's certainly taking his time rounding up the
thieves."

"He may have a lead," I offered. "Milo goes by the book,
you know."

"He's a slow reader then," Bernie asserted. "It's been a
week since the break-in at our place."

I saw the Bronskys headed our way. I could talk to Ben
later. I quickly excused myself and all but ran to the car. I
wasn't in the mood to suffer from Ed's self-absorption.

I was drinking coffee in the living room and reading the
Sunday paper when the phone's ringing brought me out of
what felt like inertia. It was Vida, and she was agog.

"A date! A break-in! Milo and Ben! We must talk!"

"Do you want to come over to what was once my happy
little home?" I inquired.

"No, no, no, you must come here. Take yourself out of
yourself. And the house, of course. Such unpleasantness! My,
my!"

I told Vida I'd come by in half an hour.

The rain had all but stopped, with the clouds lifting and even a hint of sun directly overhead. I wondered if we'd get heavy snow in the winter to come. Despite a couple of big snowfalls the previous season, the state had been suffering from drought in the summers.

Vida opened the door before I was halfway up the walk. She looked awful. Her chin was trembling, and her face was ashen.

"What's wrong?" I asked, hurrying to meet her.

"I tried to call you to tell you not to come," Vida said in a voice that was hardly recognizable. "But you'd already left."

She'd backed into the narrow entry hall. I'd never seen her in such a state. "Shall I make tea?" I asked, utterly confounded.

A whistling sound told me that Vida had already put the water on. "I'll get it," I said. "You sit."

I also felt shaken, and took extra care not to drop Vida's English bone china cups and saucers. Whatever caused her distress had occurred in the last thirty minutes. A devastating phone call, maybe. I doctored Vida's tea with cream and plenty of sugar before joining her in the living room, where she'd collapsed on the sofa, holding her head.

"Is it the family?" I inquired. "Has something happened to one of them?"

But she mouthed the word *no*.

"Buck?" I asked.

"No," she said out loud. "Nothing like that."

"Then what?"

Vida sat up straight and took a sip of tea from the cup I'd placed on the side table. "Maybe I'm being a silly old fool," she said.

"I can't tell unless you let me know what upset you so," I responded, sitting down beside her. "I take it no one died?"

She shook her head. "That's the problem," she murmured.

"What do you mean?"

Obviously, Vida was making an enormous effort to pull herself together. She even managed a croaking laugh. "I *am* a silly old fool. I'm sorry I alarmed you." She cleared her throat. "Now tell me about the break-in."

"Vida," I said firmly, "I won't let you get away with this. Something scared the hell—heck, I mean—out of you. What was it?"

She was scowling into space, apparently at war with herself. Finally she took off her glasses and began rubbing her eyes. "Ooooh . . . It's probably nothing. Maybe I got upset because of your robbery. It was bad timing, that's all."

"What was?" I'd started to survey our surroundings. A round Chippendale table was flanked by two armchairs on the opposite side of the room. A stack of mail sat next to a lamp with a crystal base. Several catalogs, no doubt enticements for Christmas shopping, along with a couple of circulars and what looked like a letter were spread out on top. "Did something come in the mail?"

Vida shot me an accusing glance, perhaps because I'd reached the right conclusion. "Yes," she said after a pause. "Marlow Whipp—or his substitute—was so late yesterday that I forgot to check the mail after four-thirty yesterday. I'd forgotten about it until I phoned you. I'd just gotten home from church, you see." She paused, taking another drink of tea. "There was a letter, anonymous. Really, it's probably someone's idea of a prank." She nodded in the direction of the round table. "See for yourself. I can't think why I let it distress me so."

I got up and retrieved the letter as well as the envelope. The single sheet of plain paper read:

I KNOW THE TRUTH ABOUT ERNEST.

The envelope, with no return address, was typed in the same font. The postmark was from Seattle.

I put the letter and the envelope back on the table. "We shouldn't touch this anymore. There may be fingerprints."

"No, no, no," Vida said adamantly. "I'm not turning it over to Milo. Goodness, such a fuss about nothing!"

But Vida was still pale, and her hand trembled when she picked up the teacup. "Let me get you some more," I said, holding out my hand. "I haven't poured mine yet anyway."

"Oh. Thank you." She tried to smile, but it wasn't much of a success.

When I returned, Vida was no longer trembling and her jaw was set. "A joke. Definitely a joke. Ernest spent his life putting up with Oscar Wilde allusions. You know—*The Importance of* . . . etc. This may be from some old friend."

My face became severe. "You know that's nonsense. That letter has nothing to do with Oscar Wilde. Frankly, I don't know why you're so upset." I had an inkling, but Vida didn't need to know that. "Ernest has been dead for . . . what? Over twenty-five years?"

"Thirty, to be exact," Vida replied. "Come January."

I'd forgotten how young Vida was when Ernest died. Meg, the youngest of the three girls, wasn't in her teens yet; Amy and Beth were in junior high and high school. It was no wonder that Vida had gone to work for the newspaper just a few weeks after Ernest's death.

I sat down on the sofa beside Vida. "Let's rule out a joke," I said firmly. "Can you think of any reason—no matter how far-fetched—why you'd receive such a letter after all these years?"

Vida shook her head. "That's why it came as such a shock."

"Do you think the letter is a prelude to blackmail?"

She looked bleak. "What a horrible idea."

It struck me as odd that Vida didn't dismiss the suggestion out of hand. "This might be an attempt to . . ." I hesitated. "To soften you up for the next letter."

Vida threw up her hands, almost hitting me in the head with her elbow. "Oh, for heaven's sake! You make me sound like a victim in a cheap detective novel!"

"Sorry. But we have to explore the possibilities."

"No, we don't," Vida asserted. She drank a big swallow of tea. "It's all very silly. I wish I hadn't told you. Let's talk about something else. Your gentleman friend, perhaps. Or the break-in."

I surrendered. The truth was I wanted to talk about Rolf; I needed to talk about the break-in. Vida, however, listened with half an ear. That wasn't like her. After about an hour, I wound down and stood up.

"I should get going," I said. "Maybe Milo has some information on the robbery. I haven't talked to him today."

"Very well," Vida said, also rising to her feet. "Let me know if you hear anything."

After I went down the walk, I glanced over my shoulder. Vida had already gone back inside. Usually she waited until her guest had driven off, waving her arms like a windmill, and shouting, "Do come back!" Farewells also gave her an opportunity to scour the neighborhood for any interesting activities.

Vida was obviously not herself.

A s I drove down Tyee Street, I realized that I had never checked out the story about Ernest's death in the *Advocate*. If I felt like it, I could call Milo from the office.

January, thirty years ago. I found the correct volume, which had not yet been put on microfiche. Kip had been working on that project for some time, but could do it only in his very sparse leisure time. I hauled the heavy book down from the shelf and took it to Scott's desk.

It didn't take long to find the story. It was on page one of the edition from the second week of the new year.

ERNEST RUNKEL
DIES AT FALLS

The article was written under Marius Vandeventer's byline. "Alpine timber broker Ernest Runkel died Friday night in a tragic accident at Deception Falls. He had been attempting to go over the falls in a barrel when the borrowed truck he had driven to the site accidentally ran over him.

"A native of Alpine, Runkel, 49, was a well-liked and respected businessman. According to his widow, Vida Blatt Runkel, her husband had harbored a longtime desire to make the falls attempt in the winter months when the water was running full spate.

"Sheriff Eeeny Moroni was called to the scene when Cornelius Shaw, Alpine insurance man, noticed a truck perched haphazardly on the edge of Deception Creek and phoned the authorities to ask them to check it out. Sheriff Moroni and Dr. Cedric Dewey agreed that the accident had occurred close to an hour before they arrived on the scene.

"See Obituaries, page 4."

I felt as if ghosts were reaching out from the past. Cornelius Shaw, Eeeny Moroni, and Cedric Dewey were all dead. Bernard Shaw's father had died before I arrived. The doctor—known as Old Doc Dewey after his son, Gerald, set up practice—had passed away a couple of years after I arrived in town. And Sheriff Moroni had turned out to be as crooked as a logging road.

I turned to the obituary. Ernest had indeed been a pillar of the community. He was an elder in the Presbyterian church, a member of the Chamber of Commerce, Kiwanis, and Rotary clubs. He'd worked with the Girl and Boy Scouts, the Future Farmers of America, and the Red Cross. He'd served as a volunteer firefighter and an organizer of Loggerama, the town's annual summer festival, which, in recent years, had metamorphosed into the Summer Solstice. The lengthy list of Ernest's survivors included, of course, his "devoted wife" Vida and their three daughters. Services would be held at First Presbyterian Church on Friday. There would be no viewing. Mourners were asked to sign the guest book, and memorials were to be sent to the Red Cross and various Presbyterian charities. A two-column photo of Ernest ran above the obit. It was a studio pose, probably taken a few years earlier, since he looked closer to forty than fifty. He was indeed a "nice-looking" man, as Mary Lou Blatt had informed me. He also appeared stolid, even a bit pompous.

I checked the following week for a follow-up story, but there was nothing further. That struck me as curious. In fact, the coverage itself made me curious. Thirty years ago, the *Advocate* had been published on Thursdays. Marius Vandeventer had five days in which to write the page-one article. Given Ernest's status in the community—and the bizarre nature of his accident—I would have expected at least a couple of dozen inches instead of a mere five.

I reread the news story twice and the obituary once. A strange feeling of unease crept over me.

But I wasn't sure why.

NINETEEN

CONFUSION CHISELED AWAY AT THE GRAY MATTER OF MY brain. I needed to stop dwelling on the *Advocate*'s coverage of Ernest's death, so I called Milo to inquire about any progress on the break-ins, mine in particular.

"As a matter of fact," he said in a rather smug tone, "we are making progress. I'll let you know by tomorrow morning."

"That's great," I replied with enthusiasm. "I have an idea what direction you're looking in."

"Thought you might." He paused. "Aren't you going to ask if I had any luck this morning?"

I'd forgotten that Milo had gone fishing. "Sure," I fibbed. There was no greater gaffe than not asking a fisherman if he'd had any luck. "Catch anything?"

"You bet. A ten-pounder. Real fight in that baby. I'm going to cook it for Ben."

"Good for you," I said, with even more enthusiasm. At least he wasn't going to cook the steelhead for me. I'm a fish lover, but the steelies don't taste as good as trout or salmon. "Martin Creek?"

"Yep. I'd only been out about twenty minutes."

"Hey," I said on a whim, "how long do you keep accident reports?"

"Seven to ten years," Milo replied. "That is, until the insurance liabilities run out."

"Oh." I was disappointed. "Were you working for Eeeny Moroni when Ernest Runkel was killed?"

"I was," Milo replied, his tone changing. "I never guessed he was such a bastard. But I was green in those days, and Eeeny was one clever SOB. Why are you asking me that?"

I made a face. Dare I suggest to Milo what I was thinking? Could I? I wasn't even certain why I felt so curious. "Were you on duty that night?"

"No," Milo said. "It was a Friday, and it was Mulehide's birthday," he went on, referring to his ex-wife, whose real name was Tricia. "We'd gone into Seattle for a—excuse the expression—romantic weekend."

"What about the other deputies? Were any of them around?"

"What year was that?" he asked.

I told him.

"No," Milo said. "Dwight came aboard a year or so later, Sam maybe five years after that, and Jack didn't join the department for another ten. Of course, Bill Blatt and Dustin Fong are relative newcomers."

Dustin had been hired a few years after I arrived in Alpine. "Who were the deputies?"

"There were only two of us," the sheriff answered. "Me, of course, and an old-timer named Zeke Zacharias. I think he was some shirttail relation of Eeeny's pal Neeny Doukas. Why do you want to know?"

I suppressed a sigh. "Do I have to tell you?"

"What's the big secret?" He sounded more miffed than curious.

I chose my words carefully, explaining first how I'd never

looked up the article on Ernest Runkel's death until now. "I'm surprised so little was made of it in the paper," I went on. "Granted, before I bought the *Advocate,* I only went through the previous year's issues. It seemed to be that Marius—like any small-town publisher—used twenty words when he could have managed with two. It's the problem of filling up the front page with local news. You give the reader more than they need—or want—to know."

"Maybe there was a bunch of other stuff going on," Milo suggested.

"No. I scanned the rest of the page-one stories," I said. "It was the usual county commissioners, school board, and timber industry news. Nothing big, no controversies. In fact, Marius ran a three-column picture of snow in Old Mill Park."

"Well," Milo said, "you know more about that stuff than I do. What's your point?"

"I'm not sure," I replied. "It just strikes me as odd. This was huge news. Not only was Ernest a native son, but his father was Rufus Runkel, who helped save Alpine. There was no mention of that in the obituary or much other background, either. I would've expected Vida to put together a foot-long death notice." I paused, my brain working double-time. "What do you remember of all this? Were you back in town that Monday?"

"Right," the sheriff replied. "We got home Sunday night. We had one of those two-night off-season deals at the Westin."

"And?" I coaxed.

"Jeez . . . It's been thirty years, Emma," Milo said. "I didn't know about Ernest until I got back. I didn't go to the funeral. I had to work, and anyway, I didn't know Vida and her husband all that well in those days. I mean, I *knew* them—who didn't?—but they weren't friends of ours. Remember, I was still in my twenties at the time."

"There had to be a buzz, especially in the sheriff's office," I said. If Milo and I had been face-to-face, I would have shaken him.

Milo made an impatient noise. "Hell, I don't remember gossip and crap like that. It's women's work. Ernest tried to pull off a lame-assed stunt. He wanted to try getting into the barrel once before they hauled it upcreek above the falls. It was cold as a well digger's ass, and he hadn't tried to get inside with his all-weather gear. The barrel was right in back of the truck, and the brakes slipped. He got run over and croaked. Sad, but true."

"Who was with him?"

"Huh?"

"You said 'they.' Somebody had to put the barrel into the creek after he got in it."

"Oh. Right." He paused, perhaps thinking through the situation in his usual methodical manner. "I'm trying to remember who Runkel's friends were, especially if one owned a pickup truck."

"It was a pickup?"

"A red Chevy," Milo said. "I remember seeing it in the impound area out back behind the office."

The impound section of the SkyCo sheriff's department was two parking spaces next to the building. "Who owned it?"

"Good God Almighty," Milo said in a low, startled voice.

"God owned it?"

"No," Milo replied, still sounding shaken. "How the hell could I have forgotten? It was Andy Bayard."

IT TOOK ME A FEW SECONDS TO ABSORB THIS STARTLING revelation. "Were Andy and Ernest friends?" I asked in a voice filled with dismay. They seemed like an unlikely duo.

"Not really," Milo replied, sounding more like himself.

"But Andy worked—*when* he worked—hauling stuff. I suppose Ernest paid him for the trip to the falls."

"What did Andy have to say about the accident?"

Milo didn't answer for so long that I thought he'd dropped the phone. "He didn't," the sheriff finally said after searching his memory. "That was when he took off. Don't ask how; I suppose he hitchhiked. Eeeny tried to track him down, but the next thing we knew he'd gotten killed in a car wreck somewhere south of Seattle. Auburn, I think."

The Runkel-Bayard connection didn't end with rumors about a romance between Ernest and Genevieve. Had Andy been so jealous of Ernest that he'd killed him? It was a horrendous thought.

"Whoa!" I blurted. "Are you saying that Eeeny didn't bother to go after Andy under such suspicious circumstances?"

Milo didn't answer right away, and when he spoke, his voice was pained. "Back then we didn't know how crooked Eeeny was. At least I didn't. Maybe Zeke did. I always wondered, but by the time I figured it out, Zeke was dead. For all I know, Andy paid Eeeny off. Looking back, there were a lot of cases that might have had different outcomes if our previous sheriff hadn't been a corrupt SOB."

Milo was undoubtedly right. He'd been young, inexperienced, maybe naive. Eeeny Moroni had been in office for years, using charm and a gift of gab to win votes in the days when the sheriff was elected.

"Incredible," I murmured. "Didn't it occur to you that Ernest might have been murdered?"

"No," Milo replied. "Everybody—including Vida—said it was an accident. I didn't work the case, remember? Hey, for all I know, Eeeny may have tried to find Andy but came up empty. It happens."

"Who told you Andy had died?"

"Oh . . . Jesus, Emma, I can hardly recall much about it. Vida, maybe. She probably got it over the wire service."

That made sense. But Vida had never hinted that foul play had been involved in Ernest's death. Nor had any such suggestion appeared in the newspaper. Quickly, I flipped through the next six issues. Nothing. Maybe I was crazy.

Or maybe not. There was definitely something crazy— besides Ernest's stupid stunt—about Milo's account of the accident.

"If Andy Bayard took off right after the debacle, who was the witness to the accident?"

"There wasn't one," Milo replied, "except for him. Eeny and Zeke must have reconstructed what happened."

That was possible. "Okay," I said, and sighed. "I'm making a mountain out of a molehill. Forget I brought it up."

"Easy to do," Milo grumbled, "since I don't remember much about it except that it was a damned fool stunt for Ernest to attempt."

I couldn't argue with that. But after we hung up, I sat staring at the article about Ernest Runkel's death.

It still didn't sound right.

IF, I THOUGHT, I COULD ONLY DISCUSS THE MATTER WITH Vida. But I didn't want to upset her or make her angry. Instead, I made a list of people who'd still remember the incident, particularly those insightful types who might have felt the coverage was odd at the time.

It was a short list, but Buddy and Roseanna Bayard were at the top. They usually stayed for coffee and doughnuts after Mass, but should be home by now since it was just after noon. I didn't like drop-in callers or being counted among them. But I was a journalist and often had to set manners aside. I hoisted the *Advocate* volume I'd been perusing, locked up the office, and headed for the Bayards' home.

The temperature had dropped in the last hour, though the sun directly overhead peeked around the high clouds. Sure enough, both Bayard vehicles were parked out front. They had a garage, but Buddy had remodeled it for storing his photos.

Roseanna didn't look happy to see me. "What now?" she asked in a weary voice.

"Some questions," I said, following her into the living room, where Buddy was watching a Seattle Seahawks game.

He moved just enough to catch me out of the corner of his eye. "Hi, Emma," he said before turning back to the TV where a field goal attempt was under way.

I knew better than to interrupt. But the Baltimore Ravens' try was good and Buddy shut off the sound in disgust. "No defense," he grumbled. "What's up, Emma?"

First, I showed Buddy and Roseanna the newspaper article about Ernest Runkel's death. Then, as tactfully and succinctly as I could, I related my reaction to the paucity of information.

"I also flipped through the issues for the next few months," I added. "There was no mention of your father's death. That's odd because Marius Vandeventer always published former residents' death notices. We still do. Can you explain any of this?"

Buddy shrugged. "Ma told me when Pa died. I suppose she got word of it from Vida. I don't think Ma gave a damn whether it was put in the paper or not, since he was drunk at the time. She'd written Pa off years ago."

That made a certain kind of sense. Perhaps Vida—or Marius—had accommodated Gen's wishes. I wouldn't have been so generous.

"To get back to Ernest's disaster," I said, turning to the front page of the second January edition, "did the story bother you in any way?"

"You bet," Buddy retorted. "I wondered how a guy like Runkel could have been such a damned idiot."

"You mean it was totally out of character?" I asked.

"Yes," Roseanna replied as she reread the lead story before looking up. "He'd talked about doing it, but everybody thought it was a joke. You know, to get a rise out of Vida."

Again, that part made sense. Maybe, in retaliation, Vida had begun to goad him, forcing his hand. People *did* act out of character now and then. If nothing else, I was beginning to get a clearer picture of the Runkel marriage.

"Honestly," Roseanna said with a wary expression, "I don't see anything peculiar. Granted, there aren't any details, but Ernest couldn't tell them, and if Andy really was there—though it doesn't mention his name—you say he ran off."

"But that's my point," I asserted. "It's what the article *doesn't* tell the reader that makes the difference."

Buddy was scratching his beard and scowling. "Thirty years ago, Marius didn't print all the news. He was . . . discreet. He didn't want to cause trouble or offend readers if he could help it. You're the one who brought a different style to the paper, Emma. You even print the names of people who get picked up for drunk driving."

"That's a matter of public record and as such, it's news," I stated. Buddy was right: Marius had definitely treated his fellow Alpiners with kid gloves. And I had been heavily criticized for what I considered my integrity as a journalist. "Okay," I said, and sighed. "Maybe it's a case of 'least said, soonest mended.' Did you know your dad was involved in Ernest's death?"

"I heard some rumors that he'd been there," Buddy

replied, beginning to sound defensive. He'd turned all the way around in his recliner, and Roseanna sat down on the footstool next to him. "To be brutally honest, I didn't pay much attention to what people said about my father. We were . . . I guess you'd call it 'estranged.' "

The bitterness in Buddy's voice made me feel sorry for him. His childhood must have been miserable, with a drunken father and an unloving mother. No wonder he was irascible at times. The family he'd built with Roseanna was a marvel I hadn't considered until now. Maybe as a lonely child, he'd determined that his life would be different, that unhappiness wasn't genetic. Maybe it was his faith, or Roseanna herself who had shown him how to love. Perhaps he'd had so much unrequited love stored inside that it had burst like a dam when he started his family.

Roseanna had moved closer to her husband. "Why are you spending a Sunday looking up all this stuff? Isn't it up to Milo?" she inquired, breaking the awkward silence.

"Of course," I replied. "But this is what's called investigative reporting. I'm not bound by such strict rules and regulations like Milo is. I also tend to look beyond mere facts."

Buddy took Roseanna's hand. "It seems to me you're looking damned hard at us."

I shook my head. "That's only because it was your mother who was poisoned."

Roseanna gave me a challenging look. "But now you've got Buddy's dad involved in Ernest Runkel's nutty accident. Is all this going into the paper?"

"Of course not," I shot back. "The only way I'd print any of this is if it had a direct bearing on who killed Genevieve."

"Rot." Roseanna swung her head around to look up at Buddy. "I'm beginning to feel persecuted."

Buddy didn't say anything, but the beleaguered expression he wore spoke volumes.

I stood up. "I should be heading home. I went straight to the office from church."

Buddy pointed to the bound volume that now lay on the floor. "To look up that old crap?"

I was the one who now felt defensive. "Aren't you interested in who killed your mother? Don't you want to know if you have a half brother?" I pointed my toe at the old newspapers. "I look for answers everywhere. You'd be surprised how many of them come from the past, especially in a small town where things don't change very swiftly."

"I still say Ma's death was a fluke," Buddy declared, rising from the recliner but keeping Roseanna's hand in his. "Come on, Emma. Why do people kill other people? For gain or for love, right?"

"True, but—"

Buddy interrupted me. "According to the lawyer, Mr. Vaughn, Ma's estate is worth—we guessed—more than two hundred and fifty thousand dollars. That's mainly for the condo, which was paid off a few years back. She had about four thousand dollars in savings, plus a fifty-grand IRA. It's enough to put the kids through college."

I didn't respond. Collecting the newspaper volume, I started for the door.

"I don't intend to share," Buddy huffed as both he and Roseanna followed me. "If this character who claims he's Ma's son ever shows up again, he'll have to prove it. Frankly, I think he's a crook. As the sole heir, I don't have to pay inheritance tax, because the estate's less than seven hundred thousand. That's the law."

Even as I turned the doorknob, Buddy continued his diatribe. "So if people don't kill for money, it's for love. I don't think Ma had a guy hanging around for the last five years. Good God, she was close to seventy. And who in Alpine would consider her a rival? Mary Lou Blatt? Darlene Adcock? Annie Jeanne? Come on, Emma, you're just looking for headlines."

On that contentious note, I headed for my car.

But I still felt sorry for Buddy.

INSTEAD OF GOING HOME, I WENT BACK TO ST. MILDRED'S. Ben was on the playfield, teaching some of the parochial school students how to make free throws. Judging from the sweat that trickled down his reddened face, this was not a day of rest for my brother.

"Want to play?" he called to me.

"No, thanks," I shouted. "Can you still dunk like you did at Blanchet High?"

"Sure, if I have a ladder," Ben replied, tossing the ball to a redheaded boy of twelve. "Are you in need of spiritual guidance?"

"Some kind of guidance," I admitted. "Can I pull you from the game?"

Ben waved at the half-dozen kids who were passing the ball around the top of the key. "Later, fellas," he called. "Keep practicing. Focus, relax at the line."

We went into the rectory, which felt uncommonly warm. "Is this the tropics?" I asked.

"Damn," Ben breathed. "Annie Jeanne's turned the heat up again. She's always cold. No body fat. Let me adjust the thermostat."

I followed him down the hall where the control panel was located just outside the pastor's study.

"Eighty-eight?" I said, leaning over his shoulder to look at the current setting. "I may pass out."

Ben led the way into the study. "I'm already hot as a fresh tamale. You want something to drink?"

"What've you got?"

"Beer," he said, turning to a small refrigerator in back of his desk. "Dennis Kelly kept chocolate in there. He swears it tastes better cold. I've got beer and bottled water and some diet pop. What'll you have?"

I grimaced. "I don't drink diet, I prefer water out of Burl Creek, and you know I'm no beer lover. But I'll drink one anyway. I feel as if I've put in a long day already."

"Who hasn't?" Ben retorted, taking two cans of Bud Light out of the little fridge. "I've got two Eucharist ministers down with flu, so I had to bring Holy Communion to the nursing home after Mass. Tonight I'm going to Monroe to say the five o'clock at St. Mary of the Valley. Their regular priest is out of town."

I was only beginning to realize the responsibilities that Ben had taken on in Alpine. Sunday was not a day of rest, nor were the other days of the week. I hated to burden him with my problems, but if he was a priest forever in the order of Melchizedek, he was also forever my brother.

So I unloaded. Ben listened patiently, sipping beer and occasionally frowning. Unlike Milo and the Bayards, he took me seriously.

"I'm not sure if I've got all this straight," Ben said when I'd finished. "You're trying to tie in a thirty-year-old accident with Genevieve's poisoning. It's a stretch. But life's a tapestry, with threads appearing and reappearing over the years."

"In this case," I put in, "it's more like a quilt. A crazy quilt."

"Exactly." He frowned again. "So what did Gen do with all the money she made off those quilts?"

"That's what I'd like to know," I responded, shifting in my chair as the afternoon sun came through the window. "Even if she could make two or three a year, she should have had more than four grand in her savings account. Buddy and

Roseanna never mentioned her being a lavish spender. Fur-thermore, she bought a relatively inexpensive condo back when prices were really low in Spokane."

"The other son," Ben said.

I stared at him. "You mean she supported him?"

My brother shrugged. "Why—if he is her son—does he keep such a low profile? That suggests something shady. Maybe Gen spent money on lawyers and bail bondsmen."

"That's possible," I allowed. "I hope Milo gets some in-formation back from Sacramento tomorrow."

"Are you thinking this Knuler character may have offed his mother for money?" Ben asked.

"Considering the modest size of her estate and the fact he'd only get half of it," I replied, "I'd think she'd be worth more to him alive than dead. She might have been his cash cow with those quilts of hers. Besides, it appears he didn't ar-rive in Alpine until after Gen died. I don't see how he could have done it—unless he got here Monday and spent the night in his car. It seems unlikely that he was the one who sneaked into the rectory kitchen and doctored the cheesecake."

"Somebody did," Ben pointed out. "What if Gen had de-cided to cut him off? There's a motive."

I sighed. "A motive," I repeated. "Any motive I can think of is weak. Buddy and Roseanna could have killed Gen for the same reason. None of it makes sense. If only I could speak freely to Vida . . ."

Ben leaned back in his chair. "There's the rub." He spoke softly and looked at me with steady brown eyes.

I shifted my gaze to a fat robin on the windowsill. "I know," I murmured. "Am I steering clear of the obvious?"

"Maybe," Ben allowed. "It's unthinkable, of course. It's also unavoidable."

Sadly, I nodded. "Vida hated Gen. She suspected Ernest

of being unfaithful with the woman. She may even have blamed Gen in some weird way for the accident. Gen's ex-husband egging Ernest on, perhaps even causing the disaster—or intentionally making it happen. But," I continued, raising my voice a bit, "even if Vida has the best motive, she wouldn't have done such a thing. Besides, she didn't get back to Alpine until after Gen died."

"Vida's hardly the homicidal type," Ben noted. "Though I understand your reluctance to bring up such a touchy subject with her."

The robin was pecking diligently at something in the windowsill's wood. "I'd never consider Vida a suspect," I stated firmly. All the same, I suppressed a shudder as I recalled the near glee that Vida had exhibited when her old enemy, Thyra Rasmussen, had dropped dead in the *Advocate*'s newsroom. I put both elbows on Ben's desk and propped up my chin. I was still eyeing the busy robin; the bird eyed me back.

"Damn!" I exclaimed, my head jerking up.

Ben gave me a startled look. "What?"

I was utterly dismayed. "Vida *did* get home before Gen died." The words dropped like lead.

Ben scowled. "What're you talking about?"

I pulled and fretted my shaggy brown hair. "She told me she got back late, but she didn't."

"I don't get it."

"It was the bird," I said, pointing toward the window. "Somebody—maybe it was Vida or possibly Bill Blatt—mentioned that Buck forgot to cover Cupcake that Monday, but Vida returned before dark to keep the canary from having a conniption fit."

Ben looked thoughtful. "In other words, Vida doesn't have an alibi for the time frame when the glipizide was put into the cheesecake."

"It's too stupid," I declared. "But why would she fib about her return?"

Ben shrugged, but said nothing.

I looked out the window again. The robin was gone. I'd probably scared it with my loud exclamation and frantic gestures.

God knows, I'd certainly scared myself.

TWENTY

B EN AND I TOSSED IDEAS AND THEORIES AROUND FOR AL-
most an hour. On the surface, we didn't seem to be getting anywhere. But my brain was stirring in some distant
place I couldn't quite bring into focus. Or maybe I didn't
want to. Vida still was the key. I was sure of that much. The
problem was how to approach her.

But first, I felt I should say hello to Annie Jeanne.

She was sitting up on the bed, huddled under a quilt—
presumably made by Gen Bayard. She seemed glad to see me.
"Sit in the rocker, Emma dear," she said. "It seems so cold
today. I was making notes on organ music for Advent, but my
fingers got so stiff I had to quit. Do you think we'll have frost
tomorrow?"

"It's that time of year," I allowed, lowering myself into
the old rather spindly rocker. "Usually, we have frost by the
end of October."

"Yes—'the frost is on the pumpkin' and so forth." She
smiled and chafed her hands.

"I was glad to see you in church," I said. "You must feel
better."

"I do." Annie Jeanne pulled the quilt closer. "I'm just cold. But I'm trying to put Gen's death into perspective. I know she's at peace with the Lord. Father Ben assures me that's so." Her eyes, which had misted a bit, roamed over the different quilt pieces. "This is a crazy quilt Gen made for me. See, she's used fabrics that symbolize our friendship."

I got up from the rocker and went over to the bed. Sure enough, there were patches with a schoolhouse, a church, mountains, trees, waterfalls, and even a small town scene.

"So clever, don't you think?" Annie Jeanne remarked. "She sent this to me for my birthday two years ago."

"She must have spent a lot of time going through fabrics," I noted. "Some of these almost look like photographs."

Annie Jeanne giggled. "They are! I don't know a single thing about computers, but Gen told me that if you manage them properly, you can learn all kinds of craft tricks. What she did was to take some of her own pictures and transfer them to plain fabric. Then she'd work them into the quilt. Isn't that amazing?"

"Yes, it is." I sat down next to Annie Jeanne and peered more closely at the different pieces. "I'm farsighted," I confessed. "I think I'm about ready for glasses."

"You'd look nice in glasses," Annie Jeanne said. "Brown frames, to set off your pretty brown eyes."

I nodded, but was more intrigued by the quilt than improving myself. "Why, this is a photo of Alpine. When was it taken?"

Annie Jeanne tapped the small-town fabric. "Before Gen moved away. It's Front Street at Christmas. See the decorations?"

The view included the courthouse, the Whistling Marmot Movie Theatre, and even the *Advocate* office. There were some cars, too, though they were too small to discern the models' age. Some of the holiday décor looked familiar. It had been only five or six years since Mayor Fuzzy Baugh had been coaxed into spending a small portion of the city's budget for total replacements.

"The quilt has a theme," Annie Jeanne pointed out. "See in each corner? There's an initial for each of us. The *A* and the *G* in the upper and lower left-hand corners stand for Amity, or friendship, and Giggles—for all the fun we had. Every piece in that half of the quilt has some reference to the two of us, growing up together—the church, the school, Old Mill Park, and so on. The *J* and the *H*—her middle name was Helene—on the other side represent Joy and Happiness. Or Health. I forget. Maybe both."

There were only two photo transfers on the right half of the quilt. One was of a church organ, right under the *J* for Jeanne. The other was at the bottom, just above the *H* for Helene. It was of a bridge with a waterfall in the foreground. I couldn't help but shiver as recognition dawned. The landscape looked like Deception Falls.

"You see?" Annie Jeanne said with a gentle poke in my upper arm. "You're cold, too. I think your brother likes to suffer. Offering it up, no doubt, for the poor souls in purgatory."

I ignored the comment. "That's Deception Falls, isn't it?" I said, pointing to the panel above the *H*. "Why is that special?"

Annie Jeanne frowned, but quickly brightened. "Picnics," she said. "Yes, of course. That must be it. We used to have picnic lunches there."

The hesitation in Annie Jeanne's response made me wonder. There definitely was a picnic area just off the highway by the falls. I'd gone there myself. It might even be true that Annie Jeanne and Gen had picnicked there. But Annie Jeanne hadn't needed to think about the other patches. I had an uneasy feeling that Deception Falls might be included for a different reason. That piece of fabric wasn't on the friendship half of the quilt, but under Joy and Happiness. Whose happiness? I didn't know how quilts were put together, but it appeared to be the last piece, way down in the corner above the *H* for Helene.

A very strange idea was forming at the back of my brain.

"Gen must have worked on this for a long time," I noted.

Annie Jeanne nodded with vigor. "My, yes. Ages, it took her. That's why I only got it two years ago. She worked on it in her leisure hours. As she told me, it was a labor of love."

I moved away from the bed. Gen's concept was charming, her execution was clever, and her workmanship was flawless. But for some reason, I wanted to distance myself from that quilt. There was a sinister quality about Gen's handiwork, though I could only begin to guess what it was.

"I should go now," I said. "I don't want to tire you out."

"Oh, I'm feeling much stronger," Annie Jeanne assured me. "And," she added with a big smile, "I enjoy the company. Mary Jane Bourgette and Betsy O'Toole are coming again tomorrow and Tuesday, but after that, your dear brother and I will be on our own."

Only a slight frown indicated that the prospect upset her. Or perhaps she was hinting that I should take over where Mary Jane and Betsy were leaving off. I didn't volunteer, however. It'd do Annie Jeanne good to get back into her old routine.

Ben was on the phone when I paused by his office. He pointed to the receiver, mouthed "blah-blah-blah," and waved me off.

I sat in the Honda for two or three minutes before deciding what to do next. If only I could fast-forward the digital clock on the dashboard and make it indicate tomorrow morning. I felt thwarted by weekend closures in high places, particularly Sacramento where questions about Tony Knuler might still be answered.

Finally, I drove out of the parking lot and started up Fourth Street. My intention was to turn left on Tyee and head for Vida's. But when I got to the intersection, my nerve failed me. I kept going up the mountainside to Fir and my little log house.

I had a limited choice of activities at home. The TV was gone; so was the stereo system and my laptop. Reduced to the Stone Age, I decided to clean Adam's room, including the closet. I'd resisted throwing out any of his belongings after he moved away to college. But nearly fifteen years had passed: Adam wasn't coming back home. In fact, he'd e-mailed me Friday from his frozen Alaskan outpost to say that maybe it'd be more convenient if he stayed at the rectory with Ben during the Christmas holiday. I'd fired off a responding e-mail, telling him that if he didn't stay with his dear old mother, I'd start nasty rumors about him and a saucy walrus named Tina Marie. My son had knuckled under.

After ten minutes, I'd managed to get rid of eleven worn crew socks, four ragged sweatshirts, and a pile of underwear so old that one pair of shorts was decorated with Darth Vader.

But housework wasn't distracting me from my obsession. Standing up from a crouching position by the closet, I vowed to confront Vida. I could do nothing else except drive myself crazy.

The phone rang as I was hauling the garbage bag out of Adam's room. Maybe it was Vida. I grabbed the receiver off the end table next to the sofa.

"Hi, Dreamboat," said Rolf Fisher. "I take it our love hasn't sunk yet. Or did we pass like ships in the night?"

It wasn't that I hadn't thought of Rolf or had forgotten

his kiss. But I'd been so caught up in the mystery of Gen's death that he'd slipped slightly under my radar screen. Or maybe I really was trying to forget about the spark he'd ignited. It'd be safer that way.

"Oh, Rolf!" I cried, and uncharacteristically burst into tears.

"Hey—what's wrong?" He sounded justifiably startled. "Are you missing me that much?"

Maybe I was. I fought for control. "It's . . . this . . . damned murder," I blubbered. "It's . . . taking me in a . . . direction I don't . . . want to go." Snorting and sniffling, I paused to blow my nose. So much for the glamorous outfit that had put me in deep debt. I sounded like a sick rhinoceros. My image was sorely damaged.

"Do you want me to drive up?"

I sighed. "Oh—no, of course not." Snort, sniffle, squeak. "The afternoon's moving along." Clearing of throat, another blast into the Kleenex. "We both have to work tomorrow. I'll be okay. Really. I'm just tired and frustrated."

I'd expected a provocative comeback, but Rolf was serious. "I get the impression your sources are unavailable on a Sunday. I also infer that you suspect someone you don't want to be the killer."

"Not really," I said, at my most piteous. "It's that I don't want to hurt or upset the person who knows the most about . . . certain events which may or may not lead to finding out who killed Genevieve Bayard."

"And that would be . . . ?"

I opened my mouth to answer, but abruptly shut it again.

Rolf waited. When I didn't say anything, he spoke again. "Your House & Home editor, the redoubtable Vida Runkel. Am I right?"

Hearing Rolf say her name out loud unsettled me. "I don't

suspect her of killing anyone," I said staunchly. "It's the background I'm trying to figure out. Only Vida may know the truth, but I'm afraid . . . Oh, why burden you with this? It's small-town stuff. Stick to your international hot spots and Beltway shenanigans."

"I think I mentioned that my beat is the Puget Sound basin," Rolf said in a droll voice. "If you want to unload, go ahead. I'm sitting here in my overpriced Queen Anne Hill condo watching the rain pelt hapless tourists at the Seattle Center."

I was tempted to take up Rolf's offer. But it would only delay my visit to Vida's. "Never mind," I said, and sighed.

"When do you want me to arrive this coming weekend?" he asked.

The query took me aback. "I . . . I don't know yet. I mean—"

He interrupted me. "Maybe you don't want to see me." He almost sounded serious.

"I do!" I exclaimed. "I do," I repeated, lowering my voice. "Friday seems so far away. Can we talk on the phone in the meantime?"

"Sure," Rolf responded. "We can do a Harry-Met-Sally thing with both of us in our beds, talking to each other and not acknowledging that we're deeply in love."

The tears had stopped. Maybe the reason I hadn't dwelled on Rolf was because he was right. I was afraid of love. It had brought me great pain. And great joy.

"Whatever we do," Rolf went on when I didn't respond, "don't let Spencer Fleetwood get the story first for KSKY."

"You know Spence?" I asked, surprised.

"Sure. You think we ignore the other media just because they're inferior?"

"No, of course not. Don't you like him?"

"All these months that I've pined for you, Emma Lord, I

figured Spence was my biggest rival. How come you two never hit it off?"

"I don't know . . . the media rivalry, maybe."

"In novels, that's what sparks passion. Hey, I better go. I think a family of four from Fresno just drowned outside the Experience Music Project. Kisses on your face and anywhere else I can reach. Bye."

Despite my brief crying jag, somehow Rolf had managed to inject steel in my spine. I put on my jacket, grabbed my purse, and drove to Vida's.

Defying the gray clouds that had begun to gather again, she was out in the garden.

"Well now!" she exclaimed. "What are you doing here?"

I noticed that Vida was wearing gardening gloves and holding a pair of shears. A half-dozen stalks of bedraggled chrysanthemums lay near her feet.

"We need to talk," I said, going down the walk. "How about some tea?"

Vida grimaced. "I really shouldn't." She looked up at the glowering sky. "It's going to rain any minute, and I wouldn't be surprised if there was snow mixed with it. The temperature's dropped ten degrees in the last hour."

"It is colder," I admitted. "Can't your gardening wait?"

Vida shook her head. "I'm picking a bouquet for the cemetery. Tomorrow is my mother's birthday. I don't want to take time off from work to do this. Nor do I relish tromping around in snow up there. The cemetery is so lumpy."

I knew what Vida meant. The local burial ground had been established over a hundred years ago just below First Hill, when Alpine was known as Nippon. The loggers hadn't yet arrived, but miners were already digging into the veins of silver and gold on Tonga Ridge. Several had died in a cave-in, and had been buried just below the mine shafts. When Carl Clemans bought his parcel of forest a few years later, he was heedless of the rocky turf and proclaimed the rudimentary site as the town's official cemetery.

"I'll ride up with you," I said. "When do you want to leave?"

Vida wiped her forehead with the back of her hand. "Oooh . . . I could go as soon as I pick a couple more mums. I have some amber ones alongside the house. Do you want to wait in the car?"

"Yours or mine?"

Vida shrugged. "As long as your car is here . . ."

"Fine. See you in a minute."

Vida disappeared around the corner of the house. I turned on the Honda's radio. It was always set to KSKY, since few other stations came through clearly in our mountain aerie.

"It's two-thirty in Sky Country, and this is Rey Fernandez on KSKY-AM, the voice of Skykomish County, with the latest breaking news. Deputy Sheriff Sam Heppner has just announced that the burglary ring which has been plaguing local residents has been uncovered by county law authorities. Two young men working as valets at the ski lodge were arrested less than an hour ago and charged with breaking and entering, grand theft, and destruction of property. As minors, their names have not been released pending notification of their families."

I punched my fist on the horn, startling myself and a Manx cat sitting in front of a neighboring house. Had Milo known about the bust when I spoke to him on the phone? He'd said they were getting close to finding the perps. But even if I couldn't get the story in the paper until Wednesday, the sheriff should have given me a heads-up.

Rey, Spence's backup DJ, had finished his bulletin and was playing the station's Sunday classical music offerings. Seeing Vida come out of her house, I switched off the radio.

"Ooof!" she cried, settling into the passenger seat with a thud. "Goodness, why are you scowling?"

I relayed KSKY's latest scoop.

"Good for Milo," said Vida. "A shame my nephew Billy isn't in town today. If he'd been on duty, he would have notified me at once."

Or else, I thought.

"I know how they did it," I said. "I'm surprised it took this long to catch those valets. They simply took the cars they parked to the owners' homes—including mine—and broke in."

"Why would they need to break in if they had keys?" Vida inquired.

It was a good point. "Maybe some people don't have all their keys on one ring. Or else the robbers thought if they broke in, they wouldn't be suspected of having any keys, let alone the customers' cars. Anyone seeing the car itself would simply assume it belonged there."

"Clever in its way," Vida murmured. "Henry Bardeen must be furious. I must call Buck as soon as I get back."

It took only five minutes to reach the cemetery and wend our way to the Blatt burial plot. Vida pulled out the vase that was installed by the monument and took it over to a faucet a few yards away. I gazed around me, aware that the Runkel plot was adjacent. It always made me sad to see the double headstone over Ernest's grave. His name and the dates of his birth and death were inscribed on the gray marble, which was only fitting. But the blank space for Vida was upsetting. I couldn't imagine her being dead; I couldn't envision Alpine without her.

"There now," she said, shoving the weather-beaten mums into the vase. "I'm afraid that's all that's left in my garden except for a few rosebuds that will never bloom fully. If we have frost tonight, they'll be blighted."

Blighted. The word stuck in my mind. Ernest, blighted and cut down in middle age. Annie Jeanne, a blighted blossom if there ever was one. Buddy Bayard, blighted in childhood by lack of love. Most people were blighted, in so many different ways. I, too, had felt an early touch of frost. But maybe Rolf Fisher was bringing some sunlight into my life.

"I see Ernest's birthday was last week," I noted. "November eighth."

"Yes." Vida was pulling some tufts of overgrown grass from around the base of the Blatt monument. "We were born just six months apart." She straightened up. "Shall we go?"

"Sure."

We both trudged uphill to where I'd parked my car at the edge of the narrow winding road. Vida chattered all the way, commenting on the various graves: Bertha May Amundson, Arthur Trews, Elmer Tuck, Old Doc Dewey. It seemed as if she knew everyone who was buried in the cemetery. I wasn't paying much attention, even as she continued her running commentary after we started to drive away.

There had been no flowers commemorating Ernest Runkel's birthday. The cemetery's groundskeepers left bouquets and plants for at least two weeks. Indeed, Ernest's headstone was surrounded by tall grass and a couple of weeds. It wasn't well-tended like the Blatt plot and even a few of the other Runkels' graves. That seemed very odd.

But the idea that had been growing in my head was far from blighted.

In fact, it was beginning to flourish.

And I didn't like it one bit.

TWENTY-ONE

"WHAT REALLY HAPPENED TO ERNEST?" I asked.

Vida and I were sitting in her kitchen, waiting for the teakettle to boil. Since returning to her house, we had talked of other things, mostly the arrest of the valet parking attendants. But I'd finally worked up my courage to ask the troublesome question that had been beating up my brain even before I read the article about Ernest.

Vida evinced surprise. "Whatever are you talking about?"

"The accident at the falls," I said, keeping my voice steady. "I went back and read the coverage in the *Advocate*. It doesn't make sense. Was Andy Bayard really there?"

Vida made an awful face. "I'm afraid so." The teakettle whistled; she got up to take it off the burner. "I suppose you're thinking there was foul play. Or that Andy caused the accident that killed Ernest."

I didn't respond. Vida put two bags in the kettle and waited for the brew to steep.

"I'm surprised you never asked about Ernest's death before," Vida remarked. "Tact on your part, I always assumed."

"That's true," I admitted. "I didn't want to reopen old wounds."

Vida nodded. "Very thoughtful. And I must confess, it was a ludicrous situation. At the time," she went on, pouring tea into our bone china cups, "there were people who couldn't talk to me about it without having to stifle their amusement. It was quite terrible."

"I imagine," I said as Vida sat down at the table.

She sighed and gazed at Cupcake, who was pecking at his cuttlebone. "We'll never know what really happened, of course. Andre Bayard was totally irresponsible. I can't think why Ernest asked him to go to the falls in the first place. Plenty of other people had trucks in Alpine. I suppose Andy had been drinking." Vida spoke in a dispassionate voice, pausing to blow on her tea. "I always assumed that Andy was also inebriated when he had that fatal accident down on Highway 18 or wherever it was outside of Seattle." She gave me her owlish look. "Did Buddy tell you about Andy's involvement?"

I hedged. "I think it was Buddy." There was no need to reveal that I'd interrogated Milo. That would further rile Vida. "You must have started with the paper just a few weeks after Ernest died," I remarked.

"Four weeks to the day," Vida said, and gave me an even harder stare.

We locked gazes for several seconds before Vida jumped up from the chair, turned her back on me, and bowed her head.

"I can't do this!" she cried, her voice shaking. "Please, Emma, leave me now."

It wasn't the reaction I'd expected. Vida's broad shoulders were quaking and she was stifling sobs. I went to her and put a hand on her back.

"Please, I didn't mean to upset you. Tell me what's wrong."

But Vida shook off my hand and stumbled away toward the back door. Speech seemed beyond her. Even Cupcake was watching his owner with a bright, beady eye.

"Good God," I murmured, pressing the hand she'd rejected to my forehead. I didn't know what to do.

Except to obey her command.

I left.

I SAT IN THE CAR FOR A FEW MINUTES, FEELING WRETCHED. Vida and I had both had emotional breakdowns in one day—and, I feared, for the same reason.

Ernest.

After five minutes of inertia, I used my cell phone to call Bernie Shaw and ask him a vital question. Bernie told me he'd have to check the records in his insurance office. The matter that I was inquiring about probably had been handled by his father, Cornelius. Would Monday be all right? I grimaced, but told him that was fine. It wasn't, but I didn't want to badger Bernie.

After ringing off, I drove to Driggers Funeral Home. With Gen's services set for Tuesday, Al might be at work. Too much time had already passed in preparing the body for burial.

"Emma!" Al exclaimed as he unlocked the door for me. "What's wrong? You look awful!"

Al never looked so good himself, having a gray complexion and wearing a perpetual air of mourning. "I have a question for you," I said, moving inside the beige foyer. Everything was beige at the funeral parlor. Except Al, of course. "Were you working for your father here when Ernest Runkel was killed?"

Al seemed struck dumb by the query. Instead of answering directly, he led me into the parlor, where he indicated I should sit on a beige love seat.

"I was just starting out in the business," he said in his doleful voice. "I went to college, you know, at WSU."

If I knew, I didn't remember the fact, but I nodded sagely.

"I must admit," Al continued as he sat down in a beige and brown bergère armchair, "I didn't work on Ernest. He'd been terribly mangled by the truck's wheels. My father didn't think I had enough experience." Al winced—or smiled. It was hard to tell. "I also think he wanted to spare me the gruesome sight. Why do you ask?"

I hesitated. But Al was discreet, even if his brassy wife, Janet, was not. "I'm trying to sort out this Genevieve Bayard homicide. It may sound crazy, but do you remember anything—anything at all—about rumors concerning Ernest and Gen?"

Al looked surprised. "Ernest Runkel and . . . No, not a thing. I assume you mean . . . *an affair?*"

"Possibly. Some intimates of the Runkels have suggested it." I paused, waiting to see if my words had evoked any long-forgotten gossip. If Janet Driggers had ever heard anything, she'd have reveled in telling her husband such a scandalous tale.

"I can't imagine," Al declared. "Ernest was a most upstanding citizen. His father—the one who started the ski lodge—helped my dad build the funeral home back in the thirties. They were always a very righteous family."

Righteous or self-righteous, I wondered. "There was nothing out of the ordinary about the burial or its preparations, I take it?"

"Not that I recall," Al replied. "Vida took over, of course. I do remember how much I admired her, under the circumstances. She was in control, not only of the arrangements, but of her emotions. I remember Pastor McLeod—he was at the

Presbyterian church long before Pastor Purebeck—saying that Vida was like a block of ice."

"And the three girls? How were they?"

"They're not cut from the same cloth as their mother," Al asserted. "All of them were extremely distraught. I believe one of them—Beth, maybe—fainted at the grave site."

I nodded sympathetically. "It was a closed casket service, I suppose."

"Definitely." Al sighed. "I wasn't spared when the next two ugly deaths occurred. Both were loggers, within a three-week period of each other. One was run over by an eighteen-wheeler, and the other had fallen from a . . ."

I wasn't listening to Al. I was thinking through what he'd told me. It was what I'd expected. And feared.

". . . get hardened in a hurry," he concluded.

"Yes," I said rather absently. "I'm afraid that's true," I added, giving Al what I hoped was a sympathetic smile before I stood up. "I suppose Vida made sure Ernest had the best of everything."

Al was also on his feet. "Funny you should mention it," he said, walking me to the foyer in his slow, dignified gait. "She didn't, actually. She went lowball. So to speak. It seemed odd at the time, but my father figured that she was so mad at Ernest for getting killed doing such a stupid stunt that she refused to spend a large amount on his burial. Not that we minded, of course. We never coerce clients into overspending."

"Penny-pinching on Vida's part does seem odd," I remarked.

Al shrugged his thin shoulders. "As it turned out, Vida was short of money. I guess she didn't get much out of Ernest's insurance. Maybe there was a rider excluding coverage from self-incurred misadventure. In any event, that's why

she went to work for the paper so soon after Ernest's departure."

"Yes," I said. "Perhaps that's it. Vida still had three
daughters to raise."

The bell chimed just as Al touched the door's brass lever.
He glanced through the peephole. "Hunh. I don't recognize
whoever this is. Excuse me, Emma."

The young man who stood on the threshold wasn't familiar to me, either. "Are you Mr. Driggers?" he inquired in a
rather anxious voice.

Al identified himself as such. The young man gave me the
once-over, then turned again to Al.

"I'm Anthony Knuler, and I've come to claim my
mother's body."

Al Driggers was schooled to never lose his aplomb. "I
see," he said, his eyes fixed on the newcomer. "Come inside,
Mr. Knuler. Ms. Lord is just leaving."

But Ms. Lord was doing no such thing. I stepped back and
rooted myself into the beige carpet. "On second thought," I
said pointedly, "I'd like to talk to Mr. Knuler. He stood me up
the other day at breakfast."

If Al was taken aback, he didn't show it. "Well. Then
both of you must come into the parlor."

But Tony Knuler was giving me a hard blue-eyed stare.
"You own the local paper?" he asked of me.

"That's right. I have to talk to you. It's important."

But Tony shook his head. "Not now. This is personal
stuff. I'll meet you someplace in an hour, okay?"

"No," I retorted. "You have a lousy track record for
keeping dates."

"Come on," Tony said roughly, "loosen up. I'm here to
get my mother's body. Don't be so mean."

"Maybe," Al put in before I could escalate matters, "we

should all go into the chapel and pray for a moment. That would settle everyone's nerves."

I knew he meant *tempers,* but I also noted the swift glance he gave me before turning in the opposite direction from the parlor. I wasn't sure what that glance meant, but I decided to play along.

"That's a good idea," I said, following Al. "Come on, Mr. Knuler, a couple of minutes of repose might do us both good."

Tony had no choice. With a reluctant sigh, he accompanied Al and me into the dimly lighted chapel. As soon as we moved down the aisle, I realized why Al had made his suggestion. At one side of the small, plain altar was a curtained room for mourners who wanted privacy but still wished to hear what was going on in the chapel. Al let me go into the front pew first. I knelt and said a quick Our Father and a Hail Mary.

"You're right," I said, leaning across Al to Tony Knuler. "I'll leave you now. I'm very sorry about your mother."

Tony seemed placated; Al looked impassive. I left the pew and the chapel, hoping that Tony wouldn't notice that I wasn't heading for the main exit.

It took me a couple of minutes to find the door to the private mourning area. The small room reminded me of a confessional, with its padded leather seats and concealing curtain. Maybe that was what I was going to hear—some kind of confession from Tony Knuler.

The first words I heard were his, and they sounded uneasy. "If you say so."

"I know, Mr. Knuler," Al replied slowly. "I've been through this countless times, trying to help grieving family members. Often, the chapel is the best place to talk. Serenity, you know, and peace of mind."

"Whatever," Tony muttered.

I figured Al's spiel was more for my benefit than Tony's. The stalling was to make sure I found the way into the eaves-dropping area. I blessed Al for his consideration, though he was probably breaking several rules of undertaker ethics.

"I assume," Al said in his most sympathetic manner, "you have legal documents proving you're the lawful son of Genevieve Ferrer Bayard?"

"You bet," Tony replied.

I couldn't see much except the two men's dim outlines, but I imagined Tony reaching into his black leather jacket and extracting some papers.

"Here," he said. "Birth certificate, marriage license of my mother and father, and my father's death certificate from two years ago. I had to go to Spokane to get all this stuff. Oh, there's some other paper showing my father's legal change of name around the time I was born."

"I'll study the birth certificate first," Al said. "I see your first name is actually Michael."

"Right. But my mother didn't want to call me Mike or Mickey or whatever, so she always called me Tony."

"Ah." Al was probably looking next at the marriage license. "I'm afraid I didn't realize your mother had remarried. Are you your parents' only issue?"

"Issue?"

"Offspring. Child," Al translated.

"Oh. You mean of my mother and father?"

"Yes."

"Yeah, I am. I know I've got a half brother here, but I never met him."

I heard the shuffling of papers. The vague outline that was Al moved in an uncharacteristically agitated manner. "I d-d-don't understand," Al said, his voice rising an octave. "This is impossible! It must be a—a mistake!"

"How do you mean?" Tony Knuler sounded annoyed.

Al took a moment to compose himself. He cleared his throat. "The name of the husband on this marriage certificate is Ernest Runkel. He died thirty years ago. I know, I helped bury him."

Tony Knuler chuckled unpleasantly. "Then, Mr. Undertaker, you buried the wrong man. Ernie Runkel died two years ago from diabetes."

I WASN'T REALLY STUNNED—JUST DISTRESSED THAT MY guesswork had proved right. All I could think of was Vida. Had she known? I was sure she did. My heart went out to her.

But I could barely contain myself in the small, rather stuffy room behind the curtain. I clenched my fists and my jaw to keep from giving my presence away. Besides, I had to listen closely. Tony Knuler was talking about his father's life with Genevieve.

"All I ever knew was that he'd skipped town and dumped his first wife," Tony was saying. "He didn't go into details, and I was just a kid. I didn't really care. The only weird part was that once or twice a year my mother's other son and his family would come to visit. Pop and I had to make ourselves scarce. I even had to hide my toys and stash everything in the basement. But Mom insisted, and there was no arguing with her. That's why I left home right out of high school. I don't think she liked kids very much."

"So," Al said in a thoughtful voice, "your . . . father legally changed his name to Knuler when you were born, which occurred quite soon after your parents married."

"So?"

"I'm sorry," Al apologized. "I wasn't casting aspersions— that is, criticizing your mother's and father's morals. I was simply trying to get the time line straight. Why Knuler?"

"It's some screwed-up way of spelling his real name,

Runkel. Besides, it's different. I've never run into anybody with that name. Hey, I've got all the legal stuff. Can I claim the body now? I know Mom would like to be next to Pop in Spokane. Or cremated, I guess. Pop's in a vase."

There was a muffled sound from Al. I didn't know if he was stifling laughter or trying not to throw up. Not only was I hearing some amazing revelations, but I was seeing—or at least hearing—a different side of our local mortician.

"Yes . . . well," said Al. "Really, we'll have to confer with your brother. Half brother, that is. You understand that what you've told me can't be confidential? There are legal issues here."

"Like what? Isn't all this stuff I showed you okay?"

"Yes, I assume it is," Al replied in a reasonable tone, "but that's not the point. From my perspective, this mortuary has buried a man under false pretenses. I have to look into our liability, perhaps even have the body exhumed for DNA purposes."

"Shit." Tony Knuler didn't sound pleased.

"Not," Al said quickly, "that it will interfere with your inheritance. Of course, you must share it with your brother, Buddy Bayard."

"That Vaughn guy in Spokane told me it can take a long time to get the money," Tony said in a petulant voice. "I need it now."

"You should ask Mr. Vaughn for an advance," Al said, his professional poise restored. "And I must beg you to be patient regarding your mother's remains. I'll have to confer with Mr. Bayard. Perhaps you'd like to join me in my office."

Al had risen. Tony didn't budge. "You're giving me the runaround," he declared.

"Not at all. There are procedures to be followed, especially in a complicated situation like this." Al was waiting for Tony to get up. "Come, Mr. Knuler, let's get started."

With a heavy sigh, Tony stood up. The two men exited the chapel. It was my signal to leave.

My brain was on overload. As I got into the Honda, I wondered if I'd short-circuit myself and explode. Unsure of what to do next, I again sat behind the steering wheel, trying to think. Big drops of rain splashed down on the windshield, distorting the trees and shrubs across the street in John Engstrom Park. Should I go to the Bayards'? Or Vida's? Or call Milo?

I chose the sheriff as the safest, least volatile person to confront. It wasn't up to me to accuse Vida of burying the wrong man or to inform Buddy that he really did have a brother. I dialed Milo's cell phone number, assuming that he might be at the office, questioning the parking valets.

I was right. But I didn't want to talk to him at his head-quarters, where we might be interrupted or overheard.

"You want me to come to your place?" he replied in a vexed tone. "I thought you were all hot to nail these perps and get your stuff back."

"I am," I said, "but I've learned something extremely important to Gen's investigation. Please?"

"Oh—hell, okay, I'll be there in twenty minutes."

Milo made it in thirty. "This better be good," he warned me, shaking the rain off his parka.

"It is. Let me get you a drink."

Milo didn't object. I poured us both a couple of stiff shots—more for my benefit than his. Fifteen minutes later, the sheriff was over halfway though his beverage and had already smoked two cigarettes. Unfortunately, so had I.

"Jesus Christ," he murmured. "You're positive about all this?"

I admitted that I hadn't seen Tony Knuler's documents, but Al had seemed convinced. "I think," I said, "I know why

Tony didn't want to meet me. He swiped that phone book from the motel to find my listing or that of the *Advocate*. I'm guessing he was looking for some background on Buddy and thought the newspaper would be a good source. But when he got to the diner that morning, he asked for a copy of the paper. Maybe he looked inside and saw Vida's name on her page. It might have spooked him. As incredible as it may seem to us, Tony may never have heard of her, at least not by name. In fact, I wonder if he sent Vida that note."

Milo scowled. "What note?"

I told him what the note had said and how Vida had reacted. "Tony seems ha ' up for money. He may have intended to blackmail Vida."

Milo held out his glass. ' could use a refill. Jesus, I can't take all this in."

"Neither can I," I said as the sheriff followed me out to the kitchen. "It's strange, but I'd never thought much about Ernest Runkel. He was so far in the background that I only considered him as some vague adjunct to Vida, like one of her hats. He was never really a *person*—if you know what I mean."

"Yeah, more or less," Milo said, leaning against the door frame. "Who's going to tell her?"

"Not me," I said, handing the sheriff his glass and adding another dash of bourbon to my own. "What's worse, how is she going to tell her daughters? I have a feeling they never knew their father wasn't dead."

"Why?" Milo asked, scratching his head as he sat down again in the easy chair. "What was the point?"

"I think I know that," I said, stealing one more cigarette from Milo. "Vida was aware that Ernest and Gen were having an affair. When did Vida not know everything that was going on? We only have Vida's word for it that Ernest was attempting the barrel stunt. Maybe it wasn't Ernest's idea; maybe it was Andy Bayard's. It sounds more like something an irresponsible drunk would do. I don't know why Ernest would go with him; they couldn't have been close friends. Maybe he went with Andy to tell him he was running away with his ex-wife. Or maybe he was trying to talk Andy out of doing the barrel trick."

Milo looked skeptical. "Are you saying they got into a fight and Ernest killed Andy?"

"No, I don't think that's what happened. There probably *was* an accident, with Andy in the barrel. And Ernest was the one who took off. Look," I said, tapping the coffee table. "If you're going to do such a wild-eyed stunt, you'd want an audience. But nobody was there except Ernest and Andy. It might have been a dress rehearsal. And when Andy got killed, Ernest decided it was the perfect time to make his exit and join Gen in Seattle or Spokane or wherever she was awaiting their baby."

"So Eeny Moroni covered for him?"

I gave a shake of my head. "No. Eeny covered for Vida."

Milo was still confounded. "I don't get it."

"Vida couldn't bear the idea that Ernest was leaving her for another woman. She paid Eeny to go along with her and bury Andy as Ernest. She had to cut a deal with Al Driggers's father, too. Not a bribe, but payback time. I didn't know until this afternoon that Ernest's dad had helped set up the senior Driggers's business. Vida had no money, because Eeny probably demanded some big bucks. I put in a call to Bernie Shaw today, but he won't get back to me until tomorrow. I'm convinced that Bernie will tell me that his office never paid any insurance to Vida."

"If Ernest was still alive, she wouldn't dare commit insurance fraud," Milo put in. "She's not a crook."

"Hardly," I said. "She's a staunch Presbyterian, and

accepting money that wasn't entitled to her would be ana-thema. Ernest was still alive—except to Vida. As far as she was concerned, once he'd abandoned her and Alpine, Ernest *was* dead."

With his third drink in hand, Milo was pondering. "Hell, I can't arrest Vida for lying. What am I supposed to do now?"

"Nothing," I said. "Even if Al digs up Andy Bayard, there's no evidence that Vida did anything wrong. She's mainly guilty of pride. But that's Vida—and I won't stand in judgment. Think of how she would have felt in this town. Having everybody know that her husband ran off with an-other woman would have destroyed her. It was bad enough that she knew. In fact, I'm convinced that she came to believe her own lie. People do that, you know."

"What about Gen?" Milo asked, lighting another ciga-rette.

"For all I know, Gen was in on it." I started to reach for Milo's pack, but noticed that he had only a couple of ciga-rettes left. I took one anyway and ignored the sheriff's frown. "Gen and Andy had been divorced for years. She wouldn't have cared if Vida herself had run over Andy with that truck. All Gen wanted was to marry her baby's father. Not that chil-dren were important to her. She was interested only in men and love and sex."

"Why don't I ever meet anybody like that?" Milo said in a mournful voice.

I smiled. "A woman like Gen would drive you nuts."

"And end up dead," Milo conceded. "Hey, this makes a great story, but it still doesn't tell us who poisoned Gen."

I sipped my drink instead of saying anything.

The sheriff, however, expected a response. "Well?"

"Tell me," I said slowly, "do you think those two kids from the ski lodge are responsible for all the break-ins?"

"It's too soon to be sure," Milo replied, eyeing me quizzically. "They're both students—more or less—and they're from Everett. They aren't real clear about Alpine addresses. 'A blue house near a creek,' 'a place by a church'—that kind of vague stuff."

"The Pikes get home from Florida tomorrow, don't they?"

Milo shrugged. "I guess so. Why?"

"I'll bet you a dinner at the ski lodge that those valets didn't hit the Pike house."

"Why not? Because of the MO?"

I nodded. "That, and the religious medal that was found there," I said. "I asked Ben to see if anyone from the parish had lost it. I'm sure he hasn't found a claimant. The initials were MAR. I figure they stand for Michael Anthony Runkel."

TWENTY-TWO

W HY RUNKEL?" MILO ASKED. "I THOUGHT YOU SAID THE name had been changed to Knuler about the time this Tony character was born."

"It had," I agreed. "But this is a Miraculous Medal, and the person who receives it has to be enrolled in the society. We don't know exactly when Ernest changed his name. It could have been after Tony was born. Maybe they never got around to changing Tony Runkel to Tony Knuler. That might explain why, when it came to religious documents, Gen used her son's birth name."

Milo finished his drink and put the glass aside. "Why would Knuler break into the Pikes' house?"

"I'm not sure," I admitted. "It probably had something to do with his mother's quilt patterns. Or maybe the ones she stole from other members of the Burl Creek Thimble Club. He might have done it at his mother's urging. If she'd passed off copied patterns as her own, she'd be guilty of fraud."

Milo laughed out loud. "So this is all about quilts? What's wrong with a good old Hudson Bay blanket? That's what I've got. Are you sure you aren't off on a spur line that doesn't go anywhere?"

I shot Milo a disparaging look. "Quilters are artisans," I informed him. "They take great pride in their work and their creativity. When was the last time you saw a plain old blanket on display at a county fair or in a museum?"

"I haven't been to a museum in twenty-five years," Milo asserted. "I went to the aquarium in Seattle a couple of years ago, though. That was really something. You wouldn't believe the octopuses."

I sighed. Sometimes the chasm between us seemed so deep I couldn't see the bottom. "Never mind," I said, standing up and emptying the ashtray into the fireplace. "I'm not saying Gen was poisoned because of her quilts." I froze next to the sofa. "Or am I?"

"What now? Was she making quilts out of hemp?"

I ignored the sheriff's sarcasm. "Never mind. I just thought of something, but it's probably crazy."

Milo looked at his watch. "Jeez, it's going on five. I should check back in at the office. Thanks for the weird story—and the booze."

"You don't believe me?" I demanded as Milo put on his parka.

"I don't know what to think," he replied. "I'll see Al and try to track down this Knuler guy." Milo pulled the parka's hood over his head. "What the hell do we do about Vida?"

"I wish I knew."

The sheriff shook his head, and left.

THERE WAS ONLY ONE PERSON IN WHOM I COULD CONfide: my priest, my pastor, my brother.

"Do you want to come for dinner?" I asked Ben over the phone.

"I'm supposed to have dinner with the sheriff," my brother replied. "He's cooking that steelhead he caught. What are you having?"

"A fit," I said. "And I don't think Milo's making dinner tonight. He's kind of busy."

"Hmm. You sound a bit peculiar. Okay, I'll be over in a few."

I had no appetite and I didn't feel like cooking. I found a chunk of beef in the freezer and decided to make stew and dumplings. The phone rang as I was taking the meat out of the microwave. It was Ben.

"I've got a problem," he said, sounding worried. "Annie Jeanne won't let me in her room. Any chance you could coax her out of there? I don't like leaving her if she's upset."

"I can try," I said in a doubtful voice. "I'll put dinner on hold and be right there."

The night was dark and wet. I forced myself to drive carefully. After three drinks, I didn't want to cause an accident and add more complications to the sheriff's already crowded plate.

Ben met me at the rectory door. "I thought Annie Jeanne might like me to pick up something for her from the store since I planned to go out," Ben explained, leading the way down the hall. "But she didn't answer at first when I called to her. Finally, she told me to go away. She was praying. That was at least half an hour ago. Now she won't answer or let me in."

"She seemed in good spirits when I saw her earlier," I said. But I, too, was worried.

At Annie Jeanne's door, Ben stepped aside so I could take over. I knocked first, hard. Then I shouted her name. A note of anxiety coated my voice.

"Do you have a key?" I asked Ben.

"No. Or if there is one, I don't know where it's kept."

The door was old, but solid.

Ben read my mind. "Do you think Dennis Kelly would appreciate me busting up his property?"

"I think he'd rather you did that than let Annie Jeanne have a complete breakdown."

Ben heaved a sigh. "Okay, here goes Superpriest."

My brother had inherited our father's sturdy build. He backed up to get a running start, then hurtled across the narrow hall, smashing against the door.

"Damn!" he cried, rubbing his shoulder.

"Are you okay?"

"No," Ben replied, testing the shoulder by moving it up and down, "but the door sure as hell is. I need some kind of battering ram."

I had moved back to the door, listening to see if I could hear any kind of reaction from Annie Jeanne. Sure enough, I detected the sound of movement. Maybe she was reconsidering her solitude.

"What about the window?" I asked. "It's not that far off the ground."

"You're right," Ben said. "I'll get the stepladder out of the storage shed."

"Maybe," I muttered, "I should wait here in case Annie Jeanne decides to come out on her own."

"Chicken," Ben murmured. "I'll get a hammer to break the glass. Poor Kelly. He should've asked for a damage deposit."

I kept my ear to the door. Annie Jeanne was moving, though the sound wasn't coming any closer. The room's sole window was just beyond the foot of her bed. I doubted that Ben could see her if she was still lying under Gen's quilt. Surely she must know that her obstinacy was causing a problem. It'd serve Annie Jeanne right if Ben's appearance with a hammer at the window scared the wits out of her.

I heard another sound, but this time it was human. Annie Jeanne had uttered a little cry. Perhaps she'd spotted Ben, although I didn't think he would've had time to put on his jacket, find the hammer, and carry the stepladder outside.

More silence, except for the rain pummeling the rectory roof's cedar shakes. I couldn't figure out what Annie Jeanne was doing. Had she gone into some kind of mystical trance? For all I knew, she was praying for the stigmata, and waiting to be pierced in hands and feet. Anything was possible, given her skewed religious ideas.

A sudden chill—both emotional and physical—overcame me. The rectory that had seemed too warm earlier in the day now felt cold and clammy. Ben must have left a door open, creating a draft. I rubbed at my arms and stamped my feet. Despite my warm jacket and solid boots, I was shivering.

At last I heard Ben calling through the window. He repeated her name loudly and forcefully. Nothing. Then I heard the smashing of glass, followed by several cuss words. Apparently my brother was having a problem getting through the broken window.

The cussing stopped. I could hear Ben's footsteps and his voice calling to Annie Jeanne more softly. Again there was silence.

"Come on, let me in!" I yelled through the door.

More silence. Finally, after what seemed like an hour but was probably no more than a minute, a stricken-looking Ben opened the bedroom door.

"Annie Jeanne's dead."

"*What?*"

Ben stepped aside as I scurried into the room. Annie Jeanne was lying in bed, with Gen's quilt pulled up to her chin. She looked very peaceful. And very dead.

I was stricken. "Do you know CPR?" I asked in a weak voice.

"I do, but she's beyond that," Ben said, his voice brisk. "I've seen too many dead people from the delta to the desert to know it'd be useless. I'll get my anointing kit."

Gingerly, I touched one of Annie Jeanne's thin hands, which lay one on top of the other on the quilt. Her skin was cold. But it had been that way when I saw her earlier. A rosary dangled on the edge of the bed. Her prayer book lay closed a few inches from her body. I knelt and prayed for the repose of her soul.

Ben returned with his case and wearing his ecclesiastical stole. I moved away from the bed to give him room. While I bowed my head as he anointed Annie Jeanne and intoned prayers, I noticed a small medicine bottle on the nightstand. The lid was off and it looked empty. My eyes as well as my mind wandered. Being farsighted, I was able to read the patient's name. It wasn't Annie Jeanne's prescription. The label had been filled out for Genevieve Bayard, and the medication was glipizide.

A s SOON AS BEN FINISHED, I POINTED TO THE MEDICINE bottle. My brother started to pick it up, but I stopped him.

"Don't touch it," I warned. "This could be evidence."

"Good God!" Ben glanced back at Annie Jeanne's body. "You mean . . ." He stopped and grimaced. "Of course you do."

"We have to call Milo," I said. "And the medics, just to go through the motions."

Ben, who had a couple of small cuts on his hands, nodded. "I'll do it from my office. There's no phone in here. I could use a couple of Band-Aids anyway."

Annie Jeanne wasn't the first corpse I'd encountered. But standing vigil was a new experience. A few hours ago, the two of us had been chatting amiably in this very room. We were there again, together, and yet an eternity apart. *The quick and the dead,* I thought, and tried to look my own mortality in the eye. It was a test of faith to not think of mundane things.

But the world infringed on my meditation. With the baby dolls and the pixie angels and the other youthful décor, I realized that this was a child's room. Annie Jeanne had never grown up; she was still a true innocent.

The piece of quilt that pictured Deception Falls caught my eye. It was a far cry from innocence. Now I knew why Gen had put it under *H* for happiness. Annie Jeanne had known, too. That was why she'd hedged when I asked her what the fabric patch had meant. It signified not only Gen's release from any ties to Andy Bayard, but also her victory in capturing Ernest from Vida.

That wasn't the only thing my straying eyes noticed. Something was sticking out from the pages of Annie Jeanne's prayer book. At first glance, I thought it was a holy card. But it was too big. On closer inspection, it looked like a sheet of stationery, folded in half.

I'd cautioned Ben about not touching anything, but I had to see if that piece of paper was a suicide note. Very carefully, I leaned across Annie Jeanne's body. I didn't want to move the prayer book, so it took some time to extract the stationery by its corners.

As I'd suspected, it was Annie Jeanne's farewell. Ben came in just as I began to read the dead woman's small, precise script.

"Dodge is on his way. So are a couple of volunteer ambulance drivers," my brother said. "No sirens. No need."

"Listen to this," I said, then frowned. "I can't read this aloud. Not in this room with Annie Jeanne lying there."

We went into the parlor. "She dated it today, at four

forty-seven." I shook my head. "That was just over an hour ago."

Ben sat next to me on the sofa. "You mean she was alive when we were trying to get into the room?"

"I'm afraid so. That's why we heard the noises."

"Damn." Ben crossed himself.

There was no salutation.

"My best friend was Genevieve Ferrer Bayard. She was like a sister to me. We told each other all of our secrets. I knew she would never repeat what I told her, and she knew the same thing about me. We had complete trust in each other. When her second husband died two years ago, I felt so sorry for her because she'd been so in love with him. But I became very upset when she told me she hadn't been going to church. Ernie wasn't a Catholic, and he had refused to be married by a priest. He'd made a terrible fuss when Gen insisted that their son be baptized and take his First Communion."

I had to stop. As concisely as possible, I told Ben what I'd learned from Tony Knuler at the funeral parlor. My brother looked dumbfounded, but withheld comment.

"Maybe," I theorized, "that explains why Gen used the Runkel name—to get even with Ernest for being a bigot." I looked at Ben. "Dare I go on?"

"You damned well better," he said grimly.

"I didn't know what to do, except pray for her. But that didn't seem to help. God works in mysterious ways, they tell me, but I made so many novenas and offered up so many rosaries and Masses and Holy Communions—and yet Gen still didn't go to church.

She even laughed about it at the Betsy party. That made me so miserable. I knew that Gen was going to hell. I couldn't bear the thought, so I decided it was up to me to help her seek God's forgiveness."

Ben was holding his head.

"Gen didn't realize that she'd dropped her medicine bottle at the Betsy party. I'd picked it up and meant to give it to her then and there, but in all the excitement, I forgot. In fact, I didn't remember until I found it in my purse when I went to the store the next day to buy vanilla for our yummy cheesecake.

"Gen called right after I got back from the store. She wanted to know if I had any idea of where she'd lost her medicine. The kind of diabetes she had wasn't as bad as Ernie's, but she still needed to take her tablets. I told her it was safe and sound on the kitchen counter. She said she'd taken the last of the previous prescription that morning, so she was glad that I'd found it. And then she said something that made me feel sick to my stomach—she told me, 'Now, Annie Jeanne, don't you go trying to save me. I'm done with religion and all that claptrap. If Jesus Christ showed up on my doorstep, I might go out with Him but I wouldn't believe a word He said.' I couldn't believe my ears. I knew then I had to act."

The word *had* was underlined three times.

"Father Fitz—rest his soul—had gotten diabetes of old age not long before he retired. One day when I was practicing the organ, he told me about it and

showed me his tablets. Father joked, 'Now don't ever touch these, because they're dangerous. I don't want you poisoning me because I can't sing very well.'

"So I took half of the pills out of Gen's bottle and crushed them into the cheesecake topping. I'd give Gen one last chance to repent, which I did just as we finished our main meal. But she laughed at me, and told me I had crazy religious notions and I'd spent too long being pure. I hadn't had any fun out of life, she said. I knew what she meant—I hadn't had sex. That was so important to her, even at our age."

I paused to catch my breath. Ben was sitting back on the sofa, arms folded across his chest, still looking grim.

"So *we* ate the cheesecake. I thought that we'd both die, and that maybe my sacrifice would atone for her sins and we'd both go to heaven. And sure enough, just before Gen collapsed, she whispered, 'Jesus Christ!' I knew then that I'd done the right thing and that Gen was accepting her Savior. Father Ben said so."

I stared at my brother. "You did?"

Ben waved his arms. "I don't know what I said. I don't re-member if Annie Jeanne told me about Gen's last words. If she did, for all I know, Gen was swearing. Annie Jeanne was throwing up and passing out and I was trying to cope. Maybe she asked if I thought Gen was going to heaven. I probably said yes. It was one big stinking turmoil." He calmed down and regarded me with anticipation. "Is that it?"

"Just about." I started reading again.

"Now I must join my dearest friend, and enter the imperishable glory of heaven just as she did, by taking her medicine. I will first say a perfect Act of Contrition. God rest our souls and all the souls of the faithful departed."

It was signed, *"Annie Jeanne Dupré, virgin and martyr."*

Vehicles were arriving at the rectory. Ben stood up. "I blame myself," he murmured.

"Why? Do you blame Dennis Kelly, too? You've only been here a month."

We went out into the hall. "I suppose I do. Maybe I even blame Father Fitzgerald. Why couldn't any of us see how misguided Annie Jeanne was? Her faith was buried under a pile of bad theology."

Milo and the ambulance drivers had arrived at the same time. I let Ben take over while I paced the parlor. The trouble was, we were all to blame. Annie Jeanne Dupré had been a one-dimensional figure. She was the inept organist who meant well. But none of us knew what she meant; we only knew how badly she played.

Ironically, only Genevieve Bayard had befriended Annie Jeanne. I couldn't help but think of Ernest. He, too, had been a cipher in my mind. But Gen had fallen in love with him and apparently had made him happy. She had practiced, not preached, her humanity.

That was more than the rest of us had done.

TWENTY-THREE

I TRIED TO TALK BEN INTO SEEING VIDA, BUT HE REFUSED. "She's your buddy," he declared. "What's more, she's a Presbyterian who doesn't think much of the Catholic church."

I argued that Vida liked Ben, priest or not. I wasted my breath. My brother remained unconvinced.

By the time Doc Dewey showed up, I was exhausted. I'd made coffee for the newcomers and fixed scrambled eggs for Ben and Milo, neither of whom had eaten since lunch. I still had no appetite. It was going on eight o'clock before they all left, taking Annie Jeanne's body with them.

"You'll be going to Vida's," Ben said. It was more of a command than a remark.

"I feel as if this day has lasted forty-eight hours," I replied, trying to avoid the issue.

"Then you'd better go before you pass out," Ben said.

He was being Ben the Priest, not Ben the Brother. Or maybe he was both. But he was right. I drove to Vida's house.

The first thing that I noticed was that the drapes were closed. Vida liked to keep them open until bedtime so that she wouldn't miss any neighborhood activity.

She didn't respond to the chime immediately. Having suffered through Annie Jeanne's refusal to open the door for Ben, I grew anxious. But after about a minute, Vida stood before me. She looked disheveled and exhausted.

"I know everything," she said, ushering me into the living room. "Al Driggers called around five. Then my nephew Billy phoned me after he got back in town."

I stopped in midstep. A large suitcase sat in the middle of the room alongside a carton that was half-full of clothes.

"What's going on?" I asked in a voice that wasn't quite steady.

"I'm leaving town," she said. "What else can I do?"

"You can't," I declared, my voice stronger.

"I must." She turned her back on me, facing the fireplace mantel. I realized that all the family photos had been removed, including Roger's baby pictures. "I simply can't endure the humiliation when word gets out about what's happened."

"Maybe it won't get out," I said.

"Nonsense. By tomorrow morning, everyone will know."

I tried a different argument. "If you leave, you'll only cause gossip and speculation. Even if the truth is never revealed, everyone in town will suspect you of something terrible."

"But I won't be here to listen to it," Vida said in a wan voice.

I went to her and put a hand on her arm. "Listen to me, Vida. What would this town be like without you? What would the *Advocate* be without you? What about Roger and Amy and Ted? And," I went on, pressing her arm, "what would I do without you? You *are* Alpine. If you left, we might as well change its name back to the original Nippon."

"Oh, come now . . ." Vida began to weep.

"You know it's true." I steered her toward the armchair

next to the hearth. "You're the glue that holds this town together. You know everybody, you know everything that's going on, you pull all the pieces together." *Like a quilt,* I thought, but didn't say so out loud.

Vida took a handkerchief out of her pocket and dabbed at her eyes. "I don't know. . . . It's so terribly upsetting."

I sat down on Vida's sofa. "Alpine is your world. Are you going to let Ernest and Gen ruin your life a second time around?"

Vida sniffed and scowled, but didn't respond.

I leaned forward on the sofa. "What if the truth about the past was never revealed?"

"How could that be?" Vida demanded. "You know how people talk."

"The body in the cemetery will never be exhumed," I asserted. "Al may have threatened to do that, but why would he want to expose his father's breach of ethics? Tony Knuler doesn't care who's buried there, and Buddy didn't give a fig about his father when he was alive. Why would he want to know now?"

"That's true," Vida allowed.

"I'm sure Buddy is concerned only with his inheritance from his mother," I pointed out. "The pity is, he won't get nearly as much as Tony Knuler will. I have a feeling that Gen put aside most of her quilt earnings for Tony. Buddy is successful. Tony strikes me as a wastrel."

"Perhaps." Vida sighed and wiped her eyes again. "Al's releasing the body to Anthony Knuler. He'll accompany his mother's remains to Spokane tomorrow morning."

I noticed that Vida referred to Tony only in the most formal way. Maybe it was her attempt at putting distance between herself and the child that Ernest had had with Gen.

I gave an indifferent nod. "Vida," I said, "there's something I must ask you. Why did you fib about when you got home last Monday?"

"Oh." She looked contrite. "That was very silly of me, wasn't it? I didn't get home early. But Buck felt so badly about not remembering to take care of Cupcake that I pretended I'd gotten home to put him—Cupcake, not Buck—to bed at his usual time. And of course Cupcake was perfectly all right, though he did give me the evil eye when I covered him for the night."

The explanation was delivered in a voice that was more normal. It gave me hope.

But it was dashed when Vida continued. "I think I'll offer to rent the house to Buck. Furnished, of course."

I was silent for a few moments. "What about your daughters?"

Vida peered at me through her orange-framed glasses. "What about them?"

"Aren't you going to tell them that their father wasn't killed at Deception Falls?"

"No. What would be the point? It would do more harm than good. Nor do they need to know about a so-called half brother." Vida's words were bitter. Speaking them seemed to cost her dearly. "That's why I'm not going to stay with any of them until I've given myself some distance."

Sadness was weighing me down. I was so tired—and discouraged. I felt numb. My own world would seem so empty without Vida. But I didn't know what else to say. It was time to take my leave. But I had no intention of saying good-bye.

On the doorstep, Vida stopped me before I could leave the porch. "What are you going to do?" she asked.

"About what? Replacing you?"

"About the story."

I hesitated. This was the biggest story of the year, the de-cade, maybe in Alpine's history. Could I call myself a journalist and keep it under wraps?

I looked Vida right in the eye. "I'm not going to do anything."

The gray eyes I was staring at again filled with tears.

Driving home, I couldn't help but wonder if Vida was crazy. Or at least unbalanced. But by the time I'd undressed and flopped onto the sofa, I realized I was wrong. Vida had kept sane—not to mention sensible, which she would consider just as important—by believing a lie. I suppose we all do, in matters great and small.

Vida didn't show up for work the next morning. When I came through the front door, Ginny informed me that Vida wasn't feeling well.

"Gosh," she said, "when was the last time Vida got sick? I don't ever remember her missing a day because she didn't feel well."

"It's flu season," I said, and without looking at Ginny, I exited the reception area.

The newsroom was empty. I felt empty. Scott was making the morning bakery run, and Leo was at a Rotary Club breakfast.

I went into my cubbyhole and stared at the phone. Should I call Vida? But I couldn't bear to do it. I was afraid she wouldn't answer—or that if she did, she'd tell me what I didn't want to hear.

The phone rang while I was still staring at it. Fearing that it might be Vida, I answered in a tentative voice.

"Have you had breakfast?" Milo asked.

"Not really," I admitted. "I was so tired that I slept until after seven-thirty. I'm not sure I can wait for the bakery run. I haven't really eaten anything since yesterday morning."

"Meet you at the Venison Inn," the sheriff said, and hung up before I could object.

Bakery bag in hand, Scott came in as I went out. Sweet rolls wouldn't do it for me this morning. I felt hollow, literally and figuratively. I knew I needed sustenance. Pancakes. Eggs. Ham. Juice. And lots of hot coffee.

I'd made up my mind that I wouldn't tell Milo about Vida's possible defection unless he asked a specific question. He caught up with me at the restaurant door. "Let's eat in the bar," he said.

I eyed him with curiosity. "You want to get hammered?"

"Hardly. It's more private this time of day. Only the serious drinkers are knocking 'em back this early, and their brains atrophied a long time ago."

So we seated ourselves, and true to Milo's prediction only a handful of morning boozers were at the bar, bending Oren Rhodes's ear and feeling sorry for themselves. They were mostly ex-loggers, driven out of work by timber troubles. One was missing a leg; another had only a thumb on the hand that didn't hold his glass. I reminded myself that they weren't merely drunks. They were like military veterans. They'd waged a war against the forest and had been maimed in their efforts. They were people, not ciphers.

"So," Milo said after Oren had taken our orders and brought coffee, "are you going public on this one?"

It was an unusual question from the sheriff. A light was beginning to dawn. He hadn't asked me to breakfast just for the pleasure of my company. "Are you?"

Milo grunted. "Do you want me to get run out of town?"

"But you have to rule on the homicide," I pointed out. "You've got a signed confession."

"I do?"

I stared at Milo. "The letter Annie Jeanne left."

"What letter?"

"The—" I stopped as Oren brought us each a glass of juice.

"Have you seen the letter?" I asked as soon as Oren had gone back to the bar.

Milo was gazing off in the direction of the Bud Light sign above the bar. "I don't know anything about a letter." He took a sip of juice. "Your brother said Annie Jeanne made a 'good confession,' whatever that means to you guys. Isn't that stuff sacred or something?"

"You're referring to the seal of the confessional," I said. "Yes, it's privileged in law, even more than doctor-patient or lawyer-client confidentiality."

Milo shrugged. "Then I guess I have to rule Gen Bayard's death an accidental homicide."

I peered at Milo, who was now lighting a cigarette. He seemed unconcerned. *Too* unconcerned. My suspicions were confirmed. "I think you and Ben have formed a conspiracy."

Milo shrugged. "The case is closed. I'm cooking that steelhead for him tonight. You watched any of the Seahawk games yet?"

"No. I like college football better than the pros, and the Seahawks aren't going anywhere. As usual."

"How about the Sonics?"

I refused to surrender completely. "Are you going to nail Tony Knuler for breaking in to the Pike house?"

"We don't have any evidence. He says that medal thing isn't his."

"He's lying. He broke in there to destroy Ethel's original quilt patterns. And maybe some of the other members', too. I understand all the quilting materials were kept at the Pikes'."

"Are we back to those damned quilts again?" Milo asked with a sigh.

"Tony may not have known that his mother was already dead," I said. "Or if he did, he was protecting her reputation as well as his own nest egg that Gen had put aside for him."

Milo gazed at me with his steady hazel eyes. "Let it go, Emma. It's over."

I T WASN'T QUITE OVER. ON TUESDAY, THE DAY THAT GEN WAS supposed to have been buried, Annie Jeanne Dupré's funeral Mass was held at St. Mildred's. Luisa Mazilli, the college's music professor, played the organ. Before the liturgy formally began, she dazzled the mourners with selections from Bach, Chopin, Mahler, and Saint-Saëns.

But what uplifted my spirits most was that Vida was in attendance. I should have guessed she'd never miss a funeral. When I saw her coming down the aisle with her head held high and her eyes darting all around the church, I knew she was going to face down any criticism or curiosity. As she progressed toward me in her black swing coat and black sailor hat with a big white daisy, I wanted to jump up and hug her. But I refrained, and squeezed over toward Debra and Clancy Barton to make room.

"Such a crowd," she declared in her stage whisper. "The Bartons, the Shaws, the O'Tooles, Jack and Nina Mullins, a gaggle of Bourgettes. And the Bayards, of course. Goodness, is that Rita Patricelli from the Chamber of Commerce? Oh, and her brother, Pete. Who else?" She rubbernecked through Luisa's Chopin prelude. The attendees were doing some rubbernecking of their own, gazing up into the choir loft with pleasurable expressions.

The procession started down the aisle. Ben looked dignified in his white vestments, which symbolize the Resurrection. It was time to think of other things, of why we were there. It was time to remember Annie Jeanne, not in her final hours, but as a person. A person we hardly knew.

THE MORNING WAS COLD, WITH FROST TURNING THE cemetery grass to silver. Ben had preached a fitting homily, basing it on accepting Christ as little children do, for theirs is the kingdom of heaven. Dennis Kelly, who had been informed of Annie Jeanne's death by Ben, sent a message citing her "simple faith and innocence."

The senior Duprés were buried not far from the Runkel plot. Vida walked right by without even a glance. When the casket had been lowered and the final words had been spoken, she turned to me.

"Your brother does a nice funeral," she declared. "I'll mention that in my write-up. And I'm certainly glad he doesn't ask members of the congregation to offer their own thoughts and remembrances. Really, it's always such twaddle."

I agreed.

"Not to mention," Vida went on as we walked uphill from the grave site, "that Luisa Mazilli played the organ extremely well."

I stopped and turned to look down at the green canopy and the deep hole in the ground. From our vantage point, the cemetery, with its headstones and markers and various family plots, reminded me of something: a quilt. Life was like that, bits and pieces, good and bad, all patched together to make a whole, often flawed creation.

"Perhaps Luisa will become the regular organist," Vida said as we continued on our way. "She has an Italian name. Maybe she's a Catholic. It would certainly be nice for you people if you could listen to such beautiful music at every Sunday service."

"It was beautiful," I conceded. Then, after a few more steps, I said what I really felt.

"But I didn't like it."